THE
SYPHON'S
DAUGHTER

THE **ELLENDRIA** SERIES

THE SYPHON'S DAUGHTER

M.E. BATT

4 Horsemen
Publications, Inc.

4 Horsemen
Publications, Inc.

4 Horsemen Publications, Inc.
1497 Main St. Suite 169
Dunedin, FL 34698
4horsemenpublications.com
info@4horsemenpublications.com

Cover and Typeset by S. Wilder
Editor Shirley Austin

Library of Congress Control Number: 2022943326

Print ISBN: 979-8-8232-0000-4
Hardcover ISBN: 979-8-8232-0012-7
Ebook ISBN: 979-8-8232-0001-1
Audio ISBN: 979-8-8232-0008-0

DEDICATION

FIRST, TO MY CHILDREN: ARYA, ERIC, and Isla. May you always chase your dreams, no matter how fantastical they are.

Second, to my husband. You never once doubted me. Without your support and unconditional love, I never would've believed in myself enough to pursue my passions.

Third, to my family. Mom, you fostered my love of reading and writing from the beginning. You always knew I'd end up here. Dad, you supported my dreams, whichever way they took me. My mother-in-law Rosann, you've always had unwavering confidence in everything I do.

Fourth, to my beta readers, child caretakers, and friends. You all were vital in this success.

Fifth, to my coworkers. Athena, you don't know this, but you inspired the main plot of this story. Roseanne and Linda, thank you for the immediate faith in this project and for bouncing ideas around with me. Mark, though you'll likely never see this, thank you for taking a chance on me and allowing me the work—life balance which made this writing possible.

Finally, to all the assholes along the way. To the ones who made high school and college Hell... here's to you. To the bad bosses, catty coworkers, and everyone who sucked the joy from my spirit, thank you. Thank you for inspiring my villains. Thank you for making me choose books over people, time and time again. If it wasn't for all of you, I wouldn't have ever made it this far. Cheers!

TABLE OF CONTENTS

Chapter 1

T HE CANTER OF HORSE HOOVES WAS not uncommon on the main road; however, this was *not* the main road. Dubbed "Nettles Lane," it was hardly a trail, squirrels visiting more frequently than man. Sunlight trickled through the canopy of branches and dotted the forest floor, highlighting patches of dark green moss and scattered piles of crisp, dead leaves. Raylyn halted, cocking her head and straining her ears. "Surely, not a rider here?" she asked, glancing at her mother.

The older of the two women hoisted a woven basket—half—filled with various herbs and mushrooms—higher onto her arm and wiped the sweat off her forehead. Squinting, she peered into the thicket of greenery, the snapping bracken and pounding hooves growing louder by the second.

"Come here," Eva urged, pulling her daughter into a shallow hollow behind a rotting log spotted with white fungus. They crouched low, baskets discarded near their feet. Reaching into a leather boot, her mother withdrew a short knife, the dappled sunlight glinting off the blade. She crouched on the balls of her feet, poised to strike if needed. The music of chittering birds and chirping insects silenced as the thundering hooves grew closer.

A high—pitched whinny cut through the air as the mare crashed into view in a bloody frenzy. The horse's spotted white coat was hard to see through thick, dripping blood. Eva appeared at the horse's side, catching its free reins in one hand while the other stroked its muzzle. "Hurry," she commanded, moving to the horse's flank. The man draped across its back was limp and lifeless. They struggled under his weight, sliding him with an ungraceful thud to the ground, their hands staining a tacky red from his blood—dampened clothes. He didn't make a noise as he landed, and Raylyn's heart raced as her mother checked for signs of life, her ear pressed to his chest. "Alive! Get the baskets. Quickly, now! He doesn't have much time."

Raylyn rushed, grabbing the baskets, and returned to her mother's side. Eva, still crouched on the forest floor, searched his body, her hands running the length of his torso. His silken shirt clung to him—saturated with blood—and she pulled at it. The fabric resisted, caught on a long laceration running the length of his torso. Fresh blood gushed.

Scanning her options, Raylyn grabbed the cloth liner from her mother's basket. She shook off the herbs and pressed it to the wound, both hands applying pressure to slow the bleeding. Her training kicked in. If the bleeding could not be stopped, he would die. *Even so, if his intestines are lacerated as well, he will die regardless ... just more slowly.* Her mother's voice interrupted her thoughts.

"Where is the yarrow?" she asked, her voice urgent as she rummaged through the scattered pile of herbs.

"Here, in my basket." Raylyn nodded toward it, not daring to remove her hands from the wound. Already, blood soaked through the cloth, dripping onto her hands.

Her mother grabbed the cluster of small white flowers and shoved it in her mouth, chewed intensely, then spit the wad back into her hands. On cue, Raylyn removed her hands. Eva applied the paste to the wound bed, holding her hands slightly above the wound. Closing her eyes, she chanted, "Heal and make whole. Goddess, help the bleeding slow. Heal and make whole. Needless be this woe." Golden light shone from her palms, illuminating the man's torso and the severity of the injury; it cut across his body from the right rib to the left hip. She repeated this process three times until paste lined the entire length of the laceration.

The golden light faded as Eva removed her hands. She knelt back, her face pale and exhausted. The man's bleeding had slowed incrementally but still streamed down his stomach and dripped onto the forest floor. The earth gulped it almost greedily, and the surrounding soil dampened to a rich, dark brown.

"We cannot save him." Eva's voice shook and her tunic was drenched with sweat. She remained on the ground next to the dying man, whose only sign of life was his faintly rising chest.

"No..." Raylyn began, gravitating toward him as if magnetized. "There must be more that can be done!"

Desperation overwhelmed her, coursing through her veins as inexplicable as the Goddess herself. Leaning forward, she pressed her fingers to his flesh, replacing the position her mother had just vacated.

"You are not strong enough. This is beyond us." She grasped Raylyn's shoulder, shaking her head. "It is our first and most important rule, Raylyn."

"He will not die today," she snapped, shrugging her mother off. Heat coursed through her body as her own palms radiated. Though a practiced apprentice, she had never felt such a primal need to heal someone engulf her. She *needed* to save this man as much as she needed air to breathe.

The golden light tied her to him, and they were no longer two separate people, but one. Through that connection, she poured herself into him, willing him to survive.

As suddenly as her desperation to save him began, it rapidly ended and was replaced by an icy realization: her energy was draining. *Mother's right. Of course I'm not strong enough*, she thought, the crushing weight of panic tightening her chest. With hands still glowing, her head slumped, and her knees buckled. Her body crumpled atop his, the golden light at her palms flickering as they dimmed. An echo of desperation again filled her mind and—not thinking, not knowing how she did it—she reached out with her mind and *pulled*.

The power which flowed into her started as a trickle, breathing life into her limbs and strengthening her muscles. Pulling herself up, she drank it in like a starving man would a goblet of wine. Soon, waves of energy and euphoria crashed over her, and the light from her palms— dimming just moments ago—blasted with a blinding force, filling the thicket with a brightness greater than the sun. Fire coursed through her veins, and she channeled it, directing it to the man in front of her. She stitched his torn intestines and knitted the muscles and skin as instinctively as breathing. Once he was whole, she closed the channels with difficulty, like shutting a door against the winds of a hurricane. Her heart pounded with exhilaration as she pulled her hands off the man's abdomen, the only remnants of his injury his drying blood.

Hundreds of soft thuds filled the air, and she whipped her head up, disoriented. The noises soon stopped, the source of the sound clear. Swallowing back bile, she stood, examining the countless bodies of dead birds scattered on the ground. The vegetation, touched by the beginnings of autumn, was now completely dead, leaves curled and dried. She spun, eyes wide with horror. Even the pine trees, always so vibrant, were brown with death. Movement caught her eye as the stranger stirred, his lids fluttering. "He *lives*? Mother, he lives!"

Eva's eyes were wide with horror. She spoke, her voice barely louder than a whisper. "What have you done?"

"I—I don't know. But he lives!" Raylyn kneeled forward to study the unconscious man. His face was no longer ashen, and his chest rose steadily with deep, even breaths. She fingered the collar of his bloodied, silken shirt. Though it was hard to distinguish through the gore, the stitching bore a repeating pattern of eagles and crowns. "He's part of the Court," she said, gesturing at the pattern. Only those of royalty and prominent members of their employ wore the emblem of the king. Intoxicating triumph rose in her once again, the dead wildlife all but forgotten.

Her mother did not move to examine this new revelation. She remained on the forest floor, a sheen of cold sweat covering her face and drenching her tunic. Trembling, her pallor mirrored that of the stranger's just moments ago. Eva steadied herself before speaking, "Go back to the village. Find your father and instruct him to assemble the council. Have him send four men and two stretchers here. You will wait for me at home." She paused for breath before continuing, "You will not leave the house until I have returned. We have much to discuss. Do you understand?"

Raylyn, taken aback, considered these instructions. She knew the energy her mother exerted had been great, but to be unable to walk the trail back to the village? Never had she seen her in such a state despite years of practiced healing beneath her. *This is worse than when the Draundy baby had croup,* Raylyn thought. The child's lips had been blue, and yet her mother was able to expel the illness from his lungs, hardly breaking a sweat. An extra serving of mince pie was all she needed for her revival that night.

And the village council? Raylyn reasoned it was to discuss the presumed royal who was laying before her. Her father had been part of council longer than her sixteen years of life. The only times they met formally were when harvest yields were low, or a crime was committed.

Instead of obeying, Raylyn went to her mother's side. Crouching, she brushed the sweaty hair from her mother's forehead. "Momma, are you okay? What can I do?" She kept her hand on her mother's skin and concentrated, preparing to channel again. Before the warmth of the golden light could shine through her palm, her mother batted her hand down as if swatting a fly, cringing.

"I will be fine. Do as I instructed." An unspoken accusation in her eyes kept Raylyn from arguing further.

Concern for her mother cast a shadow over her earlier excitement. Her soul now thrummed with an unknown energy and she felt more alive than ever. She didn't experience the same fatigue her mother did. *But why?* One moment, she felt her life slipping away... But something had changed in her mind, like a brick wall crumbling, opening an area never discovered. She took one last glimpse at the stranger and his soiled finery before hiking through the dead foliage, her crunching footsteps the only sound in the unnaturally silent forest.

Time was stagnant as Raylyn sat on her bed waiting for her mother to return. She fidgeted with her thin cotton blanket, her fingers twitching from nerves. The fall was unseasonably warm this year and her heavy woolen quilt was still stored away, not yet needed. Moisture was heavy in the air, giving the small room an added sense of claustrophobia. Scattered papers and heavy tomes littered the top of her desk, remnants of study from the prior day. Hours had passed since she emerged from the forest, returning to her village. She found her father tending his small vegetable garden behind their house and recanted a quick version of events, forgoing the mention of dead wildlife she left behind.

"How were you able to heal him when your mother could not?" His brow furrowed, and he shot her a quick look while they hurried together into the warm brick house. He snagged his small traveling pack from a hook near the door and readied himself to leave.

"I... I don't know, Father. I've never seen Mother so ill," she said, unable to meet his eyes. Omitting the truth was as deceitful as a spoken lie, and she had never been a good liar.

"Hm," he grunted. Taking a sweeping glance over the sitting room, his eyes fell upon two swords mounted above the red brick fireplace. He settled on the lower of the two, a family heirloom passed down from each father to his eldest son for generations. A small part of Raylyn's mind wondered if she would ever inherit it or if her parents would ever try again for a boy.

Though plain, the sword was sharp and well maintained. He fastened its brown leather scabbard around his waist and sheathed the weapon. "I'm going to get help. Whoever attacked that man might still be out there. You were lucky, Ray." He pulled her close as he kissed the top of her head, ruffling her auburn hair. "If something had happened to you..." He trailed off. Giving her one last squeeze, he left, the door closing with a soft *click*.

Raylyn replayed the scene in her head as she idly sat in her room. *How many hours has it been?* The light outside steadily succumbed to dusk and little stars were peeking through the evening sky. Patience was a virtue which eluded her. Hoping for a distraction from her anxiety, she picked up one of the loose papers from her desk. It was an illustration she had copied the prior night from the textbook *Useful Herbs and Fungi*. Colored images of stinging nettle, bloodroot, and farrow decorated the page. Her eyes burned as tears threatened to cascade down. Blinking, she busied herself with tidying the papers and pencils, ignoring the bubbling sense of dread in her chest.

Murmuring voices were carried into her room on the warm breeze, and papers forgotten, she bolted to the window. Two distinct figures approached on the dirt road, and though the darkness obscured their features, Raylyn knew it was her parents. Barefoot, she rushed out of the house, meeting them on the path.

She slammed into her mother with a tight embrace, relief spreading through her like mulled cider. "Oh, sweet girl," her mother sighed. "I'm okay. Hush," Eva said as Raylyn's sobs echoed into the night air. She pulled off her daughter, cradling Raylyn's face between her smooth, warm hands.

"Momma, I am so sorry. All I could think was what if—"

"Hush now," her mother interrupted, wiping the tears from her cheeks. "We have much to discuss and little time to do it. But this," she nodded to the road and open air, "is not the place." She exchanged a quick glance with Raylyn's father, who nodded curtly.

"Did you meet trouble in the forest, Father?" Raylyn asked, attempting to regain control of her emotions. The crushing weight of dread that had been pressing on her chest lifted with a dizzying relief. Her father met her gaze, and she stumbled, shocked at his expression. His face was grave; he did not smile, nor meet Raylyn's eyes. They walked the rest of the way in an uncomfortable silence. She didn't dare speak until they were back in their home, and even then she felt her father's unspoken reproach pounding in her mind.

"Sit down, Ray," her mother said, nodding toward the table and chairs nestled in the kitchen. Eva filled a copper pot with water, placing it over the cold, lifeless wood in the hearth.

Raylyn picked at the skin on her thumb, watching her mother busy herself in the kitchen. Her father appeared and sat opposite Raylyn, a smooth wooden pipe in his hand. He lit it and spent a long moment inhaling the fragrant smoke, eyes closed. When he opened them again, he stared at his wife, who was gathering a loaf of bread, butter, and the grape jam she and Raylyn canned last season. He must have noted the flameless fireplace, and—taking another long drag from his pipe—he pointed a glowing palm at the hearth. The logs smoldered for a moment before roaring ablaze.

"Thank you," Eva said, resting the tray of food on the table. There was the addition of seasoned jerky, grapes, and a hard, mild cheese. She kissed her husband, who didn't respond. Instead, he sat rigidly, staring at the pipe in his rough hands. Eva ignored his coldness, seating herself in the last remaining chair. "Eat, Raylyn," she said, motioning toward the tray of food. "You must be hungry after the magic you performed today."

It was true. She hadn't noticed her hunger; it was hidden by anxiety and fear. With the safe return of both her parents, she realized she was starving. She bit into a thick slice of venison jerky, the heavy silence returning while she chewed. Questions formed in her mind, and with her mouth half-full, she spoke, "What became of that man, Momma? Did he awaken?" She swallowed. "And you made it back okay?" Somehow eating made her even more hungry, and she grabbed some cheese and bread.

"He did. Though you healed the wound, he is still very weak. He lost so much blood..." Her mother paused, glancing again at her husband. "Your father and a few of the village guard came to us. My memory of them arriving is … hazy. You did well with my instructions." She, too, reached out and grabbed a crusty slice of bread.

"Did *well*?" Her father's voiced cracked, his eyes as hot as the fire near them. "You were near death's door when we found you, Eva. Your daughter almost *kills* you, and you tell her she *did well*?" He slammed his pipe on the table with a loud thud. At the same time, the kettle began to scream. He stood with fury, knocking his chair to the ground. Turning, he stormed to the hearth and finished making the tea, his back turned toward Raylyn and her mother.

"Charles…" Eva began. "We talked about this." The weariness in her voice matched the exhaustion on her face.

"But did we agree?" He slammed two steaming mugs of tea in front of his wife and daughter. "What you did today," he said, meeting Raylyn's eyes with an icy stare, "is beyond any atrocity I have ever witnessed." He sat down again and took a long, deep drink from his own mug. Raylyn was speechless. Her mouth hung open, but words would not come. When he was finished drinking, he took a deep breath. It was as if the hot tea melted some of his coldness. "How long has this been going on, Raylyn?"

"Wha—what do you mean?" Her voice trembled. She didn't understand what happened in the forest, and it certainly hadn't happened before. "I was just trying to heal that man. He was *dying*." Tears sprang to her eyes. Her father was known for being a lighthearted and even-tempered man, and she couldn't recall ever being scolded by him. The rarity of the situation made it even more intolerable. "I—I don't even know what happened," she confessed, looking at her mother for support. If anyone had answers, surely it was her mother.

"What you did in the forest," Eva began, setting down her bread, "is a magic which has been extinct from this world for over a hundred years ... or so we thought. I assume you recall your religious lessons, the ones from childhood. What is the first rule of the Goddess?"

Raylyn had always been an accomplished student and answered reflexively, "Transfer of energy will always reduce the lifeforce of the wielding individual."

"Exactly," her mother answered with the smallest hint of a smile. "And what is our second rule?"

"Do no harm."

Eva nodded. "The power that you have shown today... We assumed it died out with Haddeon himself, as he is the last recorded person in history to be a syphon..." Her mother trailed off at this last statement, gazing at Raylyn as if seeing her for the first time. "All power comes from a transfer of energy, a lifeforce. As you remembered, there is always a balance, as it is the Goddess's way. For healers, we must always assess the gravity of a wound and determine if we possess the strength to mend it. An overzealous healer makes for a dead one. *That* is why I could not heal the prince. His was not an ordinary blade wound. We think," her eyes darted again to her husband, "a caster put a dark curse on the sword that injured him, causing his bleeding to accelerate."

Raylyn sucked in a sharp breath. To use powers for such evil was unheard of in Ellendria. They were a peaceful and religious nation, their king righteous and just. Raylyn thought back on some rumors she heard. A few months ago, in the early spring, the traders made their way through their remote village. Reports of turmoil in the neighboring kingdom, Cystra, spread through Lakehaven like a brush fire. Apparently, they were on the brink of a civil war, groups of radicals demanding the enslavement of the non-mages. Escalating violence and depravity were causing a steady stream of refugees to cross the border, seeking asylum. The tales of horror had even led the Ellendrian king to set up a humanitarian mission, appointing one of his most trusted advisors to the campaign.

Realization struck, Raylyn's eyes growing wide with wonder. "Did you just say *the prince*? *Our* prince? In Lakehaven?"

"Yes. We haven't been able to get much more out of him yet. It's more important for him to regain his strength and rest. He's at the clinic with Annette. I'd have preferred to stay, of course, but—"

"But I made you come home. You're in no shape to be working right now, Eva," Raylyn's father interjected, taking another puff from his pipe. "I've sent guards to patrol the village perimeter as well as stationed the best men outside the clinic. Sent scouts into the forest, too. If we discover who harmed him, it might better your odds." The iciness in his voice was gone, now all business. Charles, like his father before him, took pride in his command of the village guard.

"Better my odds of what?" Raylyn asked, setting the heel of her bread down, finally full. "Can I go see him?" She tried to keep the eagerness out of her voice.

"Raylyn, the council is meeting tomorrow to determine the ... repercussions of today's events," her mother stated, tears in her eyes as she grabbed her daughter's hand. "There was no way to disguise what happened in the forest," she said, almost pleadingly.

"I don't understand." Panic spread through Raylyn's veins. She had never been in trouble before. How could they punish her for an unknown magic of which she had no control?

Her father spoke, his voice quiet, "Whether intentionally or not, you broke the first and second commands of the Goddess. And you disobeyed a master of craft today."

"A master of craft? It was Momma!" Raylyn roared, gesturing madly across the table at her mother.

"I don't care!" her father bellowed, matching her tone. "That makes it worse, Raylyn! In your rebellion, you nearly killed yourself, your mother, and caused the destruction of nearly an acre—*an acre!*—of forest. Do no harm," her father scoffed. "Do our rules and teachings mean so little?"

She stared, aghast. Fear blinded her when she ran back to the village for help, and the damage had been all but invisible to her. *Over an acre*, she thought, disgust twisting her stomach. "I didn't... I don't..." she stammered. "I don't know how it *happened*. But I saved our prince." Her voice was small and shaky, and she couldn't find the strength to look up from the table, studying the patterns in the wood grain.

Her father sighed, resting his face in his hands. Never had he looked so defeated. "What will become of me?" she asked, her voice small and miserable.

There was a long pause before her mother spoke. "We don't know for sure. I think it would be wise if... You should prepare for the possibility of the Mark." Both her parents averted their gaze, unable to look at her.

Raylyn flew to her feet. "Mother, please!" she cried. "You know I didn't mean to. I wasn't in control of it!"

Eva's sobs matched her daughter's. "I cannot save you from this," she said, her voice cracking as she strode over to embrace her. Her father remained motionless, clutching his pipe in a daze, and Eva's sobs shook both their bodies. Outside, specks of starlight shone defiantly through the blackness.

CHAPTER 2

T HE NIGHT WAS LOSING A SLOW BUT relentless battle with the morning. Raylyn lay motionless in her bed, staring up at her ceiling. Her eyes had grown accustomed to the darkness, and she watched as a small spider scurried across the wooden planks above her. Such a simple life it led. *Must be nice,* she thought bitterly, impatience growing with each passing minute.

A humorless smile crossed her face when the muted voices of her parents traveled through the wall, accompanied by a soft thud as their bedroom door closed. Willing her heart to slow, she closed her eyes, counting out fifty long, slow breaths. Shaking herself out of her reverie, she stood and grabbed the now bursting travel sack she had silently packed hours before. Despite her efforts to be as frugal as possible, there was still too much to carry and travel on foot. There was no denying it; she needed a horse.

And *that* meant she needed Braya. The thought of implicating her best friend in her escape plans made Raylyn's stomach twist with unease, but she didn't have the luxury of choice.

Not daring to breathe, she snuck lightly out of her room and down the hall, the hearth in the kitchen now mere red coals. When she closed the front door, she didn't glance back; instead, she sprinted into the gray predawn.

The air was void of autumn's crispness, and she was soon hunched over, gasping for breath. Beads of sweat dripped from her face and her chest burned. She had never been very athletic. When the other children in the village played man-hunt in the woods or freeze tag in the village streets, she was bent over a book or hiding from her parents with Braya.

Panting, she wiped a hand over her sweaty face, pushing wet pieces of hair from her eyes. She was on the other side of town and the world was still quiet. *What will happen if the council discovers I stole a horse?*

She crept off the road, keeping close to the tall evergreen trees, slowly edging toward a nearby farmhouse. A dilapidated wooden fence lined the surrounding property, a plain stable barely visible behind an expansive house. Sprawling grassy fields were pale in the weak morning light. With quickened steps, Raylyn crept toward the back of the house. Kneeling, she searched for a few pebbles in the dewy grass, and with a practiced arm, she tossed one at the rightmost window, hitting her target.

A rooster crowed in the near distance, making her jump. She looked around, anxiety making her see false figures in the long shadows. *Come on, Braya.* She threw another stone, then a third. Finally, the blonde-headed girl appeared in the window. Opening it, Braya called out three quick whistles. Raylyn matched the trill, doing her best to match that of a robin. The window closed, her friend disappearing.

A minute later, the back door opened and Braya approached, a light cotton robe draped around her shoulders. She crossed her arms in front of her chest and a small frown tugged at the corners of her mouth. "Raylyn, what in the world—" she began.

"Shh! Not here," Raylyn interjected, eyes darting between the house and road. She grabbed her friend's arm, pulling her into a small thicket of trees. Scattered orange and brown leaves crunched underfoot as they walked until they finally stopped in front of an old walnut tree. Several wooden boards, crumbling with age, were nailed into the dense trunk. She motioned to Braya, who rolled her eyes, but proceeded to climb.

Their treehouse was nothing more than five wide planks supported by three thick branches. Raylyn remembered the summer evenings they spent constructing it years ago. Braya's father had just remodeled the stable, and the old wood was destined for the fire pit. The girls had scavenged the wood for those planks with the least water damage and smuggled them into the little grove. They hadn't let inexperience hinder them as they hauled the planks up and nailed them into the tree.

Raylyn idly fingered a lone nail that stuck out, haphazardly hammered into place. "I'm in trouble, Braya." The irritated expression slid off Braya's face as Raylyn quickly recounted the prior day's events. "I *won't* be Marked, Braya. I've gotta get out of here." She tried to disguise the desperation in her voice as determination.

"Right. Where're we gonna go?" Braya was already up, toeing the edge of the platform. "We've got two mares in the middle stalls, a couple of palfreys. They aren't the fastest, but they're pretty well-built. They'll be good on the trails." She climbed down the tree, jumping the last few feet to the ground. She turned, marching back toward the house.

Raylyn scrambled down the tree after her. "Braya," she began hesitantly, "you can't come with me. *You've* got nothing to run from." Raylyn kicked at a small rock in her path, releasing some of her frustration. "I can't let you lose everything, too." Shame warmed her face, and she averted her gaze, staring ahead at the trail.

Braya snorted. "Nothing to run from... You know I've been waiting for the right time to leave the drunk bastard." Raylyn bit her lip with another rush of guilt.

When they broke through the thicket, golden light was breaking over the horizon, coloring the fields and farmhouse with warmth. Raylyn cursed under her breath as she looked up into the sky. "I shouldn't have wasted so much time. We have to hurry." Her vision went hazy at the edges, and a sudden rush of nausea made her sway. *I can't be Marked. I can't.* She stumbled, her foot snagging in a divot in the earth.

"Hey... Hey, Raylyn. You're losing it a little," Braya said and grabbed her arm. "I've got you." She pulled her in for a quick, tight hug. Instantly, a trickle of relief spread through Raylyn, like ice melting before a hearth. "Alright?" Braya pulled back, gazing intensely at Raylyn. The blurred edges of her vision refocused.

Braya sucked her cheek for a moment before speaking again. "I'll grab the horses and you wait over by the road.

19

There's this young colt by the door that spooks from just the wind. I don't want him to go off if he sees you. He likes me, though." She grinned. "I'll be back in a second."

Braya turned and jogged toward the stable, her blonde hair catching in the breeze. Raylyn watched for a moment—gratitude radiating through her—before retracing her steps toward the road.

Braya wouldn't be swayed to stay; she was desperate for an excuse to leave the ranch and slip out of her father's grip and had been for years. After her mother died, her father found his comfort at the bottom of endless bottles. Reeking of old ale, his curses would slip out clumsily, fists swinging haphazardly through the air. The first time Braya asked Raylyn to heal a dark blue bruise on her hip, Raylyn believed her when she said she slipped and fell. A week later, Braya asked for the favor again, but his time her eye was swollen and black. It was then that Raylyn knew the unspoken truth.

The years had quieted the roaring temper in her father but did not rid it completely. Sporadically, Braya would request Raylyn's help in concealing another injury, though neither of them kept up with the charade of how it was obtained. "I'll poison his drink someday," Braya would sigh. "I *swear* I will." But so far she hadn't—to Raylyn's relief. The man was an asshole, but to take a life was such an abhorrent thought it made her stomach twist.

I took lives yesterday. Not a person, but how much wildlife did I decimate?

She reached the point where the trail to Braya's house met the main road. The sun was rising higher still, and the rest of the world would be awakening now. She was uneasy standing in plain sight of any passersby, but the road was still and quiet. She sighed, sitting cross-legged in the dirt.

She drew crude maps with her finger in the dusty earth beneath her, trying to decide where to go. North was the lake, and on its opposite bank was Fremond. Raylyn knew the town was much the same as hers—they thrived on the mild temperatures and harvested the same dark-purple grapes the capital, Lendris, bought each year without fail. But Fremond was too close; she'd be found immediately. Plus, without a boat, circumventing the lake would prove difficult. Farther north would bring her near the border of Cystra, and the violence there made that a hard pass as well.

Movement caught her eye. Braya grinned as she led two saddled horses toward Raylyn. They were identical, golden-brown, and followed docilely behind her. Raylyn hopped up, wiping her hands on her pants.

"They're pretty great, huh?" she asked, handing Raylyn the reins for one of the horses before stroking her mare's muzzle.

"They're perfect." Braya had outdone herself. The beasts were equipped with sturdy leather saddles and a few saddle bags each. She peered inside one, finding oats. The second was empty besides a woolen blanket, and she shoved her pack inside with ease. "Are you sure you want to come?" Raylyn asked, glancing up.

Braya snorted again, and in a swift movement, mounted her horse. Her bedclothes were replaced with trousers and a tunic, feet clad in worn leather boots. "If you aren't here, what reason do I have to stay?" She adjusted herself in the saddle, reins held in one hand. "I snagged some jerky and bread. Some coin too, though not much. He spends it all on booze. Didn't even need to sneak; the bastard's still out cold. Drunk as a skunk." She took a bite of jerky, looking down at Raylyn. "Which way, boss?" she asked, smirking.

Raylyn mounted her horse, though without the practiced grace of her friend. "What do you think about heading south? The weather will stay mild longer, and we could lose ourselves down by Lendris."

"Ooh, we'll be city girls in the big capital, eh?" Braya crooned sarcastically. "Let's get on with it, then."

"Do you think the road will be okay? Maybe we should cut through the fields until we get to the woods," Raylyn said, chewing her lip.

"It's early yet. I'd imagine your parents are still in bed. You said they retired late? I'm sure the road will be fine."

Raylyn nodded, nudging her horse into an easy canter. Braya followed, tiny clouds of dust puffing into the air with each step. *It would be more conspicuous to gallop through town*, Raylyn thought. She was eager to distance themselves from the village but didn't want to draw unnecessary attention. Once on the outskirts, they could urge the horses into a faster trot. They only had to pass a few more farmhouses, and each step loosened the tightness in her chest. The sun crested the horizon, dispelling the morning mist, and fragrant, ripe grapes perfumed the morning air as they slowed their cantor to a walk past row after row of twisting vines.

"Raylyn..." There was an edge to Braya's voice that jolted her out of her musing. She pulled her horse to a stop. "Look," she urged, pointing ahead of them.

Raylyn did as instructed, straining her eyes, but saw nothing more than the brown dirt and scattered rocks of the road, surrounded by a sea of green grassy fields.

"I don't..." she began, stopping as her eyes caught a flicker of movement, a person appearing beneath the shadow of a boulder. She swore under her breath. They had just passed the last farmhouse, and she had fooled herself into thinking they were safe.

"What should we do?" Braya asked from behind her. Raylyn was still staring ahead.

"We continue on." She nudged her horse forward. "We can outrun them if need be." One person on foot had no chance against two fresh mounts.

She paid the person no mind as they approached, keeping her eyes straight ahead on the road. *Who would loiter on the outskirts of town, anyway?* she thought, irritation drawing her brows together. Curiosity got the better of her, and she chanced a quick glance at the figure.

Her stomach flipped, and she regretted her decision. The stranger she saved in the woods the day before was sitting on the ground, leaning against a large boulder. He held a book propped open in one hand, and upon catching Raylyn's eye, he snapped it closed, a grin spreading across his face. No sign of his injury remained, and his bloodied clothes were replaced with the simple linen shirt and trousers that her mother kept stocked for patients in the clinic.

Breaking eye contact, she mentally debated, her mind reeling. She could run from her family and the village council, but from the prince of her country? Not likely. *But he was unconscious the entirety of our encounter*, Raylyn argued with herself. *How would he recognize me?* Confidence boosting with that thought, she squared her shoulders, giving him the slightest nod as they passed, as if greeting an unwelcome acquaintance. At that moment, her horse gave a little whinny, pulling toward the prince.

She gritted her teeth and pulled the reins, heat flushing her cheeks. The mare resisted, and she heard Braya mutter, "Come on girl," as her horse, too, pulled toward the prince.

"Stop," he commanded, his voice silky and strong. Raylyn's urge to flee lessened by degrees, and the horses froze, unpersuadable. He pocketed his book, sauntering toward them, a low chuckle accompanying his smile. Stopping in front of her horse, he stroked the mare's neck, crooning softly to the animal in a slow voice. His gaze shifted upward, meeting her eyes once more. She stared back, entranced. A small, faraway part of her brain buzzed with annoyance, but it silenced as she stared back into the prince's deep brown eyes.

"I thought you'd be here sooner," he said, his tone almost questioning. Without waiting for a reply, he grabbed her hand, bending to kiss it. The pressure was soft and fleeting, and her skin tingled with the warmth of his breath. "Raylyn Ashton, I believe I owe you my life."

CHAPTER 3

Braya's barking laugh jolted Raylyn from her stupor, and she broke her eyes away from the prince's gaze, shaking her head to clear it. She raised an eyebrow at her friend, and the smirk slid off Braya's face. Realization sank in, and Braya scrambled to dismount her horse. She stumbled a little as she landed on the ground, disguising her clumsiness in a deep curtsy.

Raylyn followed suit, biting her tongue so hard she tasted blood. She despised him at this moment. They had been so close to freedom, yet some invisible force drew her toward him. Slowly sliding off her horse, she fixed her eyes at his feet, an annoying itching under her skin distracting her.

"Can I help you? We are in a bit of a rush, so if you wouldn't mind..." She gave a brief curtsy before turning back to the saddle, preparing to hoist herself back up. The day was only brightening, scattered birdsong chittering in the warm air, and each passing moment caused an increased tightening in her chest.

Without warning, a trickling heat spread through her body, calming her by degrees. The tension in her shoulders loosened, a carefree numbness replaced her roaring anxiety ... and yet ... the itching intensified, making her want to tear the skin from her body. The sudden juxtaposition of emotions unsettled her. She froze. Tales of effectors were rare and always left a bitter taste in her mouth. How had rumor of the prince's power not spread?

The internal battle to regain mastery over her emotions took only moments. She glanced at Braya, who stared vacantly, a grin spread on her face. Whipping around to face the prince, she put as much ice into her voice as possible. "If you please, *manipulator*. Release us from your spell."

His eyes widened with shock, whether from the insult or the surprise of her discovery, she didn't know. A smile played at his lips, and his eyes danced with delight, glimmering golden-brown in the morning sun. She swayed, an intensified need pulling her close to him. As if her feet were controlled by someone else, she took a few stumbling steps forward, her mind growing hazy. His smile widened as she approached him, deep under his spell.

No. She wanted to burn her skin off, it itched so badly. Balling her hands into fists, the illogical part of her mind wondered what would happen if she punched him. "Enough," she hissed, her face twisting with disgust. His cocky smirk faded, brows raising. "Braya, let's go." Raylyn mounted her mare, who remained passively pleasant. "Braya!" She was still standing in the middle of the road, stroking her horse's mane, Raylyn's orders falling on deaf ears.

"I've not come across many that can overcome my powers," the prince said, his brow furrowing. "What other secrets do you hold?"

Raylyn rolled her eyes. "Only the obvious fact that I'd very much like to be on my way, *Your Highness*."

"Interesting time to take a day trip out of town, wouldn't you agree?" He stepped around her, peering into one of the burdened saddle bags, eyeing the provisions inside with a raised brow. "Or perhaps you've planned a longer trip?"

She took a deep breath, fighting the urge to kick him. "Respectfully, it's none of your damn business. Now, end your enchantment on my friend."

He held her gaze, a look of amusement glinting in his eyes. "As my lady commands." Before he finished the last word, Braya choked out a strangled gasp, coming to her senses as the prince's influence lifted. "You aren't skipping town yet, Raylyn. Follow me." Without waiting for a reply, he strode past them, toward the expansive farms and houses, toward the Council and the sentencing Raylyn had so nearly eluded.

Resignation settled into her core, and she dismounted her horse. Word of her insolence was guaranteed to get back to her parents and the council. She couldn't imagine their faces if she came trotting into the village aback a mount with the prince walking on foot. "Ray," Braya hissed, "what are you doing? Let's just go." Her voice was a low whisper. "We could get a head start, make a run for it. Get out of his range, then—"

"I wouldn't reveal all of my schemes for listening ears, if I were you," the prince called over his shoulder. "Just my opinion, though. Divulge all you wish. But move along now. I believe we have an early appointment in the village square." And with that, he faced forward once more, not at all concerned with Braya's desire to flee.

Silence fell on the trio as they continued their march back into the village. The few miles on foot were much more taxing, and for the second time that morning, she was coated in a sheen of sweat. Fear mixed with exertion, and her heart hammered against her ribs like a frenzied percussionist. With each step, she had to resist the urge to turn around and run, despite what little that would accomplish. The prince remained several paces ahead of the girls, but he did not turn to look at them again. Effectors could feel the emotions of others around them as easily as hearing spoken words, and any snap decision to escape would be ended before it even began.

They passed Braya's farmhouse; the brightened sky illuminating the mild disrepairs that the gray dawn hid earlier. Several shutters hung crookedly, and the green paint on the front door was peeling. When Braya's mother, Anais, was alive, the front flower garden had been her pride. Raylyn remembered hiding behind trimmed hydrangea bushes smelling of sweet, warm summer when they were children. A few benches had been placed in the meandering path, and in her final days, Anais would sit amongst her flowers, watching hummingbirds flittering from one bloom to the next. Now, it was overgrown, the benches hidden beneath vines and long, untended grass. All the beauty the world lost when Anais died resurfaced in her daughter, Braya's bright hair almost glowing in the warm sun.

Raylyn eyed her, hoping she would retreat to her home. Instead of turning down the path, she gave a quick shake of her head, mouthing, "I'm not leaving you." Her face was fixed with determination, and Raylyn swallowed hard, wishing for some of the confidence her friend so easily possessed. Her mind spun, hoping the council would overlook Braya's involvement with her attempt to flee.

Too soon and an eternity later, the road narrowed, the houses growing tighter together as they approached the village square. The village was awake with the usual bustling of townsfolk commencing with morning chores, all a blur to Raylyn. She ignored the surprised stares of passersby; stories of the events in the forest just a day prior had likely spread, rumors catching like wildfire in the small community. The prince himself was enough to garner unwanted attention, as strangers were all but nonexistent. Raylyn's mother had faced similar gawking when she had arrived unannounced almost two decades prior.

"Raylyn!" her mother's shrill voice called out, cutting through the haze of anxiety which clouded her mind. Eva rushed to her side, grabbing her shoulders. "We were so worried," she said, crushing her into a tight hug. Raylyn closed her eyes, savoring the brief comfort. Her mother pulled away, eyeing the horses and Braya. Before she could form any accusation, she caught sight of the prince, still several paces ahead of the girls.

"Your Highness! You're up!" Eva exclaimed, dropping into a deep curtsy. "Praise the Goddess."

"The praise belongs to you and your daughter, I daresay," he said, stepping closer to them. "You have my deepest thanks."

A scarlet flush crept across Eva's cheeks. She laid a hand on Raylyn's arm as if afraid her daughter would disappear again. "But how do you know?" she asked, disconcerted.

"Ah, I overheard the chirping of birds while I was recovering last night in your clinic, Madam Healer." He smiled and continued, "It's surprising what people say when they think no one is listening."

Eva's face flushed a deeper red. "Oh, those girls, such little gossips! I apologize. I will be having words with them on proper conduct."

"No apology necessary. A display of power that's been extinct for a century deserves to be talked about. Especially tied with the rescue of royalty. You can't blame them." His gaze fell on Raylyn, and she shifted, uncomfortable under the weight of it. She struggled to conceal her emotions, knowing she was an open book for him to read.

"Beg your pardon, Your Highness," Eva began, turning her attention to Raylyn as well. "But where were you? We've been searching for both of you for the last hour. I wasn't expecting to find you both … *together*." A small furrow appeared between her brows.

"Of course, Madam. Your curiosity is understandable. We went for a little stroll together." His tone was indifferent, as if stating the weather was warm today.

"A little s-stroll?" Eva stammered, taken aback.

Braya snorted, rivaling that of her horses. The other three turned toward her in surprise. Raylyn was ashamed to think she had forgotten the presence of her friend and pushed the guilt down, wondering if the prince knew her thoughts.

Braya cleared her throat. "Well, it's absurd, isn't it?" she said, rolling her eyes. She opened her mouth to continue, but the loud, clear chime of church bells rang through the air, cutting her off.

Eva's eyes widened. "Raylyn, it's time. We need to go. Please excuse us," she said, glancing at the prince. "We have a council meeting, and it behooves us to be timely. I implore you, Your Highness, allow Braya to escort you back to the clinic. You were in such a frail state last night."

"Let me come!" Braya said earnestly. She dropped the horse's reins and moved toward Raylyn.

Before she could plead further, the prince interrupted. "I appreciate the concern. But I would rather like to join you for this meeting. If I'm not mistaken, I'm largely to blame for its occurrence."

Eva stood, holding the prince's gaze. Devoid of the fine clothes and gore of the day before, it was almost possible to believe him as an ordinary villager. Eva's mouth twitched downward, her disapproval visible to Raylyn's trained eye. She had received such a look more than once—usually from staying too late at Braya's farm or miscalculating ingredients for a salve to be used in the clinic.

Finally, her mother nodded. "Of course, Your Highness. Please, it's this way." She glanced at Raylyn, a glint of sadness replacing the disapproval in her eyes.

"Wait, I want to come, too!" Braya yelled, moving to tie the mares up at the trough outside the stone building where the council sat.

"No, Braya. You are not involved in this matter," Eva said. "Take your horses back to your farm. I'm sure your father could use your help in the stables."

"But—" Braya protested.

"*Go*," Eva commanded, eyes narrowing. Raylyn swallowed dryly. Her mother was one of the most respected leaders in the village and did not tolerate insolence. She could not remember the last time anyone disobeyed her, youth and adult alike.

Hot anger flashed on Braya's face, but she knew her battle was lost. Without another word, she spun on her heel, leading the horses down the road. A strange mix of sadness and relief filled Raylyn's chest as she watched her friend retreat.

"If you please, Your Highness," Eva said, her voice softening to a more respectful tone as she opened the large wooden door at the front of the building.

Raylyn was never permitted to step inside, and curiosity had clawed at her for years, wondering what secrets lay hidden within. Normally, she would have been all eyes and ears, examining every minute detail. Instead, fear dulled her curiosity and the cool air caused goosebumps to prickle up her arms. Flickering lantern light illuminated the hall, devoid of windows and natural light.. Half a dozen doors stood at equal intervals on the left side of the corridor, looming ominously over the corridor. Their echoing steps were the only sound in the otherwise empty passage.

Thirty-one, thirty-two, thirty-three, Raylyn counted her steps, trying to ground herself before she succumbed to her panic. They paused in front of the third door. A heartbeat later, a sinewy, clean-shaven man appeared, propping the door open with one hand. Raylyn recognized him as one of the newly appointed councilmen, Bennard. He was a few years older than Raylyn and worked under her father as one of the village guard. Other than that, she knew very little about him.

"Good morning, Madam Ashton," he said, nodding his head low in respect. Eyeing Raylyn and the prince, he continued, "Forgive me, but no one is permitted guests for today's assembly."

"Bennard. Good day." Eva disregarded his statement and turned toward the prince. "Please, Your Highness, may I have a moment with my daughter? I'm sure Bennard would be kind enough to find you a seat—close to the door, if you wouldn't mind—and we shall join you momentarily." Despite asking permission, Eva spoke with command. Raylyn was almost too numb to be impressed.

"Your Highness?" Bennard repeated, eyes wide. He dropped to his knees. "M-my sincerest apologies," he said, head almost touching the cool stone floor. The door he previously held swung in its freedom and hit him on the side of his face. "Oomph," he groaned, rubbing his head.

The prince chuckled. "No need, good sir. Please, rise. Let's give these ladies their privacy." Bennard did as instructed, his face red with either embarrassment or injury or both, and the pair entered the chamber.

All the while, Raylyn was staring, but hardly seeing. Her courage from the morning had dissolved like dew on grass, and the world grew foggy. She tried counting her breaths but couldn't focus and lost track. The small part of her brain that could think clearly wondered if hearts could explode because surely hers would at any moment. The pounding echoed through her ears, growing steadily louder. Each beat brought her closer to losing her entire grip on reality.

"Raylyn." Her mother stepped close and cradled her face between her palms. She pressed her lips to her forehead and mouthed words that Raylyn couldn't hear.

Instantly, warmth radiated through her body, spreading from the spot her mother had kissed. The healing spell

33

burned away some of her crippling anxiety. Its absence was jarring, as if stepping into warm sunlight after being smothered by darkness. She blinked as the icy numbness of anxiety faded. "There you are," Eva said, still cradling her face, eyes glistening with the threat of tears.

"Momma, what will happen? Please, *please* don't let them Mark me." Raylyn's voice cracked from its prolonged silence.

"I do not know if I can save you from this. Our laws have been broken—unintentionally, which, of course, may allow for your redemption." She let go of Raylyn's face and rummaged through the inside of her light cloak. She pulled out a small package wrapped in brown paper. "Take this—no! There's no time," Eva said, silencing her unasked question. "If all goes awry, you will know when to open it." She concealed it in the waistband of Raylyn's trousers. "I love you, and I will do everything I can to protect you." Without further explanation, Eva opened the door and gestured Raylyn inside.

It was the largest room Raylyn had ever seen. Though the council building was imposing on the outside, it seemed impossible that a room this expansive would fit inside. She pondered on the magics unknown that would allow such a feat as she gazed around the room.

The center of the room sank into the ground as if someone had dug a huge hole into the floor. A carved stone staircase led down to the pit-like bottom, where sat three plain chairs, empty. Every twelfth step opened to a wide tier, which encircled the perimeter of the room, bedecked with wooden benches neatly tucked beneath banquet tables. Glass water pitchers and goblets were stacked on top, catching the flickering lantern light.

Despite around forty people sitting at various levels in the room, it was nearly silent, their steps reverberating in the hollow air. She followed her mother to an empty bench, but before she could sit down, a baritone voice rang throughout the room.

"Perhaps you were unaware, Madam Healer. Guests are prohibited from this meeting today." The design of the chamber made it difficult for Raylyn to determine where the voice had originated, but movement caught her eye. Across the room on the lowest level, in what Raylyn deemed "the pit," a man stood bracing his hands on the table in front of him. He was barrel-chested, his tunic straining against the expanse of his stomach.

Eva paused, halfway to sitting down, and straightened herself up. "Young Bennard was kind enough to inform me on my entry to this chamber, Doyle. Though I think we can both agree that it is appropriate that *the accused* attend their own trial, wouldn't you agree?" Eva sat and nodded for Raylyn to join her on the bench.

"I do not agree! I'm sure we *all* disagree." He glanced around the room. "This is not abiding by our customs. We have not discussed the allegations yet, nor are we ready to hear *her* side of this mess," Doyle hissed, and though Raylyn was too far away to be certain, she thought she saw little beads of sputum fly from his lips. "And that doesn't take into consideration whoever *that* is." He motioned toward the door, where the prince idly sat, leaning back against the stone wall. "And Bennard, what are you doing? Why are you not manning the door?"

Raylyn peeled her eyes away from the fat, shouting man and looked over at the prince. Seated next to him was Bennard, who apparently couldn't help but dote on him. He froze as he filled the prince's cup with water from the pitcher on the table. With the room's attention, he fumbled, and water soaked the table, running down its sides to form a puddle on the stone.

"*Get out*! Get out and man the door, you half-witted imbecile!" Doyle bellowed.

Bennard, who was muttering apologies to the prince while trying to push the puddle away with his feet, scampered out of the chamber. "Deepest a-apologies, Your Highness," he repeated, retreating through the door.

The room was silent for a moment. "Did he just say, 'Your Highness?'" inquired an older woman, sitting a few benches down from Raylyn. Her hair was slate-gray and tied into a tight bun at the nape of her neck. Eleanor Bernshaw was one of the oldest people in the village. Her age and wisdom compensated for her minimal healing powers, and she was one of Raylyn's mentors in the clinic when she was first learning of proper hygiene and dressing changes. Her hands were mangled with arthritis, and she wouldn't allow anyone to heal them. "Don't waste youth's energy on an old lady. I'll manage just fine," she would say. Her condition went unchecked for too long, and even Eva could not reverse the damage.

All at once, the room was buzzing with conversation. Whispers of, "The prince, is it him?" and "He's found!" echoed in the vast chamber. Raylyn chewed her lip, trying to hear what everyone was saying. Though the royal family was held to high standards, people of Lakehaven were accustomed to their remote independence. She wouldn't be surprised if they tried to escort him from the chamber.

"Enough!" Although Raylyn expected Doyle's pompous tone, the voice belonged to another: her father.

Between her anxiety-ridden stupor and the intimidating conference chamber, Raylyn had failed to remember that her father—a member of the council since before she was born—would be attending. She remembered the look on his face last night, and her heart sank. If her own father thought her actions were so deplorable, what chance would she have with the council?

The din died as quickly as it started. All eyes were on Charles Ashton, High Caster, commander of the village guard. He was standing on the same tier as Doyle, though on the same side of the room as Raylyn and Eva. From the angle, Raylyn could see the back of his head, no gray visible in his thick, brown hair. "All for Prince Rowan to remain for the length of the meeting?"

To her surprise, all but a few hands raised in the air. Expectedly, Doyle huffed in his seat, arms crossed over his chest. Mrs. Bernshaw's twisted hands rested in her lap, too, and Raylyn stared in shock.

"That's settled. Let's get on with it then." Her father sat back down. Raylyn wasn't sure if she was relieved or disappointed to be out of his eyesight.

"It's not settled," Doyle disagreed. "That *girl* shouldn't be here!"

"That *girl* is my *daughter*," Charles growled, "and I expect you to keep that tone out of your voice when referring to my family. She stays." Raylyn's throat tightened. Maybe her father didn't hate her after all.

"I'll take whatever tone I damn well please, especially when referring to the little demon you've sired!" Doyle spat, a purple hue coloring the edges of his face.

Stunned silence filled the room. Heat crept up her neck at the insult. She knew the villagers would be afraid of the powers she had shown, yet she wasn't prepared to hear the accusations of evil. Shrinking in her seat, she stared at her hands, afraid to look up and meet the council members' eyes.

"No one in this room is foolhardy enough to believe my daughter is born of the darkness, Doyle. You've all known her since she was still sleeping in my wife's womb. And if you cannot control your outbursts, perhaps it is *you* who needs to be excused from the chamber." When Doyle remained silent, Charles continued, "Very well. You all are aware why we summoned you on such little notice. We must discuss the breach of our laws which took place yesterday eve."

A low murmur ran through the room and heads turned to look at Raylyn. The weight of their stares made her face burn even hotter. She knew word of her magic would spread, but to be the subject of such scrutiny was torment, and she wished she could exit the meeting on her own accord. She'd rather meet her fate blindly.

"Excuse me, Charles," Mrs. Bernshaw rose, addressing the room. "Though it is our tradition that the council head leads these trials, given your, ah, intimate relationship with the accused, we think it wise that another assumes those duties today."

"We?" Charles asked, surveying the room. "Who comprises 'we'?" His voice was steady, though his hands balled into tight fists at his sides. Beside her, Eva straightened.

Pleasant as ever, Eleanor Bernshaw replied, "Sorry, Charles. We voted on it prior to your arrival."

"Of course," he said stiffly. "Graymor, perhaps you'll take over my duties?" Charles turned, addressing the man next to him. Kenneth Graymor was her father's second-in-command in the village guard. Raylyn had known him for as long as she could remember; more times than not, he joined them for Sunday dinner.

"Unnecessary, Charles. Thank you, of course. We agreed that I will lead this meeting," Mrs. Bernshaw said.

When no one voiced their opposition, Charles nodded, returning to his seat.

"Raylyn, dear?" Eleanor Bernshaw turned, addressing her with a smile.

"Yes, ma'am?" She tried to forget the audience, remembering the countless days she spent under Mrs. Bernshaw's instruction. If her father couldn't conduct the meeting, then having to recount events to her would be the best alternative.

"Do you see the chairs at the center of the room? Make your way down the stairs, and we shall begin."

Raylyn glanced at her mother, who gave a tight-lipped nod, before she rose and strode toward the stairs. She concentrated on her feet, each step a struggle as her heart raced. Reaching the wooden chair, she sat and dared a quick glance up at the room. Instantly, she understood the purpose of the strangely designed chamber. Sitting at the lowest level, she felt like a caged animal. The few dozen council members peered down, encircling her, mistrust apparent in many of their stony faces.

"Raylyn Ashton, your charges are as follows," Mrs. Bernshaw began, grabbing a sheet of parchment from the table in front of her with gnarled fingers. Her eyes narrowed as she read. "Disobeying direct commands from a High Master or Madam, reckless destruction using unpermitted magic, and syphoning power using dark magic." She laid the parchment down. "We have all been informed of the incidents that occurred yesterday in the forest, roughly three miles west from the village. Per the reports, just over an acre of forest was destroyed, including several hundred oaks and a dozen ancient redwoods.

"Furthermore, direct commands to cease use of magic under the instruction of High Healer, Eva Ashton, were disregarded, resulting in the aforementioned destruction."

Betrayal leached like poison in Raylyn's stomach. Whatever report her mother gave the night before just seemed to incriminate her further. *So much for doing everything you can*, she thought icily.

"I am concerned, however," Mrs. Bernshaw continued, "about the legitimacy of the syphoning claim. The accusation of such evil does appear outlandish, especially deriving from one of our own." Mrs. Bernshaw gave Raylyn a small smile.

"The legitimacy?" Doyle repeated. "How many more acres of sacred forest would you see demolished, Eleanor, to be fully persuaded?"

"In all these years, the girl has never shown the slightest sign of possessing such powers—"

"Hidden by her parents, of course! Protecting the little monster! They should stand trial as well!"

"Lower your voice, Doyle," Mrs. Bernshaw instructed as if speaking to an unruly child. "It is imperative we validate these accusations prior to declaring a final sentence."

"Which is what, exactly?" Prince Rowan asked. He was lounging in his wooden chair, completely at ease. Raylyn noticed the novel he was reading on the road lay open in his lap.

"Beg your pardon, your Highness?" Mrs. Bernshaw asked.

"The final sentence, 'If *our Raylyn* here is declared guilty of having...' What did you call it? Ah, yes. 'Evil, dark syphoning powers'?" He set his book down and leaned forward in his seat, head cocked.

"Well now, that would depend on the council vote. Based on the meeting last night, we are leaning toward the Mark."

"Meeting last night?" Eva asked. "I was never told—"

"We thought it best to let you and Charles rest, dear," Mrs. Bernshaw replied without a hint of guilt.

Her father, his voice low and dangerous, retorted, "I am head of the council, leader of the village guard, and you dare orchestrate secret meetings?"

"You dare hide a monster in our midst?" Doyle bellowed back.

Her father sprang from his seat, warm light glowing from his palms. "By the Goddess, if you call her a monster one more time," he spat, the table in front of him trembling, "I will make you regret ever learning to use that vile tongue of yours."

"Aha! A threat on my person; you all are my witnesses! I'd imagine the demon inherited the power from you, eh?" Doyle was standing, too, though his palms didn't glow. Raylyn cringed in her seat, silently pleading for her father to sit back down. She had already ruined *her* life. She didn't want her father to be punished for her mistakes as well.

"Enough! Are we untrained children to act with such immaturity?" Mrs. Bernshaw asked, clearly disgusted.

The quaking table calmed as the light in Charles's palms died. "M-my apologies, Eleanor. This *is* my daughter we are talking about."

"And if it is too emotional for you to handle, you may excuse yourself. We will not make final accusations until we are finished with the trial. Another word, Doyle, and you will find yourself excused as well." Both men sat mute, glaring looks as sharp as knives toward each other from across the chamber. Raylyn glanced between the two men, wondering if she was going to get caught in their crossfire.

"Raylyn, do you understand the seriousness of your charges?"

It was the first time she was being addressed. Pulse quickening, she scanned the room. Dozens of eyes were on her, including her mother's. Eva gave the tiniest shake of her head. *No.*

"N-no, Mrs. Bernshaw." Her voice quavered, small and insignificant.

"What needs explaining, dear?"

"All of it," Raylyn said. "I don't understand anything that's going on." Her confidence grew as she spoke, and she imagined herself alone in the clinic with Mrs. Bernshaw, all other faces melting away. "One moment I was healing that man... Prince Rowan, I mean, and the next, I... I'm not sure what happened. It was like energy from around me was ... flowing through me. I don't think I could make it happen again even if I tried." Tears now burned her eyes, falling in salty drops onto her tunic.

"It has never happened before?"

"Never... The Goddess blessed me with healing powers like my mother. I have trained for years to hone the craft, as you know, Mrs. Bernshaw. Please, let me keep my healing powers. *Please.* I don't know what I'll do if you Mark me." The words poured out in a hurried rush.

"So, it's true..." Mrs. Bernshaw stared at Raylyn, at a momentary loss for words.

"I didn't know I was doing it; it was like I had no control." She sniffed, wiping her running nose. "Goddess knows I would never harm the forest."

"You belong to the Goddess no longer," Mrs. Bernshaw said icily. "I prayed it wasn't true, girl. My heart longed for another explanation."

"Eleanor, really," Eva said, standing. "We don't understand what's going on. Maybe with some time—"

"What do you hope for, Eva? To train her? Perhaps to refine this Goddess-forsaken ability? *No*. It will be the Marksmen for her, and be grateful we allow her to live."

"You don't speak for the council," her mother said, urgency clipping the words. "Allow the vote."

"Vote. Aye. Allow them to make their voices heard." Mrs. Bernshaw sat in her chair, stony faced and decided.

"W-well," Eva's voice shook, her façade of power crumbling. Her eyes darted around as if seeking an escape. "Well. Alright. All those in agreement with Raylyn's crimes?" Save her parents, every hand rose, even Prince Rowan's. She averted her gaze, not wishing to face the sentencing head-on. "All those—" Eva's voice cracked, she cleared her throat before continuing, "All those in favor of punishment by Marking?"

Raylyn didn't need to look up; her mother's sudden sobs, echoing through the chamber, were proof enough of her inevitable fate.

"Fools," Prince Rowan muttered. She glanced up, confused.

She wasn't the only one. "Your Highness?" Mrs. Bernshaw asked cautiously.

"Fools." He was reclining in his chair again, reading, face hidden behind the volume. "The lot of you, such fools... So eager to destroy the unknown rather than come to understand it."

"Indeed!" Mrs. Bernshaw gasped. Her mouth opened and closed like a fish, but she could not verbalize a further rebuttal.

"Fools are those who dance with this darkness," Doyle grumbled. "Those that justify it should burn with Haddeon himself. We are people of the Goddess and do not condone such *wickedness* in our midst," he said fervently, beads of perspiration flinging from his temple as he shook his head. "I can feel the evil radiating off her as we speak!" He stood, waving his hands around as he drew a safety sigil in the air. "Goddess protect our innocent souls!"

Raylyn shifted in her seat. Doyle was an imbecile. She heard her father complain of the man many times, especially after a mug or two of mead. His family had lived in the village for decades, if not centuries, but he showed none of the wisdom nor power of his predecessors. What he lacked in talent, he made up for in opinionated brashness.

Prince Rowan closed his book with a swift snap, tossing it on the table. "You can *feel* the evil, eh?" Without taking his eyes off Doyle, the prince continued, "Tell me, wise sir, what *else* can you feel?" Doyle's face deepened to a violent purple and sweat coated his skin in a greasy sheen. "Heart's quickening? Chest tight?" Prince Rowan smirked, arms crossed.

Doyle, however, was choking, tears streaking down his flushed cheeks. Raylyn stared at him in horror. She had read about effectors; though they couldn't physically harm people with their powers, they could manipulate emotions, increasing anxiety and panic until the suffocating feelings overwhelmed their target. This was exactly what was happening to Doyle, and the terror in his gasping face made her stomach twist in disgust.

"Stop!" she yelled, jumping to her feet. Her chair clattered to the floor in her haste.

"Why?" Prince Rowan asked, his eyes still on Doyle, who clawed at his chest and throat. He must have ended his enchantment though, for after a moment, Doyle took in great gasping breaths, wiping the tears from his cheeks.

"E-Effector!" Doyle stuttered. A few gasps echoed through the room.

"Apt observation sir." The prince's act of nonchalance broke. He stood, rolling up his sleeves. "I presume your meeting is at its conclusion, though I have a few things to add." His eyes surveyed the room and landed on Raylyn. "As Prince of Ellendria, I hereby pardon Raylyn Ashton of all aforesaid charges." Multiple people began their protestations simultaneously, but he spoke over them. "Anyone who contradicts my verdict is speaking treason, punishable by death, so *please*—Doyle, is it?—continue, by all means." He paused, willing someone to speak, but no one did. "Wonderful. Very well."

Eleanor Bernshaw rather recklessly interjected, "We do not want the girl here. You pardon her, you take responsibility for her." Mutters of agreement rang through the room. Raylyn pleaded silently for her parents to speak up, to disagree and argue her case. Neither did.

Annoyance colored Prince Rowan's voice. "What in the name of the Goddess would make you think I would leave her with you prejudiced, ignorant lot? The girl has powers that haven't been seen in a century, powers that may very well change the history of our world, and you wish to cast her out like a leper!"

Before anyone could counter, the door to the chamber banged open. All heads turned to see Bennard, breathless in the doorway.

"Sorry for the interruption! Y-your Highness," Bennard dropped into a low bow, "your guard has arrived. I've kept them at the entrance of the building, though they are *keen* to see you."

"Right on schedule. Many thanks, Sir Bennard." Prince Rowan turned back to the room. "We are done here. Raylyn, come with me." He strode toward the door without another glance. Raylyn looked at her mother, who flashed a quick smile, nodding her head. She turned, searching the room for her father. He was cradling his head in his hands and didn't look up. She hurried to catch up with Prince Rowan. If it was a choice between being Marked or leaving everything else behind, well, she had already decided.

CHAPTER 4

RAYLYN FOLLOWED PRINCE ROWAN out of the building, the sun blinding her momentarily. Though a thousand questions danced in her head, she had no time to ask. The door opened to half a dozen soldiers, brown leather armor adding to the bulk of their muscles. Scabbards were fastened to their waists, and their chest plates bore the same interlocking pattern of eagles and crowns that Raylyn had seen on the prince's tunic. Before they could take another step, all the soldiers—save one—fell upon a knee, heads bent in reverence.

"Garrick!" Prince Rowan gave a throaty laugh, clasping the arm of the still-standing soldier. "Prompt as ever, I see." He turned to the rest of the group. "Come, rise, and let's begone of this damned place." The soldiers rose in synchrony.

Garrick removed his leather helm, running a hand through sweat—dampened hair. Raylyn wrinkled her nose as the musk of body odor and horses permeated the air. "Rowan, where in Haddeon's hottest circle of *hell* have you been?"

Prince Rowan gave a humorless chuckle. "It's a bit of a story, my friend. And not for the street's ears." He glanced behind him at Raylyn and addressed her, "I believe we have use for your friend, the stablemaster's daughter?"

"Braya?" Raylyn asked, confused. No one had referred to her father as "master" of anything for several years.

Rowan nodded. "If you'd be so kind as to lead the way?" Avoiding eye contact with the surrounding soldiers, she led them down the familiar path to Braya's ranch.

As they walked, the soldiers seamlessly placed themselves around Rowan, forming a living shield. Straining her ears, she could hear the cadence of low voices behind her, but couldn't make out specific words. She resigned herself to eavesdropping later and settled into the mess of her thoughts. So much had changed so quickly. With the threat of being Marked gone, she was lightheaded, yet bordering on giddy. But why did she have these powers, and what if she couldn't learn to control them? Coming into powers at seventeen was unheard of; they often manifested in young childhood, and occasionally during adolescence, but adulthood? Prince Rowan's words from earlier echoed through her mind. *Powers that may change the history of our world... But how? And why me?*

When they arrived at the ranch, Braya was sitting amongst the overgrown garden, nearly hidden in all the foliage. She sprang up upon their arrival, her face splitting into a grin despite the presence of six armed soldiers.

"Went so well you need a private guard, eh, Ray?" she called. The smile faltered as they grew nearer. The two girls embraced, and she added in a low whisper, "Are they going to Mark you?"

Not bothering to lower her voice, Raylyn responded, "No. Prince Rowan pardoned me."

"That's amazing. I mean, he should, since you saved his life and all, but still ..."

"Saved his life?" Garrick repeated. "The fantasies these lasses contrive astounds me. Must be nice to have so much free time." The other soldiers encouraged him with laughter, causing Braya's cheeks to redden. Raylyn winced, knowing how quickly her friend's temper could rise.

Before she could retort, Rowan replied. "It's true." The men stopped laughing. Confusion furrowed in Garrick's brow, the unasked question in his eyes. "Like I said earlier, it's not a tale fit for the streets. But, that's beside the point. Miss Braya, is your father available? We have some business for the stable master."

She snorted. "The good stable master is indisposed. Can I be of service, Your Highness?"

"Indisposed?"

"Completely smashed, I'm afraid," she replied. "Face down on the floor of his bedchambers. That cheap whiskey again. The man's got no taste at all." She smiled sweetly back at the prince and his guards, as if discussing this year's crops and not her inebriated father.

Rowan paused, taken aback. "Right... Well, my men and I need fresh steeds. I was also wondering about that palfrey Raylyn was riding earlier. Is she still saddled and equipped?"

Braya stared up at the prince, face growing stony. "Yes. Wanted to be prepared, just in case."

"Wonderful, that saves some time. Bring her out, and an additional seven mounts, fully saddled. Garrick, what of the horses you rode in on? Surely you didn't come by foot."

"Stationed at the inn. A few are in rough shape; it was a hard day's ride."

"I will pay full price for the fresh horses and saddles, as well as gift you those steeds for the trouble." Prince Rowan nodded at Garrick, who withdrew a change purse from his waist and offered it to Braya.

Braya accepted the heft of coins with wide eyes. Winking at Raylyn, she turned, bee—lining to the stables.

"Go assist her. The quicker we make it back to Lendris, the better," Prince Rowan commanded of two of the soldiers. They nodded and followed Braya.

"Would you walk with me for a moment, Raylyn?" the prince asked.

"Do you think that is wise?" Garrick asked gruffly. "It hasn't even been a full day since you were attacked, and the traitors who did it haven't been caught."

"You aren't telling me anything I don't already know, Gar. We'll stay close."

Garrick huffed, shaking his head in disapproval. "Foolish," he muttered, "Don't get ambushed again."

The prince laughed in response. "Come," he said, looking down at Raylyn, grabbing her hand. The questions and fears wheeling in her mind silenced, replaced by a thrum of anticipation. She tried to ignore the prince's touch, but her skin prickled hotly beneath his hand. Needing to distance herself, she bent, dancing out of his reach, to pick a small purple wildflower. She focused her thoughts on pulling off each cool petal as they walked. Effectors could feel other's emotions, and she didn't need him to hear her unsolicited thoughts about his touch.

"Raylyn." He pulled her to a stop. "I will never be able to express my gratitude. Without you, I would be dead ... Your village leaders will come to accept you again. They are just stuck in old ways of thinking."

Without looking up, she continued to decimate the small flower in her hands. Despite his kind words, shame enveloped her. Not only had she violated her religion, but now she was ostracized by her village. Even her parents had given up on her. Purple petals spiraled to the ground as she continued to pluck at them vigorously.

Two large hands encased her own, crushing the tiny flower. "Look at me," he commanded, though his tone was soft, almost pleading.

She glanced up, his eyes searching her face. "Don't allow bigoted, outdated fools to taint your perspective. By the Goddess, you are something *special*. Remember that."

Despite logic, her heart raced, and all she could think about was how close he was and the warmth of his hands, still clasped over her own. A fluttering stirred in her stomach, and she felt her cheeks warm. He smiled, his lips curving upward, as he reached down and brushed a dark lock of hair from her eyes. Her skin tingled with longing ... and something else, the trace of magic crawling under her flesh. *Effector*.

She jumped away from him with such haste that she stumbled and fell against the meadow's fence, disgust replacing desire. "Do not manipulate me!" she yelled, sitting in a crumpled heap on the ground.

A pink flush creeped up Rowan's neck. He cocked his head with a frown. "I didn't." He held out a hand to Raylyn, who glared. Refusing to take it, she stood and brushed the dirt from her trousers.

"You're lying. I can feel it, like my skin's crawling off my bones."

He stared at her, contemplating. "If I've influenced you just now, it was unintentional. Sometimes it happens just as naturally as breathing ..." His brow furrowed. "Only exceptionally skilled mages have the ability to feel an effector's touch. I can only imagine what you'll accomplish with some training."

"Training?" she asked, keeping her distance. She tried to focus on the meadow, her boots, her hands, anything. Looking at his face made her feel exposed. Her heart was still hammering from their closeness moments before, and she swallowed, willing herself to focus.

"Yes, that's why I wanted to talk to you. I can secure you a spot at the Academy if you're agreeable. Unrestrained power is dangerous. You need to learn just how much you're capable of and how to control it."

Her heart quickened. *The Academy.* It was the most prestigious school, nestled in the heart of the country. Many of her textbooks were written by Academy graduates. To train under such masters was a secret desire she had never shared with anyone. She cleared her throat, trying to hide her excitement at the idea. "You speak to me of control? When you unwittingly play with others' emotions?"

He scowled, then closed his eyes, as if praying. "It is proving difficult around you. Your feelings are just rolling off you in waves." He opened his eyes and looked sideways at her. "It's overwhelming, honestly."

Heat rushed to her face as he confirmed her fears. Despite her best efforts, he was reading her like a book. "Is that something they can teach me? How to hide my emotions from *manipulators* like you?" She tried to disguise her embarrassment as anger, kicking a tuft of grass on the dry ground.

"I would think you'd have a little more empathy after the hardships you faced during your trial today. You fear that which you don't understand ... But to answer your question, yes. Those skilled enough can learn to block their emotions from *manipulators* like me," he repeated, ice in his voice. "No matter your choice," he continued, "We will travel to Lendris, regardless."

"If I decline? If I have no further desires for my future to be controlled by those around me?" Raylyn asked, daring to meet his gaze.

"You'll find the Academy will *open* doors for you, Raylyn, not close them. You're afraid?" he asked, raising a brow.

One didn't need magic to see the fear on her face. She blinked her eyes hard, refusing to let tears fall yet again. She must be stronger than that. "Have you ever had someone rip away your entire future?" Reluctance weighed on her chest, and she was terrified to leave everything she had ever known. She had been training to take her mother's place as high healer since she came into her powers at six years old. Despite the promise of the Academy, losing her place in her village was like a shard of glass to her heart. Her relief at being pardoned was overshadowed by overbearing loss.

"I've had people try ..." He trailed off, the silence building between them again. "Ah, the horses are ready. We have about a day's journey to Silver Keep, and we can pick up a carriage there. It will make the journey more comfortable."

Braya was waiting with the horses when they returned to the group. She grinned at Raylyn. "Where're we off to?" she asked, tightening the strap of one of her saddle bags.

Rowan answered before Raylyn could reply. "We appreciate your haste and generosity, but I'm sure your father requires you here to maintain your ranch."

"To hell with what my father requires. He's a grown man, is he not? He can tend to it himself," Braya said, brows raising defiantly. "I've got my own coin and supplies. I'm coming with Raylyn."

"Raylyn is destined for the Academy. Unless I'm mistaken, you have no powers. There is no place for you there," Rowan said curtly.

Braya was silent for a moment, a flash of anger darkening her eyes. But it passed just as quickly as it came. "Your Highness, if you want use of my steeds, you'll allow me to accompany you." Her voice dripped with sweetness.

"He's already paid you for the horses. Enough of this nonsense. We are wasting time," Garrick said, shaking his head.

"Then take it *back*!" Braya thrust the coin purse back towards the prince. "No price will pay me off. Raylyn is my best friend, and I am coming with her." When he refused to accept the purse, Braya turned to Raylyn. "You don't have to go with them. We were leaving together this morning before the trial. Let's just be on our own way."

Raylyn stared, dumbstruck. The morning seemed a lifetime ago, their plans mere children's fantasies. And the prospect of studying at the Academy was a seductive offer. There was no better education to be had in all Ellendria.

"Braya, I don't know ..." Raylyn glanced at the prince, searching his face for any sign of disagreement.

"You may make your own choices. I will not follow you to clean up any messes you may inadvertently make with your uncontrolled powers," Rowan said, mounting his horse. All six soldiers following suit without even a moment of hesitation.

She deliberated. An hour ago, she was destined to be Marked. So much had changed so quickly, and she was forced to decide her future with no time to think through all the consequences. *I would learn more than I've ever dared dream.* Knowing the pain that would ensue, she swallowed, staring at her feet. "Braya, I have to go with them. I can't pose a threat to those around me."

"You're going to leave me here with *him*?" she asked, nodding her head back towards her house, "despite everything I would do for you?"

"I—I'm sorry. I'll come back, I promise. But, I have to learn how to control it." Raylyn stepped closer to embrace her, but she jerked away, as if repulsed by her touch.

"Don't bother," Braya replied, refusing to meet her eye. "So much for loyalty, huh?" Angry tears spilled down her cheeks.

Raylyn was about to change her mind, tell Rowan to leave without her. But before her lips could form the words, Braya hopped on her horse, kicking it into a gallop. She disappeared in a cloud of dust as she retreated towards town. Self-loathing turned Raylyn's stomach to acid.

CHAPTER 5

"**W**AKE UP, WE'RE LEAVING." THE gruff voice startled her awake, her body stiffening in surprise. Raylyn groaned as her muscles protested the movement. The dark air still held the coolness of night and she wondered how many hours they were away from daybreak.

Despite her aching exhaustion, she rose from her bedroll, ducking under the flaps of the tiny tent. The rest of the party was up and mostly packed; her tent was the last to remain erect. Irritated, she started disassembling it, wondering why they hadn't woken her sooner.

"Here," Garrick said, appearing from behind a nearby horse. He offered her some jerky and bread.

She stared at it with a frown. "I still think we should've had a fire." Her stomach growled, unaccustomed to the limited food.

Garrick pulled his hand back. "Fine, I'll have seconds then, if it isn't fit for our little princess." He moved to take a bite of the dried meat.

Raylyn scrambled, nearly jumping on the burly man. "That's not what I meant!" She snatched the food out of his hand. "Sorry," she said, ripping off a mouthful. "I didn't sleep very well."

Garrick glowered at her. "Tonight, I'll give you a shift of watch duty. Then, you can complain about your sleep. I told you last night that a fire's smoke can lead brigands right to us. Not to mention any of the attackers who might know the prince escaped their ambush." With that, he walked away, shaking his head.

She watched him for a second, taking another large bite of her cold breakfast. The lack of fire made sense, of course, but it was still hard to take fictional robbers and assassins seriously when she was camping with six of the prince's royal guards. She pocketed the rest of her food and finished taking down her tent, rolling it into an impossibly small parcel which fit—with some coercion—inside her pack. Garrick had begrudgingly gifted it to her the night before when he discovered she failed to think of shelter in her runaway scheme.

They spent the previous day on horseback, covering as much distance as they dared without exhausting the horses. Raylyn's legs hardly held her weight when they stopped to make camp last night. Her inexperience presented itself in the deep bruising of her inner thighs from so tightly gripping the saddle. She cringed at the thought of mounting the horse again and the endless miles they needed to cover this day.

"Sore?" Rowan asked from behind her.

She spun around in surprise, wincing again as her muscles screamed. "A little," she lied. Her body had never hurt so much in her life.

He smiled. "It's hard on your body when you aren't used to it."

"And are you? Used to it, I mean." She looked over the ground a final time, ensuring she grabbed everything. All her belongings slimmed down into one overburdened pack.

"I wasn't always. The past year my father, brother, and I agreed it imperative to recruit for our army. Father is vehemently against going to war, but we need to be prepared regardless. We've been sending diplomats on recruiting missions, but I prefer to come along when I can to give the citizens some... uh... incentive to join up." He grinned as he continued, "I've met some very colorful characters along the way. And it *is* as good a way as any to build skill as a rider."

"Incentive? You mean you *manipulate* them. That's deplorable." Raylyn crinkled her nose, edging away from him in disgust.

Rowan sighed, running a hand through his hair. "I simply ease the fears of people who are on the fence. Give them a sense of confidence and pride. I don't force anyone who is unwilling."

"I can't imagine why this would be necessary, anyway. Why ruin people's lives just for a larger army? Our country has been at peace for decades. How could you be so selfish?"

His brow furrowed. "Selfish? We may have peace *now*, but it is a thin ledge on which we balance. It seems you and your village are quite sheltered from the rest of the world. The number of refugees crossing the border is

58

ever-growing, and we are concerned it's going to rise to ...
a *conflict* with Cystra."

"A conflict?" Raylyn asked. "Do you truly believe war
is that imminent?" She knew the conditions in Cystra
were bad, but war seemed extreme, especially after a lifetime of peace between the two nations. She couldn't
imagine the unrest a war would cause.

"When you see the conditions in which these people
are arriving, you'll understand. We want to avoid war at
all costs, but we must be prepared to defend ourselves if
unrest slips past the border."

Garrick called from across the camp, cutting off her
response. "Hate to break up the chatter, Rowan, but we
have a schedule to stick to. We've been here too long for
my liking."

She eyed her mare, loathing the idea of another long
day of riding. Fighting every aching muscle, she mounted
the horse, groaning. "I remember you saying something
about getting a carriage, Your Highness?" Raylyn said
through gritted teeth.

Trotting over on his horse, Garrick interjected, "Think
again, lass. The risk of traveling into Silver Keep is too
great with Rowan's attackers unfound. If horseback is too
much for you, feel free to stay behind." Without waiting
for a response, he urged his horse forward, leading the
party back towards the road.

"He's a bit high-strung," Rowan explained, an unspoken
apology in his voice. He turned, following Garrick. *Not
much of a choice,* she thought. Begrudgingly, she joined
the party on the road, resigning herself to another day of
discomfort.

The day dragged on much as the previous one. The terrain was flat, save for some long rolling hills that proved easily navigable. They stopped twice at streams to allow the horses to drink and to refill their canteens. Garrick stayed true to his word, and they circumvented the city, giving it a wide berth to remain unseen by fellow travelers.

"This is where we will break for the night," one of the soldiers said, pulling Raylyn from her musing. She hadn't noticed the sky turning violet, the surrounding trees casting long, tired shadows.

The obstacle of dismounting the horse rattled her, and even though the ground was just a few feet away, it might as well have been miles. She cursed Garrick and his caution, wishing for the comfort and privacy of a carriage.

"Can I help you?" Rowan asked, once again appearing with no sound of his arrival. He was occupied with Garrick most of the day, riding a little ahead of the group.

She glared at him, still irritated by their earlier conversation. The tales always said effectors were cunning, narcissistic creatures, out for their own gain alone. Raylyn had fooled herself into believing—however briefly—Rowan pardoned her out of gratitude and decency. His earlier confession to manipulating people into joining the army made her highly doubt his motives were ever so pure.

With a stubbornness her old donkey, Jimmy, would admire, Raylyn refused his offer and swung her leg over the saddle to dismount. Her muscles failed her, however, and she fell sprawling across the ground. Raylyn lay motionless, allowing the pain to wash over her and quell the tide of embarrassment which was sure to follow.

Rowan reached down, pulling her to her feet. She stood, legs wobbling like a newborn colt. "You okay?" he asked, chuckling.

"I'm fine." She folded her arms across her chest, wishing he'd leave her alone. She couldn't stand being close to him. The more time passed, the more she longed to see her parents and Braya, and ask them what they think all of this means. In front of her stood the reason everyone she loved was inaccessible, and though she couldn't condemn herself for saving the prince, she wished she hadn't been in the forest when he came crashing through, bloody and dying.

"How have I offended you?" he asked, hand still lingering on her arm.

She jerked away as best as she could manage despite her aches. "*Stop* reading my feelings." She adverted her gaze, watching Garrick a few yards away as he set up tents. If she refused to look at Rowan, perhaps he'd take it as a sign to leave her well enough alone.

"One doesn't need his powers to know you are in a dark mood, lass," Garrick called. "Rowan, leave the girl be and lend me a hand."

He gave Raylyn one last searching look before turning and joining Garrick. The two men pitched the tents in less than two minutes. Admittedly, it was impressive. She wouldn't have thought a royal-born would perform such common work.

Setting up her own small tent took considerably longer than the men because of her exhaustion. Every fiber of her being screamed yet she refused to ask for help. Crouching behind the fabric, she secured the last stake into the dry ground with some difficulty while Garrick's low voice to Rowan carried on the soft breeze.

"You haven't written to your brother or father yet? Why?"

"I didn't want word of the girl spreading ahead of me, Gar. How do I explain everything that happened with just a scriber? It's the same reason I didn't tell you about her, either."

"Aye, instead you send a vague note saying you were ambushed and escaped to Lakehaven. Left us all scratching our heads about the details."

"And what would you have thought if I sent you a scriber saying a teenage girl with extinct powers saved my life?"

There was a brief pause. "Well, I'd think you lost your mind."

"Exactly. It will make more sense to just show up and explain in person."

"And what if they take the villager's stance regarding the girl?"

Another pause. "Even so, I handle internal affairs. Brenden's opinion of that matter wouldn't trump mine."

"Nay, but the King's would," Garrick said, his voice dropping lower.

"My father won't disagree with me, Gar."

Raylyn knelt on the dusty ground for several moments after the voices stopped. Rising with some difficulty, she retrieved her pack from the horse, contemplating the men's words. She hadn't realized she was still in danger of Marking, or death. Her chest tightened with a renewed wave of anxiety. *I should have stayed with Braya,* she thought, head spinning.

A tall soldier named Bo, who rode next to her most of the day, passed by, offering yet more bread and dried meat. Apparently, Garrick was still too cautious for a fire again tonight, despite the distance they covered. Raylyn's stomach flipped at the sight of food. Declining politely, she ducked into her tent as quickly as her legs would allow. She collapsed on her thin sleeping roll, lumps of rocks she was too lazy to clear out pressed hard against her back. She closed her eyes, pleading for sleep to silence her screaming thoughts. Hours crept in antagonizing slowness before the Goddess granted her the relief of a dreamless sleep.

The next few days passed with more of the same. Raylyn did her best to avoid the prince. The soldier, Bo, continued riding next to her. He was a middle-aged man, with a well-groomed beard, and the lilting accent of western Ellendria. They made idle chatter for a time, and she learned he was widowed, his wife and son both passing during child-birth. He was also a graduate of the Academy. When she admitted her fears about the training, he shared his experience with her, showing no distaste regarding her powers.

"I was seven when my parents sent me," he told her as they trotted along the road. The air was mercifully cool, a welcome change from the blistering months of prolonged heat.

"Seven... that's quite young, isn't it? I thought most students were in late adolescence, if not adults."

"Ah, it is young. But, after I burned down half the house, they were left with no choice. The Academy's walls are made of stone, and stone doesn't catch flame," he chuckled, faint wrinkles lining the crooks of his eyes. "They couldn't risk burning to death over a temper tantrum."

She raised her brows in surprise. "You burned down your house?" His appearance held no clues about his strength; if anything, he looked completely ordinary, if maybe a bit underfed.

He nodded. "I don't remember what I was angry about, only that rage burnt through my entire body. Lucky to survive, really." He lifted his left sleeve. The skin of his left arm was a deep red, puckered and twisted. "It goes to my shoulder."

"I'm so sorry," Raylyn breathed, eyes wide. She had never seen such an extensive burn. "You're lucky it didn't fester. I've seen lesser wounds put men near their death beds."

"Ah yes, you are a healer, foremost? I'd forgotten." He paused for a moment, eyes gazing up at the clouds. "I wonder if Thorne is still the head of the healers at the Academy. I never took her classes. Mind, it wasn't my gift, but she had a reputation of being quite ruthless despite being so young. That was many years ago."

Interest peaked, she began drilling the man with as many questions as she could think: the layout of the school, the dormitories in the castle, the intensity of the classes, the examinations. His companionship helped ease her nerves. She couldn't control if the king would continue her pardon. She couldn't leave and apologize to Braya, nor seek comfort with her parents. So instead, she did what she knew best and gathered as much knowledge as she could of her situation.

Bo couldn't give many specifics on all the classes. He was a caster and didn't study healing or influencing. His powers were strictly offensive, and the ability to channel flames was his specialty. Their travels took them past a rather subdued river, its water low from the recent drought, and after much pleading on her part, Bo finally agreed to demonstrate his talents.

The glowing light from his palms was dim in the bright sunshine. Cupping his hands before him, a melon sized ball of fire sparked to existence, slowly rotating inches above his hands. Raising his hand high into the air, he blinked, and the burning sphere launched upwards, sailing through the air. It landed in the water with a sizzle and puff of steam.

As impressive as the fireballs were, they weren't the extent of his powers. He could also manipulate heat, freeze or boil water, and increase or decrease the temperature of the air in small places. "My first year at the academy, I did poorly on an examination. I was young and missed my parents. I didn't focus the way I should have. My emotions slipped when I was walking back to my dormitory." He looked down, a sudden frown crossing his face. "I boiled a squirrel."

"You..." Raylyn began, stricken.

"Boiled a squirrel, yes." He shook his head. "I was so ashamed, the blood pooled out of it, boiling on the road... It was winter."

Raylyn couldn't stand the otherwise cheerful man looking so distraught. "Well, I killed an acre of forest when I was healing the prince. I could only imagine how many squirrels that included." Bo looked up at her grimly. "I heard the birds falling dead from the trees. It will haunt me till my last breath," she said, speaking the words for the first time. She hadn't had enough time to process exactly what happened in the forest, but talking about it caused her shame to resurface.

"I will, as well. It is those mistakes which help us learn complete mastery over our powers, else the power has mastery over us." Bo smiled. "You will do well. It is in your nature, I believe."

He was a welcome companion for the remainder of the journey. He taught her a little about casting, things on which she never wasted her time when she was back home. She never thought the information applicable, as she was just a healer. Now, her powers were uncertain. She didn't want to arrive at the Academy and look incompetent. So, she listened and learned, grateful for the distraction and friendship.

During their second week on the road, Raylyn turned erecting her tent it into a game, timing herself to complete the task as quick as she could. "Two hundred and forty-four seconds!" she said aloud to herself excitedly, staring proudly at the little canvas tent.

"Impressive," Rowan said, making her jump. Though she distanced herself from Rowan as much as she was able, he still came to her at annoyingly frequent intervals.

"Why do you do that—sneak up on people?" she asked, turning around. She was mostly annoyed at herself for failing to hear his approaching footsteps.

"It's a habit, I suppose." He walked the perimeter of her tent, as if inspecting it for adequacy.

"Can I help you with something, Your Highness? Bo and I were about to go start the fire now that Garrick deemed it safe." Truthfully, Bo could start the fire himself in a fraction of the time it would take others. But, they decided earlier that day to test Raylyn's powers—Bo's idea. The histories always described syphons as possessing both healing and casting abilities, and Bo was eager to test the accuracy of the texts.

"I was hoping to discuss some things with you. I've tried a few times over the past couple of days, but you've been a bit … preoccupied. We'll be arriving in Lendris in less than two weeks, and I finally sent word ahead to my father and brother, mostly because of Garrick's incessant pestering." He forced a short laugh, too high-pitched. "I want you to be prepared."

Raylyn scanned the campsite, confused. "How did you send word? We've no scouts and all your soldiers remain. You have no raven, either."

He stared at her for several seconds, searching her face. "You truly do not know? Your parents didn't have scribers?"

"Scribers? I heard you talking to Garrick about that a few days ago. I'm unfamiliar with the term." She was intrigued now, irritation melting away.

"Come, let me show you," and without waiting for her response, he turned, leading her across the camp to his tent. It was a duplicate of Raylyn's, which gave her slightly more respect for the man. He didn't demand any indulgences. Holding the door flap open, he motioned for Raylyn to enter.

She squeezed past him, careful to remain as distanced as possible. She was unsure of the intricacies of effector's powers, but she was convinced proximity increased their abilities. During the past week, she remained vigilant to stay as far away from him as she could manage.

He followed her, proceeding to rummage through a bag at the foot of his bedroll. Their bodies filled the small space, and an undercurrent of tension weighed heavily in the air. Raylyn stood, back against the canvas, giving

the prince as wide a berth as possible. She absentmindedly picked the skin on her thumb, nervous. Wincing, she
glanced at her hand, a small bead of blood welling from the
abused cuticle. She wiped it on her trousers.

"Here we are," he said, pulling parchment and quill out
of the bag. He sat on his bedroll, folding his legs in front
of him, and motioned for her to join him.

"I'm fine here, thanks."

"Nonsense, come here. I'd imagine it would be fasci-
nating for someone who's never seen it before." He looked
up at her, eyes bright.

"I hope it lives up to expectations," she muttered, half-
joking. Two small steps closed the distance between them,
and she sat, keenly aware of their proximity. *Alone with the
prince, in his bed... well, bedroll.* The unsolicited thought
caused heat to prickle her cheeks, the fluttering in her
stomach difficult to ignore. She bit her cheek, aggravated
with herself, and tried to focus on the parchment that he
smoothed out in front of them.

"The quill and parchment are spelled and function just
like any other." With that, he wrote, *Garrick, come. It's
urgent,* in a scrawled script. She couldn't help but notice
the defined muscles in his arms as he set down the quill.

She dared a glance at him. He met her eyes with a look
that matched the intensity she was hiding. Her blush deepened, but she didn't look away. "Are you manipulating me?"
The words came out as a whisper, but she already knew the
answer. There was no crawling feeling beneath her skin, the
sign she now took as being effected.

"No, and if I didn't know any better, I'd ask you the
same thing." He leaned in closer, making her shiver.
Reaching a tentative hand, he trailed his fingers down her

cheek to her chin, tilting her head slightly, closing the mere inches between them. Her heart raced, and she closed her eyes, longing to feel the softness of his lips on hers.

"Rowan, I'm twenty feet away from you!" Garrick barked. "There's absolutely no need to send—" His voice broke off when he saw them so close to embracing, a piece of parchment held loosely in his hand. Raylyn jumped backward, the spell broken. "For Goddess's sake, Rowan!"

He grinned sheepishly. "Garrick, I was just showing Raylyn how the scribers work." He stood, grabbing the parchment from the soldier.

"Oh, is that all?" Shaking his head, he turned and disappeared from the tent opening without another word.

Raylyn watched him leave, chest tight with embarrassment. "Don't worry about him," Rowan said. "He's an old spinster. Here, look." He handed her Garrick's parchment, and the words he had written earlier appeared in a perfect duplicate.

Raylyn ran her hand along the page, half expecting the wetness of the ink to smear onto her fingers, yet it was dry. "That's incredible. I can't believe I've never read about it!" She grabbed Rowan's copy, examining both papers together. Exact replicas. "How does the enchantment work? Can anyone use them, even those with no powers? Do you have to buy them, or can a caster learn how to make them?" Her questions poured out, her eyes glittering with excitement.

He grinned at her. "Which should I answer first?" he asked teasingly. "Raylyn," his voice lowered, and he moved closer to her again, resting a warm hand on her arm. "I'm drawn to you." Her stomach fluttered, his words echoing her own emotions. "I think you feel the same?" He phrased it as a question, his brows raising. She gave a minuscule nod, not trusting herself to speak. Desire sparked to life inside her once more as he trailed his hand up her arm. Closing the gap between them, he met her lips.

He pulled her into him, his hand cradling her face with a surprising tenderness. Her fingers trailed up his chest, resting at the nape of his neck. A few seconds or an eternity later—Raylyn wasn't sure which—they broke apart, both flushed, eyes ablaze. She was suddenly shy again, his gaze too intense, and she looked away. Tilting her head up again, he smiled. "You are likely one of the most powerful beings in this entire country." He held her hand, making little circles on her skin with his thumb. "And yet you are as shy and innocent as a doe."

She laughed at that, some of the tension breaking. "I'm not as innocent as I might appear," she said, raising an eyebrow at him. "And shy? Well, I'm in the presence of my prince. I *should* be deferential to you, Your Highness," she said, lowering her head in a mock bow.

"No more of that. Just call me Rowan. The 'prince' and 'your highness' get old quite quickly."

"What a difficult dilemma to have," she said playfully.

His words were serious, the smile in his eyes gone. "Imagine never knowing who your genuine friends are because everyone puts on a façade to gain your favor... to never be able to be reckless or foolish because of your station. The responsibility of it gets heavy. Add to that the constant reminder of who you are and who you must be... Sometimes it's too much." He dropped Raylyn's hand, rubbing his face, weariness breaking through for the first time since she met him.

Raylyn wasn't sympathetic. "Imagine having an unsuccessful harvest and your children starving to death that winter," she said coldly. He lowered his hands from his eyes, staring at her. "Imagine choosing between feeding yourself or feeding your children. Or crawling with fleas and being grateful your hounds at least kept you warm at night. You are extremely entitled to have the existential problems you claim, Rowan."

He was speechless for several moments. "My people do not face those problems. We are in a time of peace and prosperity."

Raylyn snorted. "You're joking, surely? If not for the charity of the leaders in my village, do you know how many children would have starved during a low bounty season? We grow grapes in Lakehaven, process them into a fancy wine which you nobles love. Can you guess what happened when a disease ran through the plants a few years back?" He remained silent, just staring. She was getting irritated at the ignorance of the man. She took a deep breath, steadying herself. "Braya nearly died from neglect after her mother died. Her father was too drunk to earn a dime, and he beat her. This is what *'your people'* face. Perhaps you need to open your eyes and learn who we truly are."

She stood to leave. As she stepped through the tent flaps into the evening coolness, he called after her. "I knew you had fire within you."

CHAPTER 6

B O WAS WAITING FOR HER, ARRANGING stones in a large circle for the fire pit. Nearby lay a pile of various sized sticks and logs. "Ah, there you are. I was going to get it started without you—I didn't know how long you'd be occupied with the prince." He brushed his hands on his trousers, standing. "Are you ready to get started?"

"You knew I was with Rowan?" she asked, ignoring his question. She wasn't entirely sure what their kiss meant, and she certainly didn't want word of scandal to spread before she even arrived at the capital.

He grinned. "How could I not, with Garrick yelling like an enraged mother?" His smile faltered. "Though, if I could offer a little, ah, advice?"

Raylyn nodded. "Of course." She spent the past weeks with the man, learning each other's histories and aspirations. She was beginning to think of him as a friend, not just a soldier guarding her on the road.

"You'd be wise to shield your heart from him. Steel yourself against all those you will meet at Court." His voice was low, all playful banter gone.

Struggling for words, she said, "But aren't you part of Court, Bo?"

"No. I am just a soldier, here for a short time, then sent away again. These people... they are concerned for their gain—their gain alone—no matter the expense of others."

"I appreciate the concern. I do, Bo. And I will keep it in mind when we arrive."

"You need to keep it in mind *now*."

"You mean Rowan?"

He bent down, breaking some of the smaller twigs with sharp *snaps*. "Yes." He didn't look up, but continued working, placing the twigs with practiced efficiency in the center of the fire pit.

"He saved me as much as I saved him," Raylyn said, attempting to justify her actions. "They would've Marked me. I would have lost all my powers. He is quite—"

Bo cut her off. "You want to know what he is?" His voice was angry, and he articulated each word with a snap of a branch. "He." *Snap.* "Is." *Snap.* "Engaged." He threw the pieces into the pile. He glanced at her, seeing the shock on her face. "I am sorry Raylyn. I do not know why he has played with your emotions; he is not known for such behaviors. My wife, rest her soul, thought there was no greater sin than violating the bond of marriage. I believe that includes engagements as well."

Raylyn was quiet for a moment. It felt as though she had just been punched in the stomach, and she was worried if she tried to speak, she would vomit. After a few quiet minutes, she swallowed, mouth dry. "Engaged?"

"Ah, yes. It has been arranged since before the Queen's passing, Goddess grant her soul eternal peace."

Raylyn was trying to process this. If he was engaged, why would he kiss her? Why ask her to come into his tent at all? She was not sure with whom she was more betrayed, Rowan or herself.

Blinking back angry tears, she looked up, praying to the Goddess for guidance. The sky was black now, millions of specks of starlight twinkling above her. "Can we try the fire, Bo? A distraction would be welcome now." She rubbed her eyes, conspicuously wiping away a few hot tears. She would not cry over a man, not after all she'd overcome. She had a creeping feeling she was going to need to harden herself in the capital. No better time to start than the present.

"Of course. A hot meal will be a pleasant change from stale bread." Bo placed a last stick in the pit and turned to Raylyn. "I am not an educator, nor do I claim mastery over casting. I was recruited to the king's guard before I ever advanced high enough in classes. However, if anyone knows flame, it is I.

"Most importantly, you must clear yourself of emotion. Ah, I know... easier said than done, but you must *try*. If you have no control over your emotions, you have no control over your powers, no matter which power it is: healing, casting, effecting. They have all the same principles, yes? Clear your mind."

Raylyn closed her eyes and tried to do as he instructed. In fact, she assumed this was how he would begin. It was the same lesson her mother had taught her all those years ago when she first came into her healing powers. She had been six years old, a few years younger than average. Her dog, Biscuit—a huge, shaggy black mutt whom she had the privilege of naming—had run off into the woods near their house. She had been chasing a fox that kept breaking into the chicken coop, leaving a mess of feathers and blood, not to mention a complete lack of eggs.

Raylyn had waited in the doorway, staring out into the darkness, refusing to go to bed that night. She prayed in the most honest and desperate way that only a child could. And, after countless hours and tears, there Biscuit came, limping and whimpering. Raylyn had bolted from the house to embrace her best friend but discovered she had only come back to say goodbye. Confusion and pain shot through her body, coursed through her blood, pounded in her ears and her powers had blazed. But she was only six and despite her desperation, Biscuit died, leaving her broken body behind. Raylyn learned that day some wounds are too far gone to heal.

Her father had dug the hole by hand, forgoing his casting powers. They planted a rosebush atop her grave, the color of the petals so deeply violet they appeared black. And they never bothered with chickens again.

"Once you've emptied all your erroneous thoughts and feelings, focus on the one thing you desire to achieve: lighting the wood for the bonfire. Believe it to your core, feel it course through your veins. Signal to me when you are ready."

Raylyn did as he said, her eyes still closed. She shook her memories away, put her emotions in a box to be opened later, cleared out everything that wasn't starting this fire. She didn't just want to spark a blaze, she *was* the blaze, each beat of her heart a new lick of flame. Heat coursed through her with such intensity she was certain her skin would melt. Trying not to lose focus, she opened her eyes, staring at the broken bits of wood in the fire pit, and nodded to Bo.

"Raise your hands towards the wood—use both, it will make it easier—and channel that feeling to your palms, imagining the fire roaring."

She *pushed* the feelings of flame and heat, directing it to her hands. The back of her brain quietly processed that the movement of energy through her veins was like her healing ability, but with a dual pleasure-pain sensation. Staring unblinkingly at the sticks in front of her, she envisioned them burning, a ball of white-hot fire. A moment of hesitation passed before her hands glowed bright gold in the darkness, the energy releasing from her body like a long-held breath.

The smallest spark lit momentarily in the fire pit before extinguishing without even a trace of smoke.

Excitement flooded Raylyn, and she jumped up. "Bo, did you see that? Did you *see* it?"

"Ah, I did!" He was grinning. "Even the smallest spark can light a fire. You, Raylyn Ashton, are a caster."

She hugged him. "It's all thanks to you!" Her voice was shaky, and suddenly so were her legs. She stumbled, Bo catching her before she fell.

"Ah, I believe you could use a warm meal. Casting takes much energy, especially for the novice." He winked at her. "Would you mind if I...?" he gestured toward the cold, fire-less pit. "We can continue practicing after some of your strength returns."

"Of course."

In an instant, Bo had the fire burning, light and warmth welcome. The weather had finally shifted, and with the night came a coolness Raylyn hadn't felt since the early spring. She hadn't noticed the chill that prickled her arms until it was chased away by the fire's heat.

The fire held an unspoken promise of a warm meal. It lured the rest of the camp, including Garrick and Rowan. Garrick shot her an icy look as he stepped past. "About time," he said, sitting on a log and spearing a hunk of meat to roast spit-style over the flames. Though the meal was modest—quail he shot earlier that day—the sizzling meat was a luxury after weeks of stale bread and tough jerky.

"Ah, you are free to start the fire tomorrow if I am not quick enough for you," Bo said. A bottle of amber liquid appeared from nowhere, and he took a deep drink, eyeing Garrick with a flat expression.

Garrick chuckled. "Fine, then you can hunt and clean the birds. On better thought, never mind. We'd go hungry. Hey, pass that here," he said, grabbing the bottle. Raylyn watched their boyish teasing in silence, entranced by the dancing firelight. Shadows ebbed and flowed around the men. She was so tired she imagined if she lay back, she could fall asleep here in the soft grass, embraced by the flame's warmth.

"I didn't really get a chance to talk to you," Rowan said, pulling her out of the sleepy trance.

"I wonder why," she replied curtly. She didn't want to talk to him, didn't want to be near him. For Goddess's sake, she just wanted to sleep.

"Appears we were both too distracted." A smile lit up his face, but Raylyn didn't return it.

She looked at him, deadpan. "What is it, *Prince* Rowan?"

77

His brows furrowed. "Have I offended you?" he asked quietly. She remained silent. "If I was too bold, I am sorr—"

"*Your Highness*, the hour grows late and truthfully, I just want to rest. You need to speak to me about something *important*?" She was not in the mood for pleasantries or apologies.

He blinked, unable to determine the cause of her coldness. "Yes. Earlier, I told you I sent word to my father and brother about our imminent arrival. I explained the whole of what happened and what you did to save me. My brother didn't reply and the response I received from my father was rather ... short. 'We will speak more on this upon your safe return home.' I... I do not know how to interpret his words, Raylyn." He was somber.

The soldier to her right passed her the bottle, which had been making its way around the fire. She took it, tipping it back, and swallowed a few long sips. It burned down her throat, much stronger than the sweet mead and wine to which she was accustomed back home. It settled in her stomach, as hot as the flames before her. Wiping her mouth on the back of her hand, she gave the bottle to the prince. "Well Rowan, I guess we'll find out soon," she said, retreating to her tent without another word.

The last few days of their journey were largely uneventful. The blisters on her thighs from the constant riding were beginning to callus, and she hadn't had a proper bath in close to a month. She was beginning to think her horse smelt better than she. On their second-to-last day, they crossed a wide brook, and she took the opportunity to strip off her dirt-crusted clothes and rinse the sweat and stink from her body. Garrick blushed like a maid when she unfastened her trousers, and Bo averted his eyes. Rowan and the other soldiers, however, followed suit, taking the few minutes to wash.

She hadn't spoken to the prince since the night by the fire, and she tried and failed to ignore him as he pulled his shirt off in one swift motion, stepping into the water several feet away from her. His torso was just as muscular as she had imagined, all solid strength only formed after a lifetime of training. Her own body had changed over the weeks spent on the road, some of her softness hardening from the endless riding and sudden absence of her mother's mince pies.

Rowan turned as he splashed water on his face, revealing a huge tattoo that covered almost every inch of skin on his back. It was an intricate eagle, each feather distinct. Its wings were spread as if in flight, clutching a crown in its talons. Though she had seen the emblem of the king many times—embroidered on his shirt the day she saved him and on the soldiers' armor—she hadn't realized it was custom for royalty to tattoo it on their body.

She averted her eyes as he turned back around, but not quickly enough. Catching her gaze, he raised his brow, stopping for a moment in the knee-deep water. His apparent confusion wasn't surprising. She outright ignored him over the remainder of their journey, despite his annoyingly frequent attempts at conversation. She had no interest in hearing his apologies or worries about Court.

Looking away, she pretended to busy herself as he approached the shore, allowing distance to grow between them before she followed. Though the water was cool and refreshing, she was forced to pull the same grimy clothes back on, making the entire effort futile, and darkening her already black mood.

Over the past weeks, Bo continued to practice casting with her, giving her tips and advice on how to access her powers, but she hadn't so much as lit a spark since that first night. Frustration overwhelmed her, and she wondered if she had simply imagined her initial success. She voiced her fears to Bo when they were back on the road. According to Garrick, they were running behind but should arrive at the city gates before the next midday.

"No, not imagined. I believe your head may be getting in the way," he replied kindly.

Bo was getting frustrated, too. "You have to clear your mind!" he had yelled at her that morning. She never heard the even-tempered man raise his voice before. They were riding adjacent to each other, and Bo had given her a scrap of parchment. Her goal was to light it aflame, but after a few hours of unsuccessful attempts, they both agreed to take a break until nightfall.

Hours passed as they continued onwards, leaving the brook in the distance. Daylight began to fade, and Raylyn tried to deny the creeping dread that tendrilled its way up her stomach and into her chest. Bo told her to harden herself, and she was *trying*, but reality was bleak. Everything she had accomplished so far—enduring the trial, her pardon from Rowan, discovering her casting abilities, traveling farther than she ever dared dream—it would all be for naught if the king decided she posed too much of a threat.

Bo approached her as they settled into camp for the evening. He opened his mouth to speak, but she cut him off. "You're right, Bo. I'm too much in my head to show any kind of skill tonight. Let's save ourselves the frustration."

Bo nodded, a look of relief relaxing the lines on his forehead. The routine of camping down was now second nature to Raylyn. Her tent was up, her horse staked a distance away so she could graze in the dying foliage. An endless expanse of plains surrounded them, the grass dried and brown. It was completely void of tree cover, causing her to feel small and exposed, almost naked. The wind carried the promise of rain after weeks of drought, foreshadowing a miserable night.

Forgoing dinner and the warmth of the fire, she chose solitude in her little tent, wondering how the canvas would hold up against the oncoming storm. Her thoughts drifted on their own accord, fear churning her stomach at the prospect of meeting the king.

"Raylyn? May I have a quick word?" Rowan said, his body a dark mass barely visible at the tent's opening.

"If you must," she replied. The sudden percussion of rain drops on the canvas drowned out Rowan's reply. She groaned, knowing that despite the tent, she would be soaked long before morning.

Rowan ducked in, shaking some of the water out of his hair. He sat at the foot of her bedroll, remaining silent for a few seconds, as if meditating, a faint light illuminating his hands. Raylyn waited, her eyebrows raised.

"There," he smiled at her, "that should help."

She stared. "What?"

"I cast a shield over the tent." Seeing her blank look, he added, "To repel the rain. Mind, I'm not the best at shielding—that would be my brother—but it should last through the night." Sure enough, the patter of rain disappeared.

"That was ... very kind," she admitted grudgingly. "Thank you."

"Raylyn, I have been racking my brain for days. I know my problems differ from your village's. I know that some of the common folk would gladly trade their challenges for mine. I never meant to offend you. Please, if we could just—"

"Stop," she said, shaking her head. "That is *not* why I am angry, Rowan." It was the first time she voiced her feelings out loud, though he could sense her emotions on his own easily enough.

"Then *why*?" he asked, desperation in his voice. He shifted closer, reaching for her hand. "Tell me what I have done, I beg of you."

She pulled her hand away from him. "Well, for starters, you didn't tell me you were *betrothed*." Though she was trying to sound venomous, her voice betrayed her pain. "You kissed me ... and while I appreciate your pardon, if it means that there are certain ... *expectations*, I do not want it. I will hold my head high as they Mark me, knowing I saved my dignity and virtue." She had practiced this speech in her head countless times over the last few days, though in her daydreams, she had never started crying. She wiped her tears with an angry hand.

Pity crossed Rowan's face. "Raylyn," he said, moving even closer, resting on his knees in front of her, "it's not like that at all."

"Then you are not betrothed?" she asked, not allowing hope to pierce the words.

"It's complicated, truly, if you just listen—"

"Are you promised to another, Rowan? Yes, or no?"

"Well, I—"

"Yes or no?" Her voice was dangerously quiet now; she stared in his eyes, knowing the answer before he spoke it.

"Yes," he admitted a pained expression pulling his face into a grimace.

"Get out."

"Just let me explain, please," he begged. "If you would just listen—"

"I said GET OUT!" she bellowed, a rage building in her that surpassed the storm outside; a rage that shook buildings to dust, that consumed and destroyed in its insatiable hunger. The wind roared through the tent's fabric, mirroring her anger. Emotions she was trying so hard to repress burst, all her fear, anxiety, and pain culminating into a crescendo. She didn't even notice her glowing palms.

Rowan's eyes grew wide, his face stricken with panic. She was pleasantly hot now, the chill of the night melting away. Her vision ebbed, an unusual orange light blurring the edges of her sight. A small, faraway part of her mind whispered *fire* and heat burnt through her veins.

"Raylyn," Rowan murmured, his voice low, face ashen. "Raylyn," he repeated, "please, you must calm down." He moved slowly, as if he was trying not to spook an unbroken horse.

His words did nothing but incite further anger. Her mind could no longer string together logical thoughts. Instead, raw, untamed emotions flowed from her, and the wind's deafening howls almost hid the low crackle of ravenous flames. Distant shouts, so desperate and small, were lost in the duet of fire and wind. She smiled before her world went black.

Someone was shaking her. It was just the slightest annoyance; with little effort, she ignored it, slipping back into the peaceful black nothingness.

The shaking intensified, bringing a searing pain that shot through her head, pounding with the beat of her heart.

"Raylyn! Wake. *Up*!"

"Ughh." She opened her eyes a slit, but the light seared through her brain, increasing the pain tenfold. Her body *hurt*. If she could just let that soft oblivion envelop her once more...

"*Raylyn*." The voice was urgent, insistent.

Her unconsciousness resigned. *We'll meet again before long*, she reassured the beckoning darkness, and fighting every nerve in her body, she forced her eyes open.

It was Rowan of course, shaking her, pleading to her, begging her to stay. She watched him for a minute, still fighting off the darkness of the void that threatened to claim her. Tears streamed down his panicked face, and she couldn't process why he was upset. She had to say something; he was *devastated*. Because of her? Confusion muddled her mind, and summoning every ounce of effort she had, she spoke. "I'm ... okay." She tried to sit up, but absolute exhaustion coupled with a gut-churning pain, making stars dance in her vision.

He finally recognized she was back—awake, alive, whatever it was—and he crumpled atop her in a wave of uncontrolled relief. "She's alive!" he choked, his voice an octave higher than normal. "Oh, Goddess," he muttered, cradling her face in a tender embrace. "Raylyn, I am so sorry." His eyes glistened again, and he bent, kissing her forehead. Unfortunately, the touch of his lips did nothing to lessen the pain. The pounding, excruciating, debilitating *pain*.

"Hurts," she muttered.

"I am so sorry," he repeated, devastation written on his face.

"Happened?" Evidently, she was capable of only single-word sentences.

Voices emerged from nowhere and everywhere with urgent, clipped words; it was too much effort to keep track. Sounds blended into each other, worsening the pounding in her head. She fixed her eyes on Rowan's face, hoping to slow the spinning world. He continued to cradle her, protective and strong.

"Loren," Rowan said to someone out of her view, "thank the Goddess. Quickly now, she almost slipped away."

A new face emerged, thin body kneeling over her. Her eyes scanned the length of Raylyn from head to foot. "What's happened?" she asked, her voice more feminine than Raylyn had imagined, softly sweet.

"I—I hurt her." Rowan said. Loren looked at him incredulously. "She lost control of her powers; I couldn't reason with her. I knocked her unconscious, but with more force than I meant... I couldn't think of any other way."

She returned her gaze to Raylyn. "I'm going to examine you." Her hands, as soft as her voice, palpated every inch of her scalp, searching for injury. Pain within pain. She screamed, the soul-deep exhaustion the only thing keeping her from leaping away from Loren's touch. "You did a number on her, Your Highness. It seems she wasn't the only one without mastery over her powers."

"Can you help her? If I hadn't been so insistent calling her back, I believe she'd be... she would be gone," he said, his voice cracking.

Loren looked down at her with kind eyes. If it wasn't for the armor, Raylyn wouldn't have believed she was a trained soldier in the army, let alone a member of the prince's personal guard. She smiled an apology. "You have a concussion, and if I'm not mistaken, your skull is fractured. Moreover, you're near death from your unrestrained casting. I can mend the fracture easily enough, but the return of your energy is beyond my strength. I'm afraid that if I try to restore you completely, it would be my death. I'm sorry, but I will do what I can."

With that, the woman laid gentle hands on each side of her head. Raylyn closed her eyes, unable to keep them open any longer. After a moment, Loren started singing. Her voice lilted through the air as she sang her prayers, soft and soothing. *"Oh, Goddess, powers strong. Hear the calling of this song. Injured, tattered, broken bones. Inescapable pain and moans. Goddess of light, and darkness too, allow me to heal this girl through you."* She repeated this a few times over, an intense itching replacing some of the pain in Raylyn's head.

When she was done, Raylyn was still in amazing pain, but no longer felt the intense desire to dive into the void. She blinked up at Rowan. "Sleep now?" she asked.

He glanced at Loren, who nodded once. "Sleep now."

She awoke the next morning feeling like she had tried to drown herself in a barrel of ale. Her body protested every movement, stiff and angry. But she could move, and her thoughts were markedly clearer. She sat up despite her body's protest and met a heavy resistance. An arm draped protectively over her torso. Rowan was tucked against her, still sleeping, his chest rising and falling in slow, easy breaths. She watched him for a moment, the memories of last night flickering through her brain in fast succession. She remembered the uncontrollable rage that turned her blood to molten flame. After that, things became blurry—a calm darkness, debilitating pain, a soft serenade to the Goddess.

Her movement caused Rowan to stir, his eyes fluttering open. He saw she was awake, and he flew upright. "Raylyn," he said, his voice still holding the remnants of sleep. "How are you feeling?"

"Like horseshit," she replied truthfully, the sound of their voices causing her head to throb.

"Thank the Goddess you're alright. Do you remember what happened? Loren said you might not. You had a pretty severe concussion." He wiped the sleep from his eyes, sitting up straighter.

She moved slowly, trying to minimize the pain that pierced her mind. "I remember snippets," she admitted, "mostly just emotions. If you wouldn't mind explaining? And did we..." she struggled to find the words, "sleep together?"

"*Just* sleep, yes. I was worried about you. Loren is an exceptional healer, just not as skilled as some." He raised his brows meaningfully. "Last night..." He shifted uncomfortably. "Last night," he repeated, clearing his throat, "you lost control of your powers. I was insistent that you speak to me—to understand—and you reacted with your heart.

I couldn't reason with you, and there wasn't much time. I was afraid we'd all burn to death. I knocked you unconscious." He was staring at his hands, shame written clearly on his face. "But you weren't the only one who lost control. I was angry with you for not listening to me about... about the betrothal. And, I admit, I was afraid. None of us knew you had that type of ability. Completely raw, untrained, *wild* ability. But I am so ashamed to have hurt you." He looked up at her, his eyes reddened, on the verge of tears. "It's as if your emotions amplify mine, but that's no excuse. I beg your forgiveness."

Raylyn remained still, processing everything he said. The flashes of memory were a little more logical now, and a deep dread crept through her. "What do you mean, you were afraid we'd all burn to death?"

He stood, offering her his hand. "Let me show you." She stared at him for a moment, fear and pain masking the rage of betrayal she had felt toward him the previous night. She hesitated another second, then grabbed his hand, allowing him to help her unsteadily to her feet.

Ducking under the tent, she stared in horror. The breath rushed out of Raylyn as if she had been punched in the stomach. Remnants of her outburst were visible in every direction. The brown grass, dried from the decay of autumn, was nothing more than ash. The path of flames was written clearly on the ground. She turned, eyeing a pile of burnt debris. Smoke licked the canvas of her tent, singeing it with black streaks. Three tents were standing to her right, two less than normal.

Self-hatred threatened to boil over. "Did I harm anyone?"

"Thankfully, no. You are the only one who suffered any injuries from this. We're lucky to have Bo. He tamed the fires after you passed out, but we lost some supplies and a couple tents. All things that can be replaced," he added when he saw her expression.

"I... I should be Marked for this," she said, words coming from the pit of disgust inside her. "Everyone would have died if it wasn't for you." Her insides were crumbling, collapsing.

"Ah, as if we haven't all lost control in our youth once or twice," Bo said, walking up from the small cluster of tents. Raylyn had been too distracted to notice his arrival. He smiled at her. "You will do well at the Academy."

Raylyn panicked. She didn't want to access these powers again. "I think I'd rather be Marked," she muttered, still staring at the burnt landscape.

"A waste that the Goddess herself would shed tears over," Bo replied. "Powers that strong are rare, Raylyn."

"I'm eighteen. Why now? Who else do you know that has discovered they can channel at this age?" She was nearing hysterics, her voice high and tight. "The Goddess likely cries over my very *existence*."

Rowan and Bo exchanged glances. "Perhaps you should go rest until it is time for us to make the final trek of our journey?" Bo suggested, his words slow and even, as if afraid she'd have another outburst.

Taking a deep breath, she replied, "I'm okay. I'm not going to smite you with lightning or anything." She gave a small smile, trying to break the growing tension.

"Ah, speaking of violent weather," Bo said. "Do you recall exactly what you did last evening?"

"What do you mean?"

89

"I mean your casting. You set a blaze which was difficult to control, the sheer enormity of it was impressive alone. The flames were *commanded* by you. I could not tame them until you were, ah, sleeping. That is a skill of which I thought only the masters were capable, and it takes many years to be successful, especially with fire. Flames are wild, and they are not broken easily. But, that's not all. Though it was already storming last night, it was like the wind had a fury of its own." Sheepishly, he added, "Perhaps my imagination."

She stared at him, trying to put the pieces of her broken memory together. "I'm sorry," she said. "I can't remember." Truthfully, she kept thinking about a duet with fire and wind, but that made little sense, and she shook the thoughts away, wondering just how badly she was concussed.

The morning rushed past in a flurry of packing. Raylyn sat on a charred rock, instructed sternly by Loren to sit still and rest. Idle minutes passed slowly, but when they were finally ready to leave, bile rose in Raylyn's throat at the thought of being jostled for hours on her mare. Her aches hadn't lessened. If anything, the throbbing in her head was worsening. She felt like she had a massive hangover and was kicked by a horse at the same time.

Rowan saw her reluctance. "We have little distance to cover before we reach Lendris. I know riding will be unpleasant, but do you think you can manage?"

Before she could reply, Loren rushed over. "It's the after-effects, Your Highness," she murmured. "Here, take this. You will feel better." She handed her a satchel of dried herbs. She sniffed it, the mix of scents tingling spicy in her nose.

"Oh, of course!" Rowan groaned. "I should have known. Thank you, Loren." She nodded, retreating to her own horse.

"After-effects?" Raylyn asked him, confused.

"I'm surprised you don't know. When you've healed in the past, did you ever feel unwell afterward? The first time you ever discovered your healing ability, maybe?"

She thought of Biscuit's warm, dead body, fur sticky with blood. She shook her head. She had been unwell but not in the way the prince meant.

"What about after you saved me? When you syphoned energy in the forest?" Rowan asked. She thought again. She had been exhilarated more than anything. But, what about when she had returned home, awaiting her mother and father? Come to think of it, she *had* felt achy and nauseous, though to a much lesser degree. She assumed it was her anxiety as she awaited their safe return.

She nodded. "Yes. I did feel rather sick then."

Rowan grinned. "Chew that; you'll feel better before you know it."

She put a large pinch of the herbs into her mouth, pleasantly surprised by the mild taste. Though it wasn't good, it wasn't bitter like she expected. Accepting a hand up from Rowan, she mounted her horse. After a few minutes, the mare's jostling gait no longer made her head feel as if it would split open, and though not completely pain free, her discomfort was at least manageable.

The road led them through a town larger than Raylyn's village, but she didn't process the style of the buildings, or even look at the stands selling various goods in the market street, despite the hawkers' calls. Thoughts and fears tumbled about in her mind. She didn't know what to hope for anymore. Part of her was so sure she wanted to learn her powers: excel at the Academy, prove those in her village wrong. But another, louder part yelled that she was dangerous. The thought of casting again and losing control made her blood freeze with fear. What she wished, more than anything, was to go back to her normal life. Her healing abilities were like a warm blanket: comforting, reliable, known. Everything else confused her, and she wasn't a large proponent of change. She was so wrapped in her thoughts that she didn't hear Bo as he tried to catch her attention.

"Raylyn? Ah, Raylyn?" She turned, blinking out of her stupor. Bo had dropped back to ride beside her, and she did not know how long he had been there.

"Sorry," she muttered, embarrassed.

"Ah, it is okay," he said, waving her off. "You've been through some strenuous times as of late. The fact that you've remained atop your horse is impressive in itself." He laughed, running a hand through his beard. "If you look," he gestured up and to their right, "you can see the city walls."

At first, all she saw were the gentle waves of hills before them. They had long since left the other town, following the dirt road through more grassy fields. Trees, whose trunks were thicker than some cottages back in the village, were scattered with increasing frequency, providing some shade in the bright sun. All the clouds and rain from the night before had cleared, displaying a clean, blue sky.

Bo pointed again. "Just there."

She squinted, a gray rectangle distinguishing itself from the faraway hills. It was entirely unimpressive. Raylyn voiced this opinion out loud.

Rowan, a little ahead of them, turned in his saddle. "Oh, just you wait. We are hours away still. That unimpressive little blip will grow large enough to fit your village hundreds of times over." He wiggled his eyebrows, a renewed vigor in his attitude.

Hundreds of times over? She could get lost for the rest of her life in a place that size. Her headache started to worsen, and she grabbed another pinch of herbs. A renewed sense of overwhelming nausea rushed over her, and she wondered if she would need to dismount her horse to vomit.

"You will be fine," Bo said, noting her green-tinged face. "You need to conquer your emotions."

"Always been a bit difficult for me," she replied, swallowing dryly as she fought down the bile in her throat. "None of this makes any sense."

"In what way?"

She glared at him. "I think it is well established that the last syphon was Haddeon, dead a hundred years. Out of every person in this world, why *me*? Until a few weeks ago, I was completely ordinary. What if this is all a mistake?" Her face was warm, embarrassed to voice her fears aloud. "What if I'm not capable of anything great or special? What if I just want to go back to my village and train to be their High Healer?"

"Ah, well, you were effectively banished from your village, yes? *That* would be why you cannot go back." He smiled at her, trying to lighten her mood, but was unsuccessful. "We do not question the Goddess why it rains. Instead, we see the crops grow. We do not despair in autumn when the plants die and the snow comes because we see the renewal of life come spring. Who are we to question what She decides?" Raylyn didn't reply, her expression remaining dark and unwavering. Bo sighed, "You must have faith, Raylyn. In yourself as much as the Goddess."

His words did little to soothe her, and even less to answer her endless questions. A small tinge of hope kept her riding forward, toward the king and Rowan's brother, Prince Brenden. Toward streets crowded with strangers, and endless days of uncertainty and nights of loneliness. Onward she rode, in hope of discovering answers from the one place that might hold them—the Academy.

CHAPTER 7

S HE WAS AN ANT. CRANING HER HEAD
until her neck strained, Raylyn looked up, the stone
wall ahead of her rising a hundred feet in the air. It was comprised of stones ranging in size from as small as her fist to
larger than a carriage. Her eyes continued to dart upward,
studying the building, wondering how many casters it had
taken to construct the monstrosity. She searched for arrow
slits, walkways, anything—but all she saw was endless solid,
heavy stone. The two guards stationed on either side of the
portcullis bowed in reverence as they passed, each placing
a fist over their chest in respect to their prince. Rowan
nodded back at them in wordless greeting.

The lack of fanfare surprised her. She wasn't expecting
trumpets and parades, yet their march through the city
was anticlimactic. Shops and inns lined the main street,
and the bustling shopkeepers and townsfolk only spared

quick bows and curtsies as they passed before turning back to their business. None of the group seemed perturbed by the disinterest, so she kept her observations to herself as they had continued toward the castle, its bulk looking over the city as if it was resting on a throne itself.

A small shiver ran down her spine as she crossed the castle threshold, steps behind Rowan and Garrick, feeling much like an abandoned pup begging for a warm bed and scrap of food. The other soldiers parted ways after dropping off the half-abused and exhausted horses at the stables.

Bo bowed to her, low and respectful. "It was a privilege enjoying your company these several weeks." His words cut off when she embraced him in a tight hug. Though much leaner and taller, for a moment it was as if she was wrapped in her father's arms again. But the stink of horses and sweat engulfed her, so different from the smoky scent of her father, and she was pulled from her memories back into the present. The moment was over, and she was empty and alone once more. "Remember what you're capable of, Raylyn. Don't lose yourself here," he whispered, before following the others toward the lower kitchens, eager for a halfway decent meal.

Rowan chuckled, watching her as she stared wide eyed at the thick, colorful tapestries and paintings of generations of kings which lined the walls in the castle's entryway. "Still unimpressed?" he asked with a grin.

"I will admit, I was deceived," she replied. Garrick snorted, the sound echoing in the cavernous space. He continued ahead of them, intercepting a pair of servants who appeared to have tried, unsuccessfully, to make themselves scarce. Raylyn couldn't discern his words but noted the two women curtsy before scurrying down a corridor.

Garrick continued marching down the hall, leaving her and Rowan behind without another glance.

She turned back toward Rowan, noting his look of contentment. The furrows in his brow that she previously thought were permanent smoothed, and he looked several years younger. "You seem happy."

"There's nothing like coming home." He smiled until he glanced at her. "Raylyn, that was inconsiderate. Forgive me."

She forced a tight-lipped smile. "Nothing to forgive, Your Highness." It wasn't his fault she was banished from her village. He may have been the catalyst, but her powers would have surfaced eventually, regardless. At least that's what she tried to convince herself. The pity, so clear in his eyes, made her stomach churn, and she turned away, studying the nearest painting of an elderly man, golden crown nestled in neatly trimmed, snow-white hair. His eyes were the same brown as Rowan's, though lined with crow's feet, and the wrinkles on his cheeks hinted at a life filled with smiles.

"My Grandfather, late King Regalous. Hated his name, of course, told everyone that his father—my great grandfather—was a pretentious twit for bestowing it on him. We used to call him Reggie." He gave a small laugh. "He really was the greatest man I ever met. In his last few years, he started losing his mind. He was certain he was back in the war. It was a blessing when the Goddess finally called him home."

Raylyn gaped at him, speechless, but he saved her from fumbling a reply. "I've been wanting to talk to you about something." He grabbed her hand, leading her into a secluded alcove in the hall.

"What is it?" she asked, taken aback by his abruptness.

He leaned his head back, rubbing his neck as he searched for words. "It's about the other night. Before I start, is there any way you can promise me you won't burn the castle down but listen instead?" He looked at her earnestly.

She rubbed her chin. "Hm, well, that would probably lead to regicide, so I'll do my best to fight the urge," she said, disguising her anxiety with banter.

He nodded seriously. "The other night, you found out I was engaged and nearly started a forest fire. No," he said as Raylyn started talking, trying to apologize, "there's no need for that. It wasn't your fault; it was mine. But I need to explain something to you." He grabbed her hands, taking a half-step closer. "I've never even met the woman. It was an arrangement my mother made before she died, a peace offering with Cystra. I was just a child. The only reason it's still binding is because my father is too sentimental to break it."

She swallowed down a wave of nausea before speaking. "A peace treaty?" she repeated, suspicious. "Would you mind telling me her name, at least?"

He shifted uncomfortably. "Princess Aedra of Cystra."

Raylyn ripped her hands away from his. "For Goddess's sake, Rowan."

"I'll break it!" he called as she started to turn away. He grabbed her arm, turning her back around. "Treaty be damned. I'll write tonight and tell them it's off. Damn it, Raylyn, it is *meaningless* to me."

"It's not meaningless to our country!" She was astonished that she had to explain this to her *prince*. "If what you told me is true, and we are on the brink of war... you want to destroy one of the few things maintaining our peace?"

He stuttered, desperately searching for a reply. "To be frank, Rowan, this isn't the time or place for this. Let's go." She walked to the middle of the corridor, begrudgingly waiting for him to lead her through the maze of the castle. Face twisted in misery, he gave up his plight, stepping past her and continuing down the corridor.

After the fourth or fifth turn, she lost track of how many hallways they had passed. They climbed three separate staircases, all with various amounts of steps. At last, they turned left down a corridor, revealing Garrick lounging in one of several wooden chairs, padded with thick maroon cushions. A closed, heavy wooden door, ornate with a pattern of etched swirling eagles, stood grandly at the end of the hall. Raylyn could see no knocker, knob, or handle, just smooth, polished wood.

"Goddess's sake, you took your damn time," Garrick said, surprising Raylyn, who was certain he had been sleeping.

"Just enjoying being home, Gar. You didn't have to wait for us, you know."

"Ha! And save you the burden of explaining yourself to dear Daddy? No chance." He stretched, arching his back like a cat before springing to his feet. "Let's get this done. I'm starving."

Raylyn hesitated, ice forming in her chest. Behind that door was not only the king, but the determination of her entire future. She shivered, the motion drawing Rowan's attention. "Don't worry," he said, his eyes still sad. "I'm certain my father will be grateful for everything you've done. All will be well." She wanted to believe him, but his brow was lined with worry, and he didn't meet her eyes. He took the last few steps toward the door, placing his hand flat against the wood.

Red light flowed through the spiraling etchings until the glow filled the hallway. The three eagles in the design moved, slowly stirring to life. They flapped their wings, circling each other, then stopped as they perched in a line directly in front of Rowan's face. A sharp *click* and half a breath later, the door swung free. Raylyn's mouth fell open in surprise as she stared in wonder, the light slowly fading from the door. She had never seen similar magic.

"How—" she began, voice fading.

Rowan raised a hand, a bead of blood barely visible in the center of his palm. "The magic in royal blood opens the door. A form of protection. Any unwelcome guest would be unable to enter." He absentmindedly wiped his hand on his trousers, already stained and filthy from weeks on the road. Motioning to Raylyn and Garrick, the three entered the chamber.

"Rowan!" A gravelly voice boomed. It took a moment for Raylyn's eyes to adjust to the room; the brightness surprised her given the evening hour. Rapidly blinking, she noticed the small balls of light suspended in the air near the ceiling, casting unwavering illumination to the room. A small hearth in the corner was also lit, adding an almost smothering warmth. A large desk occupied most of the space and seated behind it, the king.

Simultaneously, Rowan and Garrick placed a fist over their chest, Garrick sinking down on a knee and Rowan bowing his head. Raylyn shifted her weight awkwardly, pausing barely past the doorway. She lowered herself into a curtsy. *Dear Goddess, don't offend him*, she thought to herself, trying to tame the quickly bubbling panic in her chest.

The king set down a quill and slid a piece of parchment away from him on the desk. Crossing his arms, he leaned back, eyes narrowed as he examined the group. "Well, it's about damn time," he said.

"I'm sorry, Father, there was a ... bit of a complication. I presume you received the scriber I sent?"

"Ha! Yes, *very* informative, son," he said, sarcasm dripping from his words. "Might've well sent the recipe for your grandmother's berry pie, for all the good it did me." Out of the corner of her eye, Raylyn saw Garrick's jaw clench, the muscles tensing.

Rowan cleared his throat. "Well, yes, it was a bit too complicated to hash out in a scriber. And anyway—"

"And you smell like horse shit," the king said, cutting him off. They stared at each other, tension palpable in the air. A moment passed before both men burst into laughter, tears forming in the king's eyes. He rose, stepping around the desk to embrace his son. Pulling back, he examined Rowan. "You don't look half-bad for someone who was on the brink of death, son."

"Thanks to this one over here," he said, gesturing to Raylyn. "Raylyn is the only reason I haven't made my peace with the Goddess yet." He glanced at her, gratitude glinting in his eyes.

The king turned to her, as if realizing her presence for the first time. "Hm," he muttered, his expression unreadable.

"Ah, yes, and I am just a useless steaming pile of cow dung," Garrick said, drawing all their attention.

The king roared with laughter, clasping Garrick's forearm. "Ah, nephew. You know I value you as my own. Though you *do* smell like a steaming pile, no doubt." He turned back to Rowan. "Sit. All of you. We have much to catch up on." Waving his hand, three chairs identical to those outside the room, materialized in front of the desk. "Garrick, a full report, please."

"Yes, Your Majesty." All playful sarcasm vanished from his voice. "The rounds were uncomplicated through the whole of the mission. We were still several miles outside of Silver Keep and had camped down for the night, scheduled to arrive by midmorning. We were ahead of schedule, as we had quick success in recruiting at Boreshead and Randor." He reached inside his pocket, retrieving a folded piece of parchment. "Here's a breakdown of the enlistment numbers." He handed it to the king, who scanned it briefly, eyes widening.

"A hundred and twelve new enlistees? From *one* recruitment campaign? These are impressive numbers, indeed. Well done."

The corners of Garrick's mouth twitched upward, but his face remained stern. "Yes, but it appears the people are uneasy. Forgive the boldness, but harvests are even less than last season, and the monetary incentive seems to tempt more families than last year... And of those hundred and twelve, we only got four new casters and six healers. Mages are too valued in the smaller villages to be bought."

The king sighed. "Unfortunate, though unsurprising, with the ungodly heat this season. The lack of rainfall will do its damage." He paused, chewing his cheek. "That's another problem entirely, though. You say you faced no trouble on the roads?"

"None. Normally we come across at least a bit of ... unrest. An unissued toll on the road, wool-for-brains highwaymen who don't note the Royal Sigil as we pass through. You know, the likes. But, there was nothing; it was an uneventful journey until that night outside Silver Keep.

It was near dawn when we woke to find Rowan missing. I sent half our party to Silver Keep searching, and the rest of us took to the road and nearby forest. We didn't find him."

Garrick shot a dark look over at Rowan, who was staring at the floor. "He sent a scriber that evening saying he was half a day's ride away, recovering in Lakehaven ... not that the bastard—excuse me, Your Majesty—had the decency to even mention his attack. We got to him as quickly as possible, no clues as to what to expect. The rest," he paused, glancing at Rowan, "is not my story to tell. The trip from Lakehaven back to the Capital was uneventful, thank the Goddess." He ran a hand over his face, smearing some road dust in a dirty streak across his cheek, exhaustion palpable.

The king frowned. "Thank you, Garrick. We will discuss the plans for the mage enlistees tomorrow. Get some rest. You've more than earned it."

Garrick nodded, understanding his dismissal, and wordlessly left the room. The king waited until the door was shut before turning to Rowan expectantly. "Why did you leave your guard? It's unlike you to be so foolish."

"Agreed, Father," he sighed, shaking his head. "I'm afraid my answer is severely lacking." His brows knotted together, deep in thought. "My memories of the attack are quite hazy. I remember waking in the middle of the night, and—I know this makes no sense—but I felt a *pull*, as if an invisible force was calling out for me. And I followed. I don't know why. At the time, I don't remember questioning it; I was only concerned about the intense need to go toward it."

"But ... go toward *what*, exactly?" The king interrupted, concern tugging his mouth into a tight-lipped frown.

"That's the thing. I do not know. It was as if I was in a trance. All I know is I wasn't myself that night..." Rowan's voice trailed off for a moment. "I've been deliberating on it for some time now, and I think that while unconscious, I may have effected Raylyn and her mother, urging them to heal me in a desperate attempt to save myself. Though I might be wrong, I'm curious to know if that was the catalyst for Raylyn's powers emerging." He looked up, meeting her eyes. "I will forever be in your debt."

She felt a prickle of heat warm her cheeks at the intensity of his gaze, but she fought against the urge to look away. *In all these weeks, he never mentioned effecting me that day.*

"Yes, Raylyn Ashton of Lakehaven. I believe you have earned my thanks for saving my reckless son's life. Perhaps you could tell me what happened?" He spoke to her like she was a skittish animal that he didn't want to scare away.

"Of course, Your Majesty," she replied, forcing her voice to remain steady. Her hands, however, trembled as she launched into a retelling of that day in the woods. As she spoke, a feeling in the pit of her stomach told her to reveal all, and she did, sparing no detail. She spoke for several minutes, recanting the mess of gore when she and her mother had found the prince, revealing the powers that she had so recently discovered, her exile from her home, everything.

But when she tried to recount that night in the field— her uncontrolled rage and endless fields of grassland burned—the words caught in her throat, choking her. "It seems," she began, her voice a whisper, "that I have some trouble controlling it." Hot tear spilled down her cheeks.

Horrified with herself, she turned her head, unsuccessfully attempting to hide her emotions.

The silence in the chamber was deafening. Raylyn urged her pounding heart to slow as she desperately pulled herself together. At last, she pushed the shame and guilt and worry into a small box, closed the lid, and locked it for good measure. *What's meant to be shall be, Goddess willing*, she thought, finally turning back toward the men.

The king studied her as a smile slowly spread across his face. "Well, don't we all at first, my dear? Who has ever painted a masterpiece on their first attempt?" His voice held a soft kindness, so juxtaposed from the beginning of their meeting.

Raylyn couldn't help but smile back, relief coursing through every fiber of her being. The best she had hoped for was Marking, if not execution. Definitely not comforting fatherly advice. She leaned back in her chair and felt like she could breathe for the first time in weeks.

"Garrick said you were back," came a voice from behind her. Raylyn and Rowan both jumped in surprise, turning in their seats to face the doorway. She caught the faint glow of dimming red light, fading quickly from the carved door. Blinking in alarm, she was certain her sanity had finally left her. The man entering the room was identical to Rowan, and the shock of it left her gaping.

The real Rowan gave a tight-lipped smile. "Obviously."

"Too bad." The stranger crossed the room with a carefree ease, lounging in the vacant seat. "Thought perhaps I'd finally be rid of you." He cracked a smile, but she wasn't certain he was joking.

As she stared, she noticed subtle differences between the two men: where Rowan's eyes were a golden-brown, the stranger's were blue, his hair was a few shades lighter, and he had about an inch of height on Rowan and perhaps a few more pounds of muscle. His shirt was a creamy linen, the king's emblem embroidered at the collar and wrists.

Seeing the blank look on her face, Rowan spoke. "Raylyn, this is my brother, Brenden."

"*The* Raylyn?" Brenden swept across the room, graceful and lively as a mountain cat, and knelt before her. She stared incredulously at him, her mind reeling, wondering if she should stand and curtsy. Before she could object, he grabbed her hand and kissed the back of it, mirroring Rowan's gesture so many weeks before. He looked up, his eyes piercing, and spoke. "You've saved my brother's life," he said in a quiet voice. "For that, we are all in your debt." He squeezed her hand, giving her a small, intimate smile, before rising back to his feet.

Raylyn was speechless, so lost for words that she was half convinced she became a mute. The king cleared his throat, allowing her an end to the awkward encounter.

"Brenden, I was just going to call for you," the king said. "Terach, too. Have you seen him lately? We need to discuss the details of Rowan's attack."

"He was in his study a few hours back. We were brainstorming for the competition." His eyes drifted back to Raylyn. "From what I hear, you have some impressive powers. I hope you'll be competing." He grinned, his face carefree and open.

She stared blankly again, starting to feel hopelessly foolish. "Um, sorry, what?"

Rowan sighed. "Bren, she's no clue about any of it." He turned toward Raylyn, hiding an eye roll from his brother. "It's a competition the academy holds annually. A combination of riddles and prowess. A caster and healer pair up to compete and the prizes for the winners vary each year. It's usually something—"

Brenden cut him off in an excited rush. "This year, each winning team will get two copies of an original Helena Lightier journal, as well as the regulatory bag of gold. A more precious prize to the healer, of course, but the caster can always sell their copy of the book. It's worth more than—"

"More than the bag of gold, that's for certain!" Raylyn swooned. Helena Lightier was the author of several of her textbooks back home, as well as *Useful Herbs and Fungi*—which was resting safely inside her pack. She was a renowned herbologist and healer. Though she had died centuries ago, her works were still prized as the most competent and well studied. To have an original—written in her own hand, with her own notes—it wouldn't be worth merely a bag of gold; it would be priceless. *Who knows what secrets it may hold that were deemed too incomplete to transcribe on copies?* Raylyn wondered, completely absorbed in her thoughts.

The king's laugh jolted her back to reality. "Well, seems like the book will be an adequate reward after all," he chuckled. "But back to our current issues." He shuffled papers around on his desk, revealing a small bowl full of what looked to be wooden coins. Grabbing two out, seemingly at random, he placed them flat on the desk, raising his left hand to hover a few inches above. After a second, the wooden discs started trembling until they tilted onto their edges, spinning, growing speed until they spun like a top. After a few entertaining moments, the spinning ceased, as if someone had slapped their hand over the coins, and they fell flat onto the desk, lifeless once more.

"What was that?" Raylyn asked, leaning closer to see the coins better. It was a dark cherry wood; the flat surface appeared to be etched with curving letters. She squinted, but she was too far away to discern what was written.

The king smiled, raising his eyebrows suggestively. "A little device I created." He picked up the coins, flicking them nonchalantly in the air. On their descent, they floated down slowly, like feathers, landing back in the bowl. "An inconspicuous and convenient way to request an audience with someone. Every coin here," he gestured toward the bowl, "has a twin residing with someone else. I send a signal, just as you saw, and the twin coin reacts in the same way."

"So somewhere else, another wooden coin just spun like crazy on someone's desk?" Raylyn asked, intrigued.

"Or someone's pocket, or in their pack, or on the floor of their bedchamber, yes. Wherever it may be."

"That's incredible," she said, still peering into the bowl. She had focused her studies so heavily on healing, she had neglected to learn these types of spells. Even her father, so revered in their village for his skill, could not imbed and maintain spells like this. "It must be a constant drain on your energy, keeping them linked," she said, her thoughts spilling into words.

"Ah, but there are ways around that, of course," the king said, winking.

The question at Raylyn's lips died as a quick tapping knock came from the chamber door.

"Open," the king commanded, and the door obeyed.

At first, Raylyn thought it was a matronly woman, as the newcomer's hair was entirely silver. But when she spoke, her voice was soft and delicate, and Raylyn was perplexed, guessing at her age.

"Your Highness," she curtsied low, "How may I serve you?" Though she was soft-spoken, she had an air of confidence and routine as she straightened and addressed the king.

"Talia, thank you for your haste, timely as ever. This is Raylyn." Talia smiled at her and curtsied again, though nowhere near as deep. "She is an honored guest of mine. If you would be so kind as to prepare her chambers and assist her with—" he waved his hand, "whatever you ladies need." He chuckled, a hint of embarrassment in the laugh.

The girl nodded. "My pleasure. The guest wing, Your Grace?"

"Hm." The king rubbed his face, deliberating. "I think not. She's a very *important* guest, Talia. Let's do one of the open suites in the north wing. They're much more comfortable."

Talia blinked but gave no other indication of surprise. "Yes, of course. If you will, my lady?"

Raylyn rose, her legs stiff. "Thank you, Your Highness," she said, feeling self-conscious next to the petite, well-mannered girl.

"A night of rest will do you well. Talia, make sure she eats. Tomorrow, we will celebrate. A feast in your honor." He clapped his hands with a self-satisfied smile.

"Ah, thank you," Raylyn stammered, unsure of what to say. She followed Talia out of the room, but Brenden hurried behind them, forcing her to pause at the door.

"Let me accompany you tomorrow," he said, his hand lingering on her arm. His eyes searched her face in a warm hopefulness that threw her entirely off balance.

"Accompany me?" she repeated blankly.

"Yes, to the feast." He smiled, his face lighting up. "I could introduce you to members of Court, a way of saying thank you for saving my little brother."

"Little? I'm two minutes older!" Rowan grumbled from the depths of the room.

Brenden smirked, turning his head over his shoulder. "Yeah, but physically, always smaller, eh?" He faced back to Raylyn, his eyes sparkling mischievously. "Would you give me the pleasure?" he asked, voice dropping low so only the two of them heard.

She bit her lip, trying to ignore the butterflies in her stomach. "Oh, right. Um, okay. I'm sure that will be very helpful."

Brenden trailed his hand down her arm with deliberate slowness, maintaining eye contact the entire time. He reached her hand, pressing his lips to it once more. "Until then," he said. Goosebumps prickled her skin, and she couldn't help but smile at his flirtations. She suddenly wished she wasn't covered in weeks' worth of dirt from traveling, hair knotted in a dirty tangle. She turned again to accompany Talia, who had been waiting in the hall studying the floor. Before the door had closed, she caught a glimpse of Rowan, his face darkened and eyes narrowed, glaring daggers into his brother's back.

CHAPTER 8

TALIA LED HER DOWN THE PASSAGEWAY, her footsteps quick and light on the stone floor. They hadn't made it far from the king's office when they passed an older man of medium build with dark hair. Talia paused, offering him a quick curtsy. He ignored her, passing them quickly without a second glance. Raylyn was about to ask who he was when dancing shadows caught her attention. She had expected more strangers to appear from around the corner, but realized the shadows were cast from lanterns—fire lanterns this time, not the flameless orbs which bobbed under the ceiling in the king's study. She was alone save Talia, who remained silent during their walk. Raylyn was once again unsuccessful at memorizing the way, her internal compass failing her completely. *I'll have to take time to explore*, she thought as they finally stopped in front of a large, plain door.

Talia pulled a ring of keys out, secured by a chain around her neck. She tried a couple before succeeding, the lock opening with a soft *click*. She smiled an apology at Raylyn. "It may be a little cold. We do routine cleanings of the unoccupied rooms, but we've had no time to prepare the hearth," she explained as she darted inside, quickly lighting torches on the walls.

Holy Goddess, Raylyn thought as she walked inside, exploring. "My entire house could fit in here twice over!" In the middle of the room was a proud four-poster bed with pale red curtains. It was piled with a mountain of matching pillows and thick, warm blankets. Raylyn ran a hand over the soft fabric. If she laid down, she would have fallen asleep instantly. She fought the urge to dive onto the bed and walked over to Talia, who now knelt in front of a grandiose hearth.

"Can I help?" she asked as the girl added a few logs. Talia spared her a quick glance and shook her head once. She aimed a glowing hand toward the logs, and a moment later, heat poured into the room, fighting back the chill in the air. Raylyn stared. "You can *cast*?" she asked, shocked.

Talia laughed, her brows raised. "Of course!" she said, tilting her head, examining her. "You're not from around here, are you?"

"Is it obvious?" she asked, chewing her lip. "I assumed servants wouldn't be mages."

Talia's expression darkened. "I am not a servant, I'm a *student*. I work for my lodgings and meals while I attend classes at the Academy." She shook her head. "It is quite common practice for those not wealthy enough to rent a room for the entire semester. Will you be staying with us long, Raylyn?" she asked, side-eyeing her. "These chambers are usually reserved for extended guests."

She thought about it for a moment. "I'm ... not sure. But I assume so, yes."

Talia nodded. "Then you have a lot to learn." She stood, brushing some soot from her skirts. "We'll draw you a bath, and I'll send to the kitchen for some dinner."

Talia led her to the back of the room and a door Raylyn thought to be a closet opened into an attached chamber. Inside was a large, deep tub and wash basin. A basket of linens was arranged prettily in the corner, one towel shaped into a swan. Talia closed her eyes and raised her hands in front of her. Water began filling the tub, heat steaming into the air. Raylyn's mouth hung open as the tub continued to fill, the water level rising rapidly to the top.

"Now *that*," Talia said, "was just showing off." She walked over to the faucet of the tub. "The castle is fully piped, of course," she said, a mischievous grin on her face.

"Impressive," Raylyn said, watching the wisps of steam disappear into the air. "Thank you," she added as Talia walked past her toward the bedchamber.

"I'll be back in an hour with some food. Anything you'd prefer? The food here really is divine. And some of the cooks aren't half-bad, either." She winked, and Raylyn knew she was talking about more than just their skills as chefs.

"I'm not picky, thanks..." Curiosity bested her. "How old are you, Talia?"

"What an odd question to ask a lady." She stuck out her tongue and giggled. "Twenty-two."

"No way!" Raylyn exclaimed. At a distance, the silver hair was confusing, of course, but up close, she was flawless youth, smooth skin and almond eyes. She was petite, coming up only to Raylyn's shoulders. Though her dress was plain, it was form-fitting, highlighting modest curves.

"Yes, truly," Talia said with a small smile. And, with that, she left.

By the time Raylyn was done bathing, the water was brown, and her skin was three shades lighter. For a panicked moment, she thought she'd have to cut off her tangled mess of hair, but several minutes and tears later, she combed the knots free. Talia returned with food and clean clothes, and at Raylyn's insistence, started explaining some intricacies of Court and classes at the Academy.

"Most of the students are in their late teens and early twenties. There are children, of course, but they usually come from very well-off families that either live in the capital or relocate for the semester. You can't just send an eight-year-old to live by themselves." She paused, taking a sip of tea, and Raylyn couldn't help but think of Bo, sent here on his own as a child. "It is very late," Talia said, stretching, "and we have a busy morning. Get some rest."

"A busy morning?" Raylyn asked, stifling a yawn.

"I'm to give you a tour. Castle, grounds, and Academy, at his royal highness's request." She wiggled her eyebrows, looking like a mischievous child. "You *must* tell me what you did to earn favor from such powerful people."

"You go first," Raylyn said. Both girls laughed.

"I've left you a change of clothes by the washbasin, as your belongings appear to be lacking." She gestured to Raylyn's single bag, sitting lonely on a trunk by the foot of the bed. "Goodnight," Talia said, slipping into the dark corridor.

Raylyn stared at the wooden door as it softly closed, gifting her solitude for the first time in nearly a month. The clawing anxiety that tore at her chest for so many sleepless nights was gone. The absence of its weight giddied her, and she floated to bed, sleep greeting her like an old friend.

The tour of the castle was overwhelming. With each passage they took, more appeared, as if the building was constantly growing. Talia navigated with easy steps, pointing out different paintings and doors. Offices, sitting rooms, ballroom, kitchens, dining rooms, sleeping chambers, servant quarters, grand library... the list was endless.

Her unquestionable favorite was the library. It was four stories high, with aisles and aisles of books on every topic one could imagine. Raylyn ran her hand along the tomes' spines as they walked, fingertips tingling with desire. Her collection of books at home, which she prized deeper than anything, was *nothing*—a leaf in a forest—compared to the hundreds of thousands which filled the room. Sitting areas were scattered between the shelves, bedecked with soft armchairs, a desk, and an orb-lit lantern. She was certain she could lose days here, escaping into the books.

"Raylyn, we have much still to accomplish," Talia repeated, not for the first time. After some coercion, she finally forced Raylyn out of the library, much to her chagrin. The rest of the castle was bland in comparison. They stopped in the kitchens, warm and humid. It was a commotion of action as the workers bustled around dicing and frying and stirring. Despite the obvious differences, Raylyn closed her eyes for a moment, imagining she was back home in her own kitchen, preparing for winter's eve festivities with her family and friends. A prickle of home-sickness settled in her stomach as they ate a quick lunch. She blushed into her soup as Talia flirted with one of the kitchen boys as he chopped vegetables in preparation for that evening's feast.

"What was his name?" Raylyn asked after they had walked out of hearing distance.

Talia chewed on her lip. "Actually, I don't know," she said with a small smirk. "Oh please," she continued, seeing the incredulous look on Raylyn's face, "Don't act the prude. I saw Prince Brenden flirting with you last evening."

"He was *not*! He was thanking me for—" Raylyn stopped short, realizing that she shouldn't make the attack on Rowan public knowledge.

"Yes, thanking you for saving Prince Rowan, I heard," Talia said casually, leading them through an inconspicuous door that led to the castle grounds. A paved walkway wound lazily through bushes and topiaries. Flowers that normally die by this time of year were vibrant with the unseasonably temperate air. "Saved him from what, exactly?"

Surprised, Raylyn stopped abruptly. Talia realized after a few steps and turned. "Oh, come now. I have ears. I was standing right there." She grabbed Raylyn's arm, hooking her own through as they continued down the path. Raylyn remained quiet, mouth clamped shut else she say too much. She wasn't about to risk her short-lived freedom by spilling crown secrets.

Talia sighed. "Keep your secrets then," she said, though her voice was kind. They walked for several min-utes, the humming of bees and chittering birds breaking up the silence. It reminded Raylyn of Braya's mother, Anais, knowing she would've gotten so much pleasure from these gardens.

The thought of Braya caused the breath to rush out of her lungs. She hadn't spared her best friend even a thought since Goddess knows when. The creeping tendrils of shame constricted her heart. "Who would I speak to about sending a letter?" she asked. "To someone without access to a scriber," she added, unsure how common that method of communication was here.

"Well, that depends. Is it someone inside the city or outside?"

"Outside."

"So, for far distances, we have ravens and messenger pigeons. They're near the stables. There's a very pretty bird I always choose to send letters to my parents in Randor. She never gets lost. For messages in the city, we have a few runners. Casters will sometimes help for short distances, too, if they owe you a debt or are trying to win your favor."

Raylyn was quiet for a second. "If you're a caster, why do you use the bird?"

Talia snorted. "How far is Randor from here?"

Raylyn thought, calculating the distance in her mind. "I'd say at least eighty miles."

Talia nodded. "Ninety-three, actually. But close enough. Ouch!" she cried, swatting a small bee away from her. "Damn sugar bees," she muttered, rubbing her arm. "Anyway, how much time and energy would it take to travel ninety-three miles?"

"Ah, quite a bit," Raylyn said, understanding. "I guess I thought maybe you could entice the breeze or something to fly it wherever you want. I didn't think it would require the same energy as actually walking it to your destination."

"No one can control the wind, silly," Talia said. "Anyway. There're the stables, and just beyond ... you see that building behind? That's the Ravenry." They had made their way out of the gardens, the castle slowly growing smaller behind them as they gained some distance. "We can stop there after the Academy, if you have the letter."

"I haven't written it yet, but thank you. I'm sure I'll find it again on my own."

"I wouldn't be so certain," Talia said with a laugh. Raylyn's miserable sense of direction had her lost in the library earlier, unable to find her way to the staircase from one of the upper levels. After several panicked seconds, Talia had found her in a maze of books and led her out of the library.

Their walk to the Academy was less than half an hour. Raylyn gaped as they came upon the building. It rivaled the castle in its enormity and was comprised of the same types of stones, all varying in size and color. That was where the similarities ended. They entered freely, no guards, locks, or spells barring the entrance.

"There's two separate wings," Talia explained as Raylyn stared. They had walked into a large entryway—larger than Raylyn's chambers at the castle—with high ceilings and several dozen windows. It was as bright as the daylight outside. Centered in the room was a long desk with a few people sitting behind it, heads down as they scribbled on parchment. Two long corridors opened on either side of the desk. "Come on. I'll introduce you."

They approached the desk, catching the attention of the closest person who slowly raised their head from the shaking scribble of notes. The woman's hair was gray, but unlike Talia, she was ancient, easily the oldest person

Raylyn had ever seen. Her skin was wrinkled and nearly translucent, eyes a hazy blue with cataracts. "Hello, dear Talia. You've brought a friend today?"

Raylyn bit her cheek in surprise. She had expected the woman's voice to be raspy and weak with age. Instead, it was youthful and clear. As if sensing her shock, the old woman turned her large, blind eyes to her. "Unexpected, am I?" she asked. Raylyn's heart began to race, fear and confusion spreading through her body.

Effector! Of course! she realized. The same disgust she felt when she learned of Rowan's powers rose in her throat. Violated at the intrusion of her thoughts, she took a step backward out of instinct.

"Oh, now, dear. You're knowledgeable enough to know my powers are not as distasteful as they seem. I do not know your thoughts, just your feelings and intentions. And I daresay I should be offended at your rudeness," she said quietly, her tone calm and soothing.

Embarrassed, Raylyn forced a small smile. "I'm sorry, Matron. It was a gut reaction."

The woman nodded, turning back toward Talia. "What can I do for you?"

"As you noted, I have brought a friend. Arwen, this is Raylyn." Talia leaned in closer and continued in a whisper. "His Majesty has instructed me to give her a tour of the Academy, as she is expected to start lessons."

"Of course. And which wing will it be?"

"Both." Though her voice was confident, Talia turned, looking at Raylyn quizzically, as if she was a puzzle that needed solving.

Arwen paused, then leaned closer. "I'm sorry, dear. Surely I misheard you. Which wing?"

"You heard correctly, Arwen. *Both* wings." And she kept her voice quiet, lips inches from Arwen's ear.

The elderly lady closed her eyes and leaned back in her chair. Several seconds went by and Raylyn shifted, uncomfortable. She looked to Talia for guidance, but the other girl shrugged, appearing just as confused as she. Arwen finally opened her eyes. "Oh, children, I was hoping the Goddess would take me before ... but very well." She leaned forward and passed a quill and scroll of parchment to Talia, who took it and signed her name on the paper.

Talia passed her the quill. "You've got to sign your name. It shows attendance."

"That's important?" she asked, signing the paper. The quill scratched sharply, accidently tearing a pinpoint hole in the parchment. Arwen scoffed, snatching it back from her.

"Left first. Healing is strong with her," Arwen muttered, then turned back to whatever she had been working on prior to their interruption.

"Thank you. Good day," Talia said. Arwen did not look up.

The left hall was a long and wide passage, wooden doors stationed at equal intervals to both sides. There were no windows here, and Raylyn could sense they were in the middle of the building. The ceiling was significantly lower here and orb-lights bobbed above their heads.

Raylyn waited for a few minutes as they walked before speaking. "Arwen is quite ..." She searched for an adequate word but couldn't find it.

"Unique?"

"You could say that."

"She *is* unique. If you believe the rumors, she was around when this place was built." She caught Raylyn rolling her eyes. "Oh, I was skeptical, too, but the more you talk with her, the more you start to believe."

"Her voice sounds almost like a child's, though. How's that possible?" she asked. The corridor was underwhelming, just stone wall on both sides.

Talia shrugged. "Some interesting type of magic, I'd assume. Though if she's able to alter things about herself, why not fix her eyes, too?"

"She is blind, then?"

"In a sense. But, be sure, she has other ways of seeing."

Well, don't all effectors? Raylyn thought. Just the thought of their skills made her stomach knot. *They invade your mind and alter your feelings.* She shuddered. It made bile rise in her throat.

Talia stopped abruptly, making her almost trip. "Look," she said, pointing toward a long row of wooden doors. She shifted back into guide mode instantly. "So, as you've already gathered, the Academy has two distinct parts: the left is for healers, the right casters. Our classes are divided by skill, not age, and it is entirely accepted that an exceptionally talented young child may learn alongside an adult. These front classrooms are designated to very beginner level skills, usually children. As you go farther down the hall, the classes advance."

Raylyn noted numbered plaques above the doors as they walked. "It is how the classes are differentiated," Talia said when she had asked. They kept walking, passing more and more doors. Finally, they reached the end of the corridor, door thirty-one on the left and door thirty-two on the right. Centered at the end of the hall was another door, larger than the rest. A triangle designed out of three curved leaves was painted on it.

Raylyn stepped closer to inspect the symbol. "This is the Goddess's sigil of rejuvenation!" she exclaimed, excited to recognize something.

She leaned closer to examine the painting more closely, the colors vibrant and free of age, when the door suddenly swung open, hitting her directly in the face. She flew backward, sprawling on the stone floor. Dancing stars blurred her vision as she cradled her abused nose. "Ow…" she moaned.

"Well for Goddess's sake, who lingers face-first in front of a windowless door?" a man's voice said. Raylyn was blind with pain, her nose streaming warm blood down her face.

"Are you okay?" Talia asked, crouching down next to her.

She blinked a few times, clearing the stars from her eyes. She tipped her head forward and pinched the bridge of her nose. "I'm fine," she said nasally, glancing at the stranger. He was vaguely familiar, middle-aged with dark hair. She stared for a second, trying to place where she had seen him before.

"Move out of the way," he ordered Talia, who did as instructed. Her eyes grew wide, and she bobbed a curtsy, side-stepping until her back was flush with the wall.

"Pardon, Lord Terach," she muttered.

He bent, studying Raylyn's face. He pulled a black handkerchief from an inside pocket of his jacket, offering it to her. She took it, mopping the blood off her face and shirt.

"Thank you," she said, still pinching her nose. She offered the soiled cloth back, but the man shook his head.

"You can keep it. Come inside. I'll have a healer tend to you. I am sorry, though idling behind doors is moronic. You had it coming."

She didn't know if she should appreciate his help or be offended. "I was examining the sigil," she said, defensively, "and no, thank you, I'll do it myself." Closing her eyes, she channeled, golden light radiating from her palm. Energy and warmth spread from her hand through her nose. Instantly, the throbbing dulled, pain quickly fading until it was gone entirely. She was pleasantly surprised to realize the drain on her energy was nearly nonexistent.

The man held a hand to her, and she took it, pulling herself upright. "I don't think I know you. Are you new? The semester started over a week ago."

"Yes," Raylyn began, scrambling for words. She hadn't concocted an appropriate backstory as to why she arrived after the start of term, though she assumed explaining the truth wasn't appropriate. "I ... timed the journey incorrectly."

Talia finally peeled herself off the wall. "Please, allow me to introduce you," she said in a rush. "Raylyn, this is Lord Terach, advisor to the king."

It finally clicked into place why he seemed so familiar. *Terach was the other person the king requested in his office when he did his coin trick.* They had passed him in the hall the night before, responding to the king's summons. "Pleasure to meet you, my Lord," she said, ducking into a curtsy.

"Ah!" he gasped, smile spreading across his face. "*You're* Raylyn! I've heard *all* about you." He laughed. "And you're a terrible liar. Timed the journey incorrect, *indeed.*"

Raylyn glanced at Talia for moral support, but the girl was staring at her feet. Swallowing, she put on her best smile. "Yes, I'm sorry for that, my Lord. Circumstances being what they are, I didn't think the truth was exactly ... appropriate."

"Nonsense, nonsense, no apologies needed. I was just making my way back to the castle. Would you care to accompany me? I have some questions about the—" he paused, looking for the right word, "*unique* circumstances you mention. I prefer to get information directly from the source when possible." He placed a hand on Raylyn's shoulder, already guiding her back down the corridor.

She danced away from his touch as gracefully as she could muster. "I was eager for the rest of my tour of the Academy, but perhaps another time?"

He didn't miss a beat. "I have a few minutes to spare. As head of academic affairs, I'm sure I would qualify as a sufficient guide." At Raylyn's blank look, he continued. "I oversee the education council and programs. Currently, Prince Brenden is training under me to learn the intricacies of the job."

Raylyn's brows raised in surprise. Being the King's advisor was status enough, but she was starting to understand Talia's sudden meekness. *Head of the education council.* Likely, one word from this man could determine her success or failure at the academy. "I—I would be honored, if you truly have the time, my Lord," Raylyn stammered, realizing she was standing in shocked silence for a few seconds too long.

"You may go," he said, sparing a glance at Talia.

"The king instructed me to stay with Raylyn, my Lord," she said, finally lifting her gaze from the floor.

"I daresay the king wouldn't object your leaving her with me," he replied. When Talia made no motion to leave, he rolled his eyes. "Yes, very well. Remain if you wish. It makes no difference to me." He turned, addressing Raylyn, "Have you seen the healer classrooms then?"

"We just walked past them; we didn't go inside," Raylyn replied.

"Hm," he mumbled, squinting at Talia.

"I'm not a healer," she said. "I didn't know if we were allowed to enter the rooms."

"Follow me." He led them down a few doors, muttering so softly under his breath that Raylyn couldn't make out the words. He stopped outside the door marked 25 and hesitated for a moment. "Forgive me if this class is below your skill level. I'm guessing it is, based off one healing display. Once you have undergone the testing, we will be able to more accurately place you." He led them inside the classroom. "Go ahead, look around."

It wasn't what she had expected. Back at home, they had a small schoolhouse for the children for basic reading, arithmetic, grammar, the likes. She was expecting a similar set up of rectangular tables and a desk at the head of the room for the teacher.

While there were a few long tables, they were pushed against one of the walls of the room. It was bright with natural light, the entire back wall filled with large windows and a glass door that opened to a small garden. She strained her eyes, trying to determine what types of plants were growing.

To the left of the room were four empty cots lined neatly in a row. A nearby cabinet held supplies of crisp white sheets, towels and cloths, and an assortment of bandages and gauze. It reminded Raylyn of the clinic back home, though much more organized.

She strayed to the other side of the room, pulse quickening with delight. Large glass display cases ran from floor to ceiling, stocked with what looked like every herb, fungi, and mineral needed to make poultices and salves. She whipped her head around toward Lord Terach in excitement. "May I?" she asked, hand hovering over the glass handle of the case.

"Of course, though ... I assume you are aware of proper handling techniques?"

Raylyn couldn't keep the scowl from her face. "Yes," she said giving the man a side-eyed look. One of the first things her mother taught her was to never allow skin contact with ingredients. *Always assume the following is true,* her mother's voice rang in her mind. *First, your hands are filthy. Dirty hands lead to festering wounds. Always wash, and if gloves are available, don them. Second, assume all ingredients will be caustic to your skin. Some truly are, some aren't. But always using precautions is good habit to keep your hands from being burnt.*

Raylyn opened the case, finding a box with dozens of leather gloves. She smiled at the familiarity of it all as she pulled them onto her hands. Grabbing a clear jar, she inspected the contents, unfamiliar with the dried purple spirals inside. She squinted, pulling it mere inches from her face. *Yes, there are the little yellow hairs.* "Grapeweed!" she exclaimed, nearly bouncing on her feet. She glanced at Terach, who watched her with intrigued eyes. "I've read about it but never seen it in person. I live too far north."

"Hm." He walked toward her and took the jar, examining the herb. "Do you know where it gets its name?"

"When crushed, it smells of grapes. And, left unchecked, it proliferates with abundance."

"Indications for use?" Terach asked, handing her the jar back.

"If crushed and combined with honey, it makes an excellent salve for chronic wounds. Alone, its fragrance helps mask the odors from festering injuries. Brewed into a tea, it fights indigestion." She placed the jar onto the shelf, her attention shifting down the case with curiosity.

Terach nodded approvingly. He let her explore for several minutes. She recognized many herbs and fungi, stating their names as she passed them. *A supply such as this would last years back home,* she thought, with a pang of homesickness. She closed the glass door, a conflicting battle of regret and excitement toiling inside her. *And this is just one classroom.* The magnitude of her situation coursed through her, leaving her almost breathless. Resources and knowledge she had never dared hope for were now within her grasp. Her hands and body ached with longing to *begin*, to learn and create and heal. A thrum of energy bounced beneath her skin, making her hyperaware of the power coursing through her veins.

Finally, she forced herself to close the glass door of the case, turning back to Terach and Talia. "It's magnificent," she said, trying to hide the hunger in her eyes.

Terach grinned, her excitement contagious. "I'm glad you approve, though I daresay you are easily impressed." He nodded toward the case of herbs. "And I may have underestimated your proficiency. Let me show you the Infirmary." He led them back down the hall and opened the door with the Goddess's sigil.

If the classroom was impressive, the Infirmary was otherworldly. Raylyn froze in place, drinking it in. She was on the brink of a sensory overload as the cacophony of sound and movement hit her. Dozens of people were working, bustling around. She even spotted two children hauling soiled linens, dirty bundles half as large as they, with fierce looks of determination on their faces. They disappeared behind a nearby doorway, reappearing moments later unburdened.

A few healers' stations were scattered throughout the room where several people sat, jotting notes and consulting with one another, occasional laughs at unheard jokes ringing through the room. Voices tangled together in a symphony of sound. From where she stood in the doorway, Raylyn could just make out corridors toward the back of the room, branching out like a tree. Curtains hung from hooks in the ceiling, presumably separating out temporary rooms for patients. Carts stockpiled with supplies were positioned every dozen or so feet in front of the curtained areas. There was a scent of sterility in the air that brought Raylyn back to the clinic at home. She blinked her eyes hard to make sure she wasn't hallucinating. It was the most beautiful place she'd ever seen.

"Talia!" One of the children called, skipping toward them. An older woman behind a nearby desk gave a scold '*tsk*!' and the child winced, slowing into a brisk walk, though innocent eagerness remained on her face.

"Hey, Renny," Talia replied, crouching a little to hug the girl. "How're lessons?"

As Renny launched into an extremely descriptive narrative of her latest lesson on handwashing, Terach motioned to Raylyn to follow him. They walked through the buzzing room toward the doorless corridors at the back, passing healers who nodded their heads in respect before continuing with their work.

Terach stopped her after only a few steps into the corridor, face grim. "Steel yourself, this ward is not for the faint-hearted." Without further explanation, he continued onward, giving her no choice but to follow. With each step, the air shifted, and soon the unmistakable sweet stink of slowly rotting flesh burned her nose, growing stronger when they stepped into the new room. The layout was much the same, but the atmosphere was markedly different. Melancholy was palpable, and while there were just as many healers as the previous room, they worked in near silence, faces stony. The only sounds which pierced the quiet were the soft movements of the workers and the occasional broken moan from behind a curtained area.

"The smell..." Raylyn whispered. She could think of nothing else, and her eyes began to burn from its intensity.

Lord Terach nodded. "I know." He raised his right hand into the air, his palm radiating light. Immediately, the odor lessened, and though not completely eradicated, was much more manageable. Raylyn wondered what spell he used to accomplish such a feat. "I want to show you the ward first, and once we leave, I will answer any questions. The patients here are quite ill and deserve as much dignity as possible." Raylyn nodded, matching his serious tone.

They began walking the room but didn't make it far before a lithe woman stopped them. She was wearing a black cotton dress that was only a few shades lighter than her skin. "Terach," she said with the warmth of familiarity. "Thank you for helping with the ... odor. It is an unrelenting challenge." She shook her head, a small furrow cutting between her brows. "I've not known festering wounds to be so resistant to treatment. But did you forget something? You've been gone all of fifteen minutes."

Her voice had a thick accent that reminded Raylyn of Bo, and their skin was a similar shade of deep bronze. *I wonder if she was raised in Western Ellendria, too.* Once again, she was overcome with amazement at this place. Because of the Academy, Lendris was a meeting ground for the elite to congregate. Western Ellendria was under the domain of the king in mostly name only. Hundreds of miles away and isolated by a massive mountain range, it was largely self-sufficient. Travel was said to be so difficult that citizens from the region were hardly ever seen.

"Of course, Thorne, happy to help however I can. And, no. Actually, I ran into someone very special. This is Raylyn, a new pupil. She's yet to have her testing, though I believe she will place into your upper-level class. Raylyn, this is Madam Thorne, the Head of Healing for the Academy. She teaches the most advanced classes and is also solely responsible for the unparalleled running of this Infirmary."

"Ah, but we couldn't run it without the support of you and the crown. We owe our successes to you, Terach," Thorne said, batting her eyelashes at him without a trace of subtlety.

"And you repay us by supplying highly trained mages to work for the crown. One cannot expect a horse to run if not properly fed, yes? That is our standing on the funding of the Academy. If we make no effort to train the next generation of mages, we cannot expect our armies to grow or our nation to prosper."

The two middle-aged adults stared at each other for several long seconds. Raylyn stood, feeling awkwardly out of place, wishing she could melt into the floor. "Nice to meet you, madam," she said, breaking the silence with a forced smile. The woman turned her attention to her.

"A ... niece of yours, Terach?"

"No, no, nothing like that," he said with a soft chuckle. "I'll save the fun of a full introduction for the king; he is to be presenting her tonight. I assume you've heard of the feast?"

Thorne frowned. "Yes, got my students all worked up, and no one wants to miss out. Well, *someone* must tend the patients. And besides," she continued, "if the harvests are as barren as the rumors say, it's damned irresponsible to waste it in some exorbitant display of wealth. We have emaciated refugees coming in the dozens every week. Give *me* the extra food, I'll make sure it goes to good use."

"Now, now. It's a *celebration*, my dear. And besides, there's no food shortage. That's nothing but baseless rumors brought from small groups of rebels to stir up unrest. Do you not have enough provisions and supplies for the running of your Infirmary?" he asked, gesturing toward a nearby supply cart, stocked so well it was nearly overflowing.

"Hmph," she scoffed. "Well, yes, of course we do. You keep us up and running, Terach. Apologies for any curtness." She ran a hand over her face, pulling Raylyn's attention to the dark circles under her eyes. "Some of the students are exceptional, but our workload here is ever increasing. I'm not even sure the last time I slept. In fact, I was on my way to my chambers to rest just before I caught sight of you."

"Well, don't hesitate on our accounts, Thorne. I'm just giving the girl a quick tour around the place before she jumps in with both feet. Don't want her too overwhelmed on her first day. If I can hazard a guess, I'd say she'll soon be good use to you."

Those hard eyes met Raylyn's again briefly before darting back to Lord Terach. "You have that much faith in the little fledgling? No education, not even tested yet. You are not one to heedlessly boast."

"Actually," Raylyn interrupted, "I've had quite an extensive education back home." She didn't want to be rude, but she did pride herself on the knowledge of her craft.

Madam Thorne laughed, the sound carrying in the otherwise quiet chamber. "I meant a *proper* education, you see."

Raylyn's cheeks flushed indignantly. "I was training to be the next High Healer of my village most of my life. My mother currently holds that title."

"And what is your mother's name, child?" Thorne asked, some interest lighting up her dark eyes.

"Eva Ashton, High Healer of Lakehaven," she replied, puffing up a little with pride.

"Never heard of her," she said flatly, the light in her eyes extinguishing. She turned back to Terach. "I will retire for a few hours. Shall I look forward to sharing your company over a few glasses of sweet wine at dinner?" Her voice dripped with honey, and it took all of Raylyn's willpower to not wrinkle her nose with distaste.

Terach bowed his head. "Of course, Thorne. You know how I enjoy your company, most especially outside these walls." She smiled, breezing past them out of the chamber. Terach stared after Thorne, distracted. Raylyn cleared her throat, and he glanced at her with a sheepish grin. "She has a mind and talent like no other. Learn all you can under her. Shall we continue?"

They circled the ward, and though it mirrored the previous chamber almost exactly, the atmosphere couldn't have been more different. It felt like the entire room was holding its breath in anticipation of dire news, causing goosebumps to creep up Raylyn's arms. When they approached the curtained section of temporary rooms, Terach poked his head around the thick fabric. "Mind if I pop in with one of my pupils?" he asked behind the curtain. She didn't hear the response, though it must have been yes because Terach reappeared, holding the curtain aloft for her.

An elderly man was lying beneath the bedsheets, his skin an ashen pallor which Raylyn recognized from blood loss and malnutrition. "Hello," she said delicately, stepping toward the cot. A bedside table stood next to the head of the bed, burdened with a metal bowl full of red stained rags and a half-full mug of water.

The man gave a wet, rattling cough in response, his body shaking with such force that Raylyn grabbed the mug to keep it from sloshing over. His face grew red with exertion, lips a cyanotic blue. When his coughing slowly ceased, he reached with an emaciated and trembling arm toward an unsoiled rag on the table. She handed it to him wordlessly, watching him spit a glob of bloody mucus into it, then tossing it into the bowl with its companions. "Much thanks, little lady," he said rasping. "Name's Jordain."

"Raylyn," she replied. Despite herself, she took a small step backward. She knew to be wary of a bleeding cough. She had spent an entire summer with her mother tending to a neighboring village plagued with consumption, and the rules to prevent catching the illness were ingrained in her mind. Yet here she was, not three feet from a man who appeared to be on his deathbed, with no gloves nor face mask.

"You're wise to be cautious," Lord Terach said, stepping past Raylyn to hand Jordain his mug. The elderly man gulped long sips before setting it back down. "But it is not catching."

"Lung tumors," Jordain said, "damned big ones." He laid his head down, propped up by many pillows. "Too big to fix." His eyes closed.

Raylyn's brows pulled together as she glanced at Terach. "I am so sorry. Have you tried—"

"We've tried it all, little lady," Jordain replied, eyes still closed. "If our righteous king in Cystra gave any damn at all, maybe I would've found out sooner and done something."

Before she could ask, Terach spoke. "He is one of our refugees, escaping Cystra. Every time a new group arrives, we do an extensive medical exam. Conditions have deteriorated so rapidly. Unfortunately, Jordain's illness was too far advanced by the time he reached us."

Another long, wet coughing fit prevented Raylyn from speaking for several seconds. "Do you not have medical care in your country?" she asked, reapproaching his bed. Now that she knew it wasn't anything communicable, she felt comfortable reaching out to hold the man's hand. His skin was cold and paper thin, each tendon and bone prominent.

"Ha! Medical care..." He paused, taking several shallow breaths before continuing. "Sometimes the city guards would assist with amputation if someone had a festering cut or sore. If you weren't one of their special mages, you were good as dirt. Even had livestock treated better than us." He spit again, more blood than mucus this time.

Raylyn swallowed hard, forcing down the bile that had rose to her throat. "That's deplorable!" she said, eyeing Terach with poorly concealed outrage. She knew of the ongoing civil war but didn't realize how badly it had escalated.

"Lucky to have Terry here," he gave a feeble nod toward Terach, "and all of you little ones, bobbin' around, doting on me. Past few years were damn trying... Nice to at least be comfortable as I die." Another coughing fit racked his body, and he closed his eyes, a small trickle of blood dripping down his bone white face.

Raylyn had no words. She allowed the tears that welled hotly in her eyes to fall. A rush of anger burned through her as she stared at the terminal man, his eyes still closed, his only movement his chest, which rose raggedly with each strained breath. From the look of his mottled extremities, he wouldn't have much longer in this world. Raylyn breathed deep, centering herself, allowing her anger to melt into a pool at her feet. Praying to the Goddess, she allowed herself to feel nothing but peace, serenity, and comfort. She channeled those feelings into the elderly man, wishing desperately that she could heal his lungs, but knowing that some things were too far gone to mend. His gasping breaths slowed by degrees, his jaw relaxing. She had relieved some of his pain. Temporarily.

Releasing his hand, she stepped back quietly, knowing he was asleep. She put as much distance as she could between her and the curtained area, covering her mouth as the silent sob tore through her chest.

"Ah, now, now," Lord Terach said softly in her ear. "Pull yourself together." She forced herself to straighten, though her stomach remained a pit of acid. Her face burned as she caught a few of the healers glancing at her sideways. "Come. I imagine you've seen enough for now." He led them out of the chamber, through the corridor, and back into the other ward. Raylyn stared at her feet the entire way, realizing what a spectacle she must have made of herself. At some point Talia caught back up with them, and she soon found herself back in the long stone hallway of classrooms.

"Are you alright?" Talia whispered.

Raylyn gave a curt nod, fatigue and embarrassment weighing on her chest.

"Raylyn met one of the refugees today. I daresay she was unaware of the severity of our neighbor's civil war." Terach looked questionably at her. "Did you try to heal him?"

"His spirit, only," she replied, exhaustion erasing all preface of strength. "Alleviated his pain, gave him comfort and peace."

"And left yourself depleted," Terach said, knowingly. "I am not a healer, Raylyn, but I know there is a limit to one's power, and it is nothing but foolish childishness to push yourself to that extreme." His words bit at her, and she noted the similarities between him and her mother.

"It's just emotions. I'll be fine in a few minutes. And anyway, it was worth it." She imagined she could still feel Jordain's bony hand in hers, as cold as if he had met the Goddess already.

Terach scowled at her but thankfully gave up his lecture. He spun on his heels, leading them back to the entry way of the hall. "You're in no fit condition to be seeing the caster's side of things today. Go to your rooms and get some rest."

And as spent as she was, Raylyn felt a small trickle of disappointment as she and Talia headed for the doorway, leaving the right side of the building completely unexplored.

CHAPTER 9

R AYLYN HAD REGAINED MOST OF HER
strength on the walk back to the castle, but Talia
insisted she rest before the feast. She laid in the cloud of a
bed for a few moments, and despite its comfort, couldn't
find sleep. Though the room had no windows, her body
knew it was midday and was unaccustomed to naps. *This
is useless*, she thought, tossing the covers aside.

She grabbed her pack from where it lay abandoned at
the foot of the bed and dumped it out, the contents spilling
into a disorganized heap. She had one change of clothes
still soiled from the road. Most of her other belongings
were sorely inadequate: the map and flint box she packed
remained untouched during the trip, her knife only used
to cut through tough slabs of rabbit meat which Bo overcooked. She began organizing the items, shoving most of
it into the bedside table.

The only items remaining were the dirty clothes. *Everything I own fits inside one bag,* she thought dismally, throwing the soiled tunic and trousers onto the floor carelessly. Out of the corner of her eye, something small and brown flew out of the heap, skidding under the bed.

Her eyes narrowed as she dropped onto her belly to retrieve the mysterious item. She stretched, searching the rough stone floor before finding it. Blood pounded in her ears with the sudden realization of what she grasped. She ran her fingers over the smooth brown paper and coarse jute rope tying it closed. *The package Mother gave me the day of the council trial.* One tug of the rope and it would open, revealing whatever token her mother thought important enough to give her moments before her exile. She wasn't sure how long she stood holding it, but the taste of warm metal startled her from her musing, and she realized she bit her lip so hard it bled.

Anger won over curiosity, and she threw the small box across the room. It bounced a few times before sliding into the far corner. "I needed your support, not some unexplained gift!" she yelled, emotions spilling over.

"Well, it's not unexplained," Talia said, watching her from the opened doorway. She held a bundle of various colored cloth, piled almost as high as her head. "The king sends his regards in the form of gowns." She smiled, sauntering into the room. Setting the dresses down on the table, she plopped into a nearby cushioned chair. "We had to guess at your size, and none are custom made, but I think they'll do fine for now."

Heat filled Raylyn's face at being caught in such a state. "Sorry, I didn't hear you knock."

"You were a bit preoccupied. What is that, anyway?" she asked, nodding over toward the package on the ground.

"A ... parting gift from my mother. Her form of a twisted apology for refusing to fight against my banishment, I assume." At Talia's blank stare, she added, "It's a long story." A quietness fell over the room and Raylyn sucked on her abused lip, the metallic tang hitting her tongue again.

"Well, plenty of us have parent issues, right?" Talia said nonchalantly. Raylyn smiled, appreciative of the sentiment. "But aren't you curious about what's inside?" she continued. "Because I am. Though after that throw, I'd wager it's broken, whatever it is."

Raylyn rolled her eyes, taking the other seat by the table. "I don't care. No gift can right the wrongs of her betrayal." She glanced at Talia's confused face, knowing she'd have to explain more. "To summarize, I was exiled from my village and my parents didn't really fight to keep me there." Eager to change the subject, she grabbed the top-most dress from the pile. The smooth green silk was like cool water, almost liquid in the way it slid through her hands. "Goddess," she muttered in awe. She had never seen fabric its equal.

"I know," Talia cooed. "You *must* tell me your secrets because I've been playing servant to the king for a year now and still haven't received a new wardrobe."

Raylyn pulled her gaze away from the dress, her head snapping up with surprise. "You serve the king exclusively?"

"Well, we all serve our king in one way or another, don't we?" she replied. "I think you should wear this one," she said, holding up a light-yellow dress, the color of fresh spring tulips. "It'll look nice with your dark hair."

140

"You know what I mean, though," she said, grabbing the gown that Talia pushed at her. "I'm sure not every student ends up with a position directly serving the king. How'd you manage that?"

Talia eyed her, a small smirk pulling at her mouth. "I'll trade you a secret for a secret."

Raylyn considered. "What secret of mine would you like to know?" she asked hesitantly. Though desperate for some type of companionship, she was leery of saying too much.

"Why did the king want you to tour both halls of the Academy?" She sucked her cheeks in with eager anticipation.

She debated on answering. *If the king granted me permission to study both healing and casting at the Academy, then surely my secret will soon be common knowledge throughout Court.* Forcing an air of casual indifference, she finally replied. "Because I can heal and cast." She raised the dress up against her bosom. "You really think the yellow one?"

Talia blinked. "I thought we were going to be serious," she said, frowning.

Raylyn sighed. "I am."

"No one can do both."

"I can."

"Prove it."

"For Goddess's sake," Raylyn said, flustered. She threw the dress down and stormed across the room, retrieving her knife from her bedside table. Without hesitation, she ran its blade against her palm, blood welling at the superficial cut. Talia winced and pushed herself flat against the back of her chair, recoiling.

Raylyn healed the cut as effortlessly as breathing and wiped the blood onto the pant leg of her trousers. "Shouldn't have done that," she mumbled, looking at the smeared crimson stain on her thigh. "These were my only clean pair."

"You basket case. I already knew you could heal. I watched you fix your nose at the Academy, remember?" Talia's face twisted in disgust.

"Oh, yeah," she mumbled. "I forgot."

It was Talia's turn to roll her eyes. "Well, go ahead and cast, then." She crossed her arms, eyebrows raised in mock anticipation.

While Talia's skepticism wasn't unfounded, it was annoying. "Why would I lie about something that could so easily be disproven?" She searched the room, considering. Casting wasn't second nature to her. She walked to the unlit hearth and used her fingernail to pry a small piece of wood from a log. She hadn't attempted to cast since that night in the field when she lost control, and worry soured her stomach. *What if it happens again?* She looked up, Talia watching with one raised eyebrow.

Raylyn steeled herself, hardening her resolve. Cupping the wood in her palm, she concentrated, allowing the edges of her vision to blur as she focused on the little wooden sliver. Several seconds passed, and Raylyn fought the doubt in her belly. Finally, a trickle of smoke rose from the wood before it caught fire, a tiny flame flickering for a second before it extinguished into ash.

Talia's mouth fell open in shock before she composed herself. "A bit unimpressive, wouldn't you agree?" she said, trying and failing at sarcasm. Her voice was hardly more than a whisper.

"I've only just found out about the whole casting thing," Raylyn admitted.

Another long pause fell on the room. Raylyn subconsciously twisted a dead piece of skin on her thumbnail cuticle. *Perhaps I shouldn't have said anything.* She hoped she wouldn't chase Talia away with this revelation.

"So," she leaned forward, resting her elbows on the table, cradling her chin, looking very much like a bright-eyed child. "How did you learn to do *both*?"

Raylyn relaxed, the tension in her shoulder loosening. For a moment, she thought she would have a repeat of the council meeting. "That's not the rules of this game," she said, forcing a laugh. "A question for a question, right?"

Talia brushed a strand of her silver hair behind her ear, then nodded. "Fair is fair," she agreed. "Ask away."

"How did you end up in direct service to the king?" she asked, plopping down onto her bed.

Talia gave a wicked grin. "I have some unique talents that he favors." Her smile faltered for a moment as she narrowed her eyes. "Though, perhaps not as unique as yours."

"What is that supposed to mean?" she asked, trying to make sense of her words. "What are your talents?"

"Question for a question!" Talia sang.

"Fine," she said, rolling her eyes.

"Are your parents syphons like you? And are you Haddeon's great granddaughter or something? Because then maybe you could lift the enchantment in the Hall of Sorrows."

Raylyn balked in surprise, nearly falling off the bed. "Wha—? How do you know that?" she stammered, her eyes wide. "Who have you told?"

"Oh please, everyone is going to find out sooner or later—and I'd wager on sooner." She smirked. "I think the king plans to announce it at the feast tonight." Raylyn just stared at her, so shocked she couldn't find words. "I was with him when he received that scriber from Prince Rowan a few weeks ago, explaining what happened and what you could do. Didn't know about the casting part, though," she admitted, almost as an afterthought. "There are myths that syphons possessed both casting and healing abilities, but I thought those were just bedtime stories to scare little kids."

Raylyn gaped like a fish. "You've been acting like you've had no idea this entire time!"

"Part of my charm." She winked. "It's okay, Raylyn. I don't actually think you'll call down lightning and eat my soul. You *can't* do that, right?"

"Of course not!" she yelled, throwing one of the countless bed pillows at her.

"Right." Talia nodded. "Right, figured that was a myth. Though one of these days I really *will* take you to the Hall of Sorrows and see—just for fun—if you can fix it. No one uses that part of the castle anymore because of it."

"Hall of Sorrows?"

"Yeah, you know, the rumored place where Haddeon killed his wife a century ago. It's said to be cursed or spelled or something because no caster has ever repaired it. He left nothing but a crumbled heap of stones where the old throne room once stood. Supposedly, Haddeon is the only one who would be able to revoke the curse and repair the room. Goddess forbid he sets foot in this world again." She shrugged. "Probably just some make believe to entertain the children, but *still*..." She looked at Raylyn sideways. "How interesting it would be if you *could* repair it."

"Oh, enough of that already!" Raylyn huffed, exasperated. "I'm not a descendent of Haddeon! Everyone knows his line didn't continue. Anyway, you never answered my question, not fully. What secret abilities do you have that make the king prize you as a personal assistant and confidante?"

"Fair is fair," she said again, echoing her earlier words. "Watch."

Talia closed her eyes, breathing slow and deep. For a moment, Raylyn thought this was another one of her jokes and was about to throw another pillow at the ridiculous girl. But as she turned to grab one, a sudden movement caught her eye, and she stared in amazement as Talia's silver hair shimmered and flowed, as if a creature of its own accord. The silver darkened into a raven black and flowed down past the girl's shoulders to her waist. She opened her eyes, altered to an alarming shade of purple so distracting that Raylyn almost missed the newly upturned nose and cupids bow in her lip.

"Ta-da!" she said, throwing her hands up in the air and wiggling her fingers. Before Raylyn could speak, Talia was changing again, her hair turning a burning red, skin aging with sagging wrinkles. "Do you like this one?" Her features shifted to that of a young boy, her hair shortening to an inch from her scalp. Finally, she shifted back to her normal self—what Raylyn assumed was her natural appearance—and sat expectantly.

"That was amazing! How did you learn to do that?" Raylyn asked. She resisted the urge to touch Talia's silver locks to ensure they weren't a wig and that this wasn't some impressive sleight of hand.

"Papa said some casters are born with unique proficiencies. Some can cast shields that will defend an entire army battalion from oncoming attacks. Some can manipulate a fireball with impeccable accuracy. Casting is about manipulating your power into physical manifested results. For whichever reason, I'm able to manipulate my features on a whim. I can blend in or stand out as I choose. Copy another's appearance, though I am still working on that. It's not as easy as it sounds, making sure you get just the right shade of hair or every memorable freckle."

Raylyn mulled this over for a minute, the realization dawning on her. "You're not just the king's servant. You're spy!" she squeaked. Talia smiled. "Do people know?"

"Wouldn't make for that good of a spy if people knew, would it? People know I serve him, run small errands, tend to whatever visiting lady he demands, simple things. I'm wise enough to never look like this," she waved a hand, gesturing to her hair and thin body, "when I'm on a more, ah, important, assignment."

"Is that your real hair color?" Raylyn asked, unable to contain herself. The only people she had ever known to have silver hair were elderly.

Talia laughed. "Define 'real.' It's what feels natural with no effort if that answers your question."

"Can you teach me to do it, too?" she asked, thinking about her unruly curls.

"Can you teach me to syphon?" Talia retorted, wrinkling her nose. "It doesn't work like that, the same way Arwen—the woman you met at the front desk at the Academy—and Prince Rowan can't teach you to be an effector. Some people are just born differently than others." She was playing with the sleeve of the green dress on the table idly, then jolted, jumping up to her feet. "Goddess, we need to get you ready, or you'll be late!" she said with a sudden realization.

"You know, I was thinking about maybe *not* going to the feast. Maybe they could just bring me a couple of plates of food."

Talia stood up on her tip toes, still several inches shorter than her. She grabbed Raylyn's chin in her hand, her lips pressed into a thin line and eyes narrowed. "You *will* go to the feast." Her voice rumbled, low and dangerous.

Raylyn swallowed. For such a petite woman, she was intimidating. "Joking," she muttered. Satisfied, Talia let go of her face, walking toward the pile of dresses. She hesitated before grabbing the yellow one and turning around.

"Well?" she said expectantly. "Take your clothes off."

It was unnerving undressing in front of a stranger. She fought crossing her arms in front of her chest, exposed. "Oh please, sweet girl," Talia muttered, helping her into the dress. "You aren't the first lady I've assisted, and you won't be the last." The back of the dress was a laced corset, and she worked on it for a few minutes, tightening it until it took her breath away. "Lovely. This color is perfect for you," Talia murmured with a last tight pull, stepping back and appraising Raylyn like she was a painting. She rummaged under the pile of spare dresses, retrieving a small drawstring bag. Countless different powders, lip stains, brushes, and hairpins spilled out as she tipped the bag over.

Raylyn was thankful and exhausted when Talia had finished. Her hair twisted up off her neck elegantly, her eyes lined with charcoal and cheeks blushed a light pink. "What do you think?" Talia asked, holding up a small pocket mirror.

"I don't even look like myself," Raylyn said, pulling the mirror closer to study her features. "If I didn't know better, I'd think you had used your powers to alter my features like your own."

"Just different powers. These I could teach you. Makeup and dresses can be almost as good as completely changing your face, especially if you're dealing with men. Speaking of, where is Prince Brenden meeting you?" she asked, wiggling her eyebrows.

Raylyn bit her lip, earning a quick slap on the wrist from Talia. "Don't ruin your lipstick!" she hissed.

Consciously trying to not chew her lip, she considered. "I assume I'll meet him there." She thought of Rowan's dark look when Brenden asked her to accompany her. Her stomach knotted again, and for a moment she was certain she would vomit on the floor. "Perhaps it was a mistake agreeing to attend with him. He was just trying to be friendly, but I feel as if I'll draw enough attention as it is..." She trailed off, nerves rattling her.

"Nonsense. You will be grand. Once the food is served, you'll forget all about being in the spotlight. Make sure you try the rosemary roasted duck. It is divine. Just one suggestion, if I may?" Talia reached up, tucking a loose strand of hair behind Raylyn's ear.

"Of course," Raylyn replied.

"Be wary of Lord Terach." She stepped back, looking her over. "A masterpiece, truly."

"Why? He seems kind enough. More kind than Madam Thorne." The healer's name left a sour taste on Raylyn's tongue.

"He is more than he seems. Just be on guard around him. Trust me, as a friend. But it is time for you to go."

"Wait, aren't you coming, too?" Raylyn asked. Talia was still wearing her plain gray dress, making no moves to ready herself.

"Oh, Goddess, no!" she exclaimed, laughing. "I've been to dozens of those dinners. I'm not about to sit through another if it's not required of me! Actually, I have a date with Kitchen Boy." She winked, floating toward the door. "Come, I'll walk you down."

Raylyn's stomach twisted, but she followed her down the stone corridors to the dining hall. *The hardest part is over*, she kept telling herself. She had already met with the king who assured her safety from being Marked. She could survive some attention from a few people at Court.

With a quick "Have fun!" Talia flounced away, leaving her standing alone, two young servants stationed on either side of the double doors leading presumably to the dining hall. This wasn't a room she had seen during her brief tour of the castle, and she was certain there were many other places still left to explore. *Like the Hall of Sorrows,* Raylyn thought. She stood awkwardly for a moment, too aware of her arms and legs. She felt lanky and clumsy. Clearing her throat, she approached the servants who stared at her with bored, expectant looks.

"Sorry, I've never been to one of these before. Is it okay for me to just ... go in?" she asked sheepishly. She attempted to compose herself, pushing her shoulders back, consciously standing straighter.

"And your name, miss?" the leftmost girl asked, her voice flat.

Raylyn gave her name, and she nodded, giving a small smile, the first bit of expression Raylyn had seen on her round face. "One moment." She opened the door a crack, peeking her head in for a few seconds, then reappearing. Raylyn stood, confused. "Custom to announce you, miss." As if on cue, Raylyn heard her name through the doors, which were ceremoniously swung open, exposing the bright warmth inside.

She curtsied to the girl before entering the room. "Thank you."

Chandeliers glittered from the high ceiling, multicolored gemstones casting tiny fractions of rainbows around the room. The cascade of voices lowered by degrees as a few heads turned toward her, giving her a brief glance, then returning to their respective conversations. Three long rectangular tables connected, making three sides of an open square. Instead of a fourth table completing the square, at the head of the room was an empty raised stage. She scanned the room for Prince Brenden, taking in the various shades of red and black cloth adorned by the chattering partygoers. Her bright yellow dress stuck out conspicuously.

After a moment of looking, the uncomfortable feeling of unease creeped into her, making her heart race. *Where is he?* she thought, heat tickling up her neck. Any longer and she'd appear especially foolish, standing alone in the middle of the room.

Relief coursed through her as she finally saw the prince approaching her from the middle table, walking over with quick steps. She moved to meet him. *Brown eyes, not blue.* "Rowan?" she asked. "Where's Prince Brenden?" She was already looking around the room again, searching.

"He sends his apology, Raylyn. He won't be able to make it tonight." Rowan placed a hand softly on her arm. "Shall we sit? We have a seat of honor for you, of course."

Raylyn nodded, allowing him to guide her to their seats, ignoring the small twist of disappointment in her chest. The head table was small and had the most direct view of the stage. They passed the king, who raised his wineglass to her with a wink and nod. Raylyn smiled back politely, sitting when Rowan pulled out a chair for her. He sat next to her, the seat on her right empty.

"Why couldn't your brother make it?" she asked, as a server appeared out of nowhere, wordlessly filling her wine glass with a deep burgundy liquid.

"Underlying obligations, I'm afraid. Ah, here they come with the goat cheeses. A little extravagant," he said with an apologetic smile. "But definitely a fine treat after weeks of jerky and stale bread, wouldn't you agree?"

Raylyn smiled, allowing another kitchen server to place some soft cheeses on a small plate in front of her. "A welcome change, I will give you that." The din of voices continued its hum in the background. Raylyn scanned the room, counting. A hundred people, a hundred fifty? "For some reason, I thought it would be more intimate."

Rowan bit back a laugh. "For Father, this *is* intimate. And believe me, it took a lot of convincing for him to agree to such a small number. He had asked for the ballroom. Could you imagine?" Rowan popped a cracker spread with a generous amount of cheese into his mouth.

"No, I can't," Raylyn replied, eyes wide. She had seen the ballroom, and though it was beautiful—all polished wood and wide windows—she couldn't fathom sitting at the center of attention with such a vast crowd. She grabbed a small slice of the cheese, her knife cutting into it, soft as butter. It melted with a sweet tang on her tongue. "Oh, this *is* delicious," she murmured, wiping her lips unnecessarily with a maroon cloth napkin.

Rowan watched her with a smirk. "Look at you, so proper. As if I've never seen you rip into an overcooked rabbit like a mad wolf."

"Well, aren't you one to talk? Look at *you*." She gestured to his thick robes, dripping in embroidery. "As if I've never seen you in a dirty plain tunic stolen from my mother's clinic."

"Stole is harsh. I like to think of it as forever borrowed."

Raylyn snorted, rolling her eyes. Before she could reply, the announcer at the double doors spoke, "Lord Terach and Lady Thorne." The door burst open, and the two walked in, arm in arm. They appeared completely comfortable as people's eyes turned to them. Thorne was stunning in a low-cut black dress, the hem just brushing the floor. A necklace of dark red jewels hung around her neck, highlighting her cleavage even more. Lord Terach dressed to match, black fur robes over a deep-red maroon tunic. They paused in front of the king, Terach bowing and placed a fist over his hand, Thorne curtsying deeply.

Raylyn turned to Rowan, a question bubbling at her lips. "Why is everyone wearing the same colors? Talia didn't mention that everyone would dress in red and black." Raylyn glanced down at her dress, its brightness hurting her eyes.

"It's an unspoken custom some of the Court has adopted. They think it's an honor to us, the royal line. A show of camaraderie, you could say. Complete and utter nonsense." His eyes slid over Raylyn's body briefly, making her squirm. "You look exquisite, by the way." He reached up, touching a soft curl near her neck. She fought back a shiver.

She was too aware of their closeness. The chairs didn't allow each person much room and their legs were merely inches from each other. She swam in her head, searching for words, *any words, for Goddess's sake,* to say. But before she could find them, Rowan's eyes left her face, looking past her and breaking the spell. She took a deep breath, followed by a slow gulp of wine. The sweetness moistened her dried throat. *Not as good as Lakehaven's,* she thought, *but a fair alternative.*

"Terach, Thorne," Rowan greeted them, smiling, yet Raylyn could hear the smallest shift in his voice. She turned to see the pair approaching the empty seats to her right.

"Your Highness." Terach pulled a chair out for Thorne, who sat with the grace of a cat, before taking the empty seat beside her. "Raylyn. How are you feeling?" Out of the corner of her eye, she saw Thorne's face darken.

"Completely fine, thank you," she replied. "In fact, I recovered before I made it back to my chambers." Annoyance clipped her words. It still irked her she didn't get to see the casting side of the academy.

"Truly?" Terach asked, leaning back in his chair. A servant scuttled over, pouring their glasses, and he took a big sip, studying her.

"What are you talking about?" Rowan asked. At the same time Thorne said, "Recovered from what?"

"I assisted a dying man in finding some comfort, that is all."

"Ha! Jordain hasn't slept so soundly in the two weeks that he's been here!" Terach exclaimed. "Three minutes with Raylyn, and he's out like a baby. I was worried her exhaustion would prevent her attendance tonight." He tipped his head back, finishing his glass with ease. Without so much as a gesture, the servant rushed over, filling it again.

"You didn't mention this," Thorne said in a low voice, eyeing Terach suspiciously. "It is one thing to stitch skin together, another altogether to ease aches of the soul." Thorne cocked her head at Raylyn, as if waiting for an explanation.

Raylyn caught herself chewing on her bottom lip out of habit, forcing herself to stop. "It ... just comes naturally," she replied lamely. In truth, she didn't think the healing of emotions was that big of an accomplishment.

"His Majesty, Rennald Lendrous, King of Ellendria!" the announcer called out with grandeur. All around, people began clanking on their glasses with silverware, a soft chiming filling the room, voices softening.

Just two seats away, the king rose, standing quietly until the chiming slowly died away, silence filling the chamber. He smiled as he looked over the room. "Thank you all for coming on such short notice. We gather in celebration of life and prosperity this evening, and in special thanks to one of our members seated with us tonight. As only a handful of you are aware, my flesh and blood, my son, Prince Rowan," the king turned his head, nodding toward them, "was viciously attacked on our own land some weeks ago." He fell silent for a moment as a rush of murmurs ran through the crowd. He nodded. "Yes, we are shocked and outraged at this gross assault. After a thorough investigation, we have determined a group of assassin mages from Cystra crossed undetected through the borderlands and are responsible for this egregious deed."

The murmuring crescendoed into a low uproar. Raylyn glanced around the room; people were slamming their fists into tables, a few women had leaned back into their chairs in apparent swoons. Some shouts of "*Bastards*!" and "*On our own land*!" rang above the cacophony.

With a practiced manner, the king let his people shout their outrage for a minute before raising his hands up into the air, like a puppeteer on stage. "Enough." The command calmed the chamber into submission once more. "Thanks to the action of one mage here tonight, we are aware of this attack, and our enemy no longer has the advantage of surprise. We will increase border controls, sending out another three dozen divisions of soldiers throughout the kingdom. As well, I have sent word to King Aedam to question whether this assault was at his order or a group of rebels."

Beside her, Raylyn saw Terach—who had been working on his third glass in a carefree manner—tense, his body growing rigid and hand curling into a tight fist. He caught her gaze and smiled easily, draining the last few drops in his glass.

"The Goddess smiles on us this season. Not only did She allow my son to be saved, but She brought us another gift." He turned to Raylyn, dread at what was about to happen sinking into her stomach. "Raylyn, please stand." She rose to her feet, taking a deep breath and putting a mask of confidence on her face. The weight of over a hundred pairs of eyes fell upon her, and despite her best attempts, she couldn't stop her hands from trembling.

The king swept behind her, squeezing her shoulders in a fatherly gesture. "She is the one we have to thank for my son sitting here today!" A roar ripped through the crowd.

"The Goddess looks down on our great nation with favor," he continued after the cheering finally died down. The tone of his voice shifted, his words quieting by degrees, making the room lean slightly in. It was undeniable that the king had a special talent for working the room. Despite her anxiety at being singled out, his show enraptured Raylyn. "A healer with power beyond her years... a newly discovered ability to cast... as if the combination of gifts were not evidence enough of divine touch... the first syphon to walk these lands in over a hundred years."

The room held its breath, paralyzed. Rowan stood, raising his glass to her. "To Raylyn! Hurrah!" Terach copied the motion, followed by a reluctant Thorne. And as if coming out of a daze, the rest of the room rose and cheered, her name ringing through the air.

With one last squeeze, the king released her shoulders, taking the few steps to his seat. Raylyn sat as gracefully as she could muster, relief washing through her as eyes slowly trailed back to the king. "We celebrate tonight in honor of Raylyn, and in thanks to the Goddess for gracing us with Her touch. Let us eat and rejoice! And what is dinner without a good show?"

A troop of servants appeared from hidden doors, carrying trays filled with steaming plates, dishing out foods with a quick and efficient practice. Rowan leaned toward her, lips at her ear. "You did marvelous," he whispered, his breath hot on her neck. Her belly stirred, having nothing to do with the aroma of the meal. A small, annoying voice in the back of her mind reminded her he could feel everything she felt. She forced herself to focus on the meal in front of her, and not her body's unwanted ache of desire.

As the servants finished filling plates, two women came onto the stage at the front of the room. Both were scantily clad, thin strapped dresses ending in tassels at mid-thigh. One was icy-blue, the other a bright red. Jewels peeked out of intricately braided hair. The pair stood far apart on opposite sides of the stage. She was about to ask Rowan what they were doing, but he was leaning close to the king, the two talking in a hushed, low tone. She sucked her lip, glancing back to the stage. The women began slowly dancing, the tassels at the bottom of their dresses whipping out with their movements. She watched, enraptured, as the one in red raised her hands, casting a long trail of fire into the air. The flames flickered and swirled, copying her twirling dance.

In response, the woman in blue raised her hands into the air as well, a curling jet of water streaming to meet the flames. Steam filled the air with a soft hiss, causing the crowd to clap their applause.

Captivated by their performance, Raylyn glanced excitedly at Rowan, who was still engaged with the king. She settled on Terach, turning to find him already looking at her, a gleeful smile on his face. "It is always so fun, watching the show with someone who's never seen it before." They both looked back at the stage, another louder hiss of steam filling the air. Raylyn could already feel the moist heat filling the room. The women spun faster and faster, flame and water dueling each other like scorned lovers.

"It's amazing," Raylyn agreed, eyes wide. Remembering her full plate of food, she took a bite. *Talia was right*, she thought with satisfaction, *the duck is delicious.* They ate quietly for a while, the sweet rich flavors melting in her mouth. The women on stage continued their twirling duet, their speed continuing to increase as fire and water curled and clashed together. As the women spun, they slowly came to meet each other at the center of the stage, their bodies inches from touching. Their dance ended in a finale as fire and water twisted together, rising higher and higher into the air, meeting with an angry and final sizzle. The cloud of steam filled the room with a hazy mist, obscuring the stage entirely. As it cleared, the women vanished, and the room erupted into applause.

She leaned back in her chair, plate all but empty and her stomach warm and full. "A few perks of living at Court," Rowan said. He finally began to eat, his discussion with the king presumably over.

"Did you even see them?" Raylyn asked, watching him shovel food into his mouth. The temperature in the room was almost unbearably hot, and she wiped away a bead of sweat that tickled her temple.

"I've seen that performance several times. Lia and Mia are quite entertaining. If they were any less..." he searched for the word, "appealing, they'd make fantastic mages for the army. As it is, my father thinks their skills are more apt for entertainment. Did you know they're twins?" he added, as Raylyn sat wordlessly, letting him ramble.

That fact jolted her a little. "Twins with different aptitudes? Is that normal?"

Rowan shrugged. "Goddess knows what normal even means anymore," he said, raising an eyebrow at her.

Terach leaned over. "All personal skill level is individualistic," he said. "We expect that twins, or all siblings really, would have the same ability, whether casting or healing— not both, as you're quite the exception. But excelling in any aspect of a power, like water control, as you saw from Mia, is completely random. Take the princes, for example," he said, gesturing at Rowan, whose face turned into a hard mask. "Twins, too, but Brenden doesn't possess the effecting capabilities that Rowan has."

Rowan shrugged, as if bored by the fact, and finished the last of his meal in a few quick bites. He pushed the plate away from him, tossing his napkin down and standing. "Raylyn, we should introduce you to some of the Court. I can see a few people are getting antsy." Raylyn followed his line of sight, catching a group of people staring at them, quickly averting their gaze.

Terach cleared his throat and stood as well. "Prince Rowan, if you're too busy, I can help with introductions." Thorne scoffed, crossing her arms over her chest.

Rowan stared at him for a moment. "Thank you anyway," he finally replied. "But I have time. Ready, he asked, holding his hand out for Raylyn. She grabbed it, rising out of her chair. Terach gave her a thin smile as they walked away.

Names disappeared from her memory soon after they were announced in the flurry of introductions. She never had people fawn over her, and the experience left her feeling uncomfortable. Every person they approached was lovely and polite; curtsies and bows and praises cascaded over her and Rowan.

She stifled a yawn, trying to hide it behind the back of her hand with little success. She wondered how many hours had passed. "It was very nice to meet you," she said for the twentieth time. She and Rowan untangled themselves from a few ladies, the names of whom she'd already forgotten.

"You're tired," Rowan said as they meandered the floor in front of the stage.

"Is it obvious?" She was finally coming down after the buildup of anxiety and excitement of the night. Her body and mind were both spent.

"Wait here. I just want to ask Terach a question, then I'll walk you back to your room, if you'd like."

"That'd be lovely."

Rowan made his way back to the head table, and she weaved through the crowd, searching for a glass of water. Her mouth was dry from talking, and her head was aching from the long night. She stepped around entangled couples whose voices were low and husky with too much wine, passing by rowdy groups who guffawed over unheard jokes. A servant was bobbing through the crowd with a tray full of ice waters. She grabbed one, parched. "Thank you," she said to the server, who bowed his head and disappeared. After a few long, cool sips, she ran her hand along the condensation that formed on the outside of the glass until her fingertips were cold and wet. She placed her hand on the back of her neck to cool herself. It worked a little. Placing her empty glass on a nearby table, she wondered how much longer Rowan would be. She so longed for her bed.

"Oh!" she cried, colliding headfirst with another partygoer. A chill seeped through her dress, and she glanced down at her chest. A burgundy stain seeped through the yellow fabric, making it cling to her skin.

"Oh, pardon me," the woman said. She looked vaguely familiar, with her honey-blond hair and a light red dress falling in ruffles from her waist. Raylyn was sure she met her earlier in the evening but couldn't think of her name. "I'm so clumsy! Let me help you." She leaned in with a handkerchief and dabbed at Raylyn's soiled chest, empty wine glass held loosely in her other hand. Faces just inches apart, she whispered, "Get out of here, *demon*," in a sharp hiss, before waltzing away, joining a group of women who burst into loud laughter.

Raylyn froze to the spot, heat rushing to her face. Tears burned at her eyes, but she was desperate to keep them from falling. She pulled herself together enough to hurry toward the exit, eyes glued to the floor. Just as she was slipping out the double doors, Rowan called to her from behind. "Hey, wait a moment!" He jogged up, catching her expression. "What's wrong?"

The doors closed behind them, and Raylyn paced down the hallway, Rowan pestering her the whole way. She stopped after a few feet, words spilling out as she told him about the woman and her friends, hot tears finally breaking free.

His brow furrowed. "I wish I had seen it happen. I can't place who you're describing, but I will try to find out, and there *will* be repercussions." He pulled her into a tight embrace, and despite herself, Raylyn rested her head on his shoulder. They stood like that for several moments, until the doors opened again, releasing more people from the party within.

"Come on, let's get you to bed." Rowan wiped away the tears at her cheeks with his palms. This close, she could count each freckle on his nose. If she leaned forward just a few inches, their lips would touch. A stirring desire awoke, replacing some of her embarrassment.

She knew he was reading her emotions, and his effecting powers overflowed, tickling up her thigh and twisting in her belly, multiplying her own longing. Heat burned in his eyes as he looked down at her. "Goddess, you are beautiful," he murmured, closing the gap between them. He kissed her, the taste of salty tears and wine and repressed desire mixing on their tongues. She let the stress of the evening fall away, knowing nothing but the feel of his lips on hers. Her belly ached as he pulled her closer, fingers burning a trail of heat as they danced down the delicate skin of her neck. A second or an hour later, they finally parted, and her head swam, the combination of their embrace and the wine intoxicating.

When they arrived outside her door, Rowan hesitated, and she wondered if he would kiss her again. But instead, he cleared his throat. "I'm so sorry for the way the night ended, with what that woman said to you. I should have been there."

"You won't be with me always, and if that's how your people really feel, then we should know," Raylyn muttered, one hand on her doorknob. She was exhausted, and all she wanted was to close her eyes and dream of empty blackness until morning. "What did you need to ask Terach, anyway?" she asked, curiosity getting the best of her.

Rowan shifted, eyes sliding down to his feet. "It's not ideal, with what just happened, but I was curious to know when your testing would be scheduled, as I would like to be on the committee that deliberates your class determination." He paused, looking everywhere but her face.

"And? When is it?" She knew the answer before he spoke.

"Tomorrow."

CHAPTER 10

"**Y**OU SHOULD EAT SOMETHING," TALIA said, brushing the crumbs from a blueberry muffin off her dress. "Here, try one."

Raylyn's stomach rolled. "No, I'm fine, thank you." The night passed in a glorious, dreamless sleep. Morning inevitably came, along with bittersweet memories of the feast: her ruined dress, the feel of Rowan's lips, the news of her testing.

Even her tea tasted like ashes. She pushed the cup away, gazing around the room. They took breakfast in one of the little nooks overlooking the gardens. An unassuming spot, it had just a table, two wooden chairs, and a small bookshelf nestled in the corner. Large windows surrounded them, sunlight warming the small alcove. Occasionally, a bunny or squirrel would skitter by, lingering a moment on the path, before disappearing into the thick bushes. Raylyn watched, hoping for a distraction. She had a couple hours until the testing, and time was dragging.

While Talia ate, she pulled a quill and parchment from her pocket. A letter to Braya was long overdue, but she couldn't think of what to say. Staring at the paper, words eluded her. "What's a nice way to say, 'Sorry for abandoning you and betraying our friendship?'" she asked, fighting the urge to snap the quill in two.

Talia considered for a moment, chugging her cup of tea in three long gulps. "Forgoing any backstory, I've always found it best to be direct in apologies. Don't sweeten words for a situation you both know is sour."

She chewed her lip. "Something is always better than nothing, right?"

"In most situations, sure."

Sighing, Raylyn wrote, trying to turn off her internal filter.

Braya,

Oh, my friend, how I miss you. I've fought for words for weeks, and yet they all are empty and inadequate. To say 'I hope you are well' is a gross understatement. Though we are not blood, you are my sister, and your pain is mine.

For such an enormous castle, it is lonely. You should see the stables here—they're bigger than the council building back home—though, likely not up to your standards. I wake every morning with regret I didn't fight harder for you to join me. The king agreed to my pardon, and without the fear of being Marked hanging over me, I see how irrational my actions

*were when I left. Please forgive me. Give me time to
find you a position at Court; I need you here.*

With love and remorse,
Raylyn

She stared at the letter as the ink dried, disgusted at
its inadequacy. Her fingers twitched, longing to crumple
it into a ball and set it aflame.

"If she is your friend, she will forgive you."

She nodded. "I'm going to send this off at the Ravenry."
Talia stood to follow her. "I remember the way if you have
other things to do."

She was quiet for a few seconds. "Are you sure? I *was*
hoping to catch a few hours in the library today, but if you
need help finding your way, it's not a problem."

"No, go study. I'll be fine."

Talia smiled. "Thank you. Good luck later!" She
bounded off without hesitation.

Raylyn sat for another minute, considering her letter.
She fought the urge to write to her parents, too, especially
her mother. After touring the Academy and the Infirmary,
she knew her mother would've loved to have this opportunity, this vast expanse of resources at her fingertips. She
thought of the package laying on the floor in her room.
Maybe I'll open it tonight, after the testing.

The walk to the Ravenry was cool and pleasant. The air
finally held the crisp bite of autumn, and the soft breeze
carried the earthy scent of decaying leaves. Soft white
clouds floated in the sky, casting shade whenever they
passed over the sun. She was daydreaming about Braya
receiving her letter, forgiving her, coming to meet her at

the castle. They would share adjoining rooms and learn the ways of the Court together, secretly laughing at all the pretentious ladies and their flouncing dresses. Distracted, she suddenly collided headfirst into someone just outside the stables. They both went sprawling onto the dirt path.

"Oh, Goddess! I'm so sorry, I didn't see you there!" Her stomach twisted, worried she was in for a repeat of last night. *At least I'm not wearing a borrowed ball gown*, she thought. She scrambled to her feet, brushing dirt from her trousers.

"Ah, yes, with my small stature, I am easy to miss," Prince Brenden said, standing. He adjusted a leather pack higher on his shoulder. A day's worth of stubble grew on his face and road dust coated his clothes.

She snorted, looking up. *Small stature, my ass*, she thought. He was easily six foot, and she had to crane her head up to meet his eye. "Head in the clouds," she finally said, forcing a small smile in embarrassment.

"Likewise." He glanced at the letter in her hand. "Headed to the Ravenry, then? Mind if I join you?" He opened his pack, pulling out a crumpled, dirty letter and waved it in the air. "I've got one that I've been meaning to send as well."

"That's seen better days," she said as they fell into step with each other.

"It's a bit old, sat in the bottom of my pack for a few weeks. Okay, months," he added when Raylyn gave him a sideways look. "I can be a bit forgetful."

"The same way you forgot about the feast last night?" she asked, her voice casually sweet.

He grunted, face darkening. "I didn't forget. That was a nasty little trick of my brother. But please forgive me." He met Raylyn's eyes. "Perhaps I can make it up to you."

"Perhaps..." The uncanny resemblance to Rowan shook her, yet his blue eyes were soft and searching. For some inexplicable reason, she felt at ease with him. "What do you mean, 'trick'?"

He ran a hand through his hair, further disheveling it. "He had Garrick send word of dissenters in a small encampment of our soldiers, about half a day's ride West. As I'm training to take over command, Father thought it would be appropriate I ride out there and remind them of their loyalty." He shook his head and kicked a small stone on the path, sending it sailing through the air. "All lies. They looked at me as if I had grown another head when I arrived. Decent, well-disciplined men, though," he added in a lighter tone.

Raylyn stopped dead, deceit washing over her. "How do you know it was Rowan's doing? Perhaps Garrick was playing some joke on his own accord?"

"Unlikely. Our cousin isn't the type."

Her stomach twisted unpleasantly with the memory of Rowan's kiss. "That was cruel of him," she said as they continued walking. The Ravenry wasn't much more than a large roost, hundreds of birds flittering inside carelessly. A few workers were cleaning soiled woodchips off the floor, paying them no mind as they walked into the expansive room.

"Have you ever sent a letter by bird before?" Brenden asked, cupping his hand out. An attractive pigeon stepped into it, the feathers at its head tinged an iridescent green.

"No," she admitted. "I didn't know anyone outside my village. There was never a need."

He held out his free hand, motioning for Raylyn's letter. "Who's the recipient, a suitor back home?" he teased lightly.

"Oh, please." She rolled her eyes. "My best friend. Well, she used to be. I kind of abandoned her when I came here."

"It was wise of her parents to not allow her to come with you," he said, attaching the letter to the bird with deft fingers. "Court is a dangerous place."

"Her mom's dead and her dad's a drunk." Her chest tightened. "I left her with no one. If she came with me, at least we'd have each other."

"Then, why didn't she?" he asked, eyebrows furrowed. "It doesn't seem like she has much to lose."

"She's not a mage. Which is absolute nonsense, to be frank, as people without powers are still capable of exceptional things! There *must* be a place for her here somewhere." She looked up at him, eyes pleading.

He raised an eyebrow. "Of course there's a position for her. Perhaps not as glamorous as mages' options, but that's anywhere you go. Why would you think that even mattered?"

Raylyn stood, dumbstruck. "What?"

"The amount of labor needed to tend the castle, its grounds, and surrounding estates is extraordinary. We're always looking for loyal help."

"It's not just mages who work here?" she asked, her voice small.

"Where do you think we'd find enough mages to keep all of this running?"

Her breaths were quick and shallow as anger coursed through her body, burning through her veins. "It seems," she said through gritted teeth, "your brother is playing tricks on us both." She took a deep breath. "Could I have that letter back? I need to make a few corrections."

The arena brought flashbacks of the joust she attended years ago, but triple the size. Risers of seats encircled a sand-filled field. Prince Brenden offered to escort her, but Raylyn wanted to writhe in her rage alone. *Why did he lie?* Disgust twisted her features as she walked through the gate leading to the top tier of seating.

She counted each step as she descended the staircase to the field, taking slow breaths, trying to tame the fire of rage which boiled inside. She wasn't surprised when she reached the bottom level to discover the half-dozen people waiting for her.

The group was split in two. Brenden, Terach, and Thorne seated to her left, chattering amongst themselves. Brenden looked up as she approached, offering a kind smile. To the right stood the king, Rowan, and an unfamiliar man. Heavy bags weighed beneath his deep-set eyes, and not a single hair remained on his scalp. "Our guest of honor has arrived!" he announced, rushing over to greet her. "The Goddess blesses us." He grabbed Raylyn's hands in his own, callouses rough against her skin. "A larger crowd than normal, but I know you'll do splendidly, dear." He squeezed her hands before releasing her.

She forced a tight-lipped smile, resisting the urge to take a step backward.

"Raylyn, this is Ordon, head of the caster's wing," Rowan said, stepping toward her lightly. She had never punched anyone before, but it took every ounce of self-restraint to resist throwing her fist into his deceitful face.

"A pleasure, a pleasure," the man murmured, his cheeks flushed a light pink. "Normally, the testing just consists of me and Thorne, but we are so honored with the *crown* attending today, as well. Momentous day, indeed." He all but danced with excitement.

Raylyn did her best to ignore Ordon's fawning. "Shall we begin?"

"Confident, are we?" Thorne asking as she slunk into a chair, crossing her legs.

"Just eager to be finished."

Thorne stared at her with disinterest, and her voice was flat when she spoke. "We have three stages set up, one for each of your ... abilities." Her mouth twisted on the word. "You'll begin with the closest. Examine the materials, then raise your hand to signal to us you are ready. Pay attention, as we will be instructing you as you perform. You may go." Raylyn nodded and made her way toward the sandy pit.

"Good luck," Rowan whispered. She wordlessly stepped past him, jaw aching from clenching her teeth together, fighting back the urge to scream. The nearest station was at least a hundred feet from the stands, and a tinge of worry broke through her anger as she wondered how she'd hear the instructions from so far away.

The first station contained two laden tables. On the leftmost sat three cages. She walked the length of the table, nausea bubbling at her throat when she realized the rabbits contained inside were all injured at varying degrees, the last cage a bloodied mess. Taking a steadying breath through her nose, she inspected the other table. Dozens of labeled jars of herbs, metal bowls, and pitchers of water and milk stood in neat rows. *Gauze, bandages, towels.* It was a miniature clinic. A smile played at her lips as she turned back to the onlookers and raised her right hand into the air.

Thorne's voice rang amplified through the air, clear and crisp, dissolving Raylyn's earlier fears. *What type of spell is that?* she wondered briefly. She didn't have time to ponder, as Thorne spoke again. "Heal the rabbits. Do not overexert yourself."

She knew this was coming. Unfastening the metal door to the first cage, she picked up the docile animal, its soft fur warm in her hands. There was no blood, no visible sign of injury. She gently palpated its body, searching for a mass or laceration, anything. When her hand ran over its left hind leg, the animal screamed and shook, desperate to be released. *Broken.* She had more practice with people than animals, but a bone was a bone. "Hush," she murmured as it continued to protest.

She breathed deep, centering herself, feeling the energy of her own beating heart. Focusing on the injured leg, Raylyn allowed energy to flow through her palms. She envisioned the bone joining back together, straight and strong. A moment later she was done. She placed the rabbit back into the cage, leg mended, and moved to the next.

She recoiled. The next rabbit's eyes were swollen closed, crusted with thick green pus. She cradled the pathetic thing, searching on the other table for the gauze she saw earlier. She gently wiped away as much of the drainage as she could, trying to get a closer look to what lay beneath. Her pulse quickened; eyes were more complicated than bone, their structure more intricate. If circumstances were normal, she'd recommend simply ending the creature's suffering. She covered its face with a clean piece of gauze, placing her hand gently on top. She only cared about ridding its infection; if it still possessed the ability to see afterward, that would just be a nice bonus. She channeled again, her breathing quickening as she felt a small drain on her energy, as if she had just sprinted up the arena stairs.

Removing her hand, her chest lightened with excitement. The swelling around the rabbit's eyes was gone, and the lenses and pupils were clear. Dried pus still clung to its fur, but that would wash off easily with some warm water later.

Dread filled her as she walked to the last cage. Dried blood mixed with thick pools of fresh. She pulled the limp body out, cradling its head. A deep laceration on its neck was still slowly oozing, and the faintest of heartbeats remained. She chewed her lip for a moment, wondering if it would be worth it. She thought of Jordain in the Infirmary and wondered if the Goddess had called him home yet. *Some things are too far gone to mend.* Channeling, she relieved its pain, holding it gently as it found the comfort needed to finally pass on. Grabbing a clean towel from the supply table, she wrapped it loosely around the animal's body before placing it back into the soiled cage, her heart aching at its loss.

She steadied herself for a moment, then turned to face the group again, waiting for her next instruction. She had expected Thorne's voice but was greeted by Ordon, instead. "Well done," he said, as if only standing a few feet away as opposed to hundreds. "You may proceed to the next station."

She fought a surge of disappointment as she passed the table full of unused herbs. She had been excited at the prospect of concocting a salve or potion, recipes from *Useful Herbs and Fungi* dancing through her mind. She walked for a minute before reaching the next station.

Rocks were lined in a straight row, growing from as small as a coin to one boulder that was larger than she was tall. Two straw dummies stood a few dozen yards away, red bullseyes painted on their torsos. She frowned, confidence dwindling. *No sense in biding time*, she thought and raised her right arm.

"Cast the stones toward the targets, starting with the smallest. Signal when you are unable to continue." Her mouth twitched into a frown. She had only been successful casting small flames and hadn't considered practicing with other types of manipulation. Her stomach flipped at the thought of casting again; images of burning fields and uncontrolled rage flashed behind her eyes, remembering the night she lost control.

Breathing deeply, she reminded herself of the small piece of wood she lit aflame for Talia the day before. *I can control it*, she thought, trying to convince herself. Bending to pick up the smallest pebble, Ordon's voice rang, "Contactless, please."

Raylyn straightened, the rock sitting solidly in the sand. It was becoming difficult to ignore the growing panic in her chest. She didn't know how to levitate even the smallest pebble, let alone launch it through the air to strike a target. She swallowed, her tongue like sandpaper in her dried mouth. Concentrating, she fought against her fears, focusing only on this one little rock. *It's lighter than a coin.* She stared, her eyes watering as the sun reflected blindingly off the sand, vision blurring. *Come on*, she urged. *Come on, come on.* The rock sat defiantly still.

Her eyes seared with pain from the intense sunlight, forcing her to finally blink. The stone remained imprinted on the back of her eyelids, a curious green shadow. She grabbed a fistful of her hair in frustration. If she could just focus, just will her heart to slow down ... it would take no energy at all to bend down, grab the tiny thing, and whip it towards the straw man. *If only it was as simple as healing*, she thought, rubbing her eyes, the green shadow rock appearing every time she blinked.

An idea flitted through her mind. Maybe it *could* be simple. She closed her eyes, picturing the rock flying through the air, imagining the energy flowing from her veins to her palms, through the few feet of empty space, to the rock. In a meditative state, she allowed her body to channel in an automatic, instinctual way. She felt the release of energy as it flowed through her hands. Her eyes shot open in excitement, searching the sky for the pebble. She couldn't see it, the sun forcing her to avert her gaze.

Frustration coursed through her when she saw the stone sitting completely motionless, mocking her from the sandy ground. "Damn it!" She fought the urge to kick the line of immobile stones, tasting salty metal as she sucked on her bleeding lip. She couldn't contain her self-loathing as she turned and raised her right hand, signaling her defeat.

A few seconds of silence passed before Ordon's next instructions came. "Cast a fireball toward the leftmost dummy." She stared in the direction where the onlookers sat, eyebrows furrowing. *What's the point?* She slowly turned, walking a little closer to the straw man. She raised her hands out in front of her with no expectation of anything happening. Trying to focus, she closed her eyes, willing the fire in her veins to manifest into the air before her.

An itching beneath her skin caused her to lose her concentration, scratching at her arms. An all-encompassing desire to burn, to destroy, overwhelmed her thoughts; all worries and frustration melted away in her singlemindedness. *Not right,* a tickle said in the back of her brain, but it was smothered by rage and desire, and all she saw was red. Gone was the desperate need to prove herself. And in an instant, a ball of curling flames rotated in her hands, the blistering heat welcome. It knew its master and did her no harm, and in a glorious release, she threw the ball at the target, a joyous ecstasy taking over as the crackling flames engulfed the straw man in a blazing inferno.

The consuming need to burn turned to ash with the target, her own thoughts trickling back into her mind. She whipped around, face twisted with disgust. "Stay out of my head, Rowan!" Her blood boiled hotter than before. "How dare you?" she screamed, pressure bursting behind her eyes. "My mind is not yours to warp!" Her words were close to unintelligible, her throat splitting. His betrayals flashed, one after another. Flames crackled around her, eager for fuel and impatient with the sand that refused to burn. She stared across the field into the stands, searching for his face. The fire crept forward with longing, insistent to help with her search.

The piercing ringing in her ears muted all else until a voice finally broke through. "Think of Braya!" it called. *Braya? Yes, he forced me to abandon Braya as well.* The flames shuddered. Growing. Hungry. "She'll be here soon, but not if you burn everything down," the voice reasoned. She peeled her eyes away from the stands, glancing as Brenden crept forward. He was just outside the reach of her flames, close enough she could see the reflection of them dancing in his light eyes. She recoiled in surprise, the flames mirroring her movements, shrinking inward on themselves. He didn't wrong her; it was his brother she wanted.

"Raylyn," he edged closer.

"Get back! I'll hurt you!" Her hands shook. She wanted to explode, to push out, to destroy.

"You won't," he said, stepping into the flames.

"No!" she cried. She couldn't extinguish the fire completely. It had a mind of its own, her panic inciting it further. Flaring upward, the flames danced at their meal.

Brenden smiled, closing the distance between them, completely unharmed as the fire licked the surrounding air. "Shield," he said with a wink.

Her shock broke through the uncontrollable rage as she gaped at him, the flames flickering a sad goodbye as they sizzled out. Her knees buckled, and she collapsed onto the sand. Brenden knelt beside her. "Are you okay? Do you need Thorne?" He rose, motioning to signal to the healer, but Raylyn pulled at his sleeve.

"I'm fine," she lied. There was a sharp pain in her chest, her pulse hammering. Despite herself, tears fell, silently absorbed by the thirsty sand. "I lost control again."

"Hey, it's okay," he said, his voice soft in her ear as he patted her back.

"What's going to happen to me?" She choked back a sob, hiding her face in her hands.

"If you're too spent to finish the last task today, we can always reschedule. It happens from time to time. During my testing, I passed out. Dad was not happy."

She hiccupped. "Wh—what? I almost burned down the entire arena, almost killed everyone. And I would've danced in the fire as I did it!" she admitted, peeking up at him with wide eyes.

He roared with laughter, jolting her. "There's so little that's been explained to you. I'm sorry for laughing, but ... you're just so precious. There are spells to keep everyone not on this sand," he grabbed a handful, letting the grains trickle through his fingers back to the ground, "from being hurt, both intentionally and accidentally." He stood, holding out his hand to help her up. She grabbed it, standing on shaking legs. "Come on, I'll walk you back. You can finish tomorrow." He wrapped an arm around her waist, supporting her weight, and guided her toward the stands.

"Wait, no." Raylyn slipped out of his grip. "No, I'm finishing this now." He stared at her for a moment, then nodded.

"Do you want me to leave or stay?"

It was her turn to deliberate. "Stay. Just in case," and she raised her arm into the air.

"Proceed to the next station and place yourself at the central stone," Terach said, voice echoing over the arena. Refusing Brenden's hand, the two walked farther down the field. Cages were set up, forming a large circle in the sand, at least twenty feet wide. She stepped past a cage, noting the white rabbit inside, chewing on the tough end of a head of lettuce. Another circle of huge, verdant potted ferns was centered inside the circle of cages. And inside the ring of plants was the stone.

She stepped on to it, the muscles in her arms screaming with fatigue as she signaled her readiness to Terach. "Syphon all the energy from the plants, allowing their death. Then syphon again from the rabbits, but preserve their life."

Her exhaustion made the first task easy. She opened a channel between her and the plants, her hands glowing, but instead of healing and offering her energy, she took theirs. The trickle of restoration was euphoric as strength reinvigorated her muscles, the shaking in her legs slowing. Too quickly, it stopped. The ferns were brown and curled. Lifeless. Dead.

She reached with her powers a little further until she felt the life force of the rabbits. She closed her eyes, focusing on the connection. Each tiny heart was pounding as fast as a hummingbird's wings. She *pulled* with gentle ease, unseen cords of energy flowing toward her from the animals, connecting her like spokes meeting in the center of a wheel. Eyes still shut, she drank it in, the rich energy pulsing through her veins. Her fatigue eased, soon disappearing completely as her body hummed with exhilaration.

"Raylyn." Brenden's voice was far away again. She easily ignored it as she continued syphoning, excitement bubbling out of her. Bouncing lightly on her feet, she smiled. She was carefree, she was a bird, she was—

"Raylyn! You're killing them. *Stop.*"

She opened her eyes, casting a sideways glance at Brenden. *If he could just feel what I feel, he would understand.* She was so light, so full of life.

The connections severed with a painful abruptness. She furrowed her brow, confused. Her eyes landed back on Brenden, his left palm glowing as he held it up, pointed toward her. "I told you, they were *dying*." A glare of sun reflected off the iridescent shield he cast around her. At first, annoyance overwhelmed her, but after a few seconds, she came back to herself, immensely grateful for Brenden and his shield.

As if he could see the change in her, he lowered his hand, the shield evaporating. "Did I ...?" Raylyn asked, the half-formed question hanging in the air.

"I think I stopped you in time." They both walked around the circle, inspecting the cages and finding all the rabbits still living.

Relief washed through her. "Thank you." She turned, raising her hand to Terach.

"You may return."

Physically, Raylyn had recovered from her loss of control during casting. She didn't need Brenden's support as they walked back to the group, but she took comfort in his presence, regardless.

She heard Thorne's and Terach's raised voices before she stepped off the sand.

"She's not going in that class."

"Her skills more than qualify her, Thorne. Why are you being so headstrong about this?"

"Do you not have eyes? The girl obviously has no control over her powers."

"She did perfectly well in the healing challenge. You're putting her in the class. There's nothing more to discuss.

Raylyn stepped into the group, Thorne's face twisting when she saw her. Without any acknowledgement, she left, storming up the stairs. Terach watched her leave, his mouth a tight line. After a moment, his eyes slid to Raylyn's face, and he visibly brightened. "Well done. Truly, what a show."

She gave a half smile, but Thorne's reaction was all she could focus on.

"Where'd Rowan and Dad go?" Brenden asked. Raylyn noticed their absence as well; only Ordon and Terach remained.

"The king wanted a moment alone with Prince Rowan to discuss his ... interference with the testing," Terach said lightly.

"Completely inappropriate!" Ordon tutted. He walked over and grasped Raylyn's hand. "Don't be too disappointed, dear. You've just come into your casting powers?" Raylyn nodded. "We will work on it, and in no time, you'll be advancing. Don't be discouraged." He turned, addressing Terach. "She'll be in Level One. Her power is strong, but Thorne has a point. Her casting is completely uncontrolled." He turned back to Raylyn, giving her hand a gentle squeeze. "Your instructor's name is Merrill. Will you be ready to attend class tomorrow?"

"Yes, of course! Thank you," she said, hiding her disappointment. *The lowest level.* She had hoped that the display of sheer power would be enough to convince Ordon to place her higher, but no such luck.

"And Thorne will be your instructor, Level Thirty. She teaches at daybreak and doesn't accept tardiness," Terach said. "I'll send a detailed list of classes and material information to your room." He looked her over, as if considering. "In addition to casting and healing, I'd like you to sit with me for syphoning lessons, as well."

Her heart leaped to her throat, excitement and fear weaving together. *I'm actually going to be studying at the Academy,* she thought, the reality of her situation finally hitting home.

She skipped to her rooms, the aftereffects of syphoning causing her head to spin slightly. The prospect of classes brightened her mood considerably, as she had always been a dedicated student. *Lowest level,* rang through her mind again, but she fought the negativity. *I'm learning to cast. I'm studying at the most prestigious school in the entire country.*

She took the last turn leading to her room, excited to prepare for the following day, but stopped dead when she saw Rowan, sitting in the hall, back leaned on her door. He heard her approaching, his head whipping up, a pitiful expression on his face. She considered him for half a second, before spinning on her heels, backtracking.

"Raylyn, please!" He sprang up and ran after her. "Please, just listen. Remember last time when you refused to—"

"Stop," she said as he tried to grab her arm. She shook him off with disgust. "Just stop. There's no amount of groveling or explaining that you can do to right your transgressions. Leave me alone."

"I knew you just needed a little push out there. I wasn't trying to play with your head. I just wanted to help." His eyes were filled with hopeless desperation as he tried to make her understand.

"The same way you tried to help when you forced me from my village?"

"What? I didn't force you to do anything. I offered you an escape when your precious village exiled you."

She acted like she didn't hear him. "And the same way you tried to help when you wrongly refused refuge for my best friend?"

He pulled back a little at this. "I don't understand what you mean."

"Brenden told me the truth. There was no reason Braya couldn't have joined us. He said there's plenty of non-mages who work here. You made me abandon her!"

"It's not a simple as that! I already uprooted one girl's life; it wouldn't have been right for me to upturn another's."

"You said there was no place for her here. Is that true?"

"You don't understand—"

"She understands perfectly well, Rowan," Brenden said, turning the corner and meeting them in the center of the passageway. "You took everything from her, and the least you could have offered was the comfort of a friend."

Rowan whipped around, and she was sure the two brothers were going to come to blows. "You weren't there. You didn't see how those villagers were acting. It was almost a riot as it was. If I had taken the other girl without permission? They'd have my head. Raylyn please," he said, pulling at her hand. "Please, you have to believe me."

Her anger soared, and she channeled, flame filling the palm of the hand he was holding. He yelped, jumping backward. Brenden's laughter echoed through the hall.

Pain filled Rowan's eyes. "If you think he's any better," he jerked his head toward Brenden, "you're sorely mistaken."

"At least he hasn't *lied* to me," she said, eyes downcast. Despite her anger, she couldn't extinguish her feelings for the man, which made his betrayals even more painful.

"Give it time." Cradling his burned hand, he paused next to Brenden, his voice full of malice. "You're playing a dangerous game, brother. I know what you're feeling. Don't touch her."

"Looks like you're the only one who doesn't know how to handle fire, Rowan," Brenden said, smirking.

Rowan's eyes narrowed, and he cast one more venomous look at Brenden, before sulking away down the hall.

"I love shopping!" Talia sang, jingling a coin purse in Raylyn's face. She swatted it away, raising a brow at the overeager girl. "What can I say? When you've grown up poor, you get excited about these kinds of things."

They walked side by side down the road to the city. Talia offered to secure them a couple of horses, but movement felt good. She was still jumpy from syphoning earlier, and the fight with Rowan only exacerbated matters. It was just barely midday, though it felt an entire week's worth of events were stuffed into the morning hours.

"So, you aren't upset I pulled you away from your studies?" Raylyn asked, squinting in the sunlight as they passed a prickly wildflower. *Purple thistle*, Raylyn thought, *good for painful joints*. She resisted the urge to snap part of the plant off, knowing her fingers would be sliced. Besides, there was no need. The Academy and InfirmaryInfirmary were already overflowing with every herb, weed, and fungi she could imagine.

"Let us get one thing clear: if there is ever a choice between studying and shopping, I will always choose shopping. Always." Talia jingled the change purse again, smiling.

Raylyn eyed it with a frown. "I did bring some money with me from home. I feel a little ... wrong, being catered to like this."

"Nonsense. You saved the king's favorite son's life. That's priceless. The least they can do is provide for you."

"I suppose."

Talia chattered a while as they walked, explaining how she was researching ways to split her channeling into three separate sections for the Academy competition. "If I could just figure this out, I could attack three people at once, potentially using separate elements for each! Send a fireball to the left, an ice storm to the right, and a sandblast directly in front. What a show that'd make!"

Raylyn gave her an appraising look. "It would definitely be impressive." She thought about her own inability to control even the smallest flame, incompetence weighing on her shoulders.

Talia must have realized because she reached up, patting her on the arm. "Don't be too hard on yourself. You'll advance out of level one in no time, really. And it's better to get the basics down solidly, anyway. Why don't you just compete as a healer? We could partner up."

"I have a feeling Thorne won't grant me in." Talia had been talking about the competition nonstop ever since Raylyn fetched her from the library. She had learned that every caster paired with a healer to compete as a team. Each student who participated must have the support of their instructor. And with Thorne's apparent dislike for her, she didn't think she'd have much of a chance to win her approval.

"You'll have to win her over somehow. Level thirty..." She let out a low whistle. "Did you know I'm only in

Level 26 for casting? Your mom really did teach you something, huh?"

Her stomach twisted. "She really did," she said, her voice cracking as she tried to ignore the pang of being homesick. *Mother wouldn't have walked past purple thistle and* not *picked some.* She scolded herself; she had been gone for just over a month, and yet was already taking so many things for granted.

Talia glanced at her, confusion plain on her face at Raylyn's mournful tone. She gave up the conversation, and they walked the rest of the way quietly. The road was well traveled, and Court members and students alike passed every so often, nodding their heads or exchanging a quick hello. The road widened as it met the entrance to the city, noise and foot traffic increasing a tenfold.

"I don't remember it being so crowded here!" Raylyn said as they weaved between people, Talia holding her hand and dragging her through the packed crowd.

Talia looked back at her briefly, before turning again. "It's not normally this busy," she said. "Something's going on." They burrowed deeper into the mass of bodies, Raylyn clinging to Talia's hand as if she was deep in a lake without knowing how to swim. Finally, they broke through the center of the crowd, a stage looming before them.

Four people were on the stage: two men stood on each side of the raised platform, and sandwiched between them were two people chained and kneeling. Their faces hung low, hidden in shadows.

"...must pay retribution!" the man to the far right yelled, projecting his voice so it carried far through the watching crowd. He paced, animated, as if acting in a play. "Today, these men face the ultimate punishment! And though it is a great blow, we choose to strike down two mages for the sake of justice! And you are our witnesses! In the Goddess's name!"

The crowd roared with excitement, jeers and slurs yelled out at random. A cackling, stout woman hoisted something suspiciously like a chamber pot—both in looks and smell—its contents sloshing onto the prisoners. The men were already so beaten down, they didn't even flinch as the urine soaked through their clothes.

"Let's go," Talia whispered, trying to edge out of the crowd, pulling Raylyn behind her. "I don't want to watch this, it's barbaric." But she refused to budge, mesmerized with horror and curiosity. "Come *on*," Talia urged, annoyed. She huffed when Raylyn refused to follow, giving her a scolding look as she crossed her arms in defeat.

The animated man pulled a small pouch out of his jacket pocket, then crouched close to one of the chained men. With a rough hand, he tilted the criminals head up, forcing a black powdery substance into his mouth. Raylyn waited, thinking he would spit it out in the captor's face, but instead, he swallowed with a final resoluteness that signaled his defeat. He wouldn't go down begging.

The other captive was his opposite. He put on a show for the crowd as he kicked and screamed and bit when the jailor approached with the black powder. The mob swelled again, a new onslaught of filth spewing from their mouths. A swift kick between his legs sent the prisoner sprawling breathlessly to the ground, his attempt at resisting trounced. The jailor bent, shoving a fistful of the powder roughly into the semiconscious man's mouth. He signaled for the other jailor to join him. Raylyn watched as the fourth man slowly walked over, realizing with horror who these men were. *Not just captors or guards. Marksmen.* He crouched in front of the prisoners and whispered something too quiet for her to hear. He placed a hand on top of each man's head, the glow from his palms almost hidden in the captives' hair.

Raylyn swallowed the bile that rose in her throat as the men's skin wavered under the spell. It puckered and twisted as if it were melting. They both screamed as blood dripped from their eyes, their ears, their nose. Their voices weaved together in agony, dueting with the jeering crowd. It was over in a moment, their screams lessening to whimpers. Disfigured under lumpy, bulging, scarred skin so no matter where they traveled, the world would know what they were. Criminals. Dissenters from the Goddess. *Marked.*

She didn't take a full breath until Talia pulled her into a shop a few streets over, a look of outrage twisting her face. "What the *hell*?" Talia asked through gritted teeth. Raylyn glanced over her shoulder, ensuring the men from the stage hadn't followed her. Though pardoned from the king, she didn't feel particularly safe in the riotous streets. "I'm never going to get that *stink* out of my nose." Talia grabbed a stack of blank parchment from a nearby shelf, shoving it with unneeded force into a canvas bag.

"I've never seen that done before ... only read about it," Raylyn said, trying to piece together an explanation. *That could have been me.* She thought of the council meeting and Eleanor Bernshaw and Doyle's desires to see her Marked. The horrible realization twisted her stomach, and she bolted from the shop just in time to lose the contents of her stomach into the dying grass outside.

Talia appeared a couple minutes later, tying the coin purse and securing it inside her dress. "Quite done, are you?" she asked, walking past Raylyn, who was still hunched over with sickness. She wiped her mouth, following the irate woman.

"Talia, I'm sorry. I don't know what came over me back there."

Talia rolled her eyes, hefting the burdened tote higher on her shoulder. "You got what you deserved," she said, gesturing to the pile of vomit in the distance behind them. "We've got a few stops to make, so let's get moving."

She tried to enjoy the trip and change of scenery, but the Marking burned into her mind. With the weight of her illusions lifted, she was mortified about her attitude toward her parents. For weeks, she convinced herself her parents could have revoked her banishment if they cared enough to try. But she now knew with every fiber of her being her exile saved her from a gruesome and painful fate. Allowing her to become so close and valuable to the crown was a shield she didn't realize she needed. No one would dare touch her while she remained safely in the king's protection ... but hundreds of miles away in a remote village? A flash of the men's molten skin flittered through her mind, causing her to shudder. *That could have been me,* she thought again. So lost in her mind, she didn't realize Talia was talking until she slapped her on the back of the head.

"Hey!" she said, rubbing her head. "That hurt."

"Good! I've asked you the same question three times over. If you act like this in Thorne's class tomorrow, you can kiss your chance of making Master Healer goodbye."

"Noted," Raylyn said with a grimace. "What was the question?" They had been in and out of shops for what felt like hours—Talia grabbing the necessary supplies as well as spending a fair share of the coin on her own desires—and the sun finally began to lower in the sky.

"Is there anything else you can think of?" She pulled out the list from Terach, scanning it quickly. "We've got parchment, quills, the requested workbooks, the moonstone and amethyst, some decent clothes. Everything they asked for." She shoved the list into the bursting tote. "Are we done?"

Raylyn was about to say *Yes, thank the Goddess*, but as she looked up from the dirt road, her eyes locked on to the closest shop's window, as if pulled there by an invisible force. Making one of the hastiest decisions of her life, she answered. "No."

CHAPTER 11

WARMTH SPREAD THROUGH HER chest as she cradled the tiny gray kitten. It had fallen asleep as she and Talia made their way back to the castle, its purrs vibrating in harmony with Raylyn's breaths. Talia looked at her like she had truly gone crazy. "What are you going to do with a cat? You'll be way too busy for it. Classes are super intense." But despite all her negativity, Raylyn picked up the tiny fur ball, knowing she wouldn't leave the pet shop without it. Cats of various ages, colors, and sizes filled small pens behind the shop's front window. Raylyn met this one's eyes and *knew* they belonged together, despite Talia's resistance.

She turned down her hall, bag of supplies weighing heavily on her shoulder. Talia left her to meet up with Kitchen Boy as soon as they came back, all smiles and batting eyes. The kitten shifted in her hands, stretching his little legs. "Welcome home," she murmured as they approached her room, something on her door catching her eye. Walking closer, her heart sank like the weight on the end of a fishing line.

Graffitied in huge red, dripping letters, the word *demon* was painted on her door. Her face grew hot, and she burst inside her room, embarrassment coursing through her. She glanced quickly around, making sure nothing was out of place. "I'll need to start locking the door," she said to her kitten. She grabbed a soft blanket and formed a little bed on the floor, placing the sleepy animal on top. He pawed at the blanket for a moment, before curling himself into a little ball, purring contentedly.

Raylyn watched, his simple contentment easing some of her panic. *I can't wait for Braya to get here,* she thought. She missed her friend desperately, but the knowledge of her upcoming arrival made her smile. When Brenden told her of Rowan's lies, he was more than willing to send a group of soldiers to collect Braya and bring her back. They were scheduled to leave tonight after preparing their supplies. "You'll like her," she said, reaching down to pet the kitten's nose.

Deciding to organize everything so she would be prepared in the morning, she hauled the heavy bag of supplies to the desk in the corner of the room. Her foot hit something, sending it skittering across the floor and throwing her off balance. She had forgotten about the package her mother gave her, so angrily thrown and discarded. Setting the bag down, she grabbed the small rectangular box, running her fingers over the coarse jute rope that knotted it closed. Jumping onto her bed, she chewed her raw lip and pulled the package open.

A folded piece of parchment and a metal chain with a circular pendent fell out. She grabbed the necklace, studying the pendent. It was silver, three spiraling leaves coming together to form a triangle on one side, and an eagle inscribed on the other. She had never seen it before. She slipped the chain over her head, tucking it inside her shirt. What she really wanted was a hug from her parents, but this would do for now.

With trembling fingers, she opened the parchment, her mother's familiar script a warm hello. She traced the first words with her fingertips.

My dearest,

First, I beg your forgiveness and pray for your understanding. There isn't much time, but please know that everything I did was to protect you. Your father and I love you so much, and nothing can ever change that.

This is a letter in three parts. The first: why. Why did we let our only beloved daughter be whisked away so easily? It is not without a great pain, Raylyn. We are faced with choosing the lesser of two evils, and I cannot guarantee your safety here. There are people in our village who will not rest while you reside within a hundred miles from them. We've overheard whisperings already. Do not concern yourself with the follies of them, but be on guard against those prejudiced enough to harm you. I hope the protection of the crown will shield you against any extremist who threatens. Stay vigilant and strong.

Second: how. How did you come into this power? I wish I could give you a straightforward answer. Instead, I offer nothing more than inferred guesses. What I am about to confess is my darkest secret and greatest shame. While your father's love courses through your veins, his blood does not. He was as unaware as you until this evening, when I no longer had the luxury of hiding it. As a young woman barely older than you are now, I made decisions which put me into a position of vulnerability. My innocence was taken by an evil and powerful man and there were nights I thought I would never be whole again. When I learned I was pregnant, I knew I could not remain and allow that man's evil to poison my child. You are the miracle who saved me from a suffocating horror, and I thank the Goddess every day for you.

I cannot imagine the pain this revelation may cause, but I tell you it with a purpose. I do not know what your sire's powers may be, though I know they are great. My knowledge of the Goddess and our history leads me to believe that he can syphon, like you. I didn't recognize this at the time, but in hindsight, it answers many unresolved questions I've been harboring. Please, learn from my past and do not allow your naivety to blind you to people's true natures. Not everyone will be cheering for you, my dearest, and some may try to use you in ways that violate the Goddess. Do not allow them that satisfaction.

The third: where. I've included a relic I almost couldn't find; I've had it hidden for such a long time. It was mine a lifetime ago, procured in the same place you prepare to study. I do not know if your birth father remains or not, as I have done everything in my power to stay far out of the Court's overreaching hand. But be cautious of any unwarranted attentions, as he may seek you out, knowing your powers are a mirror of his. If all else fails, my dearest, leave. To hell with it all—let that place burn, if need be—but run to save yourself. This pendant will secure you a position anywhere in this country or others. If you must leave, wear it with pride and make yourself anew.

I pray every day and night for your forgiveness and safety. May the Goddess watch over you and greet you with open arms many, many decades from now.

With love and remorse,
Mother

Raylyn stared at the letter until her eyes grew hazy with tears. *So much I never knew.* She set the parchment down on the bedside table, her limbs heavy and clumsy, and scooped her kitten from his blanket. "Will you stay with me?" she asked him. He purred his response, rubbing his tiny face into her hand. Curling up together, she stared at the ceiling for a long time before sleep took her.

Door Thirty loomed in front of Raylyn, and she was thankful for the small cluster of students with whom she entangled herself. They all slipped through the door, the sun not yet risen over the horizon. *Terach wasn't lying when he said Thorne doesn't tolerate tardiness*, Raylyn thought. The classroom was already full, nearly a dozen people sat behind desks, all pointed toward a large blackboard at the head of the room. She gripped her books tighter to her chest as she looked for an extra desk, trying to convince herself that no one was staring. There were no empty seats. She stood awkwardly in the back of the room, waiting for Thorne.

Thankfully, no one was bold enough to turn all the way around in their seat to stare at her, so Raylyn decided it wasn't too bad of a spot. She tried to guess the ages of the other students, but the backs of their heads didn't give much away. At the very least, there was one man who was starting to bald. Besides the blackboard and a large desk at the head of the room for Thorne, the rest of the room was strikingly empty. She tried to repress the creeping disappointment, thinking about the classroom that she toured with Terach with the large glass cases of herbs and mock InfirmaryInfirmary beds.

Thorne burst into the room a couple minutes later, her dark hair twisted on the top of her head. She was dragging a wooden chair behind her with a careless attitude. Spotting Raylyn in the back, she smiled. "Ah, you did show up. Here." She nodded at the chair. Raylyn scrambled to the retrieve it. "You may observe the lesson silently from the back of the room. But, please," she paused, placing a hand on Raylyn's shoulders as she grabbed the chair. A look of sincerity softened her eyes, and she gave her a warm smile, "feel free to leave when the material becomes too advanced."

The classroom was silent, which may have been worse than someone daring to laugh. Raylyn gave a curt nod, picking up the chair and walking it to the back of the classroom. She felt eyes on her and tried to ignore them. *If there's anywhere I truly belong, it is here.* Balancing her textbook, parchment, and quill in her lap was not easy, and the chair wobbled, one leg a little shorter than the rest. She took a deep breath, refusing to be perturbed.

"Last session we reviewed the traditional healing chants and the reasons they are becoming outdated. Who can tell me why?"

Half a dozen hands shot into the air, and Thorne called on a woman at the front of the room whom Raylyn couldn't see. "Older generations have learned to ground themselves with the chants. They also believed that chanting and songs were a way to pay respect to the Goddess for their powers. However, we have determined that grounding is all about mental state, and while spoken word may help with external distractions, it does not amplify or increase openness. As well, the Goddess hears our silent prayers, making external vocalizations futile as well as attention-seeking."

"Precisely, Pria. These incantations do nothing; they do not invoke more power or accuracy or energy. If you find yourself having issues grounding and opening your channels, meditate for a moment, clear your mind of all else. It is a much more effective and less silly way."

A few people took notes, the scratching of their quills filling the silent air, but most remained motionless, heads looking up at Thorne. Raylyn shifted in her seat as she wrote, her chair wobbling. Her mother still spoke the prayers as she channeled.

"Today, we focus on what can increase the potency of our spells. The Goddess blesses us with medicinal plants and herbs that can treat many of our illnesses. When we combine that with our channeling, not only do we save ourselves much energy, but we also save our patient potentially weeks of recovery time." She turned her back to the class, writing with chalk on the blackboard. This time, a dozen quills scratched in synchrony.

"This," she said, pointing at the board, "is the recipe for the most potent antimicrobial salve to date. Research is constantly underway, so mind you, there may be a better medicine by tomorrow, for all we know. But for now," she tapped lightly on the board, "this is the best. As you see, some of these ingredients are rare, which means limited supply and outrageous demand. This is used for the direst of circumstances, gangrenous wounds requiring limb amputation, a lacerated bowel, eye infection leading to blindness."

Raylyn was copying the ingredient list with haste, as Thorne was already moving to erase it. Her textbook slid from her lap, landing to the stone floor with a loud thud. A few heads turned back in surprise, causing a low growl of disapproval from Thorne. "Sorry," she muttered, cheeks warming.

Thorne didn't reply as she continued with her lecture. She explained the ingredient ratios, how to apply to the wound, how much energy to channel to push the patient's body toward healing. "Once the salve is mixed, it is important to keep it in an airtight glass jar. If not sealed properly, not only will it lose its potency, but it also has a chance to become contaminated. Metal canisters will not do; the minerals may seep, causing a host of other issues.

Remember the second rule of the Goddess: Do No Harm. Even unwittingly, if your actions cause your patient to worsen, the fault lies with you."

Raylyn stared, her mother's voice echoing in her head, *"And what is our second rule?"* She had asked these words the same night Raylyn saved the prince; she could even see the small smile on her face, and her father raging in the background. *He must've just found out that night,* she thought, chest aching. *How badly did it hurt discovering I wasn't truly his?*

"Your assignment is to bring me completed samples of this salve by next class." Raylyn shook away her musings. "And stay diligent with your preparations for the competition. Term's end will approach us quickly." With that, she swept out of the room, leaving the students to gather their things.

"Hello." Raylyn had just bent down to retrieve her fallen textbook when the voice spoke. She glanced up to see a red-haired woman standing in front of her, large smile on her pretty face. Hundreds of freckles were sprinkled over her nose, and her almond-shaped eyes were a bright green. "You're new. Don't worry about the chair thing. She does it to all of us, an initiation of sorts."

"Well, that's comforting," she said, standing. She adjusted the books, cursing herself for not bringing the canvas bag. "I'm Raylyn."

The woman smiled and opened her mouth to reply when someone yelled across the room. "For Goddess's sake, Ana! That's *her*, the syphon!" She spat the last word with disgust. Raylyn looked around and found the speaker, her stomach dropping when she realized it was the same woman who had spilled the wine on her at the feast. *Demon.*

She glanced back at the woman, Ana, trying to find words to explain she wasn't some evil entity. But she had already turned, red hair bouncing as she bolted away. The few people left in the room stared at her, and she felt every inch of her skin redden with shame. Keeping her eyes on her feet, she scurried out of the room, desperate for solitude.

There were few spots to hide inside the academy—no alcoves or aisles of books or sitting areas like the castled—so Raylyn took refuge outdoors. The crisp air soothed her burning cheeks; despite the sun, the weather remained cooler now. Most of the leaves littered the ground, trees all but barren. She positioned her back against one of them, its trunk wide enough to hide her. She steadied herself, slowing her breathing. *I don't blame them*, she thought, picking apart a crispy orange leaf. *If I was in their position, I'm sure I'd feel the same.* Every book she ever read which mentioned syphoning called it a manifestation of evil, citing the long list of people who went power-hungry and manic because of it. She brushed her hands on her trousers to get the small crumbles of leaves off. *That won't be me.*

She reviewed her notes from Thorne's class to pass the time before the Level One casting began. She recognized the herbs listed, but she was puzzled as to the necessity of a few ingredients. She didn't think there were any healing properties to crushed rosemary, and she was *certain* ragweed causes rashes on most people. Its use in an antiseptic ointment made no sense. Classes were held every other day, so she would work on it more tomorrow.

Gathering her books, she stretched, brushing the dirt from her trousers. She eyed the Academy building warily, once again praying she wouldn't be tied up and burned alive. The threat of ostracization couldn't suppress her mounting excitement as she walked back inside toward the caster's wing. She hadn't been able to explore it yet and was eager to uncover the secrets to casting mastery.

When she entered the classroom, she was greeted by riotous laughter of children. The room was alive with activity, and she stood dumbstruck as two young boys ran past her, chasing each other in a game of freeze tag. This version appeared to have actual freezing, though, as the smaller boy yelped in delight at the icy touch of the other. Farther in the room, a circle of girls were playing a clapping game that involved some long and twisting rhyme, a few others were seeing who could jump higher, and in the far corner of the room, a boy with black hair was reading quietly to himself, the volume thicker than Raylyn's textbooks.

The children were young; the oldest of the group couldn't have been more than eight. Raylyn glanced around, wondering where to sit. There were no chairs, desks, or tables, but a dozen multicolored cushions were thrown haphazardly on the floor. A shelf containing bright blue bins rested against a wall, an older woman with plaited hair searching through their contents.

Some children stopped to glance at Raylyn, but most continued playing, completely unaware or unconcerned by her presence. The woman with the braid turned. "Oh, come in! You must be Raylyn! I'm Merrill." She pulled another bin out off the shelf. "Ah, perfect. Okay class!"

Raylyn was shocked when they all listened, dashing to sit on the cushions. Finding an empty one, she sat, crossing her legs, feeling much too large.

"Are you a new teacher?" A blonde-headed girl said in a loud whisper. "If you are, I think you're supposed to be up there with Miss Merrill."

"She's not a teacher, Lainy. She's a student, like you. Everyone, say hello to Raylyn. She will be joining us for a while."

A chorus of *hello*'s rang out. "You're kinda old to be here, aren't you?" Lainy whispered again.

"Lainy!" Merrill scolded. "We all start in different places with different abilities, right?" Lainy nodded, staring at her feet.

Raylyn's heart hurt for the girl; she was so young, maybe six. "Hey, it's okay," Raylyn whispered. "I *am* kinda old to be here." The girl perked up, smiling.

"We are going to talk about our emotions today, and how they can help us or hurt us when we are trying to control our powers. I want you each to take a pack of color cards." Merrill placed the bin on the ground in the center of the room. The children swooped in like vultures, snatching packs of cards. Raylyn followed suit. "Each card has a different color on it. I am going to say an emotion, and I want you to show me the color that you think of when you hear it."

Raylyn stared. *Surely I'm in the wrong class,* she thought. *They expect me to play children's games?* Merrill saw the look of disbelief on her face and gave her an apologetic smile. The kids were eager for the game, sorting their cards.

"Are we ready? Okay. Happiness." The group picked out their cards, ranging in colors from yellow to pink to green. Raylyn raised a pink reluctantly, feeling incredibly foolish and out of place. "Wonderful. How about sad?" This time, blue won the majority, with some black and gray mixed in. "Angry?" An astounding number of them raised their red cards, though the little boy with black hair held up a black. "Now, I want you to tell me *why* you're choosing the color with this next one. Excited?" And on and on it went, Raylyn pulling out her cards with the rest of them.

When the class finally dragged to its close, Raylyn held back as parents came to the door to grab their children. She was careful not to make eye contact with them to avoid another "demon" situation. "Merrill?" she asked when the last of the children, the little black-haired boy, was finally gone.

"Yes, Raylyn? Did you enjoy your first day?" She already replaced the blue bin of cards and was collecting the cushions, piling them neatly in the corner of the room.

"I think there's a mistake. I know I'm not completely controlled with casting, as I'm definitely having some difficulty accessing those channels, but surely I shouldn't be in *this* class?" Raylyn laughed. "I mean, they are *young* children."

Merrill straightened, brushing her bangs out of her eyes as picked up the last of the cushions. "You belong in this class." Her voice was warm, but unyielding. "I've spoken to Master Ordon, and he informed me of your complete lack of control. It would be best to open yourself to these lessons. They *will* help."

"We did nothing but speak of colors today," Raylyn replied flatly.

"See, that's not true. We explored our emotions and the connections we make with them. I'm curious as to why you have such difficulty with this subject. Try to really *honor* your emotions over the next couple of days, recognize what you're feeling. We can talk about how you did next class."

Raylyn was speechless. She nodded, hugging her unused books to her chest as she left the classroom, her heart sinking. *Disappointment*, she recognized begrudgingly.

She spent the rest of the day researching the ingredients in Thorne's salve and playing with her kitten. She still hadn't decided on a name for him, so she stuck with "Little Guy" for now.

Talia popped in a few hours later, wrinkling her nose when Little Guy pawed at her leg. "Ouch! His claws are sharp!"

"Well, yeah, he's a cat."

Talia stuck her tongue out at her as she flopped down on her bed, peeking into her textbook. "It's like a different language," she said, scanning the page of different medicinal fungi and their indications for use. "How's it going? Big day, huh?"

Raylyn snorted. She recanted her classes, including the woman from Thorne's class who was busy convincing the Court she's a demon and the color cards from casting class. She buried her head in her pillow at this last bit. "She told me to practice *honoring* my emotions."

"I can't believe you're in the baby group! I mean, I knew it was Level One, but that's an actual nursery class!"

"You're making it worse," she moaned, hitting her with the pillow.

"I'm just ... surprised, that's all. Anyway, I can't stay long. The king has been obsessive over his afternoon tea and gossip." She winked. "I'll see you later."

The afternoon dragged. She looked up every ingredient in the salve and was certain ragweed shouldn't be
included. She searched through all her textbooks, as well
as the few library books she snagged on her way back from
the Academy. None of them had any information about it
containing useful medicinal properties, unless you wanted
to give an enemy an itchy rash.

She all but skipped to Terach's study when evening
fell, twisting down several long halls. The instructions he
left with her were precise, but her sense of direction was
largely nonexistent. After three wrong turns, she finally
found herself outside the correct door in a completely isolated part of the castle. There wasn't even another room
down the passageway.

"Ah, there you are. I was beginning to think you forgot,"
Terach said, raising an eyebrow as he let her in.

"Of course not! I just had a bit of trouble finding my way."

"It *is* a little secluded. When I first began teaching at
the Academy many, many years ago, this was one of the
overflow offices for new instructors. Over the years, the
king offered more prestigious spaces, but I've grown to like
it here. Few people go out of their way to come bother me."
The room was small, all four walls completely covered in
floor-to-ceiling bookcases, packed until they overflowed. A
small, worn sofa sat near a fireplace, and a desk with two
wooden chairs filled the other corner. There was hardly
room to walk.

He stacked some papers on his desk, revealing its
wooden surface beneath. "Come, sit. I want to pick your
brain for a bit."

Raylyn sat, taking a curious peek at the scribbled
pages of notes. The handwriting was a looping mess that

she couldn't make out, and she thought it may have been written in an unfamiliar language. She pulled her attention back to Terach as he sat in the chair in front of her, steepling his hands before him. He stared at her for a moment, his eyes narrowed slightly as if he was trying to piece together a particularly difficult puzzle.

"Was there something you wanted to know?" she asked when the silence became unbearable.

"Many things!" He clapped his hands together and leaned back. "Thousands, no doubt. But let's start with some that are easily answered. Tell me about your upbringing. I recall you saying your mother is a proficient healer?"

"Yes, she's the High Healer of Lakehaven. I was apprenticing under her since childhood."

"Hm. And your father?"

Her stomach twisted. "Leader of our village guard. A skilled caster." The words from her mother's letter echoed in her mind, but she stifled them. Blood be damned, he was the man who loved and raised her. He *was* her father.

Terach nodded. "It's very interesting." He grabbed a thick book from his desk, flipping to a flagged page. "The past few days, I've been researching syphons. The line should have died with Haddeon. But here you sit." He eyed her, and she fought the urge to squirm. "Perhaps it is a true miracle from the Goddess? Some type of retribution for forsaking him all those years ago?"

Raylyn recoiled. "Forsaking him?" she repeated, stunned. "You blame the Goddess for Haddeon murdering his wife and unborn child?" She looked away, disgusted. Just the insinuation would be enough for the church to kick his door in.

"You think it blasphemous? Here." He picked up a smaller book from his desk, tossing it to her. "Take a look at this."

She caught it, the cover smooth, worn leather, void of any title or author. Puzzled, she opened it, the yellowed pages crisp and musty. She glanced up at Terach, who grinned like a little boy on winter solstice morning. "What is this?" she asked, squinting at the tiny script inside.

"From what I've studied, that is one of Haddeon's last journals before he died."

She dropped the book instantly on his desk as if her hands had caught fire. "Not truly?" she asked, horrified.

"Oh, come now. You possess his powers, you must realize many tales of his descent are completely falsified, turned into bedtime fables to scare children into behaving."

She gaped at him. When he had suggested they study the lore of syphoning together, she hadn't expected it to turn out like this. He was proving to be a complete radical, and she wondered how he could even pray to the Goddess with ideals such as these. "I believe the Goddess is good and merciful, and she blesses us with life and the means for prosperity. Haddeon was the devil come to walk the world."

"Haddeon was merely a man, perhaps led a little astray, and abandoned by the Goddess in his time of need."

She could feel her face growing warm with passion. "You question our entire religion." Her words were sharp with accusation.

"Indeed! You should question *everything*. Create your opinions based on facts, research, and *evidence*. Don't just regurgitate the words of those elder to you." Her face was still hot, and she didn't want to look him in the eyes. Instead, she glanced toward the door, wondering if she should just leave. "How about this?" he suggested, seeing her reluctance. "Tell me what you know about Haddeon and his fall."

"He was born to a farmer," Raylyn said, chewing her lip. "But he was very charismatic and worked his way up to the Court. He married the youngest princess but killed her and their unborn child in a fit of rage. The texts say his syphoning powers were a curse and poisoned his mind until he finally broke."

Terach leaned back, running a hand through his beard, contemplating. "Hm. Anything else?"

"They say his conception was the result of adultery, allowing the Devil a vessel to walk the earth."

Raylyn jolted as Terach roared with laughter, tears welling in his eyes. She watched him, tightlipped and unamused. "It is common knowledge," she said defensively.

He wiped the tears from his eyes, a grin still on his face. "You are very young and *very* sheltered. What if I told you syphons were once more persecuted than effectors?" She didn't reply, scowl still firmly fixed on her face.

He stood, slowly pacing the wall of books behind the desk. He grabbed one, then another, making a small pile in his arms. Returning to the desk, he laid them in front of Raylyn, putting the old leather journal on top. "Don't make that face," he said when she wrinkled her nose again. "I want you to take these and at least skim through them before the next time we meet. You need to learn there's more than one perspective in life."

She had never been one to refuse a book or an academic challenge. "Okay," she said reluctantly. "Does this mean we're done tonight?" She didn't know if it was relief or disappointment pressing in her chest.

He studied her, delaying his answer. "I think so," he said. "We will make no headway unless you open your mind. Sometimes the things you readily accept as truth are nothing more than pretty lies."

She nodded halfheartedly, feeling very much like a failure. Scooping up the books, she balanced the leather journal on the top of the pile, trying hard not to touch it with bare skin.

She was already halfway into the hallway when his voice called, "Raylyn?" Propping the door open with her foot, she turned, eyebrows raised. "What did you say your mother's name was again?"

CHAPTER 12

"THERE YOU GO! YOU'VE GOT IT!"
Brenden said.

Raylyn looked up smiling, but her concentration broke and the flame she cradled in her cupped hands flickered and died, extinguishing with a small puff of smoke. "Damn it." She wiped a bead of sweat from her temple. "This isn't working."

"You're making progress." Brenden sat on the sand, stretching his legs out before him. "Go on, try again."

She shot him a dark look before closing her eyes and forcing herself to concentrate. Opening herself to her feelings as Merrill instructed, she tried to untangle the knot in her stomach. It was an interwoven mess of anxiety (*I'll be stuck in Level One casting forever!*), embarrassment (*Can't even maintain the smallest of flames!*), and self-consciousness (*Does he have to watch so closely?*). She tried to process each emotion before shoving it down, leaving nothing but concentration and her obsessive desire to become a proficient caster.

She opened the channel, a trickling drain on her energy as a lick of fire sparked in her palm. Increasing the connection, she fed the flames, marveling as they began curling, forming a floating ball of heat hovering less than an inch above her skin. She smiled at Brenden again, careful to keep her mind on the tiny fireball.

"Watch out!" a voice called. She looked up, confused, as the flame extinguished again. She was suddenly pulled to the ground, tumbling on top of Brenden, who had a firm grasp on the hem of her tunic. At the same time, soaring shards of ice sliced into the air where her head was just a heartbeat before. They flew with a deadly velocity until they hit the invisible edge of the arena field, shattering.

Breathless, she glanced wide-eyed at Brenden. "Thanks," she said, blushing. She moved to climb off him, but he held her waist for an extra second, keeping her there a moment longer than necessary. Her skin tingled where his fingertips slipped past the hem of her tunic, and another surge of heat filled her cheeks, entirely unrelated to her embarrassment.

"Sorry!" A group of three women approached, led by the same one who spilled her drink on Raylyn at the feast. Raylyn scrambled, righting herself. "Vonn lost control. You know how it is." She curtsied low to Brenden, who was still lounging on the ground, as comfortable as if he were in bed. "Such a pleasure, Your Highness." She batted her eyes, dark lashes enhancing the blue of her irises.

"Pria," he replied coolly. "Ladies. Careful where you're aiming."

"Of course, such an oversight. You know how Vonn is. Half the reason I'm here is to heal her *accidents*." The two girls behind her giggled as they pranced off.

"Nobles' daughters," Brenden said, pulling himself off the ground. "Pria's a bit of a..."

"Bitch?" Raylyn said.

"Yeah, that about sums her up. Do you want to give it another go? You were doing well that time."

"I think almost getting my brain speared by ice is a good signal to be done, don't you?" she said, making Brenden laugh. "Anyway, she might try it again. I get the feeling she would dance around my dead body. Let's go."

They made their way off the sand, and once they stepped onto the stone floor of the arena seating, Raylyn remembered a question that had been bothering her. "How does the shield work, anyway? I thought all spells required an energy source. Is there someone who always maintains the shield? Where are they?" She started scanning the seats, wondering if she had just missed a caster hanging out in the stands.

"It's actually ingenious how it's accomplished. Come on, I'll show you." He grabbed her hand, leading her halfway up the stairs. She glanced back down at the arena, watching the different groups of students practicing. A couple people were launching attacks on a straw man who had seen better days. Fire attacks were quickly extinguished by streams of water, sending clouds of mist into the air. A few hundred feet away, Pria's group of friends were practicing their shielding defenses as Vonn rained hail down on them. She hadn't realized how frequented this area was until Brenden offered to help her practice.

"Here. Look at this." They were close to the top of the arena. Brenden was kneeling in front of one of the long wooden benches, fumbling with something. Raylyn stepped closer, trying to see what he was doing. "There!" he said. An inconspicuous door opened, all but invisible in the wood, smaller than the cover of a book.

Nestled inside the bench was what looked like a black rock. "What is it?" she asked, feeling a little dumb.

"Well, come here." He grabbed her hand, pulling her into a crouch beside him. "Terach calls it a power stone. It's his invention." He grabbed it out of its hiding spot with surprising gentleness. "Touch it; it feels just like glass."

She stared at him for a moment, suspicious. "Is it going to shock me or something?" she asked, picking at the skin next to her thumbnail.

He scoffed. "Of course not. I'm holding it, aren't I?"

Curiosity won, and she ran a finger down the stone's surface, surprised at its heat, as the day was chilly. The sunlight illuminated hidden specks of silver. "It's warm."

"I know. It's great, right? Terach says the warmth is a byproduct from the spell."

She chewed her lip for a moment and tentatively reached out with her powers. If this thing really powered the shield, then it had some inherent energy stored within. She carefully opened a channel between her and the stone, with no intention of healing, casting, or syphoning. Just feeling.

She gasped, recoiling. The most chaotic energy all but burst from the stone. "How is that possible?" she asked, stumbling backward.

Brenden shrugged, putting the stone away. "Terach's very secretive about the process of crafting one. Between you and me, I think it makes him feel important," he whispered with a wink.

"Right, because being the king's advisor and head of academic affairs isn't enough."

"You forgot lead military strategist, as well." Chuckling, they climbed the last few stairs of the arena. They walked down the road toward the castle in quiet companionship for several minutes before Raylyn spoke again. "Thanks for trying to help me today, but I think I might be hopeless at casting."

"It was my pleasure. We all agreed you'd benefit from extra practice, anyway."

"And you drew the short straw?"

He snorted, glancing down at her, squinting in the sunlight. "I'm quite proficient with my shielding abilities if you remember from your testing. I thought it might come in handy in case you lose control again. The shield around the arena is powerful enough, but that wouldn't stop you from hurting others who were inside."

The image of the flying ice shards flashed through her mind. "Oh, so you're not just a tutor, but a nanny as well?" She was trying to lighten the mood but struggled with the idea she was nothing more than a burden.

"Goddess strike me down as a sinner if that were true." Raylyn glanced up at him, perplexed by the vigor in his voice. She didn't know how to respond, so they fell into silence once more. "Why is Pria trying to get her friends to kill you, anyway?" he asked, finally breaking the strange tension after a long minute.

"Ah, likely because I'm a demon syphon come to suck out the souls of children," she said flippantly. A small, sharp pain forced her eyes down, a drop of blood beading at the corner of her thumb nail. Again. She forced her fingers to be still.

"She's a prejudiced imbecile." He glanced at Raylyn's grim face. "Surely you don't take her words to heart."

She shrugged. "I'd believe similar if I were in her position."

As they approached the castle, Raylyn hesitated. She still needed to make the salve for Thorne's class. If she took the path toward the Academy, she could save nearly half an hour of walking back and forth. She voiced this to Brenden.

He frowned. "I'm sorry I can't accompany you. I have to meet with Terach to go over some business of state. With winter approaching, there's been some concern among the nobles about the refugee influx and its demand on our supplies." He shook his head, rubbing his brow. "It's ridiculous, honestly. They are so worried about the possibility of their five course dinners dwindling to merely *three*. I'd say the majority would be fine with letting them starve if it meant they still had their choice cuts of beef."

Her chest tightened. "Is that truly a concern, though? I overheard Terach at the feast say the crop shortage was just a rumor."

"The drought we've had definitely caused smaller yields. Whether a true shortage... that remains to be seen. But regardless, if we continue to get this quantity of people coming over the border for asylum, we will have trouble keeping up." A small line appeared between his eyebrows as he looked down at her. "It would be wise not to repeat that bit of information, though. The nobles are tense as it is; additional rumors would be detrimental."

"Of course, not like I have anyone to tell."

"Braya will be here before you know it. My men estimate their trip will take around three weeks." He gave her a small bow before they split paths.

Raylyn smiled, the reminder of his rescue mission sparking some hope. He had sent three men on horseback to retrieve Braya, and such a small number could ride swiftly. The trip with Rowan had taken a week longer, but Raylyn was largely inexperienced with riding, and they slowed their pace for her. She sent a letter to Braya, informing her of their impending arrival, instructing her to prepare for the journey. The guilt of abandoning her still fermented in her stomach but was lessened by degrees knowing they'd be reunited soon.

She glanced behind her as Brenden retreated toward the castle, gratitude making her flush. As if feeling her eyes, he turned too. A grin spread on his face when he caught her watching him, and he waved before turning back around. *Maybe I'm not completely alone*, she thought, a smile playing at her lips. With a touch more vigor, she continued toward the Academy, knowing with confidence that her notes for the salve were perfect.

It took her two tries, as the first batch she mismeasured the amount of water, causing the salve to be a runny mess. But her second attempt was thick, smooth, and filled the glass canister halfway. She was all but skipping when she made it back to her room, the sun already low beneath the horizon. She scavenged a crusty sandwich from the kitchens and was brushing off the last of its crumbs when she approached the door of her room, confused. The bright red lettering had gone—no trace of the word "DEMON" remained—and on the ground lay a cluster of flowers. She glanced around the corridor, looking for the culprit, but no one was there. *Purple hyacinth*, she thought, bending to pick it up. As soon as her fingers brushed the soft petals, the flower shuddered, shifting into a group of amethyst butterflies launching into the air like confetti. *Brenden*. The image of him smiling and waving popped into her mind, and she smiled as the butterflies flittered through the air, light and carefree.

"Take your seats. No, no, keep your salve; silly girl, why would you think I want them piled on my desk?" Thorne scolded one of the younger girls, who flushed and scrambled to her seat, tips of her ears turning pink.

Raylyn's janky wooden chair remained, but she refused to be perturbed by the continued lack of desk. She set her pile of books and parchment next to her, cradling the glass jar on her lap. Thorne's eyes glanced over her as she scanned the room, waiting to begin.

"Last class I left you with the assignment to mix up a potent healing salve to be used in conjunction with your channeling to heal gangrenous wounds. Is there anyone who could not complete this?" No one dared raised a hand. "Good. Today we will be using this on a few patients in the InfirmaryInfirmary who were injured in their escape from Cystra. Who feels like they followed the directions exactly and are confident in their concoction?" This time, eager hands shot into the air, pleading to be acknowledged by the Master Healer.

Thorne looked around, her eyes narrowing at Raylyn, whose hands remained holding the canister in her lap. "Ah, our little prodigy. I'm surprised to see you back. Did you have some trouble?" Her condescension made the hair on Raylyn's neck prickle.

"Yes, Madam," Raylyn said, ignoring her racing heart. She forced her words to be steady, faking a level of confidence as her classmates swiveled in their seats, a mixture of pity and amusement on their faces.

"Is that right? Were the instructions too complex?"

"No, Madam."

"Trouble finding the ingredients?"

Again, she replied, "No, madam."

"Pray, tell, what was the problem?" Thorne asked, eyes narrowing.

She took a deep breath, praying she was right. "The addition of ragweed, Madam. While every other ingredient had its purpose, there are no beneficial medicinal properties to ragweed. In fact, its inclusion at best would aggravate the wound, and at worse, trigger an allergic reaction to further complicate healing."

The room was silent as several heads snapped toward Thorne to watch her reaction. She stared at Raylyn for a moment, cocking her head, face unreadable. Then, she gave a miniscule nod, turning toward the rest of the class. "That's correct. Who else caught the trick?" No one else moved, and Thorne's expression turned gruesome. "Level Thirty... You are Level Thirty healers, and you didn't bother investigating the ingredients yourselves?"

Though Thorne didn't complement or congratulate her, neither did she show her as much scorn as the others. They spent the rest of the lesson reviewing the importance of common sense and research, and Raylyn was disappointed they didn't go to the InfirmaryInfirmary as promised.

Casting class with Merrill and the children did nothing to lighten her mood. They played a game called *Feelings, Attack!* Raylyn was paired with the little black-haired boy, and they took turns guessing each other's emotions using the dreaded color cards.

"How is your assignment going, Raylyn?" Merrill asked once class mercifully ended.

"Pretty well," she said, trying to mask her irritability. It was a waste of time sitting on the floor playing baby games for an hour and a half when she could have been practicing in the arena with Brenden.

"I want you to keep working on it, okay? Try to process and feel each emotion. If you want to master your powers, you must first master your mind."

Raylyn did everything in her power to not roll her eyes. Forcing a smile, she nodded and slunk out the door. All she wanted to do was get back to the castle and check in on Little Guy, and maybe grab a bite to eat.

Pulling open the heavy door of the Academy, she stepped outside, shivering in the cool air. Each day was markedly colder, and she peered into the cloudless sky, wondering how long it would be until snow fell. She tried to recall the last time it even rained but couldn't remember. The ground was hard and dry, and road dust carried into the buildings. *Better than being caught in a storm,* she thought as she rubbed her hands on her arms, trying to use friction to warm up. If her bag wasn't so laden with books and notes, she would've jogged back to the castle. Instead, she walked as quickly as she could, shivering when she finally opened the door to the small alcove she and Talia had shared before.

She almost fully collided with Rowan, who was standing on the other side of the door. "For Goddess's sake," she muttered, abashed. She hadn't spoken to him or even seen him since their fight the day of her testing. Other than cursing him for his lie about Braya, he hardly crossed her mind, the business of the past few days giving her little time to ruminate.

"Raylyn! Talia told me you like to use this entrance. Oh, please wait!" She was just about to dash around him, but the dismay in his face made her pause.

"What is it, then?" she asked, eyes sliding to the floor.

"I just... I miss you."

She glanced up, surprised. The desperate sadness in his face fissured her resolve. He must have sensed the shift in her because he took a half step closer, his hand reaching out tentatively, fingers trailing up her arm. Her pulse quickened as he leaned closer, their faces inches from each other. "I'm so sorry," he breathed.

And with that word—sorry—the spell crumbled. His betrayals, lies, and manipulations cascaded down, causing her to break out of his grasp. She wordlessly pushed past him, ignoring his cries as she ran back to her room desperate for an escape.

The tears slipped out unbidden, and she furiously scrubbed at her face. She was quick to make it back to her room and in her haste, she nearly missed the hyacinth, laid in the same spot as the previous day. She hiccupped, scooping the flowers up, marveling at their seamless transformation to butterflies. Brenden's kindness made her smile despite everything, knowing she had at least one honest companion here.

You have Talia, too, a small voice in the back of her mind said as she unlocked her door, Little Guy perking up from his blanket bed on the floor. *Talia's basically paid to spend time with me; it's not the same.* She flopped onto her bed, Little Guy pouncing up to join her, so light that she didn't even feel him land. He started purring as she stroked his head, nuzzling his face into her hand. "You're right," she said, nodding at the kitten. "I have you, too." She rolled over, trying to get comfortable, and her eyes landed on the pile of books from Terach. *Not tonight*, she thought, pure exhaustion taking hold. Snuggling closer to Little Guy, she closed her eyes, letting the darkness take hold.

Her days started to fall into a reliable pattern; every other day was filled with classes and lore with Terach. She was upgraded to a real desk in Thorne's class, which she took for a huge improvement, despite the healer refusing to further acknowledge her. They even visited the InfirmaryInfirmary several times, though the extent of their contributions was limited to the most superficial of ailments: diarrhea, nausea, mild colds, and the like. She was desperate for patient interaction, and those classes spent wiping out emesis basins were some of the most interesting to her.

Merrill advanced her to Level Two casting class with a lingering snippet of advice. "Don't forget, truly *listen* to your emotions." She nodded, smiled, and all but ran the few feet down the hall to the next classroom. Though her peers were still significantly younger than she, they no longer played games or used the dreaded color cards. Instead, they practiced finding and opening their channels, and soon she mastered casting a flame every time, though how long it lingered still varied by a large margin. She had a hard time maintaining full focus on the open channel connecting her to the casting, and scattered thoughts often caused her to lose the connection altogether.

She spent her "off" days training with Brenden. He continued to anonymously leave flowers at her door. It was their unspoken secret, and she worried that talking of it would spoil its mystery. So she kept her delight at the morphed butterflies to herself, enjoying his easy companionship and ceaseless encouragement as they practiced in the arena.

The rest of her time was dedicated to Little Guy—she gave up searching for a more appropriate name—and studying. She launched into the thickest book Terach had given her, which gave a haphazard genealogy of syphons throughout history, ending with Haddeon. She was shocked to learn that once, their numbers were just as great as casters or healers, but as time went on they dwindled. Whether due to persecution or some genetic component—or something else entirely of which she hadn't thought—Raylyn wasn't sure. The book was nothing but names, birthdays, deaths, and relations. Hard, indisputable facts. She was pleasantly surprised by it.

Several weeks passed, and she was finally growing more confident at the Academy, despite Pria's continued attempt to isolate her. Thorne's class had just ended, and she bent to clear her papers and textbooks. Thorne was the first to leave, as was her custom, and some of her classmates were chattering idly as they gathered their supplies.

"...been reading all night and day," Pria's voice carried to the back of the classroom, self-important and pitchy. Raylyn rolled her eyes, making a beeline for the door. "One must be as prepared as possible if they have hopes to win the competition, right? My father won when he was enrolled in the Academy."

Raylyn was too busy mentally mocking Pria—or Miss Priss, as she had aptly nicknamed her—that she ran straight into Thorne, who reappeared in the doorway. "Sorry, Madam," she said, side-stepping back into the classroom.

Unsurprisingly, Thorne ignored her and turned, addressing the class. "I forgot to mention," she said, tapping a blank piece of parchment on her desk, "The competition is in a little more than a month. We will be sending invitations out to families, so for those of you who wish to share this experience, jot your name down. It doesn't matter if you're competing or just watching in the audience. We extend the offer regardless." Without waiting to see if there were any questions, she flounced away again.

Raylyn's eyes followed her as she walked the few feet from the classroom to the InfirmaryInfirmary door, wasting no time. It was hard to know if Thorne despised teaching or if she was just spread too thin. The influx of refugees continued to increase, many in poor health from lack of medical care or badly injured during their escape. There were too many patients and not enough healers, and Thorne spent day and night working. Her exhaustion was evident in her temper and impatience with their class.

A line formed as students rushed toward the parchment, eager to add their names to the list. Raylyn watched for a moment, torn between adding her nam, and bolting out the door. *I can't face them,* she thought. Turning, she paced down the hall, her throat tight. Nausea boiled in her stomach as her father's face, twisted with betrayal and hurt, flashed through her mind.

She settled onto the only bench in the foyer of the Academy, longing for an escape from the painful memories of her parents. It was too cold outside to sit under her tree, the ground frozen as autumn slowly lost its battle with the ever-approaching winter.

Reaching into her bag, her fingers brushed the old, smooth leather of the journal Terach had given her. *It's just a book,* she thought, pulling it out with a shaky hand. It had been weeks, and Terach was growing impatient with her for ignoring it. The cover opened smoothly, its weight oddly comfortable in her hands. She had to all but bury her nose in it, the font was so small.

> *I fear I am losing her. Every morning when we wake, her tension and pain is so palpable, I've begun to think of it as my own. For several weeks now, I've channeled to her in secret while she sleeps, as she would be livid to know the amount of energy and exertion I've used.*
>
> *I can feel the baby, too. His emotions are harder to read, but I believe there is an overall sense of content-ment. His pulse is like the beating of a humming-bird's wings. It slows when Tralene's pain is the worst, and speeds again after I heal her. I pray nightly—*

"Goddess, protect us from this evil!"

Raylyn peeled her eyes from the text as Pria and her trail of followers passed. They waved their hands in front of them, drawing safety and protection sigils through the air. They had started this new habit last week, and Raylyn fought the urge to hiss at them for fun. Brenden suggested she ignore it, else deal with worsened ramifications. So, instead, she gave them a sickly sweet smile, much to Pria's horror. She glared at her through narrowed eyes before scurrying out the door, an icy breeze sneaking in from outside, prickling Raylyn's skin. She turned back to the journal once they were safely out of sight.

I pray nightly she and the babe will make it another month. She's nearing full term. The midwives say any sooner than this, and our child will have no chance of survival. As it is, Tralene is belligerent about her prescribed bedrest and is eager to do something. They've provided her with knitting, and after a dozen tiny socks, she has lost interest in it altogether. Rumors of her condition are spreading through the Court, though it is becoming twisted and malformed. There are whisperings saying I am tainting her mind, bending her to my will. Oh, Goddess, if they only knew how it is she who has complete control of me!

Even the king is looking at me with suspicion as he watches his youngest niece battle for her life. Do they not realize I would gladly give her mine, if it would mean her safety and health? The war does nothing but raise tensions, and I told Voend the dispute over the sect of land wasn't worth the battle. But fertile land is ever-sought, the greedy always wanting more.

And who am I to place judgement, when just a year
ago I felt the same incessant hunger? And now, as I
write, watching over her sleeping body, her stomach
swelled with our tiny miracle, oh, how my desires
have changed.

She stirs, and like the doting nursemaid I've
become, I am off.

Raylyn stared at the page for several minutes after she
finished reading the entry, her heart in her throat. The
words were not what she expected, and certainly didn't
sound like they belonged to a lunatic. She turned the
book over in her hands, wondering about its credibility.
Who's to say some nutter of a scholar didn't forge the book
in a twisted type of social experiment? She placed it back in
her bag, chewing her lip in concentration as she walked to
casting Level Two.

She was a few minutes early, and a line of parents gathered in the hall outside the door. Her classmates were still
laughably young, ranging in ages from ten to twelve. Some
of the older kids stood by themselves, though most were
accompanied. The side-eye glances and straight-up intru-
sive staring hadn't diminished much, the adults worse than
their children. *What's taking so long?* she thought, just as
a shrill voice cut through the air.

"I'm just not comfortable with it! We should have been
notified. We should've had the right to choose if that *thing*
was allowed to study with our children!" A woman's voice
yelled from the front of the line.

225

Raylyn's stomach sank as a few heads turned to her. She met each person's eye, causing them to turn away. *I'm just a person, for Goddess's sake.*

"Each pupil is perfectly safe in my class, and respectfully, the details of your son's classmates are not inherently yours," her instructor, Master Aerile, replied in his calm, even tone.

"He will *not* be studying in the same room as that monster." Her voice wavered and cracked.

"Of course, I understand. Please know, however, that if you pull him from the class, he will have to undergo another round of testing before we grant re-entry."

The woman muttered a curse as she pulled her son from the line, her fingers clasped around his arm.

"Momma, please, I want to stay. I'm doing really well!" He tried to break free of her grasp, but her grip was steadfast, and the child was too small. Realizing the futility of the situation, he began to cry, tears streaming down his cheeks in defeat. The woman slowed as she walked past her, hatred and fear twisting her face. She spit on the ground at Raylyn's feet, before rushing off, the boy running to keep up.

Heat crept up her neck, and she carefully stepped past the spit on the ground as she moved forward in line, the other children filing into the classroom. Despite the glances from the onlookers, Raylyn kept her head up, fighting the urge to vomit. *I'm just a person*, she thought again. Aerile gave her a sad smile as she passed the threshold. Her mind replayed the scene throughout the entire class, and she couldn't channel even once, the connection unattainable.

CHAPTER 13

TALIA WAS WAITING FOR HER IN HER room when Raylyn stormed in after class. "What's wrong with you?" she asked, looking up in surprise as Raylyn slammed the door closed and locked it for good measure.

"Bad day," she mumbled, dropping her bag and joining Talia. She sat cross-legged on the floor, watching Little Guy eat a plate of salmon and rice, cooked specially for him. Despite her initial misgivings, Talia formed a bond with the cat, and her connections to the chefs in the kitchen resulted in high-quality meals.

"Oh, I almost forgot," Talia said, looking up. "When I got here earlier, someone left some flowers. I picked them up, meaning to put them in a vase for you, and the strangest thing happened! They—"

"Turned into a bunch of butterflies?" Raylyn smiled, her dark mood lightening.

"How'd you know?" she asked, her eyebrows disappearing beneath her newly cropped bangs.

"It's been happening for some time now," she said picking up the empty plate from the ground as Little Guy finished his meal.

"It's a very clever spell. I can't seem to wrap my head around *how* it's done."

Raylyn shrugged. "I can't even do the simplest of casting consistently, so it's way beyond me."

"What do you mean? I thought you've been doing well! I've seen you in the arena practicing with Brenden. Your fireballs are coming along so nicely!"

"Aerile said fire is the most basic element to cast. All it needs is air and energy. The ten-year-olds are better than me. That's no achievement," she huffed.

"You just have to keep practicing. Your doubts get in your way."

Tired of the ceaseless advice, Raylyn shifted the conversation. "How is your training going? You spend more time in the arena than the kitchens now." It was true; most of the time, she only saw Talia during her sessions with Brenden, secluded in a segment of the arena working on her own casting. In truth, she worried a little for the woman; dark circles took permanent residence beneath her eyes, and she was paler than normal. Her continued efforts toward perfecting her competition performance were taking their toll.

"It's okay. I'm not competition ready, that's for sure, but hopefully in another month, I'll have it. I guess it helps that the king hasn't needed me much anymore. Honestly,

I should be heading back down. I just wanted to see how our little prince was doing." She scooped up the cat, kissing him in the middle of his head.

"Oh, so he's *ours*, now, huh? Maybe I'll join you. Class was useless today. I couldn't find the connection even if you handed me a map." Raylyn moved toward the door, following Talia.

Talia stalled for a moment, hand lingering on the door handle. "Aren't you supposed to meet with Brenden today?"

"No, we practice tomorrow, my day off from classes."

"I thought you were supposed to find out about your friend?"

Raylyn slapped her forehead. "Holy Goddess, I completely forgot! What would I do without you?"

"Be late more often, I daresay." Talia grinned, waving as she left.

Raylyn glanced down at her clothes, her tunic and trousers dusty from the road, a small stain on her shirt-sleeve from Little Guy's salmon plate. Deciding to change quickly, she rifled through the wardrobe, choosing a long-sleeved red dress, miniscule flowers embroidered at the cuff. She had been longing to wear it, picturing the look of surprise on Brenden's face when he saw her. She lived in plain clothes; the last time she dressed up had been the feast. Her hair was a knotted mess, and she combed her fingers through it, trying to separate and define the curls. Between the anticipation of spending some time with Brenden *not* training, and scribing to Braya, the sour events from the day slipped away, and she left her room, humming as she continued down the hall.

Brenden said he received a scriber from his men the day before. They were scheduled to arrive in Lakehaven by midmorning and would send word once Braya was safely secured. She hadn't received a letter back yet from her friend, and the availability of the scriber meant they would be able to write to each other instantly. She recited in her mind everything she would say, making a conscious effort to not sprint down the hallways as she headed toward Brenden's study.

As she turned the last corner, she almost crashed into him, resurfacing the memory of them both falling outside the stables so many weeks prior. "I'm late," she said, giving him an apologetic smile. Her face fell when she caught his expression, his eyes wide, lines creasing his forehead. "What's wrong?" Her stomach flipped as he wordlessly handed her a piece of parchment.

Your Highness,

We arrived to Lakehaven this morning, void of any difficulties on the road. The directions led us to the burnt wreckage of a manor, the bones of the described stable still standing, but barely. We've inquired with the townsfolk, who admit the fire raged weeks prior. Only one body was claimed in the disaster, assumed to be the master of the home. The girl, Braya, hasn't been seen since the eve prior to the incident, though there is a warrant out, questioning her involvement in the death.

We can search the surrounding wood, though the lake prevents us from heading north, and the mountain ranges to the east border Cystra. Please advise.

Her eyes scanned the page with such speed, that she reread it twice to be sure she understood. Blood pounded in her ears as she looked back up at Brenden, horrified, the world crumbling away.

"What should I do?" he asked, helplessness straining his words. "I'll send them to search, but if what they say is true, it's been weeks. She could be anywhere."

She glanced back down at the parchment, head muddled. The air was thick, time slowing. *She's gone. She's gone, and it's all my fault.* Black speckles dotted her vision, and she was certain she would succumb to the suffocating weight of this revelation, but a small voice in the back of her mind spoke, a little more confident than previous times. *It's Rowan's fault, not mine,* and the sudden spark of anger melted her panic and grief. It strengthened her, rushing through her body, as life-giving as her blood.

"Do you know where your brother is?" she asked, her voice distant in her ears.

Confusion crossed Brenden's face as he replied. "He was in the library, but Raylyn, what should I do—"

She brushed past him, twisting down the halls. The world was tinged in red, but she hardly noticed as she burst into the library, scanning the room in haste. The door slammed shut behind her, echoing in the quiet chamber. Heads of those nearby snapped toward her in surprise.

"Rowan!" More people turned toward her, concern plain on their faces. Her voice carried far, ringing through the air, and he appeared on the second level landing, extracting himself from behind an aisle of books.

"Raylyn? What's wrong?" He hurried down the staircase, taking two steps at a time.

Her hatred boiled hotter with each step he took, and he startled when he got close enough to see her expression. "What's happened?"

She shoved the parchment at him, snarling. "Look what you've done!"

He read the page, looking up. "I'm sorry about your friend, but I didn't *do* anything. I'm not responsible for some housefire that happened a hundred miles away." He offered her the paper back. "Truly, I am sorry. I hope she's okay."

"Not responsible? Ha!" she shrieked, hysterical. "It's entirely your fault! If you had just let Braya come, this wouldn't have happened! She wouldn't be missing!"

Rowan glanced around as a small crowd gathered, enthralled by their argument. "Could we please go somewhere private to talk about this?"

"I'm not going anywhere alone with you, *manipulator*." She sharpened her words to cut him; if she could hurt him even a fraction of the way he injured her, she would be satisfied. "Goddess forbid your façade cracks, and they see you for the lying narcissist you are!" She waved the parchment in his face. "You need to fix this! You *owe* me."

His eyes narrowed, ripping the paper out of her hand in annoyance. "It's not my fault your friend finally had enough of her abusive father. At least she tried to make his death look like an accident. I hope they are merciful when they find her."

It was the wrong choice of words. The anger she was just barely containing broke free, rushing with a burning pleasure through her veins. The glowing from her palms was a sweet release, and nearby bookshelves began to tremble, a few volumes crashing violently to the floor. The shaking intensified, and Rowan stared at her with wide eyes, taking a few clumsy steps backward.

"Raylyn, I didn't mean that. I'm sorry. It was said in anger." She envisioned him crushed beneath a shelf, smiling. "Raylyn, please," he stumbled, falling to the ground, the entire earth shaking with her rage. The frightened screams of bystanders fell on deaf ears, and they rushed tripping to the exit. She took a step closer to Rowan, who remained splayed on the ground. "Don't do this," he said, eyes searching her face. "This isn't you."

She was prepared to prove to him *exactly* how wrong he was, when the violent trembling ceased, its sudden absence jolting her. Rowan's body sagged with relief. Confused, she turned, Brenden emerging behind her.

"For such scrawny legs," he said, panting, "you run quite fast." His hands were raised, light radiating from his palms.

"Lower your shield!" she demanded through gritted teeth.

"Are you going to kill my brother?" A small smirk lit his face.

"Yes!"

"Then sorry, no. He might be a pain in my ass, but he's still my brother."

"Ahhh!" she yelled, stamping her foot. Rowan pulled himself off the ground, and she launched at him, deciding her fists would work nearly as well as her magic. Hitting an invisible force, she flew backward, collapsing to the floor. "Damn it, Brenden!" she groaned, not realizing the extent of his abilities.

The library was empty besides the three of them; everyone else fled at the onset of Raylyn's earthquake. Her anger fizzled, and as she sat on the floor, completely helpless, she began to cry. Rowan came as close as he dared, crouching in front of her. "Raylyn, I swear I will find her. It was a mistake not to bring her with us, and you *must* believe me if anything happens to her, I will carry that burden with me for the rest of my life." He stood up to leave and nodded reluctantly to Brenden as he passed him. "I guess I owe you one," he said before slipping out of the room.

As soon as the door closed, Brenden released the shield around her, and he rushed to her side, wiping the tears from her cheeks before wrapping his arms around her shaking body. "I'm so sorry," he said over and over, as her sobs echoed through the chamber.

They stayed like this, time meaningless as her tears slowly dried. Sniffling, she met his gaze, his blue eyes soft with kindness. She was suddenly aware of his warmth, the feel of his heartbeat through their clothes. Her stomach knotted as he reached down, wiping a remaining tear from her cheek. Without thinking about the ramifications, she closed the small gap between them and kissed him.

"You're not going," Talia said, crossing her arms as Raylyn scurried around her room, shoving various possessions into her bag.

The previous night passed with dreams of earthquakes as she succumbed to overbearing exhaustion. As dawn broke, the sun barely cresting the horizon, she itched to be on her way before Rowan and his soldiers left. Her stomach recoiled at the thought of him, the pain from his lies rippling through her like a wave.

She shot the woman a glance. "I am," she said, grabbing her spare cloak from the closet and fighting it into the bag.

"Do you have some secret tracking power, too? Are you a hound, going to pick up her scent and sniff her out? Just let Rowan and his guard find her." She bent down, picking up Little Guy who was mewing at her feet. He started associating Talia with mealtime and couldn't understand why his fish wasn't appearing. "And what about him?" she said, gesturing to the cat. "Are you just going to leave him to starve? You have *responsibilities*."

Raylyn hesitated. "You'll have time to stop and check on him while I'm gone, right?"

Talia screwed up her face as she flopped onto the bed in a mock swoon. "Alas, I do have the time. The king isn't requesting my services at all anymore. I don't understand it." She glanced at Raylyn, a spark of concern crossing her face.

"I'm sure he just knows how busy you are, preparing for the competition. So, you will watch Little Guy then?"

"No! It was your brilliant idea to get a cat. That means you can't just go running off whenever you'd like."

Raylyn sighed, setting her overfilled pack on the ground, hopping up onto the bed next to her. "I'm not 'running off.' Braya is *missing*. I chose this place over her once; I won't do it again."

"Ray, they aren't going to let you go," the voice from the doorway said, making both girls jump and Little Guy mewing with disapproval at the sudden commotion.

"Bo!" she rushed to the door, attacking the soldier with a hug.

"I'm sorry about Braya," he said, giving her a little squeeze. "We will do everything we can to find her."

"I have to help," she replied, searching his face.

"Your friend is right. Your place is here, training and learning. Rowan told me how far along you've come. I am so proud of you."

Raylyn suppressed a grimace at the mention of Rowan. "But maybe I can—"

"And what would happen," Bo began, cutting her off gently, "if you lose control again, especially now that your powers are even stronger? Who would search for the girl if you inadvertently killed us all?" She opened her mouth to argue, but he continued talking. "No, it is more important for us all that you stay and master these powers. Do not make me have the king order it himself, for he will. It is in everyone's best interest that you stay."

"Why is it suddenly so vital I master my powers? That could take *years*. Meanwhile Braya is out there somewhere, maybe hurt, maybe *dead*!" She stormed away from Bo, disappointed by his response. She tightened the string of her pack in a futile attempt; it was too burdened to close. Her face burning, she kicked it, scattering her possessions across the floor.

Bo sighed, closing the door with a soft click. "We are potentially on the cusp of war, and you may be the advantage that tips the outcome in our favor. Moreover, word of your abilities hasn't spread from the capital. Do you understand? This is larger than all of us."

Raylyn stared at him, stricken. "Surely, that's an exaggeration."

"The king questions whether rebels attacked Rowan or if it was foreign insurgents. Though we see no troops marching toward our land, my instincts say it was a failed assassination attempt. How truthful do you think King Aedam's reply will be?"

She thought of the feast, when the king announced his plan to write Cystra inquiring about the attack. Her stomach sank. "Maybe they will be dissuaded by their failure."

"For a time, perhaps. Forever? Unlikely. Your existence and skill alone could potentially end a war before it even begins, Raylyn. Do you understand that? You have the ability to destroy battalions of soldiers at once if you gain control of your powers."

Chills prickled her arms, and she couldn't suppress the shudder running through her body.

"Told you, *responsibilities*," Talia chimed in, watching their exchange cross-legged on the bed while Little Guy curled in her lap.

Raylyn rolled her eyes. "Did you know about this?"

"Isn't it obvious? Doesn't everyone? That's why you have these fancy rooms, a designated lady's maid," she gestured to herself with a wink, "and extra training sessions with the prince and the king's advisor. Surely, you didn't think this is *normal*?"

Raylyn flushed, her ears burning. In truth, she thought it was all a reward for healing Rowan. She sat next to Talia, deflated. "But Braya..." she said defeatedly.

"We are leaving now to search. I came to say goodbye and to ensure you aren't planning to follow us." Bo raised one heavy eyebrow, making the edges of her lips twitch upward. "This is for you." He set a roll of parchment on her table.

"What is it?"

"A scriber, so we can write. I know it's pointless to say, but try not to worry. We have some of the best trackers, and I'm confident we will find her."

She swallowed past the knot in her throat. "Thank you, Bo. Be safe, okay?"

"You, as well. Don't forget what I told you before. Don't lose yourself here, Raylyn." He disappeared as the door closed.

She turned to Talia. "I can't fight in a war!"

"Well, obviously not yet. That's why you need to keep training."

"Did the king tell you about this?"

"The king doesn't really tell me anything anymore, but I *may* have overheard a conversation or two a while ago."

"How could you not tell me?" Her fingers twitched with the urge to strangle her.

V"Ray, I seriously thought it was obvious. What does Terach teach you, if not schemes of war?" A small furrow appeared between her brow.

Raylyn's eyes slid to the journal on her bedside table. She hadn't read the next passage yet, half convinced it was a forgery. "History, mostly," she mumbled. She ignored the twist of guilt in her stomach, as she hadn't been taking her lessons with Terach very seriously. Ever since their first session, her misgivings about his abstract ideas of Haddeon and the Goddess left her distracted and unfocused.

"Can't see how that's helpful," Talia said, stretching as she stood. "Time to check in with His Majesty, though it's likely futile. Do you think he'll see me if I bring him a cup of his favorite tea?"

"Don't you think you're overreacting about this a bit? Perhaps he knows how busy you are with the competition. Or maybe he's distracted with the threat of war looming over us."

"Oh, silly girl, there's always threats of war, or famines, or disasters... No, this is different. He's acting ... cold." Her voice fell to a whisper. "I've been serving him for over a year. My father is a distant cousin to the crown, and with my abilities... well, my placement was an obvious choice. His mood has never been so friable, nor has he ever demanded such solitude. The only people he admits for audience lately are the princes and Terach. It's strange." Her face shifted, and she grabbed Raylyn's shoulders, a fire lit in her eyes. "Swear to me this stays between us. If word spreads I'm gossiping about the king's behavior, worse things will happen besides me just losing my position."

"Oh, come now, who would I possibly tell?" Raylyn asked, trying to shake her grip off with a small laugh.

Talia's fingers tightened painfully, her nails digging into her skin. "Swear it," she insisted.

"Goddess, *ouch*. Okay, I swear it." Talia released her, her expression a touch more relaxed.

"I think I will stop and get his tea and butter him up, so to speak. And just in case you get any ideas, I *will not* feed Little Guy if you still plan on sneaking after Rowan."

Raylyn stuck her tongue out to Talia's back as she left. She stared at the closed door a few moments before collapsing onto her bed, chest tightening with a growing sense of helplessness. If anyone else came to her with the same advice, she wouldn't have listened. But it had been Bo, and she trusted him fully. This didn't make her inactivity any easier. She lay in bed, studying the swirling patterns on the ceiling, as the weight of her uselessness crushed her.

Mew. She ignored the cat, who called up to her from the floor. She had a mind to just leave him there to jump up himself. *Mew. Mew.*

"Alright, fine," she muttered, rolling over and stretching to reach Little Guy. Just as her fingers brushed his fur, he darted under the bed. Unwisely, she stretched farther, hoping to grab him without getting up. Gravity won, and she fell, sliding off the bed and crashing her shoulder on the corner of the bedside table. The clutter which previously resided on the table scattered onto the floor with the sharp cracking of breaking glass.

"Damn it," she moaned, curling into a ball on the floor, her shoulder searing with pain. Little Guy stayed silently remorse under the bed as she straightened, wincing. "*Damn* it," she repeated, eyeing the mess of glass and papers. The pieces of the broken goblet were sharp, and she was careful not to cut herself as she picked them up. Her heart sank when she grabbed the leather journal from Terach, terrified it was damaged. Holding her breath, she turned the book over in her hands, inspecting for torn or wet pages. Mercifully, it was unharmed, the crisp yellowed pages still dry.

She moved to close the book, but the passage caught her eye. It was opened to a random entry about halfway through the tome.

They've taken her from me. Oh Goddess, I'm going to lose my mind, for they've taken her, and no one will tell me where! The king says it's for her health, but if he only knew! He thinks he hides his emotions, but I still sense his distrust, his fears.

These healers don't have my strength or ability. How long will she and the babe have without my constant diligence? Days? Hours? I need to find them, but everyone around me is suspicious; they think her illness is my doing, but no one will say it outright. I feel their fear and judgement and suspicion everywhere I go. Their eyes betray them as well—narrowed, cutting looks. But I swear this to be true: if they do not tell me where she is, I will turn into the evil thing they think I am. I will be the product of their creation. Goddess, they took her.

Bile rose in the back of her throat as she snapped the journal shut, tossing it onto the table as though it would burn her hands. She could feel his angst and though a hundred years had passed, it was as if his words leapt through the page to pull at her emotions, begging her to help. She couldn't read any further. It was torturous. *Mew.* Startled, she whipped her head around. Little Guy sat on the pillow on her bed, grooming his paw in a relaxed, dignified manner.

"You little stinker," she said. "*Now* you can get up here just fine, huh?" She picked up the remaining mess from the floor, mind still on the passage. *He was an effector, too.* None of the histories she read mentioned this. Had it been a secret? Or did the detail get lost with time? *He could feel the emotions of his unborn child.* Pain dripped from his words, coming to life after a hundred years. It wasn't the ramblings of a crazed and delusional murderer, and he certainly didn't seem like the devil she was taught to fear. *What if understanding him is the key to understanding myself?*

She grabbed the journal before she shot out of her room. Due to the commotion the day before, she missed her session with Terach. Racing through the chilly stone halls, her throat constricted with hope. She was still leagues away from controlling her casting powers and barely used her syphoning abilities. *What if everything he's saying isn't radical nonsense? Maybe he knows how I can control it.*

Two girls scuttled past her in the usually abandoned corridor leading to Terach's study. Tears streamed down the shorter girl's face, and she gripped a thin, gray shawl tightly around her shoulders. The other girl was whispering to her in a soothing voice, one hand on her shoulder, guiding her.

"Are you okay?" Raylyn asked, stopping as they passed. They didn't acknowledge her as they raced by, intent on their departure. Her brows furrowed in confusion as she watched them retreat down the hall. The wing was empty besides Terach's office; in the weeks of her studies, she had never encountered another soul down this hall. She turned, deciding the girls probably slipped down here for a private conversation, away from the whispering walls of the busier sections of the castle.

Terach opened the door after the first knock, his eyes widening when he saw her. "Raylyn, I wasn't expecting you." He ran a hand through his hair, smoothing some of the disarrayed strands. "Come in." He stepped back, making room for her to enter as he fastened his shirt, unbuttoned at the collar. The office was a chaotic disaster, books and parchment strewn haphazardly on the floor. "Just tidying up a bit. Missed you last evening." He bent, sweeping up the papers and piling them on the desk. Raylyn helped, grabbing the discarded books from the floor, perplexed by their abuse.

"I was a bit ... indisposed," she mumbled lamely, placing the precarious pile on his desk.

"Hm, yes, I heard all about your little temper tantrum in the library. Luckily for everyone, Brenden was there to shield you." He sat lazily in the chair behind the desk, unrolling his cuffed shirt sleeves absent-mindedly.

"I—it—" she stammered. "It was *not* a temper tantrum." Her voice raised an octave. "My best friend is missing because of Rowan's lies. I was angry. I *am* angry."

"Did you lose control of your yourself because of your emotions?"

"Well... Yes, obviously."

"Temper tantrum, like a toddler." He grinned, as if pleased at his own joke.

She rolled her eyes and wondered if she made a mistake coming here, but her grip tightened on the journal, and she sat opposite Terach, determined. She shifted the book between her hands, setting it gently on the desk between them. "How truthful is this?" she asked, eyes boring into his face, searching for a trace of dishonesty, a twitch, anything to give away some hidden deceit.

"I told you when I gave it to you. I believe that is one of Haddeon's journals from the time of his fall." He stared back at her, unwavering. "Why would you think otherwise?"

"Because it goes against my beliefs and the lessons I've been taught. Haddeon was supposed to be the devil, evil reincarnated. Not some man," she gestured to the book, "anxious about his wife and unborn child."

"Interesting, isn't it, how history becomes so twisted? You can typically find pieces of the truth if you dig hard enough."

"But it doesn't make sense. Why villainize him? What did society gain from it?

Terach leaned back in his chair, eyes narrowing as he studied her. "We are feeling exceptionally inquisitive today, hm?" It was true, her demeanor shifted. She normally sat through these lessons, half-listening as Terach rambled on about genealogy and how syphons slowly died out.

Stony-faced, she nodded. "I am hoping there's some secret in here," she tapped the journal lightly, "which will make all of this make sense. My abilities, my emotions, maybe even the war. I'm not making the kind of progress for which I hoped, and I need learn how to master all of this, and quickly." Braya was center in her mind. If she read through the journal a month ago, maybe it would've shown her the key to unlocking her full powers. But she wasted time, squandered it away with biases and prejudices. "I just won't be fooled again," she said resolutely, hands tightening into fists. "So, if what you're spewing is pretty lies to ease my discomfort about syphons, please enlighten me now. If this is fake," she nodded at the journal, "take it back and burn it, for all I care. I need the truth."

"You're very passionate," Terach mumbled. He picked up the journal, thumbing through the pages with a sort of familiarity. "Why would I waste both our time with lies? Everything I teach you is to help you learn. If I reserve a few scraps of information here and there, well, be assured it is for good reason. All truths make themselves known with time. I *am* curious what brought about this sudden change of heart? You should have made your misgivings known weeks ago."

Bo's words echoed through her mind, her stomach flipping. "A reliable friend mentioned the king's intentions of using me as a weapon against Cystra. But how am I to fight when I can only cast if I'm raging with anger? And I've only syphoned a handful of times. I don't even know the extent of what I can do!" Blood rushed to her cheeks as she admitted this, worried her words were self-important and vain. *I may as well let it all out*, she thought, rubbing her temples to ease the low throbbing in her head. "And I don't particularly want to keep almost killing people on accident," she added.

Terach was silent for a long time before he replied. Her headache pounded in synch with her heartbeat as she sat, self-conscious and vulnerable. "In a matter of months, your entire identity has shifted. What you're feeling is completely normal and expected. The doubt, the confusion. I understand your mistrust, but I'm confident you can take the words in this book to heart. You're certain that neither of your parents has your ability?" he asked, not for the first time.

Raylyn nodded, the motion intensifying the throbbing in her mind. "My mother was just a healer. She was frightened the first time I syphoned. I saw it in her eyes." It took all her concentration to form the words.

"And your father?"

"I don't even know—" She caught herself at the last moment, almost revealing her unknown paternity. *If my head would just stop hurting*, she thought, desperately scrambling for words. "I don't even know how—how he really felt about my abilities. I didn't get to talk to him much before I left my village. But no, he was a caster, definitely only a caster." For half a heartbeat, she thought she saw a strange glint in Terach's eyes, certain her secret was discovered. She blinked, and his features were cool and relaxed as normal.

"It must be difficult, having no one like yourself with whom to connect. Finish reading this. I don't know if it will contain the answers you seek, but perhaps just understanding one person with the same powers as yourself will help put some concerns into perspective for you. As for the war and the king... Those are matters for the future. Last I heard, His Majesty believes war is preventable, and will do everything in his power to not overlook any indiscretions of Cystra and King Aedam."

"But," Raylyn interjected, "they sent an assassination attempt on Rowan! Not to mention the endless stream of refugees we are harboring, healing, and feeding. It can't go on like this forever."

"Indeed, it cannot. The king has reasons, however trivial, for his decisions. And while I'm in agreement with your assumptions, the assassination attempt hasn't been declared as an outright attack from Cystra. But these are not your problems to solve. You need to focus on your training and self-discovery for a while." He stood, running a hand through his hair again. "I do have to get to work, Raylyn. I have an idea for next lesson, however, and it has nothing to do with books. I'll meet you tomorrow evening at your room."

CHAPTER 14

THE WALK BACK TO HER ROOM TOOK ages, head throbbing with each step. She passed one of the few outside windows in the corridor, her eyes watering in the stream of bright sunlight. She typically trained with Brenden before midday, but if she couldn't get her headache to ease, that would be impossible. Pausing in a small alcove, she held her head between her hands, trying to feel the cause of her pain. She always struggled healing her own headaches. Was it from lack of sleep, overexertion, dehydration, stress? There were too many variables, and she was too biased.

Warmth flowed through her palms as she channeled, addressing all the likely problems. It was worth the drain on her energy to forgo guessing which issue caused her pain. A long minute passed as the aching lessened by degrees before it dissipated completely. As if a fog lifted, her focus sharpened, the light no longer blinding her. *Haven't had a headache like that since ... the night before arriving to the capital.* Hot flames dancing in the roaring wind flashed in her mind. *I'll need to buy some of that herb Loren gave me for the after-effects next time,* she mused as she walked back to her chamber, wondering if there was any stocked in the casting wing at the Academy.

It was past time to head down to the arena; Brenden was likely already waiting. But what was the point? All the practicing and classes yielded little results. Chewing her lip, she debated, stomach churning, thinking of the night before. She had rushed out after their kiss, embarrassment and misery tangling together in a knotted mess. *Why did I do that?* she thought bitterly. He didn't seem to mind, though. She could almost feel the ghost of his fingers twisting through her hair, pulling her closer. And then, she had bolted from the room without another word. *The library is much more appealing than facing him right now.*

She found one of the many small reading nooks on the second story of the library, deep in the back of the chamber. Sitting down into one of the plush chairs, she opened the journals. Her worries about Brenden and what their kiss meant, Rowan and his lies, and even Braya faded away as she lost herself in the small curving script.

> *Voend had the audacity to come to my chambers this morning, urging me to join the front. Casualties are mounting on both sides—such unnecessary death, to what end? He said it would be a reprieve from my incessant worrying about Tralene and the baby. Would it stand to say I acted out of anger when I attacked him? If the hall had been empty, perhaps*

Voend would have brushed it off as soon-to-be father jitters. But alas, it wasn't empty. Now he is in the InfirmaryInfirmary, and I have two guards stationed outside my door.

The effect is diminished, though, as I can nearly taste their unease through the wall. And rightly so! What chance do they have if I decide to turn against them? Even the best shields can't pull their defenses in time. Perhaps the mutterings in the halls about me are sound. Perhaps I am turning into the demon they say.

Raylyn turned the page, brow furrowing as she studied detailed sketches of bedroom furniture, insects, the sun. *A way to pass the time?* she wondered as she flipped through, finally landing on the next passage.

Three days. I've been locked here for three days without the whisper of how they are! Meals brought to me like a prisoner. After all I have done! Would he sit on the throne if not for me? It's obvious they need me to win this border dispute!

I'm done. I warned the guards I will be seeing her before the sun sets, damn the consequences. If they do not bring her to me, I will pull the castle down around me until she is found safely.

More blank pages.

He speaks as if she is not long for the world, and we are to make haste.

"Who's *he*?" Raylyn muttered to herself.

It is with trembling hands I write. But why? For my words will likely be burned as sacrilege. Me, Haddeon, the demon come to eat souls and decay the world ... and what did I do, but prove them right?

Mere strands of life were all that held her here, so pale and weak and heart nothing more than a soft fluttering. And I reacted—Goddess, I reacted— and he was in the room, though I screamed at him to leave. But, it was his niece, and he was scared ... and now the king is lifeless next to me, but Goddess, her heart is beating like a ram, and there is color prickling her cheeks, and there! The baby—our baby—gaining strength as well. But will I see his birth? Will I watch him grow? Or will they hang me for regicide?

But Goddess, I screamed at him to leave.

Raylyn stared at the passage in stunned silence, breathing quickly. *If this is true, then Haddeon killed the king, too. Did Terach tell anyone else? What would they think about him possessing such a book?* She turned the page.

I thought her smile would save my soul from dam- nation when I first saw it. Two years prior, when I finally battled my way to Court. The rumors of her beauty traveled to the edges of the world, of course, but to behold her was another thing entirely. And to speak to her was to fall in love. Deep brown eyes and chestnut hair with a patch of silver above her right ear—kissed by the Goddess, they said. But she told me in confidence, it was just a birthmark, like any other.

When she woke and saw me, oh how her smile melted my anxieties, and I knew in that instant all will be well, as long as we are together ... until her eyes landed on the corpse of her uncle. I was ready with a dozen excuses, a hundred lies, but the words wouldn't pass my lips, and she already knew I was to blame, she always knows...

She won't voice it aloud, but her resentment is building. She recoils at my touch. Her eyes grow dark and distant, her answers short and clipped. Her lies convinced the guards I am blameless. And who would question her? She is naught but an angel come to walk to earth, loved by all.

Perhaps it was retribution, the king's death. Payment for the torture of our separation. The repercussion for believing the superstitions the Court is singing about me. And in the end, does it matter, if she is alive and the babe is healthy? For this is all I ask, all I need. What a fool he was, for whisking her away! They are mine, and I will protect them, no matter the cost.

Goosebumps climbed Raylyn's arms as she continued reading, the entries starting to ramble, the writing growing tighter together as she grew closer to the end of the journal. She skipped past a rough week's worth of rambling about the princess's illness as it continued to wax and wane. Haddeon's musings began to go around in circles as he repeated the same qualms about whether Tralene would ever forgive him for accidently syphoning the king's life. Raylyn was about to put the journal down, but the next entry was much clearer.

The midwives came to our chamber this morning. They gave Tralene a canister of herbal tea and told her it was time we meet our son. A few weeks too early, in my opinion, but a man's word is nothing in these matters. They tried to dismiss me from the room, ha! As if I will leave her side again! We will meet our son soon, and the world will begin to right itself.

Raylyn chewed her lip, her eyes narrowed. The princess supposedly died while pregnant—there were no reports the baby was born. She turned the page eagerly, nearly ripping the fragile paper.

It was blank. She kept flipping, but there was nothing else, the text ended with no explanation, no closure. She snapped the journal closed, unsatisfied. *What good did this do?!* she thought, scowling. She debated going to Terach's office to berate him but decided against it. He likely wouldn't still be there, and she would see him tomorrow evening anyway. She went back to her room to study, surprised to see the flowers she came to expect were inexplicably absent. *Brenden must be offended I didn't show up.*

Thorne stormed into the classroom carrying a mug and a stack of papers, her mouth twisted into a scowl. The low mutterings in the classroom ceased immediately, sensing her dangerous mood. She took a deep drink, eyes closing for a few seconds before turning to address the room. "We are in desperate need of some additional help in the InfirmaryInfirmary," she said, rubbing her face in exhaustion. "I've been working the past two nights with a few minutes' sleep scattered here and there. Three of you will be chosen within the next month for night shifts. You will, of course, be mentored beneath our seasoned healers, but please prepare yourselves for the upcoming responsibility."

Raylyn nearly sprang from her seat in excitement. *Finally*! Their sessions in the InfirmaryInfirmary were too few and too brief. Changing linens and emptying chamber pots was important, of course, but offered nothing in terms of expanding her abilities.

A murmur ran through the room as her classmates turned toward each other, whispering. Raylyn watched, in stunned surprise, as Pria raised her hand and began speaking. "Madam, sincerest apologies, but did you say *night* shifts? Because overnights are quite inconducive to my current schedule, and my father—"

Thorne's eyes were narrowed slits. "Let me make this very clear. I don't give two dead rats who your father is." The air stilled as everyone held their breaths. "If overnights aren't *conducive* for you, then very well." Pria let out a sigh of relief, relaxing back into her chair. "You may leave."

"What?" Pria asked blankly.

"Go ahead, there's the door. You think you should be handed your success and position? If you want to become half the healer your father is, then you will work your way up, just like the rest of us." Thorne stared the woman down. "Well?" she asked when Pria made no motion to leave.

"I'll stay," she quipped, voice small. Raylyn fought to suppress a grin. It was about time she was knocked down a notch or two.

Thorne's eyes swept over the rest of the room. "That goes for everyone. If anyone here thinks they deserve special treatment, please, save me the wasted time and leave." No one moved. "Very well. Let's begin.

"Today we are going to be examining how to assess when a wound or illness is too advanced to treat and how to use our skills to comfort the dying, as opposed to fighting the inevitable." The lesson was arduous, referencing multiple of their textbooks, including a section from *Useful Herbs and Fungi*. Helena Lightier studied complex illnesses and the healing properties of different organic materials, but even she understood certain diseases were too intricate to heal. "You can read and study for years, for your lifetime, but one of the best ways to learn the right action is by practicing," Thorne said, sitting on the top of her desk at the front of the room. "There is a certain *feel* about a person who is close to the Goddess's door. Almost an aura about them. You must attune to your patient's auras, or you will be incapable of identifying this."

Raylyn paused while taking notes, her ink-stained hand starting to cramp. She could usually sense exactly that which Thorne described, never realizing it was a special skill. It came as naturally to her as her vision.

"What are some common terminal diseases which would kill a healer if they tried to cure them?" Thorne rarely allowed class engagement; they typically sat silently at their desks taking notes. It was no surprise when a dozen hands shot eagerly into the air, desperate for a scrap of praise from the instructor. Raylyn, knowing her participation would do nothing but provoke Thorne's anger, sat still in her seat. Thorne picked students at random, writing their answers on the board. *Advanced Tumors. Falling Sickness. Withering Disease. Lockjaw. Black Fever.* The list continued. Healers were capable of incredible things, but they didn't have the strength of the Goddess.

Thorne continued writing, even after people stopped shouting out answers. The room was quiet, save the scratching of quills as they copied her writing, adding to their notes. Diseases Raylyn never heard of—*Infantile Paralysis, Phthisis, Apoplexy*—were scattered amongst others she was familiar with.

She jotted the growing list down, pausing for a moment when she arrived at the word *Consumption*. She chewed her lip, perplexed at its addition. Consumption was curable. Difficult to treat, of course, but curable, nonetheless. *Another test?* she wondered. With slow reluctance, she raised her hand in the air, waiting nearly a minute before Thorne turned, seeing her.

"Are you having trouble understanding the material, Miss Ashton?" Thorne asked, raising her eyebrows pointedly.

Raylyn ignored the insult. "I was just curious, Madam, why you included Consumption." She ignored her classmates as several turned in their seats to stare at her.

"Because we are learning about terminal illnesses," Thorne said flatly, turning back to the board with an air of dismissal.

"It's not terminal, though," Raylyn insisted. "A few years ago," she continued, "a neighboring mountain village implored my village for help; they had an outbreak of a very catching coughing fever. I went with my mother and a group of our healers to help. It took weeks of consistent treatment, but we cured them."

Thorne didn't miss a beat. "If they were *cured*, then it wasn't Consumption."

Raylyn tried to fight her increasing frustration with the healer. "It *was* Consumption! They had all the symptoms: weakness, fever, bloody cough lasting for weeks. We could feel the damage in their lungs when channeling."

"Enough!" Thorne said, slapping her hand down on her desk and causing her mug to slosh. She took a deep breath, sighing before she spoke again. "There are many illnesses which can cause similar symptoms." Her voice was clipped and strained, as if it was taking all her self-control to keep from screaming. "You think you know better than all the master healers? I've had enough of your interruptions."

"We actually did reference Pleore's text, *Pulmonarious and Tussis,* for our treatment practices, and his method *was* successful."

"Get out!"

Raylyn jolted. "But, I just—"

"Out!" she repeated, gesturing a sweeping hand toward the door. "Apparently, there's nothing I can teach you, wise *Madam* Ashton," she sneered, her eyes angry slits again. "Don't bother wasting any more of your time coming back."

Blood rushed in Raylyn's ears, distorting her hearing as if submerged under water. Arguing further would only exacerbate Thorne's anger. Dazed, she scrambled, shoving her books and notes into her bag. Most of her classmates sat in fake obliviousness, eyes fixed to their desks. Pria met her eyes, smirking and gave her a small wave goodbye when Thorne turned her back.

Raylyn stormed down the hall, irate with the injustice of the situation. *Thrown out for questioning blatant inaccuracy? The last time this happened, I was awarded a desk.* Seething, she replayed it over in her mind. Thorne wasn't angry because Raylyn was obstinate. It was because she was proven wrong and had her errors put on display for the entire class to see. Banishing Raylyn was nothing more than petty revenge.

She took a steadying breath as she escaped outside. Exhaling, the air steamed into a miniature cloud around her face. Tiny flakes of snow drifted lazily from the sky, and she watched them for a moment, surprised. It was the first precipitation in weeks. Shrugging on her cloak, she hastened back to the castle, ignoring the pang of guilt at skipping her casting class. The desire to distance herself from Thorne outweighed her worry about absenteeism. *Probably wouldn't be successful casting, anyway*, she thought scornfully, pulling up her hood as the snow began to fall harder.

The stone of the castle halls locked in the frigid air. She brushed the snow from her shoulders, leaving a slowly melting puddle behind her. Warmth seeped from the kitchens and the enticing scent of simmering stew and fresh bread pulled her inside. The kitchens were always active, reminding her very much of a beehive. But today, there was an increased vigor about the workers, who didn't acknowledge her as she approached. The nearest stove held the slowly bubbling stew, equipped with bowls, spoons, and sliced airy bread. It was usually kept stocked with a simple meal for servants and students alike to serve themselves. She ducked forward, dodging a woman juggling two trays of towering glasses. She danced past Raylyn with a practiced ease. "Be quick about it, eh? We got work ta do, His Majesty and his demands." Using her hip to open one of the double doors, she disappeared into the inner kitchens.

Raylyn ladled a bowl full, topping it with several pieces of bread, sucking her belly in as a man passed behind her in the same fashion as the woman before but carrying plates instead. Raylyn marveled at the enormous pile—stacked nearly four feet high—and wondered how it didn't topple over.

"He's a caster," Talia whispered in her ear, making her jump and spill some of the stew. "Such simple things mesmerize you."

"Damn," Raylyn swore, swooping to clean the mess on the floor. She could only imagine the reprimand from the kitchen supervisor if she caused someone to slip. *I'll be banned from the kitchens, too,* she thought bitterly. She glared up at Talia. "You snuck up on me!"

Talia shrugged and jumped up to sit on a nearby counter, swinging her legs. "Shouldn't you be at the Academy right now? And hey—toss me some of that," she said, pointing to the loaf on the stove.

"Thorne kicked me out," she replied, handing her some of the bread. Talia ate it in three large bites, hardly pausing to breathe.

She swallowed, wincing. "You really got on her bad side, huh?"

"Obviously. What're you doing here, anyway, visiting a *friend*?"

"Alas, I have broken Kitchen Boy's heart. Apparently, it's rude to forget someone's name after spending so much time with them." She shot Raylyn a devious grin. "No, I'm waiting for the king's tea. He's very particular on how it's prepared."

"So, he's still seeing you then!" Raylyn said. "That's great—"

"Shh!" Talia hissed, her face darkening. "The walls have ears here."

Raylyn rolled her eyes and ate the rest of her meal in silence. Just as she was taking the last bites, a motherly looking woman with a soiled apron busted through the doors, carrying a silver tray loaded with a kettle and small teacups. "Much thanks, Ri," Talia said, hopping up to grab it.

"If I have to tell you to stay off my counters one more time, I'll get the switch out! Stop trying my patience, Talia!" The words were menacing, but the woman's voice was warm with affection. She kissed the top of Talia's head, gave Raylyn a warm smile, and disappeared back into the depths of the kitchen.

"Who's that?" Raylyn asked as they left, the coolness of the halls pricking her skin with goosebumps after the warmth of the kitchens.

"That's Ri, she's basically in charge of running the kitchens... She's like my makeshift mom here. Took me under her wing when I first arrived."

They walked in quiet companionship for a few minutes, Talia glancing over her shoulder a few times. Apparently satisfied by their seclusion, she whispered, "He's not right. This," she raised the tray up slightly, "is the only way I can get him to admit me. And even then, I set down the tray and am dismissed almost immediately."

Raylyn chewed her lip, thinking. "Is there anything you may have done to offend him somehow?"

"No! And it's not just me he's refusing to see, it's almost everyone. I just *know* something's not right."

"Should we... I don't know, maybe tell someone?" Raylyn suggested, unsure how to help.

Talia looked at her as if she had grown a second head. "We would be toeing the line of treason, spreading accusations about the king's behavior. And anyway," she continued as they climbed the staircase leading to his study, "who could we tell?"

"What about Terach?" He was the king's advisor, after all; if anyone would be able to help, it would be him.

"Raylyn," Talia said, frowning, "I told you to be careful with Lord Terach; he's dangerous. And definitely not trustworthy."

She bit back her reply. Talia wasn't one to change her mind easily, but Raylyn couldn't see any reason to not trust him. He was kind and knowledgeable and welcomed her with open arms. Pleading his case would only cause her to close off again, and this was the most open Talia had been in weeks. "Maybe Brenden, then?" she asked reluctantly. The thought of approaching him with qualms about his father didn't seem very appealing, to say the least, but if something was truly wrong with the king, then someone needed to intervene.

"Hm. Maybe," Talia muttered as they approached to door to the king's study. Two guards were stationed on either side of the entrance, though Raylyn couldn't reason their purpose; the door was enchanted somehow to only admit royal blood or those authorized by the king. The men were large, hulking figures, muscles well-defined beneath their leather armor. No swords hung at their belts, but she was certain their casting abilities would make up for lack of weapons.

"You should go," Talia whispered, hardly glancing at her. Pushing her shoulders back, she raised her chin slightly as she approached the guards, carrying the tray as if it were a precious treasure.

"See you later," Raylyn said, but Talia was already halfway through the doorway and didn't bother to say goodbye.

She continued back to her chamber, melancholy settling into her chest. Her rage at Thorne dissipated, leaving a hollow ache for that which she had lost. *No more healing classes, no assisting in the Infirmary.* It was a cruel joke; she was inches away from unlocking so much knowledge—on the verge of honing her craft—and it was all snatched away in a moment. As she approached her room, her chest ached a little more when she noted the threshold void of the purple flowers. *It's my fault*, she thought as the entered her chamber, stomach twisting as her kiss with Brenden flashed through her mind. In that moment, there was nothing she despised more than herself and all her foolish decisions.

Tap, tap, tap. She jumped up, rushing to the door. *Finally.* She was waiting the better part of an hour for Terach to show up for her lesson. The afternoon had dragged in the slow guise of studying. Talia never showed up to tell her how her meeting went with the king. Brenden didn't bother coming to ask where she was the last couple of days. Her disappointment sent her into a sour mood, darkening her thoughts until she could focus on nothing else, settling to lie in bed and ruminate on all the choices she ever made.

She ran a quick hand through her hair, smoothing the strands down and hoping she didn't look like someone who sulked in bed all afternoon. Pulling the door open, she forced a smile for Terach, who waited expectantly.

"Good evening, Raylyn," he said, inclining his head in greeting. "Are you ready?"

Despite the weeks she lived here, there were still several sections of the castle she had yet to explore. Classes and training took up most of her time, and the free hours she did have were spent with Talia or Little Guy. She was familiar with the path Terach took, leading her down to the first floor of the castle, past the occasional table laden with ancient pottery, hidden alcoves with soft seating, reading nooks tucked into corners. The castle was beautiful, if too lavishly decorated.

They made it to the main foyer, the paintings of past kings gazing down over the room. Terach turned to her, smiling. "Just a bit farther," he said, stepping up to an intricate tapestry. The stitching was marvelous, and from a distance, Raylyn mistook it as a watercolor painting of a thunderstorm, a single tree struck by a bright bolt of lightning. Terach lifted a segment of the tapestry, revealing a plain wooden door. "After you," he said, his grin widening at the shock on her face.

She entered, a blanket of darkness enveloping her. She stepped hesitantly, the small illumination from the foyer did little to penetrate the endless blackness ahead of her. "It's quite dark—"

Several balls of clear, bright light momentarily blinded her, cutting off her words. Terach winked, his hand raised in front of him, palm glowing. She watched as it faded, signaling an end to his casting. And yet, the orbs remained suspended in the air above them. "How did you do that?" She had been wondering since her first night here how the orbs were powered. They had a seemingly endless supply of energy.

"A little trick," he said, reaching into the pocket of his cloak. He handed her a smooth, black stone. "Be careful with that: it's worth quite a bit."

"It's like the one in the arena!" she exclaimed, feeling foolish for not realizing sooner.

Terach looked at her with a raised brow. "Yes, though I'm curious how you know about that. These stones aren't common knowledge."

Subconsciously, she began picking the skin around her thumbnail, realizing her mistake. "I, uh, was curious about the shield around the arena, and asked Brenden about it," she admitted reluctantly, hoping Brenden wouldn't be reprimanded.

Terach nodded. "I should have known with your curious mind you would ask about things most people don't even notice." He gave her a small smile, and her muscles relaxed with relief. He began walking, the orbs moving in sync, illuminating the passage. It was narrow, just wide enough for her and Terach to walk side-by-side, and the stone floor and walls were icy, sucking the heat from her limbs. She shivered, pulling her cloak tighter around her arms.

After several minutes, they arrived at another wooden door, identical to the one at the start of the passage. Terach opened it, the orbs shooting into the new chamber. It was a disaster. The room had imploded on itself—the walls and ceiling were caved in, massive stones and fallen masonry scattered on the floor. Dust coated everything, as if no one had stepped foot inside since its demise.

"The Hall of Sorrows," Terach said, stepping around her into the chamber, leaving footprints in the thick dirt coating the floor. "This once was a prominent part of the castle; records show it used to be the grand ball room ... It's rumored to be where Haddeon killed his wife, Princess Tralene." His words were soft as he paced, his footing occasionally sliding in the rubble.

Raylyn watched him, breathless at the level of destruction. "I don't think he killed her," she said quietly, finding a large piece of stone and sitting on its ledge.

Terach appraised her. "Indeed? Why is that?"

"If the journal you gave me was truly written by Haddeon's hand, it proved his love. He wouldn't kill her."

"Interesting theory," he sighed, sitting on a stone adjacent to her. "What else have you gleaned from the journal? I assume you've finally finished reading it?"

"I have," she said. "Mostly, I feel disappointed by its ending."

Terach nodded wordlessly, surveying the room and its destruction. "Dozens of people have tried to restore this part of the castle, until about twenty years ago when we gave up, deciding to live around it. It was in here I found the journal."

Raylyn, who was absent-mindedly drawing her foot through the soot, looked up in surprise. "Really? I wouldn't think anything could be recovered in this mess."

Terach gestured to the small area where the rocks were unnaturally orderly. "We've tried over the years to excavate the area, but it's cursed. We can shift some of the smaller boulders around, but after time, they migrate back to their original positions. It was during one of those excavation attempts the journal was unearthed."

His words reminded her of something Talia said weeks prior. "Stories say the only one able to repair it is Haddeon himself."

Terach raised an eyebrow at her. "I'm surprised you've heard those tales."

Raylyn smiled, and the two sat amidst the destruction, their silence an ode to the lives lost. The air held the ghosts of memories: parties filled with echoing laughter, string quartets and sopranists, dancing... It was all muted beneath a silent pulsing of raging pain. "Why would Haddeon's journal be located in what used to be a ballroom?"

"I have a theory this is where Haddeon and Tralene were when their child was born," Terach replied solemnly.

"Tralene is said to have died while still carrying the unborn baby," Raylyn argued.

Terach stared at her for a moment, his face unreadable, and her eyes fell to the floor. It always made her insides squirm when she looked too long into someone's eyes, as if trying to read their soul. "I'm *quite* sure Tralene did birth the baby, and there were severe complications. You read yourself the pregnancy took a heavy toll on her. Without Haddeon's continued intervention, they never would have survived so long. Haddeon's powers were other-worldly, almost a God himself." Raylyn fidgeted, uncomfortable with the outrageous claim. Terach must have noted her sudden discomfort. "Or demon-like, whatever have you. I imagine he tried healing his wife and child, but their ailments were too severe. What happens if you attempt to cure an illness too advanced?"

"You risk advanced energy expenditure, up to and including your own demise," she said softly, her eyes large with wonder.

"Right. Imagine having powers of a God—fine, demon—and losing the love of your life and your newborn babe. I think Haddeon reached out seeking energy sources but was channeling them into the bodies of those already deceased. And he kept syphoning, spreading death and destruction throughout the castle until there was no one left." He paused for a moment, his eyes fixed to the ground and staring far away. "It's a wonder he only demolished a portion of the castle and didn't level the entire thing to the ground."

It was an interesting theory, Raylyn had to admit. The journal did substantiate several of his ideas, but a large portion was speculation. *What good does it do to wonder about such things?* She stood, brushing the dirt off the seat of her pants, and walked in the small clearing, examining the boulders and rubble. The biggest piece of stone was in the center of the room, and it appeared to be a large, solid portion of the ceiling. Raylyn stared, wondering how much a piece of rock that size would weigh.

Terach appeared at her side. "Are you ready to practice?" he asked.

"Practice what?"

"Syphoning."

"Here? But how? There's nothing here to syphon from." She looked at him quizzically. Unless he meant for her to syphon *him*, which she absolutely wouldn't do.

"I have a second theory: that you may find power within the stones themselves." Now, she was certain he was crazy, fear prickling in her stomach. Talia had warned her to be careful around him, and now she was isolated in an abandoned part of the castle with someone who may have lost half his mind. Whether he sensed her unease or realized how bizarre his words sounded, he continued. "Just open a connection to the stones. If I'm wrong, we can go to the pig pens and assist the butcher with the next slaughter. But at least *try*."

"Okay," she said hesitantly, turning to the enormous central stone. She closed her eyes, focusing, and the channel opened just as easily as it had during her testing, as instinctual as breathing. And then it hit her, a chaotic disarray of screaming power... anger, sorrow, *pain*. She stumbled as it slammed into her, falling hard to her knees. Severing the connection, she gasped, trying to catch her breath. She knelt as her heartbeat slowed, ensuring the only emotions she felt were her own. She glared up at Terach, who watched her with wide eyes. "Did you know that was going to happen?"

He blinked a few times, as if dazed, then reached down, offering her a hand. "What exactly did happen, besides you falling?"

She accepted his assistance and pulled herself up. A couple spots of warm blood seeped through her trousers at her knee, and she reached down, brushing away the gravel embedded in the fabric. "It was as if a thousand voices were screaming at me. Like a thousand people's emotions released at once."

He shook his head slowly, his eyes wide with innocence. "I did not know... Are you ready to try again? Perhaps start with a smaller rock." He backed up a few paces, then nodded at her encouragingly.

She swallowed, forcing the bile back down in her throat. The prospect of encountering the distressed energy again made her sick. And yet, she was more terrified this would be another skill she couldn't accomplish, another aspect of her powers she wouldn't be able to control. *I know I can do this*, she thought, and focusing on a much smaller rock—one about the size of Little Guy—she channeled again, opening the magical connection.

And again, there was a rush of tangled energy, slamming into her chest and knocking the breath from her lungs. But it was less consuming this time, and with a concentrated effort, she tamed it, trusting her instincts opposed to any form of skill. Heat and power rushed into her, filling her, until she thought would surely explode with it. *Too much.* With difficulty, she opened another channel, this time to cast. Manipulating the influx of energy, she threw the stone, launching it through the air where it whooshed, defying gravity, to the jagged edge of the ceiling, sticking as if sewn back in place. Both channels broke abruptly on their own, but the stone stayed fixed in the ceiling above. Despite her unease at the weird angry energy, Raylyn filled with triumph at the accomplishment, a renewed sense of confidence melting away her previous qualms.

"Amazing," Terach breathed, staring at her with adoration in his eyes. "Let's go again."

She didn't know how long they continued; it could have been minutes or hours or days. By the time they finished, a small portion of the ceiling had flown back into place, joining together like the most intricate puzzle. When they finally made their way back down the narrow hall, she wondered out loud, "You said the stones always revert back to their original position; how long do you think they will stay in the ceiling?"

"I don't know," he replied. "No one's ever been able to put them back in place before."

She swelled. *No one has been able to repair the damage in a hundred years,* she thought. *How amazing would it be if I could do it myself?* Unbidden, Talia's words echoed in her mind, "*Are you sure you aren't Haddeon's great grand-daughter or something?*" and the goosebumps that raised up on her skin had nothing to do with the cold stone surrounding her.

The halls were nearly deserted as Terach escorted her back to her room, and the one servant they passed scurried away wordlessly, her eyes glued to the floor. "How're your other classes going?" Terach asked, breaking the growing silence.

Raylyn cringed. "Not very well at the moment," she said, launching into the story of getting kicked out of healing class.

Terach stopped dead in his tracks. "Surely, she just dismissed you for the day. Thorne has been under a bit of strain with the Infirmary lately. It was likely just her temper flaring."

"Well, she told me not to 'waste my time coming back', so no, I think she permanently expelled me." Her eyes prickled with shame, and she was grateful for the dim lighting in the hall.

Terach grunted. "Follow me." He spun on his heel, heading in the opposite direction. Raylyn raced to keep up with him. After a few turns, he stopped in front of a door, pounding on the wood with a closed fist.

Muffled clattering and curses sounded through the door, and a moment later it opened, Thorne's face shifting from an icy glare to surprise at seeing Terach. "Well, this is unexpected," she murmured, her voice low. "Finally come to apologize then? I'd think you could've picked a more decent hour." She leaned on the doorframe, a black silken robe thrown hastily around her shoulders.

Terach took a step back, revealing Raylyn behind him. Thorne made a noise that resembled a cat spitting up a hairball, and she pulled her robe tightly around herself, crossing her arms. "What in the Goddess's good name is going on?"

"Did you dismiss her from your class?" Terach asked flatly.

"Yes. Did you really need to wake me for this? I have to be back to the Infirmary in three hours." She moved to shut the door, but Terach stuck his foot in the way, stopping it.

"You cannot make that decision without consulting me! I am the head of academic affairs. What is her offense?"

Thorne rolled her eyes, remaining obstinately silent.

"What was her offense?" he growled, his voice growing dangerously low.

"*Madam* Ashton," she began in a condescending tone, "spoke out of turn."

"You know as well as I that is not an acceptable punishment."

"The child thinks she's smarter and more proficient than everyone," Thorne snarled, almost spitting. "She has no sense of modesty."

"She is more proficient than most, Thorne. You aren't being reasonable."

They stared at each other for a minute, anger simmering on both sides. Finally, Thorne replied. "I have nothing left to teach her."

"You know very well the next step is apprenticeship. Why are you making it so hard on the girl?"

She didn't reply. Instead, she shifted her icy gaze to Raylyn. She spoke through gritted teeth, her voice dripping with disapproval. "You will have night shift duty three days a week, directly supervised under a preceptor. Come sunrise, you will remove yourself from the Infirmary—I do not want to cross paths with you. You will start in two days. Any tardiness, any attempts to break away from your mentor, and you will be removed. Do you understand?"

"Yes, Madam," Raylyn said, ensuring her voice remained strong and steady. Thorne rolled her eyes, then slammed the door closed, sending a small gust of breeze that ruffled Raylyn's hair.

She smiled in appreciation at Terach, whose face was drawn into a frown, small lines appearing at the corners of his mouth. "I'm sorry," she muttered, seeing his distress. "I'm causing problems for you."

He smiled at that. "Trust me: you are the least of my problems. Thorne is just stubborn." He ran a hand through his hair. "It's getting late, and we should get you back to your room." He led her back down the hall, despite her insistence that she could make her own way.

She nearly skipped with excitement. *Two days. Two days and I will be working as a real healer, at the most advanced Infirmary in the entire country!* Little Guy purred approvingly when she forced herself to bed, anticipation and excitement holding sleep at bay. She grinned at the ceiling, fantasizing about earning her Mastery of healing before she even turned twenty, until finally, sleep claimed her.

CHAPTER 15

"**W**E MISSED YOU LAST CLASS," Master Aerile said, stopping her with a light hand on her shoulder.

Raylyn turned, swallowing dryly. She spent the better part of the morning worrying about this confrontation. "I'm sorry, Master," she said, lowering her gaze with a guilty expression.

"You have people who care about you, Raylyn. If something is going on, you can tell me." He squeezed her shoulder, then released her, a small smile on his face.

"Thank you," she said, sighing with relief. "I'll remember for next time." *That was easy*, she thought. She pulled her books from her bag, stifling a yawn.

The prior day was spent preparing herself for her upcoming shift in the Infirmary, compiling her most important notes and texts, and imploring random servants for any spare healing aprons. She hoped Talia would stop by, and she even hunted the main parts of the castle for her, but the woman was either busy or avoiding her. Raylyn had no one to share in her excitement. Trying to train her body to sleep during the daylight hours and stay awake the entire night was the hardest part of her preparations, and she woke several times during the early afternoon, dreaming of knocks on her door.

"Today we're doing a training method to help with control," Aerile said, passing small tufts of cotton to each of the students. He walked back to the front of the room, holding his own tuft in the air. He released it as his palm began to glow. Instead of falling to the floor, the cotton shot straight up in the air, as if being drawn my a string to the ceiling. "Perhaps not as eye-catching as the flames we previously used, but a more complex method of channeling. Your connection is with the surrounding air as opposed to the cotton itself." Hand raised, the cotton began to make circles in the air, spinning faster and faster until it was nothing more than a white blur. The children around her cheered in delight, grabbing their own tuft in anticipation. Aerile gave a few words of instruction, then set them free to work at the task, pacing the rows of desks.

Raylyn mentally opened a channel, allowing herself to connect to the air around her. She jolted in surprise when the cotton shot high in the air on an invisible breeze. Aerile nodded in approval as he passed her, checking in with the students, adjusting postures and offering words of encouragements.

They practiced for the better part of an hour, Raylyn making her cotton dance in figure eights, to the nearby children's delight. A knock on the door made her look up, breaking her concentration and causing the cotton to fall naturally to the desktop in front of her.

"Continue practicing," Aerile said, heading toward the door. Raylyn did as instructed, about to form the connection, but Aerile's words made her look up again.

"Your Highness," he said, folding into a low bow. "To what do I owe this pleasure?"

"Oh, for Goddess's sake, Aerile, you don't bow to me." Brenden's voice carried across the room.

"How many years has it been since you stepped foot in this class?" Aerile asked with a soft chuckle. "Quick wit, you were."

"Ah, must be around ... close to a dozen, if my math is right."

"A dozen!" Aerile shook his head softly. "Ah, the years escape me, like sand through my fingers. But I forget myself. Is there something with which I can assist you?"

"If not too much trouble, Master, I was hoping to steal Raylyn away." Heat filled her face, all the way to the tips of her ears. She slouched low in her seat, thankful, at the very least, that her classmates were too young to pick up on the exchange.

"Of course, of course. We have mere minutes left, besides. Come along then, Raylyn," Aerile said, waving to her, somehow knowing she was listening. As nonchalantly as possible, she walked toward them, pulse quickening as she thought of the last time she saw Brenden, the memory of his lips on hers making her stomach tighten. "Well done today," Aerile said as she passed him, giving her a little wink. She forced back a smile, closing the door softly behind her.

"So, you *are* avoiding me," Brenden said as she stepped out into the hall.

"What? No, of course not," she replied, feigning interest in the stonework of the floors. "Just busy, you know."

"Then why won't you look at me?"

She glanced up. "I *am* looking at you," but her eyes were pulled back to the floor. *How could I be so stupid to risk our friendship?* "About the other night... I wasn't myself. I shouldn't have done that." Her face was on fire. "I wish I could take it back."

He was quiet for a moment. "Do you mean trying to attack my brother or kissing me?"

Still staring at the ground, she bit her lip. "Well, both, I guess."

Another pause. "Hm. I don't think you're being honest with me." He stepped closer to her, tilting her head up with one finger under her chin, forcing her to look up. Her heart raced. "That's better," he murmured. A glimmer of hope surged through her. *Maybe I didn't ruin everything,* she thought, losing herself for a moment in his clear blue eyes. "Are you *sure* you regret it?" he asked, his face inches from hers, breath warm on her skin. "Because I don't."

She answered by closing the remaining space between them, their lips pressing together softly. Kissing him was like coming alive, every nerve in her body tingling awake, eager, *hungry*. It could have been seconds, minutes, or hours, but when they finally parted, she was breathless and dizzy, a small part of her still insatiable, desperate for more. "Let's walk," he suggested, linking his arm through hers.

They lazily headed toward the castle, in no hurried rush. The chilly air gave them an excuse to walk close together. "So, how've you been? Why aren't you coming for practice anymore?"

Raylyn launched into a retelling of her last few days: Thorne's banishment, the Hall of Sorrows, Terach's intervention. It spilled out from her, and she realized how much she missed his companionship. "Tonight's my first shift," she continued, "and I spent most of yesterday trying to change my sleep schedule."

Brenden peered down at her. "Is that why you didn't answer the door when I came to see you?"

She laughed. "Well, that explains those dreams."

They entered the castle arm in arm, passing a small group of lower nobility. They bowed their heads in greeting, Brenden pausing, giving a brief *hello* as they passed. Raylyn smiled, trying to be friendly. While the servants and many of the students had been kind enough, the members of the Court seemed to look right through her, never really acknowledging her in their passing. Whether this was out of fear or disdain, she wasn't sure.

Just as she was about to turn to look back to Brenden, she locked eyes with Pria, two of her frilly friends dangling on each of her arms as if they were accessories. The woman's eyes narrowed as her face contorted with obvious disgust. "Goddess save us!" she said, signing a safety sigil in the air. Heads turned toward her, confused at the outburst. "It's the demon, enchanting our very own prince! Paralleling the destruction Haddeon brought to our nation. Have we not learned from our past mistakes?" She swooned, her ladies screeching under the sudden burden of her weight. Raylyn's face heated with anger as she watched Pria continue the charade, several men rushing to assist her to the ground.

Brenden hesitated. "Let's go," he whispered, lips at her ear, guiding her down the nearest side hall. They took a few turns, leading to one of the many sitting alcoves, a small couch nestled against the wall. "Are you alright?" He sat, pulling her next to him.

"She's terrible," Raylyn said, "but I'm fine." Moments before, she was seconds away from casting a fireball aimed for the woman's head, and she would've laughed as her hair burned and skin melted. But distance helped, the heat in her cheeks cooling as her embarrassment dissipated.

"She speaks utter nonsense. You know that, right?"

"You mean I'm not Haddeon reborn? *Damn*, and I had my plans for world domination finalized and everything." She smiled as Brenden laughed, though her words were hollow. After everything she and Terach talked about in the Hall of Sorrows, she was beginning to believe Haddeon was as misconstrued as Pria was making her out to be.

A quiet moment passed as she fell into her thoughts. Brenden's touch pulled her back. He played with a piece of her hair, hand trailing to her neck. "You know," he said, fingers dancing at her shoulder, "I was going to ask you to the feast tonight, to try to reconcile for standing you up last time."

"Feast?" she asked. She wasn't aware of any feast being planned or that there was cause for celebration. According to Bo's last message, Rowan and his crew were still searching the borderlands for Braya, and they were on the brink of war. What was there to warrant a feast?

"A last minute whim of my father's. The poor fools in the kitchen are going crazy with preparations."

That explains the frantic staff the other day, Raylyn thought. "I can't go, Brenden. I really should get some sleep before my shift."

"Can't you delay your shift by one little day?" His fingers danced to the nape of her neck as he moved even closer, sending a visible shiver racking her body. "I'll have you know I'm an *excellent* dinner companion."

"Thorne would throw me out faster than a flea-ridden blanket," Raylyn replied, searching hard for the words.

"I could talk to her, convince her," he murmured.

She laughed. "The Goddess herself wouldn't be able to change Thorne's mind."

"Hm." He sighed distractedly as he swept her hair up in one hand, twining it around his fingers. His mouth followed the earlier path of his fingers, planting a dozen tiny kisses from her shoulder to her neck.

The heat that burned in her belly had nothing to do with her earlier embarrassment, and she moved toward him, meeting his lips. Her racing mind slowed, knowing nothing other than this moment, and reflexively, her hands reached into his hair, pulling him closer. Desire surged. She nibbled his lip before resurfacing for air, breathless, moving to his ear, then neck.

Brenden groaned, then shifted, pulling her hips down so she lay on the couch beneath him. Her fingers found the waistline of his pants, pulling his tunic free. Delicately, deliciously, her fingers slipped beneath the cloth, feeling the hard muscle of his torso, then chest. It was his turn to shiver, his body trembling beneath her touch. Time was nonexistent and her body would have been happy spending the night with him there ... but a small voice in the back of her mind eventually made her break away. They were both breathless, chests heaving in a duet of passion. "I really should go back to my room," she said reluctantly, fingers tracing a circling pattern on the hot skin of his back.

Hunger flashed in his eyes. "I could walk you," he said, intentions clear on his face.

With every ounce of willpower, Raylyn shook her head. "I don't think that would be a good idea," she said, her body protesting the words.

He nodded, brushing a strand of hair behind her ear, then untangled himself, tucking in his shirt with a sheepish grin. "You're certain you won't join me tonight?" he asked.

Raylyn wasn't sure if he was referring to the feast or his bed. Either way, the answer was the same. "Not tonight."

"Marginally better than the other ones. At least your hair's pulled back," Madam Creena said, inspecting her with a narrowed eye. The woman's hair was pulled into a tight bun at the back of her head. A silver chain circled her neck, Master emblem hanging proudly. "Hands?" Raylyn held them out as ordered, the older woman pulling them close to her face, inspecting her nails. Seeing the reddened and broken skin on her thumb, she tutted in disapproval. "Now really girl, bandage that up before you get an infection." She tossed her a roll of gauze. Raylyn quickly wrapped her thumb, then pulled out a small pad of parchment and her quill.

Creena was already pacing away, and Raylyn raced to catch up. "Night shift is always short on staff, so don't expect students to come and empty your chamber pots for you. Tonight, it's just you and me in the main ward, so be prepared to work. And if you think you're above doing the dirty jobs, you can think again."

"I've no problem with chamber pots, Madam."

"No doubt you'll end up cleaning vomit and blood, too."

"That's why I've my apron, Madam," she replied with a smile. The Infirmary was darker than during the day; more than half the orbs which normally illuminated the ceiling were unlit to promote higher quality sleep for the patients. *I wonder where the power stone is kept*, Raylyn thought subconsciously as they paced.

"You already know where the soiled linen and garbage go," she muttered, passing the appropriate doors. They walked a little farther, reaching another door in the corner of the chamber. "This is one of our supply rooms. We get the joyous responsibility of stocking the carts so dayshift can be nicely prepared, spoiled lot they are." She led them inside the room, shelves lining all the walls, towering from floor to ceiling. Raylyn stared in wonder at the excess of linens, bandages, gauze, towels.

More stock in this one room than in my entire village, Raylyn thought excitedly. When she was apprenticing under her mother, there were times when they allowed a wound to go an extra day without a dressing change because of gauze shortages. Often, her mother suggested to their patients to use clean cloth to wrap a wound. To have such resources at her disposal was a privilege.

"We've got the more common salves over here. Willow balm for pain, aloe for burns obviously, yarrow cream helps in a pinch with chronic bleeding ulcers." She continued to point out the different salves, Raylyn scribbling in her notepad as fast as her hand would allow.

They continued the tour for over an hour. Though she had been in the Infirmary several times during Thorne's class, it was always menial tasks. Her nerves calmed as the tour continued. Creena showed her the location of the medicine cabinets, charts hung next to cabinets for quick reference; introduced her to the record keeping at one of the healers' stations, explained the importance of documenting patient conditions and interventions throughout the shift.

"We'll round on the patients, give you an idea of what we're working with here. But be sure to keep quiet; we've got a few restless ones I'd rather you don't wake."

The curtains which provided a façade of privacy to each person were a nauseating floral pattern. Creena pulled each one back with a delicate hand, giving a brief overview on each patient's condition. Festering wounds, red fever, hypothermia. The list continued. "They're so sick," Raylyn breathed, stomach knotting. How could King Aedam allow such conditions?

Creena cocked her head. "These are the healthy ones. When you eventually get to the other wards," she nodded toward the hall leading deeper into the Infirmary, "that's when you'll find the sick ones."

Raylyn kept herself busy as the night passed, responding to the low moans of patients as they woke, stocking supply carts, reading prior notes in the patient's records. Creena didn't let her out of her sight, but she expected nothing less. No healer would allow a novice free rein, especially not a Master.

The skylights set into the ceiling allowed the gray pre-dawn light to filter through, illuminating the room by increments as the sun approached the horizon. She rolled the dirty linens from Bed Six into a small ball, red stains spreading through the cloth like a watercolor painting on canvas. Wiping a bead of sweat from her brow with the crook of her arm, Raylyn dropped the laundry in the appropriate bin. Creena was true to her word; there was vomit and blood as well as other unpleasant excrements.

Her mentor appeared, a glean of sweat on her face as well. She sighed, rubbing her face. "Twelve years of night shift, and you'd think I'd be accustomed to the exhaustion by now." She glanced at Raylyn. "You look like you belong in one of those beds, girl. How 'bout you take off and get some sleep? Did fine work tonight."

Raylyn gave a tight-lipped smile. "I didn't really do much." The most exciting part of the night had been reapplying a bandage on Bed Six's leg wound. Creena allowed her to hold the man's leg in the air so she could dress it, rectangular cotton pads placed over the weeping ulcers, held firmly in place with three rolls of gauze.

"Some nights are quieter than others. You take the slow ones with a praise of thanks to the Goddess. Here." She handed Raylyn a torn scrap of parchment. "Those are my shifts for the next few weeks. If I work, you work, understand?"

"Yes, Madam," Raylyn said, studying the scrawled writing.

"And no more of that 'Madam' nonsense. It's Creena. See you tomorrow night."

She hardly had the gumption to pull her soiled apron off before she fell onto her bed, ignoring Little Guy's mews for food. *First full night done*, she thought with a small smile. Her head spun from lack of sleep and her feet throbbed, unaccustomed to the constant standing for hours on end. Chilled from her walk back to the castle, she wrapped herself in the thick woolen comforter, and fell into a dreamless sleep.

Bang, bang, bang. She buried her head under a pillow, only half-waking. Sleep pulled her back down, gently cradling her in dark oblivion.

Bang, bang, bang... Bang, bang, bang. "Oh, for Goddess's sake!" she swore, ripping the covers off as she stumbled out of bed. "Is there a reason you're trying to knock down my door?" she asked testily as she yanked it open, her eyes still heavily lidded from sleep.

"Not a morning person. Duly noted," Brenden said, bright smile on his face. Her tiredness dispersed like mist in the hot sun, and she was acutely aware of her ruffled hair and bare legs. Her eyes darted to the pile of dirty clothes at the foot of her bed, stripped off and discarded in her exhaustion.

"Coffee?" he asked, offering her a steaming mug. His eyes trailed to her bare legs, and he raised a brow, smile shifting to a devious smirk.

Raylyn grabbed it, closing the door until it was open no wider than a crack. "I was sleeping," she said rather dumbly, the weight of his eyes still lingering on her skin.

"I can tell," he said with a chuckle. "Terach sent me. We've got some things to talk about. I'll wait out here while you get dressed." His voice lowered to just louder than a whisper, "Unless you prefer I come in?"

"The hall is fine," she squeaked, her voice cracking. She rushed to close the door, sloshing coffee onto the floor. Flustered, she grabbed her dirty apron from the night before and wiped up the mess. *What could Terach possibly need to talk about?* She dressed quickly, pausing for a moment to drain the cup of coffee, wincing at its bitterness. Little Guy mewed, watching her leave. "Sorry, bud," she mumbled, reaching down to scratch him on the ear before she left.

Terach's office was hardly large enough for one person, let alone three. Already, Raylyn's face flushed in the heat of the room, wondering if it would be rude to prop the door open for some airflow. She absentmindedly picked at her thumb as she sat on the small couch, leg pressed against Brenden's. Between the unexpected summons and Brenden's proximity, her pulse raced, making it difficult to focus her stream of thoughts. The memory of his hands dancing on her skin made her blush, and she glanced at the door again, the heat oppressive.

Brenden caught her hand, studying her abused thumb with lowered brows. "Stop that," he said, separating her fingers with his, holding her hand close to his body. Her face grew hotter at being caught.

"There!" Terach said, setting his quill down with a flourish. "Sorry about that. Needed to get these written up and sent out." He waved the parchment in the air to dry the ink.

"You said we needed to talk?" Raylyn probed. She was growing restless waiting.

Terach and Brenden exchanged a tense look. "We do. Last night was ... eye opening, to say the least."

She stared blankly, thinking back to her relatively uneventful night in the Infirmary. "In what way?"

Brenden shifted, releasing her hand as he spoke. "The feast..." He ran a hand through his hair, then looked at her, frowning. "The issue is, Raylyn, what we are about to say must remain in this room, do you understand?"

Her pulse quickened. "Yes, of course."

His face twisted, as if sucking on a lemon, his next words coming slow and strained. "While I trust you completely, I am going to have to ask for more than just your word."

"I—I'm sorry... I don't know what you mean."

Terach cleared his throat. "Brenden developed a way to make a promise binding through casting, Raylyn. In this instance, we just require your discretion, which will prevent you from relaying the information we are about to tell you."

Her eyes darted between the two men, wondering if this was some sort of joke or training exercise. They were both staring back at her, expressions so serious they looked almost grim. "Does it hurt?"

Brenden laughed. "Of course not. And since I'm initiating the spell, it will be on my energy demands, lasting until I break it."

She was quiet for a moment, considering. Whatever they wanted her to know was obviously confidential, and her chest was tight with excitement, a little thrill jolting through her at the thought of being included. Refusal didn't seem an option, as it would deem her untrustworthy, or even a threat. "What do I need to do?"

The tension broke on their faces in unison. "It's very simple," Brenden said. "I'm going to open a channel between us. I will manipulate the spell, casting it to you. All you need to do is accept it." He paused, biting his lip. "It might feel a little ... intimate," he said, color rising to his cheeks. "Ready?"

She nodded, and he grasped both her hands, his eyes closing in concentration. An itching sensation came over her body, much like when she was being manipulated by an effector, and she fought the urge to squirm away. Brenden's eyes opened, staring into hers, desire burning. She felt his wordless request, bobbing at the end of the invisible connection between them. This time, she closed her eyes, trying to make sense of what to do next. *I accept?* she thought, feeling a little ridiculous.

Energy and heat boiled through her blood, burning out of her skin in a rush. A million invisible cords tied her to Brenden, pulling her very essence until it met his. All traces of her earlier exhaustion vanished, each nerve of her body humming with a tense energy.

As suddenly as it began, it ended, the link severing with a jolt. Her chest heaved with a tingling remnant of desire. The room tilted as if she were intoxicated. Brenden seemed similarly affected, his cheeks flushed and breath coming fast. His grip on her hands tightened as he leaned in closer, his eyes bright and eager.

"You'll feel better in a moment," Terach said, making her whip around in embarrassment. She had forgotten he was there. Already, her vision and thinking were clearing, her breathing and pulse slowing. Brenden released her hands with a sheepish smile.

"Wonderful!" Terach said, clapping his hands together as he leaned back in his chair. "Now that's taken care of, Brenden, why don't you go ahead and explain what's going on?"

Brenden nodded, staring at his hands for a moment before he began. Finally, he looked up, his face drawn with concern. "There's no easy way to say this, but I think my father is going mad."

Her mouth popped open with surprise. She didn't know what she expected from this meeting, but this *wasn't* it. She glanced at Terach, whose face was grim as well. "Why would you say that?" she whispered, hoping there was a spell sealing the door from eavesdroppers.

"He's impulsive and reclusive, which never was his nature. And last night he announced he received word from King Aedam. He claims the attack was a group of rebels and in no way connected with the crown."

"But that's great news," she said. "It means we don't have to go to war!"

"It would be wonderful if it were true," Terach said from behind his desk. "Unfortunately, my spies tell me otherwise. Which makes one wonder what His Majesty's reasoning is behind ignoring an outright attack on one of his sons."

"But that doesn't make any sense. What happens when they bring their armies to our borders? How will he deny it then?" she asked, glancing up at Brenden.

"I don't know. All I can think is his mind isn't right. He never acted like this before. He made his announcement last night and then started ... rambling. It didn't even make sense. I had to escort him out of the dining hall." He shook his head in disgust. "Tried to blame it on too much wine, but how long can we hide such a change in behavior?"

Raylyn chewed her lip in silence for a few minutes. It coincided with Talia's mounting fears, and her stomach knotted with guilt for not putting more faith into the woman's concerns. Her voice echoed in the back of her mind. *"Be careful with Lord Terach." If she was right about the king's sickness, is she right about Terach, too?* She shifted, a growing sense of unease making her uncomfortable. "Why tell me this?" she finally asked, breaking the growing silence.

The men exchanged another quick glance. "It was my idea," Brenden said quickly. "If his newfound behavior doesn't improve, then we'll be forced to intervene. We don't know how the Court will react, and I want to make sure you understand our reasoning."

"Intervene how, exactly?"

Terach stood, shuffling the stack of now dried parchment into a pile. "If the king is indisposed, Brenden would assume his duties. We would be able to head off the likely approaching attack."

"Perhaps it was just the alcohol, though?" Raylyn reasoned. "Does he have bodily ailments, pain, lethargy?" They both shook their heads. Raylyn's brow furrowed, confused. "How do you plan on convincing a mad king he's mad?" Brenden looked down at his feet, not meeting her eye. She turned to Terach. "Well?"

"You see the difficulty of our situation. Time would undoubtedly be the downfall for His Majesty. The court would see that his outbursts and behaviors are more than just eccentricities or overindulgence in drink, but from my correspondences, we don't have the luxury of time. That's where we need you."

Raylyn snorted. "What could I possibly do?" The second the words were past her lips, dread spread through her, icing in her veins. She knew what they were requesting of her before Terach said the words.

"We need you to weaken the king."

CHAPTER 16

THE WEATHER GREW ANGRY OVER THE next few weeks, making up for the earlier draught. Snow piled past Raylyn's knees, turning the trek between the castle and Academy into a chore. Ice storms were more common than not, and the tiny sharp shards whipped on the wind, slicing into any exposed skin.

She tugged, opening the castle door as she fought against the wind's resistance. Clambering inside, she shook the accumulated ice from her cloak, fur-lined to fight the bitter cold. Despite the miserable weather, excitement raced through her chest. *Level Three!* she thought, all but skipping down the hall. The weeks of practicing with Brenden in the arena, along with slowly repairing the Hall of Sorrows helped her overcome the mental block that so often kept her from accessing her casting powers.

Terach stood in front of the kitchens, arms crossed and a scowl firmly lining his face. "You're late," he accused.

She grinned widely, ignoring his attitude. "Aerile held me after class. I've been promoted to casting Level *Three*!"

The annoyance slid off his face as he returned her smile. "Excellent," he said, clapping her on the shoulder. "You're making tremendous progress. Speaking of, should we get on?" he gestured to the kitchen doors.

Raylyn grimaced, nodding reluctantly, and led them through the kitchens. This was her least favorite lesson, but she understood its necessity. They passed through the inner belly of the kitchens, the massive stoves heating the room. The staff didn't spare them a second glance, accustomed to their frequent comings and goings.

Cool air chilled her face as she opened the door to the glassway. The walls and pitched ceiling were made of large panels of glass, allowing daylight to pour into the space. Lettuces and herbs cluttered the area, leaving a narrow walkway through the center of the hall. When the sun shone, the room filled with a moist heat, condensation budding on the glass panels. But the current storm hid the sun, depriving the glassway of natural warmth. *At least it blocks the wind and ice*, she thought. Small heat orbs bobbed every few feet, providing just enough heat to keep the plants from freezing.

"Damn," Terach muttered as they continued down the hall. Raylyn glanced up, watching as Terach approached a small cluster of shriveled plants. He bent, sifting through a container of extra soil and retrieved a small black stone, tucking it in his pocket. Catching Raylyn's glance, he shrugged. "Spell went dry."

Over the past few weeks, she tried relentlessly to uncover the secrets of Terach's power stones, but the man was unyielding. No amount of pestering, nagging, or persuading would make him talk. "Maybe I'll tell you on the day I embrace the Goddess. Or maybe not," he had said with a wink.

The glassway was several hundred feet long, and there were at least a dozen total scattered on the castle grounds. The glass design, coupled with Terach's added heat spells, allowed the kitchens to grow fresh vegetables and herbs during even the harshest months of winter. Some provided a connection to different parts of the castle, making interesting shortcuts, while others connected to nothing and stood freely on their own. This one provided a quick and efficient route to the butchery.

"Hello, Tom," Raylyn said as they walked into the cold room. There was no hearth, as too much heat would spoil the meat. Terach told her even in the summer, the room was kept unnaturally cool.

The butcher looked up, dropping a rag into the bucket next to him, wiping his hands absentmindedly on his thick apron. Two long stone counters ran parallel to each other on either side of the room. One for processing, the other for packaging.

"Back already?" the butcher said, his gravelly voicing causing Raylyn to smile.

"Unfortunately," she replied, ignoring Terach's disapproving look.

"Well, you know the way," he said, picking up the cloth and wringing it into the soapy bucket.

She swallowed her nausea down, her feet dawdling.

"Come on," Terach urged as he strode to the back of the room, opening another door. Raylyn hurried behind him, stomach churning.

The next chamber was the cause for her recent insomnia. Her overnights in the Infirmary already caused a bone-deep exhaustion, and the scant hours of sleep she stole during the day were plagued with recurring night-mares of this room. A row of empty metal pens lined one wall and hooks larger than a man's hand hung from the ceiling on the other side of the room. Cold stone sur-rounded them, and there wasn't a trace of comfort to be found. Lanterns flickered, glinting off the metal, providing the only illumination in the windowless room. A second door was set at the far side of the room, daylight creeping through the cracks.

Terach went to that door, disappearing. He returned just a few heartbeats later, an adolescent boy following, coaxing a huge hog through the doorway. He kept his eyes glued to the stone floor as he led the animal into one of the pens. As soon as the gate latched, he bolted from the room.

"Ready?" Terach asked. Raylyn didn't reply, staring into the pig's intelligent black eyes. *As smart as a dog, Father used to say.* It was oblivious to its fate, nose searching the floor in hopes for something edible.

Terach sighed, resting a hand on her shoulder. "We've had this conversation over and over now. These animals are headed to the slaughter, regardless. Might as well get the practice."

He was right, of course. "The chickens were easier, especially the one that pecked me," she muttered, absent-mindedly rubbing the light scar on the back of her hand.

She took a deep breath, steadying herself, then nodded to Terach.

He casted, encasing himself in an invisible shield. The precaution was hardly necessary now that Raylyn had gained more control. She turned to the pen. "Sorry, buddy," she mumbled softly. It continued to sniff around, unaffected as she opened a channel, connecting them. Using the link, she mentally searched, unfamiliar with the pig's complexity. After a moment, she found its pulse and the flow of lifeforce to and from its heart. Delicately, she *pulled*, a thread of energy syphoning to her no faster than water dripping from ice. The pig didn't react. *Good*, she thought. Her goal was discretion.

She pulled with a touch more force, aiming at the pig's heart, slowly blocking the outflow of energy, and redirecting it to herself. It was an intricate way to syphon, resulting in a much smaller energy surge and much less suspicious death. The pig's pulse began to slow, and it stumbled, folding to the floor. Gradually, its breathing slowed as well. She glanced at Terach who nodded, signaling her to finish. Pulling once more, the pig ceased breathing, calm and still in its death.

"Fantastic! You're really coming along," Terach said, his voice a cheery juxtaposition to the morose loss of life. He passed her, peaking out the door and calling the boy again. "Let's go again."

With effort, Raylyn blocked out the screaming portion of her mind that so readily rejected the killing. She continued in a rigid, conditioned manner, refusing to stray from the task. After what felt like hours of intricate work, she turned to Terach, all ten pens filled with silent and still bodies.

"You're ready," Terach said, eyes glinting in the torch-light. "Come to my study tomorrow evening, and we'll go over the plan."

Her body was tense with fatigue and apprehension, the short nap she took after her night in the Infirmary doing little to quell the tide of exhaustion. She didn't remember walking through the halls or passing anyone after leaving the kitchens, as her body carried her subconsciously back to her room. A fresh coat of paint was still tacky on her door, "demon" painted hastily, drips splattering the floor. Pria's harassments hadn't lessened with time. Raylyn couldn't even muster enough energy to sigh over the graffiti, mentally noting to take care of it after she got some sleep. She unlocked the door with a jiggle of the key, heart aching for the enchanted purple flowers that never arrived anymore.

A figure sat on her bed, Little Guy nestled in her lap. Raylyn shrieked in surprise, opening a channel to cast an attack.

"It's just me!" Talia said, leaping off the bed to Little Guy's displeasure. He slunk under the bed in irritation.

Raylyn put a hand to her chest, willing her racing heart to slow. "The door was locked!" she said, trying to reason through her bewilderment.

Talia rolled her eyes. "Any caster with half an ounce of worth can pick that lock. Anyway," she pulled a necklace of keys from underneath her tunic, "I have a key, remember?"

Overcoming her initial shock, Raylyn crossed the threshold, collapsing next to Talia. She closed her eyes, relishing in the warmth and comfort of the bed. *I could fall asleep right now,* she thought.

"Hey, get up," Talia said, poking her forehead.

Raylyn cracked open an eye, annoyed. She was desperate to just lose consciousness for a few hours, escaping her growing apprehension. "Why?"

"I've missed you."

Raylyn grunted. She had only seen glimpses of Talia over the past few weeks. Though she tried to convince herself it was because she was too busy training for the competition, a creeping suspicion made her wonder if the woman was just growing tired of her company. She was hurt at first but now just felt relieved. The lack of her presence meant it was easier to conceal her upcoming plans for the king.

"Ri told me you and Terach have been spending a lot of time together." The tone of her voice shifted, and Raylyn sighed, resigning herself to being awake.

She sat up and rubbed her face, shaking off the traces of sleep that so quickly tried to consume her. "So? He's helping me train, that's all."

"You're not only doing those history lessons anymore, huh?" She gave Raylyn a sideways look, her head cocked.

Does she know? Raylyn thought, forcing her breathing to stay steady. "History lessons continue. We've also been exploring the intricacies of my syphoning power, as well. Which you would already know if you didn't completely disappear for weeks on end."

"That's not fair," Talia said, raising her eyebrows. "The competition is in one week, and more than that—"

"More than that, I'm nothing more than a job to you. Without the king's enforcement, there's no reason for you to continue to dote on me. It's fine. I completely understand." She flopped back down, burying her face beneath a pillow, annoyed.

Talia ripped the pillow off her, flinging it to the floor. "Listen here," she said, face contorting. "First of all, how insulting. A *job*? I've grown to think of you as a dear friend. And second, I'm not the only one who's been busy. Do you know I've come to your chamber four times in the past week? Four! This time I decided to wait, and I've been here for *hours*."

Raylyn averted her gaze, chest tight. Giving a half smile, she asked, "Any chance you caught sight of who vandalized my door?"

Talia stared at her blankly. "What?"

"Doesn't matter," she muttered, but Talia was already crossing the room to examine the door.

"Bitches," Talia muttered. She raised a hand, palm glowing, and the paint liquified, running down the wood like water, where it pooled on the ground. Once the door was cleared again, she directed her attention to the red puddle, which began to congeal and raise into the air, a circular ball of dried red paint.

"Thanks," Raylyn said once Talia had finished.

"I wish I would've caught them," she said, shaking her head. "Teach whoever it is a lesson."

"Start fights now and you'll get yourself disqualified from the competition," Raylyn replied. "Anyway, it's Pria. This is the fourth time she's done it."

"Bitch," Talia repeated as she resumed sitting next to Raylyn on the bed. They were quiet for a minute while they sat, Talia examining her fingernails with feigned interest. Finally, she spoke. "I'm worried about you."

"What? Why?" Raylyn asked, her voice unnaturally high. Her earlier anxiety resurfaced, panicked that her schemes were discovered.

"It's about Terach..." Talia said, making her chest tighten. "There's been a lot of rumors..."

"About what?" she asked sharply as Talia trailed off.

She must have heard the panic in Raylyn's voice because Talia looked up, her brow furrowed. "I *told* you to be careful around him. You're already working in the Infirmary. That's more than enough compensation for your room and meals. There's no reason to feel obligated to... to do *those* things with him."

"I ... what?" Raylyn asked, confused. Talia's concern was palpable, tears welling in her eyes. It wasn't the accusation of treason she expected.

"We all try so hard not to talk about it. So many of the girls are ashamed and deny it when asked... I mean, he's the head of academic affairs, and the king's advisor to boot. I know it's intimidating, but you can just say *no*." Tears trailed down Talia's cheeks as she spoke, and she slowly curled in on herself, hugging her knees to her chest.

"That is *not* what's going on!" Raylyn said, stunned.

Talia looked up, wiping her cheeks with the back of her hand. "It—it's not?" she said, sniffling.

"Absolutely not! Terach wouldn't do something like that. He's a decent man, and he's at least as old as my father!" Disgust welled in Raylyn's stomach as she wondered how far those rumors traveled throughout the castle. It must be a believable tale to have Talia in tears, as she had never seen the woman cry before. She could foresee Pria adding the word *"slut"* to her door next time. *Wonderful.*

Talia's face darkened. "If you're being truthful, thank the Goddess. But please don't discredit the truths so many of us have faced. Terach is a *predator*, Raylyn."

She fought her initial urge to argue in favor of the man. He was kind and considerate, filling in a void which surfaced in her ever since she left her parents. Her mind wanted to reject the idea he was abusing his position of power to take advantage of students in such a way. But Talia's red splotched face caused her to remember those two distraught servants she passed in the hall so many weeks ago when she was going to Terach's study. His disheveled appearance, the mess of his office. But no, this was Terach. She'd spent countless hours with him over the past couple months. *There's no way.*

"I don't believe it, Talia. How do you know someone like Pria isn't making these rumors up just to stir trouble? I *know* Terach. He's not like that."

Talia slowly shook her head, her eyes narrowing. The tears had dried, leaving a bitter and twisted expression. "There's a special place in Hell for people who discredit victims' abuse."

"I'm not discrediting anything, I'm just saying you shouldn't believe everything you hear."

"What about what I've seen? What about what I've lived through? Am I allowed to believe *that*?" Her words were clipped with anger, and she was bordering on yelling.

Words were hard to catch. "I—but... but you didn't tell me that," Raylyn stammered, torn. "I'm... I'm so sorry, Talia." She wasn't fully convinced, but this didn't seem like the right time to sort it all out. Talia just nodded once, her eyes staring at nothing.

They sat in silence for what felt like hours, the tension slowly dissipating.

"So..." Raylyn began, hoping to repair some of the damage. "How's training going?"

Talia looked up from petting Little Guy. "Really well, actually. I've been able to maintain the three connections every time, sometimes I can even split them into six, but not consistently. I think I have a good chance this year."

Six different channels at once? "That's amazing."

Her smile faltered, falling into a grimace. "I wish my efforts with the king were going even half as well."

Raylyn's stomach twisted again at the mention of the king. "Still no luck?"

Talia snorted. "None, whatsoever."

"I figured." It didn't come as a surprise. Through the past several weeks, he had become more reclusive and volatile. The single instance Raylyn saw him out of his chambers was during a fit of rage, when he upturned his entire tea tray, spilling boiling hot water onto a servant. She rushed over and healed the servant, but the image of the girl, writhing on the floor in pain would forever be imprinted in her memory. "Actually, Brenden and—" Her voice cut off suddenly, as if her throat closed. She was about to tell Talia that Brenden shared her fears about the king's shift in behavior, as well, but the words wouldn't come out. "Bren—" Tightness squeezed her throat as if a fist was wrapped around her neck and painful tears prickled in her eyes. *The spell!* she remembered, and instantly dismissed the idea of disclosing information to Talia. Breath rushed into her lungs as the invisible hand released, and she subconsciously fingered her throat in relief.

"You okay?"

"Yeah, just ... choking on my spit, apparently... Anyway, you were saying?"

Talia's brows knotted together in thought. "I'm giving it one last shot with the king before I completely give up. Ri said I can help her in the kitchens if needed, so if my position as spy is done, then so be it. But I have this insane theory..." She trailed off, her eyes growing distant again.

"What's the theory?" Raylyn urged, curious to know if Talia knew of the king's rapidly increasing madness.

"I'll tell you if it happens to be true." She climbed out of the bed. "I'll let you get some sleep. Sorry to intrude... I really did just miss you." She gave Raylyn a small smile as she left.

Nightmares of metal hooks and faceless girls writhing in pain plagued her few hours of sleep, and after waking—covered in sweat for the third time—Raylyn gave up the notion of rest. She washed and dressed warmly for her anticipated hike through the snow. Though she loved her shifts in the Infirmary, the prospect of a night off with Brenden caused her pulse to quicken with excitement. Wishing the wind wasn't so harsh, she knotted her hair into a bun, knowing any other style would turn into a tangled mess from the wind.

Her hand was on the doorknob when a faint glow caught her eye. She turned, seeing the scriber on her desk glowing red. It had been a few weeks since Bo last wrote. She raced across the room, excitement and fear tangling together.

Raylyn,

There are no words to soften the following fact. We cannot find her. The snow has masked any trail or lead that we had. We've been searching the borderlands for nearly two months now and have been heading back south for a few weeks. There are only a few vague rumors—even amongst the larger cities we've traveled—and none of them have any substantiation. While we will continue looking as we get closer, odds are not very great.

—Bo

His extended silence made sense, then. He was afraid to disappoint her until it was absolutely necessary. Her eyes prickled, but she fought back the tears. *He promised he would find her,* she thought, Rowan's vow popping into her head. *How shocking, he lied again.* She tried to take comfort in the fact that no reports of a dead or murdered girl were circulating. It was the only hope she had left.

CHAPTER 17

BRENDEN SWUNG THE DOOR OPEN AS she approached, the ice storm raging relentlessly. "Here," he said, holding out a hand to help her up the steps. They fell together in an embrace as he shut the door against the wind. The cabin's heat was glorious, and she kicked off her heavy, snow-trodden boots and cloak, rushing to the hearth to warm her pinkened, tingling fingers.

A weight touched her shoulders, and she looked up from the dancing flames to see Brenden draping a heavy fur blanket around her shoulders. "It's definitely brutal out there," he said, rubbing her arm through the blanket.

"If it weren't for the wind, it wouldn't be so bad."

"Are we really talking about the weather?" He snuck under the blanket, wrapping his arms around her waist, pulling her tightly against him. The heat from his body was almost hotter than the fire, warming her chilled skin. He tilted her head up, hand cupping her chin, then frowned. "What's wrong?"

She bit her lip, not knowing where to begin. "Nothing. Everything." She slipped out of his embrace, taking the blanket, and settled onto the plush couch. They had been frequenting this cabin for a few weeks now. It had once been a ranger's, back before the new barracks was built. Brenden told her it sat abandoned for several decades and had it furnished especially for her.

The entire structure was smaller than her room at the castle, containing little more than a table, couch, and bed. *He definitely went overboard*, Raylyn thought, peering around at the dozens of lit candles and vases of flowers. She reached forward, fingering the red petals on the roses. "I'm surprised you didn't choose purple hyacinth," she said, glancing up at him. It was the first time she acknowledged the anonymous gifts, and she couldn't contain her curiosity about why they stopped.

His brow furrowed. "Is that your favorite? I'll remember for next time." He sat beside her, pouring two glasses of wine.

"You ... weren't the one leaving me flowers by my door, were you?" she asked, realization dawning.

He was silent for a moment before he sighed, handing her a glass of wine. "Did the flowers stop around the same time my dear brother left on his rescue mission?"

Heat prickled her cheeks, and she didn't answer, choosing to stare into the glass of wine instead. Tipping it back, she emptied it in several quick gulps.

The silence was heavy for a few minutes until he grabbed her empty glass, filling it again. "So ... bad day?"

"It was syphoning practice again today." She sighed. "And they can't find Braya."

Brenden set the bottle down, wrapping an arm around her shoulder. "I'm not surprised. The storms usually hit harder up by Lakehaven around this time of year, so if our weather is any indicator, they've had a bad few weeks."

Heat filled her cheeks. She hadn't thought about how hard it must be traveling in these conditions. *How much cold would a thin tent stave off?* She ran a hand over her face, ashamed of what she had put Bo and the other soldiers through. *At least Rowan deserves it,* she thought, halfway through her second glass of wine.

"Hey, easy there," Brenden said with a soft chuckle. "It's not a race, right?"

Raylyn looked up at him, his sharp blue eyes causing her mind to go blank for a moment. This was the reprieve she needed from the barrage of worries and pains ceaselessly running through her head. Without hesitating, she reached up and stroked his face, the stubble of his beard prickling her hands. The soft kindness in his eyes shifted to a hungry desire at her touch. She leaned forward, their lips connecting softly. He pulled her closer, their bodies pressed together, and their kiss deepened. His hands slipped under her shirt, creeping up her waist, tickling over her belly, gently caressing her breasts.

She could think of nothing but want, and she shifted herself onto his lap, reaching down and tugging off his tunic. Her belly tingled at the sight of him shirtless, and she trailed her fingers over the defined muscles of his chest and abdomen. She stopped, fingering his beltline, a shy yearning making her pause. He leaned back, a ragged sigh escaping.

"Raylyn," he said, voice strained and raspy. "Maybe we should slow down a bit?" He leaned forward, holding her in place on his lap with one hand, and drained the last of his wine.

"I don't want to slow down," she said breathlessly. It wasn't the first moment passion heated up between them; she figured the entire point of coming to this secluded cabin was to maintain some discretion. Frequenting the prince's chambers at night would lead to a host of added rumors neither wanted to deal with. But Raylyn stopped them every time before things went *too* far. She had never bedded anyone before, never even came close to it.

Her words must have stirred the longing in him because he set his glass down, then began working on the buttons of her shirt, exposing first her neck, then chest, then belly. She shrugged the fabric off her shoulders, and it slid to the ground as goosebumps prickled her bare skin. Brenden's lips found her neck, trailing down to her collar bone, setting her skin ablaze. He reached up, pulling her hair free from the bun. It fell in a cascade around her shoulders, and he ran one hand through it, continuing to kiss her body without pause.

Suddenly, he stood, lifting her into the air. She gave a little shriek of surprise, then giggled, wrapping her legs around his waist. He walked her over to the bed, laying her down with a surprising gentleness. Her heartbeat quickened as he climbed atop her, their bare chests touching. He shivered as her nails gently ran the length of his back. Shifting, she moved her hands between their torsos as she worked on unfastening his belt.

Brenden paused, his entire body growing rigid. He grabbed her hands, stopping her. "Are you sure?" he whispered.

She met his gaze, leaning forward just a bit to kiss him again on the lips. "I'm sure."

They laid together for a long time afterward, skin bare and warm beneath the fur blanket. The fire had burned itself low, and he kissed her one more time before getting up, fastening his trousers as he threw another log into the hearth. "Might as well have another glass of wine," he said, glancing out the window. "I think we're stuck here for the night."

Raylyn got up, blanket draped like a gown. "Really?" she asked, peeking outside. The ice storm strengthened to a blizzard, a wall of white encasing the cabin. She rushed over to the door and opened it a crack, peering out. The wind gusted with fury, whipping flakes inside. She shut the door quickly. "I'd say you're right."

"Can I ask you a question?" Raylyn said, sitting onto the couch.

"Sure." He sat down next to her, staring into the fire.

"Have you heard any ... rumors ... about Terach?" She chewed her lip, searching his face.

His head snapped toward her. "What kind of rumors? Do you think word about our plan has gotten out?" he asked in a rush.

"No, no. Nothing like that." She searched for a moment, trying to find the right words. "Rumors about his ... private life."

He stared at her, face blank. "Could you be more specific?"

She sighed. There wouldn't be a delicate way to phrase this. "Does he force students to sleep with him?"

"Oh," Brenden leaned back, relaxing. "That."

"How can you be so casual about it?" Raylyn asked, appalled.

"I'm sorry if it sounds like I'm being flippant. I thought for a moment we were all going to be hung for treason. Let me breathe for a second." He chuckled, moving to fix the blanket sliding off her shoulder. "It's a bit of a story, but since we're in no rush ..." He poured them both another glass of wine and continued, "Terach went through a pretty bad phase about ... two decades ago."

"What do you mean, 'bad phase'?" Raylyn asked as he paused to take a sip.

He swirled his glass. "He was in love with my mother."

"I—what?" she asked, taken aback.

"I think that's probably the most important part of his story. He was deeply in love with my mother, though I don't think he has ever voiced those words out loud."

They were quiet for a minute, the only sound coming from the crackling of the flames. "How did she pass?" she asked quietly.

"*That* is a debatable question, and the answer changes depending on who you ask. My father claims it was a mysteriously rare and incurable illness. Terach believes she was poisoned. The accepted answer at Court is the former, of course." He took another long sip, then looked at her sideways. "It's funny for this to come up tonight. Her birthday is tomorrow."

"I'm so sorry," Raylyn whispered, her voice cracking.

He shrugged. "I was a kid." His eyes stared into the distance. "She went to Cystra, hoping to stave off a war. Tensions had been escalating over the border—like always—and she told us she had this perfect plan to secure the peace."

Something clicked inside Raylyn. "Your brother's engagement."

"Huh, I didn't know you knew about that," he said, brows raised. "But yes, you're right, of course. I still remember the morning she left. *'Behave for your father, and don't argue with your brother.'*" He laughed. "We were swinging punches before her carriage even disappeared." He finished the remaining wine, appraising the near-empty bottle. "Good thing I came prepared," he said with a wink.

He walked over to the table where a large basket rested and pulled out another bottle, followed by some cheeses, fruit, and bread. She watched him, his upper half still bare, as he made up a large plate.

"Here," he said, pressing a strawberry to her lips. She took a bite, juice dripping down her chin. "Goddess, you're distracting," he murmured, and kissed the juice off her chin, leading to her lips. The warm tingling filled her lower belly again, and she allowed herself to fall into a hazy state of oblivion for a few minutes, the taste of berries and wine mixing as they kissed.

Her stomach growled, and they both laughed, breaking apart. She grabbed a piece of bread. "Where was I?" he asked, swallowing a slice of cheese. "Mom's trip, right? When she returned, she was so changed. Her skin was ashen, some of her hair had fallen out... she couldn't even walk by herself at that point. She told my father no one was

310

to blame, and she secured the treaty. She made him swear on her deathbed he would uphold the peace.

"Terach was furious. I remember him shouting at my father, saying it's obvious someone from Cystra poisoned her. He offered to lead the armies himself, but Father refused. Whether out of denial they were the cause of her death, or due to the promise he made, I don't know. What I *do* know is Terach never treated my father the same after that day. I think deep down, he despises him."

Her mind raced, processing this information. So many things clicked into place—the king's reluctance to war, Terach's underhanded comments, even Rowan's continued betrothal. "So Terach became depressed?" she asked, trying to understand where this tale was leading.

"He definitely didn't cope well when she passed, and who could blame him? Imagine the love of your life taken from you, and no one caring to seek vengeance. I think his inability to persuade my father to fight left him feeling powerless. And he did whatever he could to feel in control again." He paused, touching one of Raylyn's curls with fondness. "I hope you don't think I'm excusing his actions; they were wrong. But he isn't the same man he was back then. Any rumors you hear about forcing women to bed him are speaking of the man he once was, not who he is today."

She mulled this over. It made more sense, though didn't explain Talia's firsthand accusations. "I didn't know about your mother. I'm so sorry," Raylyn finally said, her stomach twisting. Indecision still twisted in her mind, and she didn't know what to believe about Terach.

Brenden shrugged. "Other than my brother, father, and Terach, no one else knows."

Her pulse raced. *Such a secret.* "I won't tell," she promised.

He laughed loudly. "Of course you won't. You couldn't, even if you wanted to."

She raised a brow. "What does that mean?" she asked, biting into another berry.

"The spell, remember? You won't be able to tell people my secrets unless I unbind you."

A wave of horrified understanding washed over her, the blood draining from her face. She was too aware of her nakedness, of their proximity. She shifted backward, putting space between them on the couch. *He could do anything to me right now,* she realized, *and I wouldn't be able to tell a soul.*

He must have sensed the change in her because his eyes mirrored her horror. Running a hand through his hair, he shook his head. "Raylyn, that came out wrong. It's not like that. I would never do anything to hurt you."

"Is all of this just... just a weird power trip for you or something?" she asked, wrapping the blanket tighter around her shoulders.

"Of course not!" he insisted. He reached up to comfort her but thought better of it and lowered his hand. "Raylyn, I *care* for you. Too much, I think."

She looked at him, suspicion still clear on her face. "Right." She stood, picking up her shirt and trousers, donning them.

"You seriously don't believe me?"

"Ever since I came here, all people do is lie to me." She should have realized his affection was insincere. "You're just like your brother," she hissed.

Jealousy darkened his face, and he rushed over to her and grabbed her arm. Her anger melted into fear, and she flinched backward, unable to break his grip. "I thought so," he said. "What *exactly* is there between you and my brother?"

"Nothing." She tried to squirm away, but his hand tightened. "Just like there's nothing between us."

His hand that held her glowed, and she felt a channel open, connecting her to him. She didn't have time to react. Every nerve inside her was alive, on fire, tingling. It stopped suddenly, and Brenden released his grip. He turned, collapsing onto the couch, his head cradled in his hands.

Raylyn stood, dumbfounded. "What did you just do?" she asked quietly, already knowing the answer.

"I released you from the spell," he muttered, not looking up.

"Why?"

"Goddess, Raylyn, isn't it obvious?" He threw his hands into the air in exasperation. "I don't want you to feel like my prisoner. The fear in your eyes makes me want to vomit!" He shook his head slowly as he regarded her. "If anyone is bound, it's me."

Her breath was coming fast, making her dizzy. She sat on the bed, staring at him from across the room. "What do you mean?"

He met her eye, pain clear on his face. "Damn it, Raylyn. I'm falling in love with you."

✧

"Sorry I'm a little late," Raylyn said, as she rushed into Terach's office. She threw her workbag on the ground. She would have to go straight to the Infirmary for her shift after this meeting. "Had to feed the cat." Brenden smiled at her as she sat down next to him, then kissed her cheek. If Terach was surprised by their exchange, he didn't show it. Instead, he raised a hand toward the door, his palm glowing. Raylyn didn't see anything happen and raised an eyebrow, questioning.

"Just giving us some extra privacy from any unintended audiences."

"Oh." She swallowed, her throat dry as she remembered the seriousness of this meeting. She stared at Terach for a few extra seconds, trying to see him in a new light, as everything that Talia and Brenden told her was fresh in her mind. He looked back with a smile, his eyes kind. While she didn't think Talia was lying, it was easy in that moment to dismiss her accusations as misunderstandings. Terach was like a doting uncle, not a power-abusing predator. *Everyone makes mistakes*, she thought.

"So," Brenden began, as he grabbed Raylyn's hand, intertwining their fingers. "Terach told me you've really progressed with your abilities." He looked down at her, his eyes warm. A trickle of heat cut through some of her anxiousness, warming her belly as memories from the night before flashed through her mind.

"I guess so," she said, looking away. His eyes were too distracting.

"Don't be modest," Terach said. "You've mastered intricacies I didn't even know were possible with syphoning."

"Not like we have copious amounts of information on the art," Raylyn said, snorting. "There's no *Syphoning for Beginners* books in the library. I've searched."

"Regardless," Terach said, waving a hand. "You're ready. We need to set our plans into motion." He grabbed a piece of parchment from his drawer, scanning it quickly. "My sources in Cystra informed me of three different battalions that have emerged, and at least two of them are moving eastward toward the border. If we don't act now, it will be too late."

A wave of nausea came over her. Brenden gave her hand a squeeze, sensing her nerves. "We know Raylyn needs to weaken my father, but she needs to be free of suspicion. If word gets out she visited his chambers and suddenly he's incapacitated, rumors *will* emerge that it was her doing."

"Whispers of his behaviors are already spreading through the Court, especially after what happened to that servant," Terach replied, shoving the letter back into his desk. The image of the burned girl flashed through her mind. Thankfully, she had been passing through the hallway with Brenden at the right time. Though she was able to heal the girl, leaving her skin free from any scars, there was little she could do to help the emotional toll of the incident, and the servant resigned, leaving her position to go back to her parents' farm.

"Even so, we need to take precautions. I am going to send Thorne to give him another full examination, ensure again there isn't some curable ailment before we move forward. You will go with her," he said, nodding to Raylyn. "Once the exam is finished, if nothing is found contributing to his madness, then you will intervene. The goal is only to weaken him. His death would lead to an extensive investigation which we do *not* have time for."

Raylyn's blood froze to ice. "There must be another way. Thorne despises me. She won't agree to my presence."

"She *will* agree, as I will order her to do so. You've made yourself known as one of the most prominent healers amongst the pupils of the Academy. A special regard won't seem so unlikely. It would be easily dismissed as additional instruction in identifying rare conditions." He crossed his arms, apparently pleased with this rationale.

"Perhaps, if everyone didn't already know she absolutely abhors me! It's a running joke in the Infirmary that I must leave before the sun breaks the horizon, else I risk running into her! Her recent trip has been such a reprieve." Thorne was requested to a nearby city to give a presentation to their school, due to soon return. Her absence lightened the mood in the Infirmary considerably, and even Creena was whistling while she worked the other night.

Brenden cleared his throat. "I think Terach's plan makes sense. There's little to no chance of you approaching the king on your own, not with the way he's acting. He won't even see *me* anymore. It isn't so hard to believe the head of the healing wing would make amends with her most proficient student."

Two against one. "Let's hope Thorne can figure out what's wrong."

Terach smiled. "It will go smoothly, and as soon as you're out of his chamber, your role will be complete. Brenden and I will move forward with the Court."

"When will I begin?" Raylyn asked, throat tight.

"Thorne should return tomorrow."

One more day, she thought, head spinning.

"Thank the Goddess you're finally here," Creena said. Her cheeks were flushed, and the hair at her temples was damp with sweat. "Well, hurry up then," she muttered as Raylyn tied on her apron and knotted her hair off her face. "We've another wave of refugees, and they didn't fare well in the storm last night."

Raylyn glanced around, noting the chaos. The beginning of her shifts were usually busy as patients finished dinner and the more senior healers finished charting. Now, at least double the amount of patients crowded the ward, every bed filled. A few cots bordered one of the healers' stations. Apparently, there was an overflow.

"Take group C. Vivvy has report."

"My own assignment?" she asked, excitement tightening her chest.

"You can manage!" Creena called from across the chamber, disappearing behind a curtain.

Vivvy, a few years her senior, gave her a brief overview on her group of patients. All were newly arrived since her last shift. Hypothermia and frostbite were the main conditions, along with one boy with a broken leg.

"Goodnight Viv," Raylyn said, waving as she left. Starting her routine, she grabbed a cart of linens and towels, and stocked each of the patient rooms, introducing herself as she went along.

I'll have to grab more cloths, she thought, pulling the last curtain open. "Good evening," she said for the dozenth time, setting the linens next to a washbasin, her back to the patient's bed. "My name's Raylyn, and I'm going to be taking care of you tonight. I've brought some fresh bedding, and I can help you get cleaned up if you'd like." She shifted through the stacked pile of cloth, pulling out the clean sheets and blanket.

"Raylyn?" a familiar voice said from the cot behind her.

It can't be. She whipped around, her heart stopping. "Braya!" She rushed to the bed, embracing her friend as tears cascaded down her cheeks. Braya hugged her back, giving her a little squeeze.

"I'm so sorry," Raylyn said, pulling away. She wiped the tears from her cheeks, but more fell, making the effort futile. "I tried to write you, to tell you to come, but I think you were already gone. I never should have left you," she continued in a rush. "And how did you end up here? Are you okay?" Her mind raced, trying to remember the report Vivvy gave her.

Braya laughed. "I'm okay." She held up her foot. "Frostbite," she said. Her toes were bright red.

"Oh, Goddess," Raylyn muttered, inspecting her foot further. The skin was shiny, like a newly formed scar.

"You should've seen it last night. It was black," Braya said. "One of your healer friends did a really good job, said I should've lost at least half my foot."

Raylyn stared at her, half convinced she was hallucinating. "I just can't believe you're finally here. I'll have to tell Bo!"

"Who's Bo?" Braya asked, swinging her legs over the side of the bed. "And do I have to stay here another night? Look, I can move all five toes." She wiggled her foot happily. Raylyn watched closely, the baby toe hardly twitching.

"Get back in bed! Are you crazy?" Braya didn't move, so Raylyn picked up her friend's legs, swinging them back onto the cot.

Braya smiled. "Goddess, I've missed you."

"You have to tell me everything! And your house, your father—I'm so sorry," she said, words flowing out like water from a broken dam.

"The house was unfortunate, but Dad deserved his fate. And before you ask, no. I didn't set the fire. Though, I wish I had." She rolled her eyes. "At least then I'd be persecuted for a crime I actually committed."

"You don't have to explain that to me," Raylyn said. "I offered to poison him ages ago." They laughed, and for a moment it was like no time passed at all. Raylyn felt as if they were back in their old tree fort, hiding from their parents.

The curtain ripped open, making Raylyn jump. "What are you doing?" Creena asked, eyes wide when she saw Raylyn sitting on the bed next to Braya. "You've got two patients ringing for you! Tonight's *not* the night for reunions!"

Raylyn smiled an apology to Braya. "I'll be back, and then you have to tell me *everything*."

A few hours before dawn, the last of her patients finally fell asleep. His frostbite must have been worse than Braya's because three fingers on his left hand were missing, areas of black and purple spreading to his palm. They would likely need to take his entire hand. She placed a cool rag on his forehead, then stepped into the hall. "I think his wounds are festering," she said quietly to Creena.

The older woman nodded. "They'll amputate it in the morning. For now, we'll keep his fever at bay."

Normally, Raylyn would have thrived in the busyness of the shift, and she had ached for the freedom of her own assignment for so long. But she was frustrated, as she could only get snippets of Braya's story as she bounced from patient to patient. With everyone sleeping now, she peeked into Braya's room to find her friend also passed out from exhaustion. She quietly pulled a chair into the room, so she could chart her shift notes while keeping a close eye on Braya. She worried to look away or turn her back for too long, lest Braya would disappear again.

She passed reports on to Vivvy, who chugged coffee while taking notes, deep circles set beneath her eyes. "Try and get some rest. Will you relieve me again tonight?" she asked as Raylyn gathered her supplies and stuffed it into her bag.

"I'm off tonight," she said. "But I'm actually not leaving. My friend is in bed twelve." She turned, almost missing the shocked expression on the healer's face.

"You're still here?" Braya asked, stretching as Raylyn ducked through the curtain.

"If you think I'm ever leaving you alone again, you're wrong." Braya smiled. "Anyway, you didn't finish telling me how you ended up with a group of foreign refugees."

Vivvy stopped by, offering them both a breakfast tray with a wink. Braya tore into the food with ferocity. "Don't judge," she said, her mouth stuffed. "They told me to eat a lot. It'll help with the healing or something."

Raylyn appraised her, realizing how much weight Braya had lost. The light cast shadows in the hollows of her cheeks, and her arms were thin, some of the muscle wasted away. "No judgement. I'll just sit back, so you don't accidently mistake me for part of your meal."

After a few minutes, Braya was satisfied. "I did receive your letter," she said, pushing the breakfast tray away from her. "And truthfully, it likely saved my life."

"How so?" Raylyn asked, raising a brow.

"I was preparing to come. As if I would wait for an escort." She rolled her eyes. "Don't you know me?"

Raylyn grinned. She was concerned Braya would attempt to make the trip alone when she sent the letter.

"Anyway, I'm not proud of this, but I was stealing some supplies from Miss Bernshaw—come now, don't look at me like that! I knew the warm weather wouldn't hold forever, and that woman is ancient. What would she need a traveling cloak for, anyway? I had a little pile of things to bring with me stashed away in the stable: saddle bags packed full of bread, jerky, you name it. The last thing I wanted was just a nice cloak. You know how threadbare mine was.

"Anyway, I was only halfway back to my house before I smelled the smoke. Went up like tinder. Some of the village guard sounded the alarm, and all I could think of was my pile of goods that didn't *quite* belong to me. So, I ran. Fully stocked horse and thick new cloak." She shook her head. "I should've realized how it would make me look. So worried about being caught a thief that I earned myself the title of murderer." She snorted. "Could've killed him a hundred times over if I had the notion to, but I didn't. And they all turned a blind eye every time I showed up battered and bruised. But, oh no, let's all mourn the abusive alcoholic's death!" A few tears trickled down her cheeks, and she wiped at them ferociously.

Raylyn sat on the bed next to her, grabbing her hand. "I'm so sorry, Braya," she said, her voice a whisper.

She collapsed into her, sobs racking her body. "He was a bastard," she said, sniffling, "but he was all I had left." They stayed there for a minute, before Braya pulled away. "Guess I've got you back, though."

"We've been looking for you for months," Raylyn said. "I never gave up. If they would've let me, I'd be gone right now, searching!"

"Good thing you're not," Braya said with a smile.

"Where did you escape to?"

"Ah, now, *that's* quite the story."

They talked for hours, Braya explaining her escape across the border into Cystra, and Raylyn sharing the woes of her first few months of training. Though free from Brenden's binding, she didn't reveal the plot against the king; there were too many ears around.

"It's bad over there, Ray," Braya continued. "Non-mages are treated worse than dogs. I tried to find work, especially on the rural farms, thinking away from the cities would be best." She snorted, shaking her head in disgust. "No one would have me, especially not when I asked to be *paid*."

Vivvy pulled open the curtain, causing both girls to turn. The healer took her time inspecting Braya's foot, poking each toe with a tiny pin. "Ah!" Braya said, jerking her leg away. "That tickles."

Satisfied with Braya's healing, Vivvy turned to Raylyn, cocking her head. "Aren't you going to get some sleep?"

"Don't worry about me, Viv. Just catching up." Vivvy gave a disapproving shake of her head and rolled her eyes. "Guess I'll bring you a lunch tray, too," she said, disappearing around the curtain into the bustle of the Infirmary.

Braya sat up straighter in bed, kicking off her covers. "I was traveling south for at least a month, continuously rejected as a farmhand. I didn't realize I was heading straight for the fighting." She shook her head with a sigh. "That first night I camped maybe half a mile into the forest, lit a fire, the works. Well, someone saw the smoke because next thing I remember, I woke up laying on the ground, beaten, and my horse and supplies were gone."

"You're lucky you didn't get killed!" Raylyn said with a little gasp.

Braya nodded. "I know... I ran into this crew the next day. They helped me find some of the Ellendrian soldiers assisting refugees at the border. Non-mages are being forced out of their homes, their assets seized. It's disgusting."

Vivvy came back with lunch, and the girls ate quietly, fatigue washing over Raylyn as the shock of discovering Braya faded.

"What I've been wondering," Raylyn began, swallowing the last of her sandwich, "is how the influx of refugees continues? Every week we get a new wave of people, but doesn't King Aedam want to keep his citizens? Aren't they trying to limit people from escaping?"

Braya stopped chewing, a look of thoughtfulness crossing her face. "From what I've overheard, it's harder to leave the cities with more guards to keep an eye on people. King Aedam doesn't agree with the enslavement of the non-mages, but what is he to do? He can't punish or imprison every mage and noble, or he'd have nearly a third of his population in the dungeon." She glanced down at her lunch, grabbing the glass of water, and drained it in four long sips. "I think people are going to keep slipping out until the entire government is overturned."

A chill washed over Raylyn, prickling her skin. It had been centuries since slavery was abolished. "We should be helping them," she said in a hushed voice. Even if the attacks on Rowan weren't ordered by the king, the country was falling apart. *How many innocent lives will be lost or enslaved because of this madness?*

The curtain opened again with a rustle, and Raylyn expected to see Vivvy coming to grab their empty trays. Instead, it was Terach, whose surprise mirrored her own. Slowly, understanding washed over her as she remembered Terach often visited the wounded refugees, offering kind words and traces of hope.

"Raylyn," Terach said, brows raised, "didn't your shift end this morning?"

"It did," she said, smile spreading on her face, "But look who I've found!" She stood, grabbing Braya's hand and squeezing it.

His blank face stared for a moment before understanding crossed over it. "Surely, not your missing friend?"

"Yes!" she said, her voice high and squeaky with excitement. "This is Braya. And Braya, this is Lord Terach, the king's advisor, head of academic affairs, and my mentor."

Braya laughed. "That's a mouthful of a title." Raylyn shot her a look. Braya always was a bit of a nuisance with authority figures; she thought it a game to make them as irate as possible. But then Braya smiled up at him, her blue eyes sparkling and for a moment, the striking girl was back, and it was easy to forget she was a malnourished, injured escapee.

"Indeed, it is," Terach said, returning her smile. "Raylyn, I implore you to get some rest. You have a busy day ahead of you. Thorne should be arriving soon." His eyes narrowed, and she understood the meaning.

"Right," she replied, warmth heating her cheeks. She forgot about their plan. Her stomach twisted as anxiety's creeping tendrils took hold. She turned to Braya. "Do you think you'll be okay without me for a little while? You have to *promise* me you won't just disappear again."

Braya stuck out her little finger. "Pinky promise," she said with a smile. "Though if you could please convince your healer friends to release me, the pattern on those curtains is starting to make me nauseous."

"They'll discharge you as soon as they see fit," she replied as she left. "I'll come check on you at dinnertime."

CHAPTER 18

"**WAKE UP! WAKE UP, WAKE UP, WAKE** *up!*"

Raylyn startled, bolting upright, nausea rising in her throat. "What's wrong?" she asked, looking around wildly, traces of sleep vanishing.

Talia had jumped on top of her in the bed, her eyes wide, all color drained from her face. "I've figured it out!"

Raylyn rubbed her face, trying to shake off her exhaustion. "Figured what out?"

"The *king*," she said meaningfully, her voice lowering. "It's poison. In his *tea*." She said the last word gleefully, as if she just found the answer to a riddle.

She stared at her. "What?"

"Get up, I'll show you."

Raylyn raced down the hallway as Talia led her to her chambers. "I've been spying for a month now, impersonating a guard," she whispered as she unlocked her door. "Should've seen me sneak the armor." She grinned. "But anyway, it didn't make sense, his sudden shift in behavior, so I watched for a while, trying to find any type of weird pattern. But there was nothing." Opening the door, she led Raylyn inside. A subtle scent of wood lingered in the air accompanied by rustling and intermittent squeaks, and she glanced around, stunned at the dozen cages occupying most of the room's floor space.

"What's with the rats?" she asked, peeking inside the closest cage. The large, white rodent was sifting through the woodchip bedding with its pointy nose.

"Right, I'm getting there. There was no common thread, except for his daily requests for tea! So, when a servant brought it up last week, I swapped it out, replacing it with some I brewed." Her face twisted with guilt. "I suppose it was my fault that girl got burned because when the king realized the tea wasn't correct, he completely lost it."

"Wait, you knew about that?" Raylyn asked. There was no one else around that day besides her, Brenden, and the two guards.

She wiggled her eyebrows deviously. And then, like rippling water, her face shifted and took the form of a burly, heavily mustached man. Raylyn's mouth popped open in surprise. She shifted back to her normal features with a wink. "So, I took his special tea, and I decided to conduct some experiments. Hence, the rats. And look!" She rushed to the farthest cage, and Raylyn followed, the squeaking and rustling growing louder.

"Goddess," she said in a hushed voice. The rat was thrashing about, throwing itself on the bars, and occasionally biting its own leg. Drops of blood were scattered on the woodchips.

"It's the one I've been feeding the tea."

"We have to find Brenden."

They ran toward his room, not bothering to hide their haste. A few passersby stared at them in confusion, but no one stopped to ask why they ran. Turning a corner, Raylyn skidded to a stop, tripping in her haste. Thorne and Terach also stopped, arm in arm, staring at her with confusion.

"We were just coming to fetch you for your additional training," Terach said, one eyebrow raised as he watched Raylyn pull herself up from where she fell on the floor.

Sucking in huge breaths from the exertion, she gasped, "We ... need ... to ... talk."

"What is it, *Madam* Ashton?" Thorne said, her face twisted with distaste. "Always one for such drama."

"They are matters best told in privacy," Talia chimed in, her breathing even and calm.

"And who are you?" Thorne asked, continuing her condescending tone.

Oh, enough of this nonsense, Raylyn thought. "It's about the king," she said, seething.

Terach's eyes narrowed, and he wordlessly grabbed her arm, all but dragging her down the hall to his office.

Once inside the room, Terach spun at Raylyn. "What is going on?" he hissed through gritted teeth.

She glanced at Talia, who began talking in a hurried rush, eyes on her feet. "I've been suspecting for some time, my Lord, the recent changes in the king's demeanor were not natural. I believe he is being poisoned."

"Ha! Nonsense! He's been examined thoroughly multiple times. Are you implying that Madam Thorne is incompetent in her ability to detect poison? And who are you to think you know so much about him?"

Talia flinched, shrinking in on herself, but remained silent, refusing to reveal her position as spy.

"Absolutely absurd. And you," he turned to Raylyn, lip curled in anger. "I expected so much better from *you* than some childish game of detective."

"Terach, she has *proof*."

"Proof? *Very* likely—"

"What kind of proof?" Thorne asked, her voice even and calm. Both Raylyn and Talia's heads whipped up in surprise.

"I've conducted an experiment on rats, Madam," Talia said, her voice growing steadier. "I stole a pot of his tea on a hunch, and over the past three days, I've fed it to two of them. One has died; the other is erratic, biting itself as if rabid."

Terach stuttered, spitting in anger, but Thorne held up a hand, silencing him. "It will do no harm to investigate this. Do we know who prepares his tea?"

Talia swallowed. "I do, Madam, but I'm certain she isn't part of this. Someone else must be adding something, or—"

"Send a message to this person to make another batch and have it brought to me in my office at the Academy," Thorne said, cutting her off. "I will test it myself."

Talia gave a curtsy, then darted from the room. Raylyn turned to follow her, but Thorne grabbed her shoulder, stopping her. "How are you involved in this?" she asked, her voice low.

Raylyn's eyes inadvertently darted to Terach, thinking of their plan. "I—uh, Talia is one of my closest friends. She confided in me, and I rushed to ... Terach, thinking he would be the best person to intervene."

Thorne studied her, trying to uncover the hidden lie in her face. Raylyn stared straight back without flinching, until the older woman slowly nodded. Taking that as her dismissal, she began to turn, but Thorne stopped her again. "Have your parents arrived yet for the competition? I saw many families traveling into the capital when I returned."

Raylyn's brows furrowed in confusion. "I didn't sign up for my parents to be invited." There was little point. Not only was she not competing in the competition, but she also had qualms about seeing her mother and father again. A few letters from home came over the past weeks, her mother's looping script clearly addressing her name, but she piled them on her desk, unread.

"Hm, I recall your name being on the list." She smiled, a glint in her eyes, and Raylyn took her chance to fly out the door, heart in her throat. *She wouldn't write to my parents without my consent, would she?* Dread flowed through her veins. She wasn't ready to see them, especially not with everything going on.

She jogged down the hall, hoping to catch up with Talia, finally finding her when she arrived at the kitchens. "Did you fly here?" Raylyn asked, breathless again. Talia gave her a side-eyed look, tears streaming down her face. "What's wrong?"

"It's Ri," she whispered. "She's going to be blamed for this." She wiped her face on her sleeve, glancing up at Raylyn. "I feel like I'm setting her up."

"You're not," Raylyn reassured her. "We have to figure out what's going on. Are you certain Ri's not behind this?"

Talia glared at her. "Of course she isn't!" A kitchen worker bustled through, carrying a tray of dirty dishes, and they paused, holding their tongues until he passed. Once safely out of hearing distance, Talia continued. "She has no motive, it's a good life here, and why would she try to..." She gave Raylyn a meaningful look, too cautions to voice the words "kill the king" out loud.

"What if someone else put her up to it? Threatened her, maybe?"

Talia didn't respond as she chewed the inside of her cheek. "I don't know. Maybe." Her face crumpled in misery at the thought.

"Here ya go, sweets," Ri called, the inner kitchen doors swinging as she bustled toward them, metal tray balanced casually in her hands. "What's the matter?" she asked, seeing the look on Talia's face.

Talia didn't respond, and she looked to Raylyn for help. "Ri," she began, her voice a quiet whisper, "who gave you the recipe for the king's tea?"

"What a strange question," she replied without missing a beat, "it's a family recipe, passed down for generations on my mother's side. Why do you ask?" Though her words were confident, the color began draining from her face.

"Ri, I think the tea's making him sick," Talia said, tears sliding down her face.

"If someone's told you to add something, you need to tell us."

She was quiet for a minute, her eyes growing wide. "I was told—" Her voice cut off, her mouth open, but no sound coming out. Clearing her throat, she tried speaking again. "He—" This time, she began coughing, a look of horror crossing her face as her airway closed, spittle dripping down her chin as her cheeks began to turn a bright red, then purple.

"What's happening to her?" Talia shrieked as the woman collapsed to the floor, still clutching her neck in a futile attempt to breathe.

"Ri, stop trying to speak!" Raylyn commanded, dropping down onto the floor next to her. "It's a spell," she said, glancing quickly at Talia. "Whoever is behind this spelled her to keep her quiet." The seconds were long as they waited helplessly by Ri's side. Finally, she gasped in a shaking breath, burst capillaries tinging her eyes a bright red.

The inner kitchen doors swung open, a few of the workers peeking in to see what the commotion was about. "Just ... swallowed the wrong way," Ri coughed, waving them off. "Back to work, go on now." The curious faces disappeared.

"What are we going to do?" Talia hissed quietly, pulling Ri up from the ground. "She's obviously going to be framed for this!"

Raylyn tried to slow her breathing; her head was spinning. She experienced the same choking suffocation weeks ago when she tried to reveal details of Terach's and Brenden's plan to Talia ... *before* she was released from the binding. *How many people know how to do that?* They made it seem Brenden developed the spell himself. She shivered, realizing both women were staring at her, waiting for an answer. Feigning confidence and trusting her instincts, she eyed the women. "Follow me."

Raylyn rushed the tea tray to Thorne, wondering if her delay would be obvious. She hadn't had much time to think or prepare, but Ri's position as head of kitchens worked to their favor, and she gathered plenty of food, disguising it as another request of the king. *Who would think to look for them in the Hall of Sorrows?* Raylyn thought, trying to comfort herself. She left both Talia and Ri there in the deserted chamber, equipped with candles, bread, and water.

"Took your sweet time," Thorne muttered from behind a small desk piled with neat stacks of papers. Raylyn had never been in her office, and she stared, dumbstruck. Glass vials, tubes, and beakers lined a long counter to the right. Orb light glinted off glass cases filled with labeled jars, mounted high on the walls, and encircling the room. The rest of the space was filled with bookcases, and she squinted, trying to read some of the titles.

She set the tea tray down on the counter, careful to avoid the glassware. "You may leave," Thorne said, catching the curious look on Raylyn's face.

She bit back a reply and wordlessly slipped into the hallway. *At least her office is right next to the Infirmary*, she thought, racing through the door.

"Braya, ready to get out of here yet?" she asked, popping behind the curtain. "I think—" The words died at her lips and icy horror froze her into place. Two healers, Vivvy and a woman she didn't know, who stood on either side of the cot glanced up as she approached. "What's going on?"

Vivvy shook her head, stepping away from the bed. Braya's face was ashen with deep purple hollows beneath her eyes. She held her breath in fear until she saw her friend's chest raise and lower. *Still alive*, she thought with a rush of relief.

"We're not certain what's happening," Vivvy said, her voice soft and low. For the first time, Raylyn noticed the fine lines around her mouth and eyes, and it seemed the woman had aged a dozen years within a day's time. "She was doing so well yesterday and this morning. But after you left, she ... took a turn. Hasn't woken yet, but her vitals are mostly stable, pulse is a bit low."

"Is it an infection?" she asked, "Perhaps from the frostbite?"

"We've checked. She has no fever, no signs of infection, no other injuries. Her lungs are clear. It's as if her body is just giving up. Everyone's condition is deteriorating." She glanced towards the curtains, her brows knotted together as if anxious to check her other patients.

No. Raylyn placed her palms on Braya's chest, light glowing off her skin. She opened a channel and *concentrated*, searching. Mentally, she ran through the length of her friend's body, looking for signs of weakness, disease, anything. She stayed like that for several minutes, inspecting every organ, every inch of vein, hope slowly dwindling. Vivvy was right, it was as if a deep fatigue set over Braya, her heart straining with the effort of beating. "Did you try healing her?"

"There's nothing to focus the energy on, Raylyn," Vivvy replied. "It would do no good."

Shooting her a dark look, Raylyn turned, focusing her attention back on her weakened friend. She closed her eyes, allowing her energy to pour through the channel. Braya's heart began to beat with increased vigor. More and more energy flowed through her, and for a brief second, she considered syphoning more. *But from who? My friends and colleagues? The other sick and dying patients? No.* She broke the connection, panting as she wiped away the beads of sweat at her temple.

Many times, healing a patient without a focus of how and where would result in the energy dissipating into the air, leaving the healer weaker and the patient no stronger. This was *not* one of those times. Braya's pulse continued with renewed strength, and her coloring slowly improved. Vivvy gave a small gasp as Braya's eyes fluttered open.

"What ... the *hell*?" Braya asked weakly, glancing around the crowded room. Raylyn snorted in laughter.

"How?" Vivvy said in wonder, "I'm so sorry. It doesn't usually work—"

"It's okay," Raylyn said, cutting her off. "Go to your other patients. I've got it from here." Vivvy nodded, and she and the other healer left, glancing back over their shoulders in wonder as they slipped behind the curtain.

"Scared me half to death," Raylyn said, as Braya sat up, rubbing her head. "You okay?"

"I'm ... fine. Just a headache, and I think I might—" Raylyn rushed over, passing her an emesis basin just in time. "...puke," Braya finished, wiping her mouth with the back of her hand. "Eh, I feel a little better now."

She handed her a mug of a water. "Has this happened before? This ... fainting spell?"

"No, never," she said, scrunching her face up in concentration. "Though one time my father pushed me into the wall, and I saw stars ... but this was different."

A creeping suspicion rose in Raylyn's chest, but she couldn't place what was wrong. She struggled with herself, trying to find the answer to the puzzle. But like an itch just out of reach, it was inaccessible. She rubbed her face in frustration. "Do you remember anything before you passed out? When I left you earlier this afternoon, you were completely fine."

"Nothing really. Your fancy friend made rounds, introducing himself to all the patients here. I got tired. Figured I could take a quick nap, there's nothing else to do here ... and I guess I just now woke up."

Raylyn thought on that for a minute. "I'll be right back. I need a word with the healers."

Braya nodded, then leaned back, closing her eyes.

She found Viv a few rooms down standing over a patient's bed, hands laid gently on the person's chest. She approached, noting the hard white cast on the boy's leg. He couldn't have been older than ten and was even more emaciated than Braya, with cheek bones so prominent, he looked almost skeletal. The glowing in Vivvy's palms ceased, and she acknowledged Raylyn, eyes still locked on the boy's face. "I don't have the reserves you do, and healing this many patients, well... I can only spare so much."

"Are they all like this?" Raylyn asked, her voice shaky. She stepped closer to the boy, watching his steady breathing.

"Most. A few retained consciousness, but they all complain of the same symptoms: lethargy, muscle fatigue, headache." She shook her head. "Something similar happened on the other ward, but the patients there were so sick, we didn't think anything of it..."

Raylyn chewed her lip, thinking. "Some type of catching illness that spread?" she asked, already dismissing the idea. Vivvy shook her head, too. If it *was* that catching, at least some healers would be ill, as well. And besides, when she channeled, she felt no presence of infection or disease. *What could cause dozens of people to nearly die on the same day, with the same symptoms, no presence of disease?* She stood in silence, hovering over the little boy's body, his chest slowly rising with each breath. For a second, Raylyn was reminded of the hog she had syphoned, its breathing slow, energy depleted, but otherwise no sign of injury or weakness.

Hot, metallic blood filled her mouth as she inadvertently bit her lip, slicing through the already delicate skin. *It's impossible,* she thought, shaking her head. *There're no syphons other than me, and who would target a group of injured refugees?* Dread poisoned her stomach and bitter bile rose to the back of her throat. *Unless the man who raped my mother is still here.* She had tried hard to dismiss her mother's letter, refusing to dwell on its contents. It sickened her, knowing she was a child of violence. But it all added up: the weakened patients, their symptoms, the lack of causative illness.

Vivvy was placing a wet rag on the child's forehead with delicate hands, completely oblivious to Raylyn's internal battle. "Hey Viv," she begun, swallowing hard, "have there been many visitors to the Infirmary lately?"

"Just staff... No one here has family or friends to come visit."

Deflated, Raylyn nodded, and followed the healer out of the room. She popped her head into Braya's room. "Do you think you can survive for a few hours while I go write a letter?"

"Can't I just come with you?" She sat up hopefully.

Raylyn considered. Braya seemed mostly recovered, and if her suspicions were correct, getting out of such a vulnerable place would be best. *But what if I'm wrong?* She thought. *What if it's some elusive illness and taking her will risk her life?* "Try to go a single night without losing consciousness, then we'll talk." Braya flopped backward, burying her face in her pillow with an exaggerated groan.

"I'll be back before you know it," Raylyn promised before racing out of the building. Once outside in the dark, cold air, she stopped, spinning into a mound of snow, and vomited.

I should be in better shape by now, she thought, as she sucked in huge breaths, her chest burning. Little Guy mewed at her, weaving between her legs as she entered her room.

"I'm sorry," she said, as he continued to look for his meal. "Later, okay?" She grabbed the scriber off her desk and the spelled quill next to it.

Bo, this message is a day overdue, but Braya is here! We can speak more on her miraculous arrival when you return, but there are insidious things happening that I need to address, and my trust is shattering with those around me. I do not know to whom else to turn, and though he has deceived me in the past, Rowan's lies have never intentionally caused the suffering of innocents. The king is being poisoned, an attack on Cystra is looming, and—I know how absurd this sounds—I am certain another syphon resides at Court, feeding off the suffering of others. Please make haste in your return, for it feels as if the world is crumbling.

A knock on the door caused her to jump, and she slid the parchment into a drawer, slamming it shut. Her heart hammered as the knob of her door jiggled, and it slowly opened. Brenden's head peeked through, his lips curving into a smile when he saw her. "Where have you been? You missed our training session."

Realization spread over her like cold water. Time hadn't stopped, and she had inadvertently missed casting class, as well. Brenden glanced into the hall, then proceeded into her room, closing the door, and locking the bolt. Little Guy slipped through her legs, disappearing beneath the bed. Her heart hammered, the image of Ri suffocating on the kitchen floor flashing through her mind. "I—I must have lost track of time... Braya's here."

He rushed at her, scooping her into a tight embrace. She resisted the urge to flee from his touch. "That's amazing! Where is she?" He glanced around the room, as if expecting Braya to emerge from the air.

"The Infirmary." At his confused glance, she added, "It's a long story."

His face crumpled. "I wish I had the time." He sat on the edge of the bed, patting the mattress next to him. "Come, sit. We need to talk. Ouch!" he yelped, pulling his feet up off the floor. Raylyn could see one of Little Guy's paws peeking under the draped quilt.

"Yes, we do," Raylyn agreed. She kept her face blank, but inside, her heart raced, accusation bubbling at her lips.

"We've received word that one of Cystra's battalions is due to cross the border in only a few days' time. I'm going to rally our troops and lead in the attack. We won't just sit by and watch our country fall." It was customary for royalty to fight, and unwillingness to participate in the battles was cause enough for another to lay claim to the throne.

Raylyn startled. She wasn't expecting this. "But what about your father? He hasn't given the word to take up arms against them. What about the treaty?"

Brenden stared at her. "You took care of that ... barrier ... didn't you?"

"I—*what*? No! Thorne's still testing the tea for poison!"

His mouth fell open, but words didn't come out. He closed his eyes and ran a hand through his hair, taking a few deep breaths. "Terach didn't tell me. But regardless, we no longer have the privilege of time. If we don't move to defend ourselves, they will commit a massacre on our people."

Raylyn stayed silent for a moment, wheels turning in her head. "Terach didn't tell you the plan was on hold?"

He shook his head, not meeting her eyes.

"But you don't seem shocked to learn your father's tea has been poisoned."

"You said Thorne's still testing it. The theory isn't confirmed yet." His words were convincing enough, but he still didn't look at her.

"How many people have you spelled into silence?"

"What are you talking about?"

"The spell you placed—and lifted—on me, to keep me quiet about our plan. How many others have you forced to do your bidding?"

He finally looked up, eyes narrowing. "I don't force anyone to do anything. It is the way of the spell. If it isn't willingly accepted, it holds no power."

"I'm sure a threat from the prince of Ellendria would be enough motivation for anyone to accept it, especially a non-mage working in the kitchens." She tried to stand up and put distance between them, but he turned, grabbing her wrists, forcing her still.

"You have to understand," he began, voice low and pleading. "My father was going to let this country fall. I did what I had to do to protect us. Do you want to live under our enemy's rule? Have your friend enslaved because she has no powers?"

She tugged at his grip to no avail. "You poisoned your own father!" she hissed. "Moral people and just rulers don't go around poisoning their way to the throne!"

He laughed, rolling his eyes. "Oh, you are so sweetly naïve." She flinched as he leaned down, kissing the top of her head, then released her hands. She flew away from him, back against the opposite wall. "Raylyn," he said, shaking his head, "I would never hurt you. Don't you know that by now?" She didn't reply. "I'm leaving now. I think the distance will give you time to think things over, understand my decisions. When I return, we will talk again." His eyes searched her face. "I love you, you know that?" Again, she remained silent, and he gave her a sad smile before walking out the door.

"Brenden!" she called, stopping him. He looked back at her, hope simmering in his eyes. "Is Terach a syphon?" The words slipped from her lips before she had time to analyze if they were wise.

Brenden snorted, raising his eyebrows at her. "No." He turned back, sweeping across the floor toward her. She backed up until she was flush with the wall, with nowhere else to run. Reaching down, he caressed her face, leaving a tingling trail down her cheek. "You're the only one blessed with that special power," he promised, kissing her full on the lips. "I'll come back to you," he promised, kissing her forehead softly. He left, but Raylyn was frozen in place, staring at the door. His assurance didn't ease her suspicions, but she did believe if Terach was truly a syphon, Brenden was oblivious.

"You still holding up?" Raylyn asked as she sat next to the cot. Her voice strained with the effort to sound normal, relief cascading through her at finding her friend still awake and relatively healthy.

"Perky as a peach." Braya sat up, her face serious. "I can't take another night here, Ray. Please, get me out of here."

"Let's just see how this night goes," Raylyn said, ignoring her friend's groan. "Listen, we have no idea why everyone became so ill, and we have to make sure it doesn't recur."

"What's your theory?" Braya said, leaning forward.

"How do you know I have one?"

"You always have a theory about something."

She smirked; it was true. Ever since her childhood, she was investigating the cause of things. Why the sky was blue, why the leaves changed colors, why boys were always pulling on Braya's curls when they were children. And she always uncovered the answers. "I think there's another syphon," she whispered, voice as soft as a breath.

"That's a good one." She leaned back, hands behind her head, contemplating. "Alright, give me the argument. What caused you to come up with that?"

Raylyn crinkled her nose. "Well, for one, my mother hinted that my real father had the same ability, and that he might still be here, at Court."

Braya startled, slipping halfway off the cot. "Damn, that's heavy," she said, shaking her head. "How long have you been carrying that?"

"Couple months."

"I'm sorry. You know Charles will always be your real father, right?"

"I know."

Jolting awake, Raylyn's heart pounded, confused by her unfamiliar surroundings. As if a fog was lifting, the scenery clicked into place. She didn't remember falling asleep, but the night was late—or very early morning, it was hard to tell—and Braya sighed softly in her sleep next to her. Raylyn slowly untangled herself from the cot they shared, stretching, her muscles unaccustomed to such tight quarters after the months of her enormous bed. Her stomach growled, reminding her of the meals she had missed over the past few days. Remembering the sweet pears she handed out during her last shift, she tiptoed around the curtain, heading toward the snack cart.

A flash of movement caught her eye, and she turned to see a shadow across the chamber materializing into a tall figure in a dark cloak, back turned to her as it retreated in haste toward the exit. The person passed under one of the dimly lit orbs near the door, light giving detail to the form: tall, short dark hair, slim.

"Hello?" Raylyn called softly, trying to keep from waking the rest of the ward. The person either didn't hear her, or ignored her, and with another flick of his cloak, the man disappeared into the hall, dropping something in his haste. It fell to the floor with a muffled thud.

She rushed across the room, scanning for any healers. There were none, which was unusual. There was always supposed to be at least one healer—preferably a master—on the unit in case of emergencies. Spotting the dropped object, she bent, retrieving it from beneath a linen cart. *A power stone?* She turned the palm sized rock in her hands, heat radiating from its core. A dozen accusations raced through her mind. There was no one else who would have reason to carry around a power stone besides Terach. A small piece of her mind desperately wished to find some other answer and absolve him of any guilt. He was her mentor, her confidante throughout the past couple months, and her chest ached at the unspoken accusations accumulating within her. *Maybe he was here to replace a power stone that went dry*, she thought without conviction. She tucked the stone into her pocket, the heat seeping through the fabric and tingling the skin of her thigh. Opening the Infirmary door, she peered into the deserted hallway, nothing more than a corridor of blankness.

"Everything okay?"

Raylyn whipped around in surprise. Creena was behind her, drying her hands on her apron, a brow raised as she caught Raylyn's startled expression. "Did you see who that was?" she asked, gesturing towards the door. "The man who just left."

"What are you rambling about?" she asked, scowling. "No one was here. Especially not at this hour."

"Yes," Raylyn insisted, "it was a dark-haired man. Where were you?" Though she tried, she could not disguise the accusation in her voice. If Creena had just been here, maybe she could've verified her suspicions.

Creena's face darkened, her eyes narrowing. "Answering nature's call, if you must know. And listen here, if you're so concerned about it, you can throw your apron on and give a hand. I've been at this alone all night and Goddess forgive me for stepping out for a bit of relief." Her words were short and sharp.

"I... I'm sorry, Creena. I'm a bit on edge lately." Her eyes glanced back to the door. "I can help if you need me. I just didn't bring my work bag."

"We have spare equipment. Come on." She led her into one of the supply rooms in the rear of the chamber. Once inside, the anger in her expression melted. "Here, this will do," she said, pulling out an ancient brown apron, with a single large pocket sewn into the front. Raylyn wrinkled her nose, earning her another scowl. "It's not a blessed beauty contest."

Raylyn tied it on with quick, practiced fingers. "How is everyone doing tonight?" she asked, knotting her hair back.

"Surprisingly well, with all things considered," she said as they returned to the main chamber.

The rest of the night dwindled quickly, and the bustle of the morning was a welcome distraction to Raylyn; once she stopped moving, she would have to deal with the implications of what she saw. Creena was right, all the patient's conditions were much improved, and the day-shift healers praised the Goddess as they received report, thinking it a miracle those who lingered on their death-beds the day before had recovered so incredibly.

Braya snorted as Raylyn brought in her breakfast tray. "You can never just rest, huh?"

"Says the kettle to the pot." Raylyn pulled the curtain closed, then joined Braya for the meal of porridge and fruit. "Listen," she said, her voice quieting. "I saw someone last night." She proceeded to tell Braya of the dark figure and the power stone. She had forgotten that Braya didn't know what a power stone was, so the conversation deviated for a few minutes.

"That is incredible," Braya said, eyes wide. "Imagine your lanterns never running out of fuel! Remember when the Draundys' fireplace was blocked, and they froze half to death two winters ago? They had to stay with Bernshaw until the first melt. All they would've needed is one of those rocks, and it could've warmed their whole house!"

"I don't know about that. Maybe a room. But the spell isn't cast forever. Terach says the stones run dry. Just the same as burning through all your firewood."

"Their house was hardly bigger than a single room anyway," Braya continued.

"You're missing the *point*," she said. "Terach's the only one who makes them. They do no good in anyone else's hands. Which means the person I saw last night must be him."

Braya scratched her cheek, thinking. "Someone could be stealing them, you know. Even if they don't have the knowledge to make them, and even if it wouldn't last forever, having a device like that could change people's lives."

Raylyn stared at her for a moment. *Perhaps I've gotten too accustomed to the niceties of Court.* Braya's suggestion hadn't even crossed her mind, and the ever-persistent tendril of guilt wrapped itself around her gut, squeezing. Had she already forgotten what it was like, when crop yields were too low, and they didn't have enough to barter for lantern fuel? Did she not remember the impenetrable darkness after the sun set in winter, and being grateful for the candlelight sparking the smallest glimmer of hope in the compressing blanket of blackness?

"Maybe," she said finally, wishing her heart believed it. She chewed her lip, thinking. The threads of an idea, which she had been so consciously ignoring throughout the morning, were weaving together. "Braya, what do you think about getting discharged today?" she asked, already knowing the answer.

"Hell yes," she said, jumping off the cot and jostling the near-empty breakfast tray. She smiled sheepishly as the dishes clattered to the floor. "Can we go now?"

"Just keep your head down," Raylyn mumbled, pulling the hood lower over Braya's face. "We're almost there." She repeated the motion with her own cloak, not just trying to block the wind. The less people who saw and recognized her, the better.

"This way." She led Braya through the side entrance through the gardens. Not only was it closer than the main doors, but it offered more seclusion.

Midday offered the best protection at discovery, as students were typically engaged in classes or training, and the nobility of the Court were convening about business matters or taking lunch. The castle was blessedly empty, and they crossed the halls to the entry chamber with no issues. She pulled back a portion of the tapestry, ushering Braya inside the hidden door, unseen. The darkness blinded them for a moment, and Raylyn raised her hand, casting a shaky ball of light. Though her casting skills had improved significantly, she still struggled with control, and it took a concentrated effort to keep the orb hovering over their heads.

"Hidden passages," Braya muttered, her voice carrying in the stone corridor. "It's just like the bedtime tales our mothers used to tell us, isn't it?"

"It's much darker," Raylyn said, referring to more than just the light. "You aren't going to like what I'm going to tell you, but there were too many people around to explain earlier." She took a deep breath, mentally preparing the argument ahead. "Obviously, this isn't the way to my bedchamber. This is the Hall of Sorrows, and no one knows the state it's currently in. I have a couple friends hiding here right now, and I want you to stay with them."

Braya's silence stretched so long that Raylyn started to wonder if she had even spoken the words aloud. She was going to say it all again, wondering if she had become half-mad from chronic sleep deprivation, when Braya finally spoke. "Okay."

"Okay? I was prepared for an argument," Raylyn said, shocked.

"This is your world, Ray... It's not pleasant to admit, but what chance do I have surrounded by a bunch of mages?

You have yourself tangled in a mess, and I can't do anything to help free you."

The orb bobbing above them flickered as Raylyn's concentration broke, taken completely off guard by Braya's words. They had been friends since infancy, brought together by their mother's friendships, and not once did Braya ever express any jealousy or longing for Raylyn's powers. It was accepted as readily as the differences between their hair color. They always just fit together. Raylyn didn't know if it was her own anxieties, or if Braya felt the tension in the air as well, like a hairline fissure forming in a boulder.

A single, massive stone remained in the center of the Hall of Sorrows, the last piece to be placed. Raylyn had spent several days trying to tame the rageful energy inside the rock to guide it back into its place in the ceiling. She wasn't successful. The darkness hid all the work she had accomplished, the small orb providing just enough light to walk forward without tripping over their feet. Knocking on the fourth door on the right, she called, "It's just me," and was acknowledged by the clicking of a bolt.

"Is it over?" Talia asked anxiously, opening the door. "Did they figure out who did it?" Her eyes fell onto Braya, and her brows pulled together, confused. "What's going on?" Torch light poured from the sitting room, and Ri approached the door, as well.

"It's a bit of a story, and I don't have a ton of time. But first," Raylyn gestured to Braya, "some introductions. This is the infamous Braya."

Talia's jaw fell open, as her eyes darted between the two of them. "How?" It was all she could manage to say, her mouth opening and closing like a fish.

Instead of answering, Raylyn pulled the pack from her shoulder, producing a wrapped loaf of bread, a bag of sweet pears, and a heavy waterskin. "I have a lot to cover with little time, so let's get started."

It took a little over an hour to update them on everything she had discovered and was planning, but it was time well spent, and she felt secure in the three's safety. Not even Terach had kept up on her progress within the Hall of Sorrows, and she was certain the record of the inner rooms was lost with time. Even if someone found the passage and discovered the wreckage almost completely repaired, the hall was lined with dozens of doors, and the sitting room locked from within.

She had forced herself to sleep, choking down a draft of valerian and lavender. If her plan was to work, she would appreciate the rest later. The knot in her stomach tightened as she slipped into the Infirmary, keeping her hood tight around her face. It was a few hours into night shift, dinner trays already came and went, and most patients were already sleeping. She glimpsed Creena at one of the sinks, scrubbing a pile of metal instruments.

"Creena," she whispered, placing a hand on the woman's arm.

"Goddess above!" she yelped, dropping the pair of surgical scissors with a loud *clang*. "What are you doing, sneaking about?"

"Come here." She pulled her into a nearby supply room, glancing around before closing the door.

"What in the—are you *well*?" Creena asked, placing the back of her hand on Raylyn's cheek. "You're acting as if you have brain fever."

"What I'm going to say is going to make you even more suspicious of that illness," Raylyn warned with a humorless smile. "I need a bed."

"A bed?" Creena asked flatly. Raylyn nodded, eyebrows raised meaningfully. "A bed here? You *are* unwell!"

"I'm not sick, Creena. Just listen." She broadly explained her suspicions and her plan within two minutes, hardly wasting time to breathe. Terach's name didn't surface, as Raylyn was still clinging to the hope of his innocence. She didn't think she could handle losing both Brenden *and* Terach.

Creena was slowly shaking her head as Raylyn finished, which wasn't a good sign. "You mean to catch this mystery syphon in the act, and then what? Confront them? You've had a few months of training, and this person—*if* they exist—theoretically could have years, if not decades?"

Raylyn swallowed, nodding. "I have a backup plan in place in case I am ... incapacitated."

She rolled her eyes. "You are still a *child*, and a willful one at that. How about you grab an apron and help me out again tonight? You can have all of group C again." She moved to open the door, and Raylyn put her hand up, stopping her.

She bit back a clipped reply, the "child" comment irking her. "I need your help, Creena. Most likely scenario, nothing happens, and I look a fool spending the night in an Infirmary bed. *Please*."

The furrow between the woman's eyes deepened, the weight of the decision clear on her face. Raylyn held her breath, waiting, until Creena finally threw her hands up with an air of exasperation. "Fine, fine. Ridiculous, and you're lucky your friend's bed is still open, else you'd be sleeping in front of the healers' station. Now move and let me *work*." She pushed past her, annoyed, and Raylyn could see the tension in her shoulders, her brow still furrowed.

Her pulse raced as she ducked behind the curtains, finally lowering her hood as she settled into the freshly made cot. But as the hours passed uneventfully, her heart slowed, and she began to think the entire scheme worthless. There was no telling if the person would be back tonight or not. The dim room was quiet, save Creena's steps, and the occasional muttered moan or snore behind one of the curtained rooms. Her lids began to sink, and it was a struggle to stay awake despite her earlier nap. *Would an hour really hurt?* she thought groggily, blinking hard to rid the grittiness in her eyes.

Her curtain shifted, making her sit up in alarm, but it was just Creena. "There's an emergency on the other unit; two patients are deteriorating quickly, and the girls need extra help," she said in a rush. "I know you're doing your little," she waved her hand in the air, searching for the right word, "*test*, but would you just keep an ear out for a few minutes in case anyone needs something? I've just rounded, so everyone should be okay."

Raylyn rubbed her face, shaking away the tiredness. "Of course." Creena nodded, pulling her curtain fully open so she could see the room, then disappeared.

Her head throbbed from straining her ears all night, awaiting the silent steps of the stranger who had yet to arrive. She tried to hear past the whooshing noise that pounded in her head and swung her legs over the side of the bed in defeat. *This wasn't a good plan at all,* she thought, grinding her teeth in frustration. *All these hours, and no one showed.* Appeasing herself with at least being able to help Creena, she was just about to hop off the bed when she caught the almost-silent click of the Infirmary door closing, her head whipping up in surprise. In one swift movement, she slid back into bed, pulling the covers up to her chin, peering beneath her lashes.

It wasn't the best vantage point. Lying fully prostrate, the linen cart outside the room blocked her view of the left side of the chamber, including the Infirmary door. She tried to peer through the stacks of towels but couldn't discern anything. Turning slightly, she shifted her gaze to the right, the curtained rooms and supply closet doors at the back of the unit clearly in view.

She waited, holding her breath as the cloaked figure came into view, slowly circling the room. He paused at each set of curtains that separated the patient rooms, disappearing behind them for a moment, before continuing onward, his movements silent. Every nerve in her body was alive as he came closer, her chest tightening almost painfully. Two rooms away, one room away. *Here.*

As soon as the figure stepped in front of her, she bolted upright in her bed, throwing the covers off. She raised a glowing hand and heard him make a surprised grunt. "Pull back your hood," she ordered, voice low and dangerous, "Or I'll attack. Now!"

He chuckled softly and complied, and her heart sank as Terach's face appeared. "Easy, now, Level Three caster. I wouldn't want anyone to get hurt."

"I *knew* it was you. I didn't want to believe it, but I knew..." Her hand faltered, lowering slightly.

He gave her a sad smile. "Too clever for your own good." Raising his hand, she didn't even have time to react as she hardly saw his palm glow, before a hazy dizziness took hold of her mind, and all went black.

CHAPTER 19

T HE FIRST THING RAYLYN WAS CON-
scious of was the incessant pounding in her head.
She struggled to open her eyes, her lids weighing a hundred pounds. She finally succeeded in opening them but with great difficulty. Her head was foggy, and she couldn't understand what she was seeing. Beneath her was a red cushion, not the thin white pillows of the Infirmary. A towering line of bookshelves filled the far wall, instead of the floral patterns on the curtain dividers. The effort to sit up was mountainous, and she tried for a desperate minute before a wave of nausea made her give up as she began dry heaving.

"Woah, there," a voice said soothingly, placing a cool cloth on her forehead. "Let's not try getting up just yet."

Terach's voice triggered her memory, and her eyes shot open, wide with panic. "You..." was all she could get out, frustrated and pained tears burning in her eyes.

"Truly, I didn't want to do that," he said, tucking a stray piece of hair behind her ear with gentle fingers. "But you were getting quite loud, and we couldn't risk waking everyone, could we?" He leaned over, grabbing something out of her sight. "Here, drink some." A mug appeared, and Raylyn turned her head toward the back of the couch, lips clamped together tightly. "I could have killed you in the Infirmary and saved myself the trouble of carrying you here. Why would I poison you now? Just drink. It'll help with the nausea."

She fought for another useless minute, his insistent pressing forcing her lips open, and she sputtered as the warm liquid filled her mouth. A warmth flowed through her body, and true to his word, the urge to vomit dissipated. He helped her sit up, propping another pillow behind her back. "Let's talk."

She cringed away as he sat on the edge of the couch next to her, wishing she had the strength to bolt from the room. "About what?" Raylyn asked sharply. "About how you've been syphoning from the patients, nearly killing some of them?"

Heaving a heavy sigh, Terach nodded. "I can imagine how it would seem that way, if you didn't understand."

"What is there to understand? I should've believed Talia. You're nothing more than a predator." She glared at him, disgusted at the tears filling her eyes. *Months of trust wasted on such a horrible person. When will I learn?*

His eyes narrowed, and Raylyn bit her tongue. This wasn't Terach the mentor anymore, and she'd do well to remember. If he chose, he could end her life now, ensuring his secret remained safe. "A predator?" he mumbled, a brow raising. "No. Everything I'm doing now is to better this country. Those refugees, they're *not* our people. They're nothing more than an added burden, an additional expense. It's all a ploy of King Aedam to weaken us. Nothing but underhanded blows, and we keep ignoring them as if nothing is wrong. How many more years would this go on until we finally crumble? What harm is there in funneling their energy for our own gain?" His hand waved up at the ceiling, where several glowing orbs hovered.

"That's the secret behind the power stones? It isn't just a complicated spell... You've been transferring their syphoned energy into them." A chill ran over her, goosebumps prickling her arms.

Terach nodded. "I can teach you how, as well," he said, mistaking her quiet tone for awe. "Between the two of us, we could accomplish wonders."

Raylyn's face twisted with disgust. "The second rule of the Goddess is do no harm. I would *never* commit such atrocities."

Terach sighed again. "You think me a monster, without knowing everything Aedam has done. War has been overdue for too long."

Horrified realization dawned on Raylyn. "You sent Brenden to defend us from their attack, but they were never leading their armies here, were they?"

His eyebrows raised in surprise. "You *are* clever. The attack on Rowan this past autumn should have been fuel enough to set this war ablaze. Hell, the death of the queen two decades ago should've started it. I've had enough waiting. The king and his promises..." He shook his head.

"I've half a mind to convince your lady's maid to join the cause as well. I can't seem to figure out how she discovered the poison." He cocked a brow at Raylyn, as if expecting her to explain.

He chuckled as she stayed silent, refusing to answer. "I could convince you to talk, if you won't do so willingly."

Fear constricted her throat. She didn't know how to get control over the situation. As fatigued as she was, she could hardly move her arms, let alone try to attack him. "You tricked Brenden into poisoning his father," the accusation spilled out, giving Raylyn a desperate thread of hope for Brenden's redemption.

Terach snorted. "No, he did that on his own accord. He, at least, understands the threat at our borders."

"What threat?" she cried. "You've sent him to face an opponent of your own creation. Those people in the Infirmary aren't your enemy! They're victims escaping a civil war!"

"A civil war spilling onto our lands, Raylyn! Don't you see?" He ran a hand over his face in exasperation. "The skirmishes at the border, the attack on Rowan. How long until their king is disposed? Slavery of the non-mages is on the horizon, not far away. What will stop their new regime from bringing those beliefs here? You really want your little friend enslaved? We can stop them."

"How can you speak as if you are free from blame? You are sucking the life from those people! Hurting them when they are at their weakest. I'd rather be enslaved than be tortured!"

Anger flashed on his face, and he stood, looking down on her with a furrowed brow. "You are too valuable to squander, Raylyn. All you need is a bit of ... *persuasion.*"

The dizzying sensation returned, and Raylyn's strength drained as if she were hemorrhaging. "Such energy I sense in you, and yet, you're so easy to overpower. Sleep on it, *daughter*," he murmured, his words muffled as if she were under water. Black spotted her vision until unconsciousness claimed her again.

Bang, bang, bang.

Raylyn's eyes fluttered open at the noise, trying to shake off the disoriented fog. She shivered, her skin slick with a cold sweat. Blinking hard, her vision refocused, the blurriness around her clearing. Terach was at his desk, looking at the door with a scowl.

Bang, bang, bang. This time, the pounding was accompanied by a voice. "I know you're in there, Terach, and if you don't open this door, I will get a group of casters to smash it apart!"

"Goddess's sake," Terach muttered, pushing his chair back from the desk with a sigh. He opened the door a crack. "What is it, Thorne? I've got a week's worth of work to do now that forces are deployed."

"I know. Your burdens are *so* much heavier than anyone else's." She pushed her way past him into the room, and Raylyn allowed her lids to fall closed, succumbing to the utter exhaustion. "The tea was poisoned, and whoever did it was exceptionally talented—" Her words cut short. "Seriously, Terach, I thought you were well past these ... *behaviors*." Her voice was far away. "Leave us, Raylyn."

She opened her eyes, struggling to remain conscious. Another wave of cold nausea rose to her throat and despite her efforts, she couldn't even lift her head from the couch. Giving up, she relaxed into the cushion and closed her eyes, taking comfort at the image forming behind her lids. The Goddess, surrounded by a soft, warm light, reached forward, caressing her cheek with a loving tenderness.

"What's wrong with her? Terach, what have you *done*?"

Raylyn smiled, warmth spreading from her cheek through her veins. She reached up to embrace the beautiful deity, joyous tears filling her eyes. But the Goddess shook her head, pointing toward the pocket of her pants, before taking slow steps backward. "Wait," Raylyn cried, reaching out. Pain seared through her muscles. "Come back!"

"Shh, Raylyn, you're okay." She opened her eyes again to the harsh realities of Terach's office. Thorne crouched over her, her hand channeling warmth and energy. Her muscles came alive with a sore lethargy, but at least she was able to move again. Her cheek still tingled with heat from the Goddess's touch, and her thigh was so warm, it nearly burned. Reflexively, she reached down, worried her skin would blister. Her fingers stumbled upon a lump in her pocket that she had forgotten, and she quickly moved her hand, afraid to draw attention to it.

Apparently appeased by her renewed condition, Thorne stood. "Raylyn, leave us. Lord Terach and I need to have a *private* conversation." Raylyn scrambled at the chance, fighting the fatigue in her legs as she stood.

"Sit. *Down*," Terach said through gritted teeth. Raylyn froze, paralyzed with fear.

Thorne spun at him. "If you do not allow the child to leave, I will scream for the guards to come witness this disgusting scene! It's been *years*. I thought these, these ... *tastes* ... were behind you!"

He rolled his eyes. "Thorne, calm yourself. It's not what it seems—"

Thorne bolted to the door, throwing it open. "Guards! Help!" she screamed with a crazed vengeance, her eyes narrowed with a scorned hatred.

"Damn it!" Terach cursed, raising a glowing hand.

Her eyes widened with surprise. "You have the gall to try and attack *me*? They'd Mark you, for sure, casting with such violence." She turned her head back into the hall. "Guards!" she cried again.

"Good thing I'm not casting," he muttered, and without a trace of effort, he syphoned.

Thorne tripped, catching the doorway for balance, her mouth opening with shock. The color drained from her face and she stumbled, falling to her knees. A few breathless seconds passed, and her eyes rolled backward in her head before she collapsed into a heap on the ground. Raylyn stared in horror, praying the woman was still breathing.

"I didn't want to do that!" Terach hissed, crossing the room in a few quick steps, and slamming the door shut again. He knelt next to Thorne, his back to Raylyn.

Raylyn's heart was pounding, the weight of her fear nearly crushing her. She glanced at the doorway, wondering if she would be quick enough to slip out while Terach was distracted. But no, she was exhausted and slow, Thorne's healing giving her just enough energy to sit upright. Even if she were to try and syphon, Terach would quickly overpower her.

She shifted, her thigh burning from the power stone's heat. *Of course*, Raylyn thought in a rush of excitement, pulling the stone from her pocket. It was just like manipulating the power stored in the boulders and wreckage of

The Hall of Sorrows, but instead of directing the energy elsewhere ... she pulled, the confused rush of power unnerving. It renewed her, invigorating her limbs, clearing the shroud of mist from her mind. Terach was still bent over Thorne, cradling her body in his arms, oblivious to this exchange. There was no time to waste. She connected several channels, linking her to Terach, then with all the force of her anger, pain, and betrayal, she *pulled*.

He whipped around, still holding Thorne, a cry of outrage pouring from his lips. She pulled harder. With ease earned from weeks repairing the Hall of Sorrows, she opened another channel, casting and throwing him backward. He slid on the stone floor, his body hitting his desk with a loud crash. Raylyn continued syphoning, the energy becoming too much, and she redirected it into the stone grasped tightly in her hand. It buzzed with vibration. She advanced on him, looking down as his body shook on the floor. His eyes flickered closed, his pulse slowing as his heart fought against the strain. With effort, she stopped, cutting off the channels before she took his life. For good measure, she landed a kick square in his gut, and he didn't flinch.

Good enough for me, Raylyn thought, assured he was unconscious. Dropping the stone, which left red blisters in her palm, she rushed to Thorne, praying she was alive. Her hands poured light as she laid them on the woman's skin, searching for a strand of life, a single heartbeat. She closed her eyes in concentration. *Please*, she begged, *please ... there!* Her pulse was thready and weak, and Raylyn almost missed it. She poured energy into Thorne, sending wave after wave, until color prickled in her previously pale face.

Her arms shook with exhilaration as warmth returned to Thorne's skin.

It wasn't until pinpricks of black dotted her vision that Raylyn realized something was wrong.

She lost her balance, the room spinning, and fell off her knees onto her side. So anxious to tend to Thorne, she forgot to draw the energy from the power stone she dropped on the ground in haste. She reached a shaky tendril toward it in a last effort to syphon, but the growing blackness consumed her once again.

Voices woke her, and she shot up, adrenaline coursing through her veins. Looking around wildly, she realized she was in the Infirmary, Braya and Talia watching her with amusement.

"Easy there, killer," Braya said, putting a hand on her shoulder to keep her from climbing out of the bed. "Everything's okay."

"But Terach—and Thorne was--where are they?" She pushed Braya off her, climbing out of bed.

"Terach's in the dungeon; they've already Marked him. It was too dangerous to wait for the official trial," Talia said, standing up. "You really should lay back down."

"Thorne was dying, and I tried to help her but—"

The curtain opened, Thorne smirking with amusement from the other side. "Your concern for me is surprisingly endearing, if unexpected," she said, guiding Raylyn back to the bed. "Now listen to your friends and lie down. You've been out for two days and need to build your strength back up."

"Two days?" Dread filled her. "But we have to stop Brenden! We have to tell Rowan or the king; Terach lied to everyone, the Cystrian army isn't marching toward us to attack!"

They were all silent, Braya and Talia exchanging anxious looks. Thorne closed her eyes, taking a deep breath. "*That* is a concern." Without another word, she spun on her heel, racing out of the Infirmary.

"Are you guys alright? What's been going on?" Raylyn said, rambling to distract herself from the growing horror of impending war.

"When you didn't return by midday, we followed your instructions, writing that note on your magic parchment." Braya's eyes grew wide with excitement. "Imagine how useful something like that would've been when we were kids! Anyway, we sent the message to your guard friend, and he wrote back they were only a day's travel away. They showed up yesterday." Braya wiggled her eyebrows suggestively as she continued, "I *knew* there was something simmering between you and Prince Rowan from the first day you met."

Talia snorted,. "It's not Rowan she was close to—it was Brenden, the one leading the army."

Braya turned to her. "Then why did Rowan sit by her bedside all night, praying?"

Raylyn felt heat rise to her face. "He did *what*?"

Braya shrugged. "If it wasn't for the ill king, I daresay he'd still be here, whimpering."

The king. "Is he going to be okay? And what about Ri? Did they clear her of the charges?"

Talia nodded. "Yes, to both. The king is markedly better for just a couple days of recovery, though he's withdrawing from the substance severely. Thorne testified to the Court that when she discovered the poison and confronted Terach, he tried to kill her, and she found you half-dead, too. Ri was found completely innocent, but she's shaken from the entire ordeal. Left last night for her family's country estate." A flash of pain lit her eyes, but it was gone before Raylyn could say anything. "But that isn't all of it, is it? He really was the one syphoning from the refugees, wasn't he?"

Raylyn was acutely aware of her quickening pulse. *They think Terach poisoned the king.* No one even suspected Brenden. Raylyn chewed her lip, conflicted. Finally, she nodded. "Yeah, he was. He used their energy to make the power stones that fuel all this." She pointed to the light orbs hovering at the ceiling. "He also called me 'daughter,' so I guess that solves another mystery." She swallowed, disgust and pain of the revelation making her throat tight.

Neither of the girls looked surprised, and Raylyn guessed they figured it out already on their own. She fought her guilt, unsure why she was protecting Brenden. *Terach polluted his mind over the years, as well, but with a poison no one can prove.* A wave of dizziness made the room spin, and she lay backward, resting in the pillow.

"Here," Braya said, handing her a glass of water. "Drink some." She complied, and they sat quietly for a few minutes as Raylyn processed everything. If only they could stop Brenden from attacking. The treatment of the non-mages across the border was horrendous, but instead of launching war, they could assist the king to take a stand against the radicals who were trying to install slavery. Despite everything, her eyes were growing heavy, a bone-deep exhaustion weighing on her.

Talia nudged Braya, and the pair exchanged a wordless conversation. Braya cleared her throat, then stood. "Ray, get some rest. No," she continued as Raylyn tried to argue, "you're not going to save the world today, and worrying does no one any good right now."

"You've always been too bossy," Raylyn muttered, but she didn't argue further, knowing there was no point. She needed rest to rebuild her strength. Terach was Marked, the king was safe, and there was still the small chance Brenden could be stopped. She clung to that hope as her friends waved goodbye, ducking behind the curtain. Sleep blessed her soon after.

"You can do this," Raylyn said. Talia stared back with wide, terrified eyes. "Listen, don't you think bringing the king's assassin to justice is a bit more daunting than some silly Academic competition?"

"Yeah, we've got this, Tal," her partner said, a middle-aged male healer, whose job was to keep her alive despite the barrage of attacks from the competition.

Talia peered out at the crowd, ignoring them both, a shiver racking her body. The air was enchanted warm, and Raylyn was awed as the heavy snow melted instantly on the shield engulfing the arena like a large, warm bubble. They were in a small room below the stands, a short ladder with a trap door above their heads separating them from the rest of the stadium. "This is much harder," Talia finally muttered, her blazé attitude crumbling under the pressure. "Look at the amount of people out there. I didn't have an audience when I discovered the king was poisoned!"

"You've made it this far and are totally fine. What's changed?" It was the second day of the competition and the fifth and final round. Talia made it look as easy as breathing, out-competing older and more experienced mages, all while hardly breaking a sweat.

"I'm just so close..." she mumbled. "I don't want to choke now, when I've almost won."

"Well then, make sure to chew thoroughly," Raylyn replied, snickering at her joke. Talia glared at her, humorlessly. A bell rang, the vibration ringing in Raylyn's chest. "Alright champ, that's my cue. We're all rooting for you." She scrambled up the ladder, taking the arena stairs three at a time to get back to her seat.

She nearly fell down the steps in shock when she saw her parents chatting with Braya as she neared her seat. "Momma? Father?" Her throat knotted as they both turned to look at her, their smiles faltering at the expression on her face. "What're you doing here?" The first few days after she was released from the Infirmary, her heart raced at every corner, expecting her parents to show. The castle was packed with families arriving, but as the days passed with no news, she began to think they just gave up on her.

"Raylyn!" Her mother rushed toward her, pulling her into such a tight embrace, the breath rushed out of her. "Braya was telling us you've gotten yourself mixed up in some trouble!"

"Ow, mom... crushing me..." she sputtered, breathless.

She pulled back, her hands falling to hold Raylyn's as tears streamed down her face. "You never even *wrote*," she said accusingly, pain evident in her eyes.

367

Raylyn chewed her lip, ashamed. After everything that happened—how close she came to dying—her feud with her parents seemed so childish. "I'm sorry, Mother. I was so angry. I felt like you didn't even want me anymore after I discovered ... my powers," she said lamely.

"Oh, Raylyn, no." She shook her head. "You've got it all wrong, sweetheart."

Her father walked over, scooting past Braya, who watched as if this was the most engaging performance she ever saw. "We knew you couldn't stay in Lakehaven, Raylyn," he began, pulling her into one of his signature, one-armed hugs. "And neither could we."

They both smiled, and Raylyn's eyes darted between them. "What do you mean?"

"I had to train my replacement before we left, since you were always the one destined to take my role. It was a heavy task." Eva rolled her eyes. "But I think they'll manage alright."

Raylyn continued to stare uncomprehendingly, until her father spoke again. "We sold the house, Raylyn. Packed up the bit we needed to bring. Carriages don't travel fast in this weather," he said as he looked up. The snowflakes melted on the invisible shield, little rivulets of water rolling down the sides of the shield like a thousand tiny waterfalls. "I decked Doyle square in the face the day you left, and then I was ... relieved ... of command duty, so I didn't have *that* tying me there, either."

"Father, I'm so sorry," Raylyn said, her eyes burning. "If it wasn't for me—"

"If it wasn't for you, my life would be much less joyous," he said, cutting her off. He wiped the tears from her cheek with his thumbs, pulling her in close. "You're my daughter, through and through, Raylyn. Don't ever forget."

The second bell rang, making them both jump in unison, and they laughed as they took their seats next to Braya, who gave Raylyn a wink as she sat. Her stomach knotted as she realized how lucky she was to have her parents, when Braya was alone. "Should be a good show," Braya said, pulling her legs up under her and sitting on her heels. She leaned forward excitedly as Talia joined the center of the ring with the last two contestants. A hush fell upon the crowd as everyone waited for the third bell.

Ding. The arena roared with excitement. Cheers, screams, and applause joined together in a crescendo as the contestants took their places in the sand. "Raylyn, can we talk?" Her head whipped up in surprise as Rowan stood over her, dripping in finery for the event.

Heat creeped up her neck, which worsened when her parents—spying the prince themselves—began to fawn over him, her father taking a knee on the stone floor. She nodded, bolting out of her seat, desperate to get him away from the embarrassment of her parents.

She had done so well avoiding both the princes for the past week and hadn't imagined either would make such a public scene. Following up the stairs, he led her inside a private room, a glass panel allowing a clear view of the arena below. The seats were covered in plush cushions, and in the center was a circular table filled with assorted wines, cheeses, and meats. She expected to see Brenden and the king, but no one else was here.

"You're avoiding me," Rowan said, sitting on one of the cushions. The words echoed Brenden's, all those weeks ago. Raylyn stared through the glass, watching as one of

369

Talia's opponents—a middle-aged, bald man—casted what looked like a lightning bolt at her friend. Raylyn winced, but Talia blocked the attack, redirecting the bolt back at its caster. The man dove, rolling sideways in the sand as he narrowly avoided the attack. "Raylyn," he urged, forcing her to turn.

"I ..." She sought the words, struggling. "*Yes*. I've been avoiding you. I couldn't figure out how to phrase, 'Thank you for searching for months in the snow for my best friend, and sorry the entire endeavor was pointless.' Oh, and let's not forget, 'It's a miracle you were able to get to your brother in time to stop a war.' And 'Sorry I seriously considered killing you in the library a few months ago.' I just seem to get it wrong around you, Rowan. It's not easy to admit."

Rowan laughed. "Okay, so is it my turn? Thanks for saving my father's life; thanks for discovering the truth about Terach—I always knew he was a sneaky bastard. Sorry for inadvertently effecting you and forcing my emotions on you." His voice grew low, and he looked away from her, his cheeks flushing.

Raylyn chewed her lip. "I ... don't know how much was caused by your influence and how much was my naivety," she admitted, sitting on the cushion next to him. "We definitely got off to a bad start." A roar through the crowd made them both look up, and she saw Baldy lying on the ground, immobile. "Yes, Talia, get 'em!" she called, a grin spreading across her face. "Talia said if she wins, I get her copy of the Helena Lightier book," she said, wiggling her eyebrows in excitement. "How is the king doing, by the way?"

"Recovering, thank the Goddess. Is it selfish of me to say I'm grateful I wasn't around for the worst of it?"

Raylyn shook her head. "No. I think it would make you a glutton for punishment if you wanted to witness the madness he went through." They sat quietly for a moment, watching Talia dance with her last opponent, a woman in her twenties with inky-black hair. "I thought Brenden would be here to spectate, as well," she said, trying to keep her tone casual.

A look of pain crossed Rowan's face, but Raylyn blinked, and it was gone. "He's ... pretty shaken up about Terach's betrayal, and I think he's seeking solace in solitude," Rowan muttered, staring at his hands. "He was closer to Terach than our father, in truth. If positions were reversed, I daresay I wouldn't handle the blow nearly as well as he has."

Raylyn nodded, not trusting herself to speak. Though she hadn't been ready to confront either prince, she continued to have a lingering hope that she and Brenden could reconcile. Her stomach flipped, remembering their last conversation. *I'll come back to you,* he promised her. His eyes had been so desperate for her understanding, so anxious to fight against an enemy that didn't even exist.

"Are you ... in love with him?" Rowan's voice was strained with pain, causing her chest to tighten. So unaccustomed to his presence, she had forgotten his effecting ability. There was no point in lying, her every emotion was on display for him to see.

"Rowan, I—"

Suddenly, the crowd thundered again, the sound so deafening Raylyn clasped her hands over her ears. They both jumped from their seats and rushed to the window, fingers digging into the sill. There, in the center of the arena, stood Talia, victorious. Raylyn screeched with excitement as Talia reached both her hands up and casted three separate jets swirling into the air like tornados: one fire, one ice, one white-hot lightning. The cheers intensified, and Raylyn looked up at Rowan, huge grins plastered to both their faces, their previous exchange forgotten for a moment.

"ROWAN!" a voice from behind them shouted through the chaos. Turning, Raylyn saw Garrick, his face grim.

"Gar, what's wrong?" Rowan asked, raising his voice above the noise.

"It's Terach…" He shook his head with disbelief. "He's escaped." Horrified disbelief rushed through Raylyn's veins, and her mind froze with the shock.

"He's gone? That's impossible! He's Marked! How could he escape?" Rowan was halfway out of the room, but Garrick put a hand on his shoulder, stopping him.

"Rowan, that's not all. He took your brother. Brenden's gone."

The End Of Book 1

BOOK CLUB QUESTIONS

1. How does Raylyn change over the course of the novel?

2. What mythology did you identify throughout the novel?

3. What was the catalyst for Raylyn losing control of her powers?

4. For which love interest where you rooting? Why?

5. What is your position regarding the civil war in Cystra? How does this relate to events in history? How does this connect to current political affairs?

6. In which ways do Braya's and Talia's friendship help Raylyn throughout the story?

7. Many of the characters are morally "gray." Describe how this is a reflection of real life.

8. Which of the characters is your favorite, and why?

9. Do you think anyone can reach redemption, regardless of the significance of their mistakes? Why, or why not?

About the Author

M. E. BATT IS A YOUNG ADULT AND Adult Fantasy romance author with a deep fascination for magic systems and love triangles. Born and raised in a small village outside of Buffalo, NY, she is a large proponent of chicken wings with bleu cheese, not ranch.

Besides working full time as a nurse and trying to tame three wild and tiny humans, she spends her free time delving into the depths of other worlds. Some of her favorites include the *Inheritance Cycle* by Christopher Paolini, *Handmaid's Tale* by Margaret Atwood, *Mistborn* by Brandon Sanderson, and *Red Queen* by Victoria Aveyard.

More books from
4 Horsemen Publications

Young Adult Fantasy

Blaise Ramsay
Through The Black Mirror
The City of Nightmares
The Astral Tower
The Lost Book of
the Old Blood
Shadow of the Dark Witch
Chamber of the Dead God

Sins of The Father:
Story of Silas
Honorable Darkness: Story of
Hex and Snip
A Love Lost: Story of Radnar

**Leslie &
Janice Sommers**
Brighde Reborn

C.R. Rice
Denial
Anger
Bargaining
Depression
Acceptance
Broken Beginnings:
Story of Thane
Shattered Start: Story of Sera

M.E. Batt
The Syphon's Daughter

Valerie Willis
Rebirth
Judgment
Death

Discover more at
4HorsemenPublications.com

CPSIA information can be obtained
at www.ICGtesting.com
Printed in the USA
BVHW051324281122
652930BV00004B/21